MY ALIEN MATES
COMPLETE COLLECTION

BOOK 1-3

MAGGIE ALABASTER

STAR WARRIORS

MY ALIEN MATES BOOK 1

To the readers, I wish health and happiness.

1

MY FIRST TIME seeing Earth from the window of a space shuttle freaked me the fuck out.

I mean, who wouldn't be scared? I'd spent the last twenty two and a half years on the rock. It was home and I was going a long way away. So far, I could barely wrap my head around it.

"Are you o-okay?" A voice with a hint of a stammer broke through my uneasy thoughts.

I turned and forced a nervous smile, which probably looked like I needed to pee.

The guy who spoke was absolutely gorgeous. He was also blue. I don't mean he was cold either. His skin was steel blue, with a slight sheen that almost looked metallic. He was definitely not from Earth, but his brown-green eyes were surprisingly like a human's in shape and colour. Right now, they were locked on me. He seemed concerned, even anxious.

I met his gaze and my stomach fluttered. Nerves. It was just nerves. Yet the fluttering continued and I struggled to look away.

He cocked his head and I realised I hadn't responded.

I cleared my throat and willed my stomach to stop behaving like a silly teen. Hot guys like this didn't go for girls like me.

"I was thinking about," I swallowed down a knot of emotion, "leaving Earth." The last word choked out, as though saying it might make all of this more real.

I glanced out the window—or was it a porthole—and caught a glimpse of the edge of Africa. My breath caught in my throat. I blinked away a tear.

"I suppose that is a lot t-to think about." He looked down at his booted feet and shifted in his seat.

I wiped away a tear and took a moment to get a good look at him. Apart from his skin, he didn't seem that different to me. He was around the same age, with the short hair and the uniform of the military arm of the IF—The Interstellar Federation. A badge pinned to his chest marked him as an ensign.

"Yeah, it really is," I agreed. A whole hells of a lot.

He lifted the side of his face and looked at me with one eye. "I'm sorry, I'm not good with— with—"

"Aliens?" I suggested lightly. I probably looked as strange to him as he did to me.

He shook his head. "Conversation," he said finally. "Talking is..." A darker shade of blue crept up his cheeks.

"Difficult?" I said.

He nodded vigorously. "Yes. I could have been an ensign sooner, but I'm..." His head jerked up and his eyes widened apologetically. "I'm sorry. Here you are, leaving your home planet, and I'm babbling on."

6

"It's all right," I assured him quickly. "You're helping to take my mind off things. Stuff. Everything." *Very eloquent,* I told myself. "I'm Edie. Short for Edith." I grimaced. My parents were big fans of history and older style names. My brothers Julius and Horatio were even less lucky than I was, except in the middle name department. Mine was a closely guarded secret. Yes, it's that bad.

I held out my hand.

He stared at it, brow furrowed. "I'm sorry, I'm not sure what..."

"Oh." I realised the reason for his confusion. "You're supposed to shake it. It's an Earth thing, I suppose." I shrugged. I was about to pull my hand back when he gripped it and shook it so hard I thought my wrist might tear away from the rest of my arm. He stopped still and held on to my hand for longer than necessary.

"Not like that," I said. I gave an awkward laugh, although to sit like this, hand in hand, felt natural, like we'd done it a hundred times before.

My face heated.

His mouth formed an O and he released my hand like it was too hot.

"I'm sorry," he said for the third time in as many minutes. "I barely passed alien etiquette."

"It's okay." My skin tingled. "Plenty of humans wouldn't pass human etiquette. Here, let me show you." It was *totally* for educational purposes, not because I wanted to hold his hand again. Or so I told myself. I ignored the fluttering which now felt like backflips in my belly.

I held out my hand, but this time when he gripped it in his, I shook it gently.

"Just like that, see?" Oh yes, purely *educational*. So why did my stomach feel as if an impromptu dance-off was taking place in there?

He smiled, showing two rows of even, white teeth. "This is called the sh-shaking of hands." He seemed very pleased with himself.

I chuckled. "Something like that." I took back my hand regretfully. "What's your name?"

"Danec, son of Jaec," he declared. He glanced down at his palm, a smile on his lips.

"Where are you from, Danec, son of Jaec?"

"Freytauri, a few st-stars over." He jerked his head in what I suspected was the wrong direction.

I smiled. "Is it nice there?"

"Nicer than Earth," he replied. His jaw dropped and he looked mortified. "I mean, um, it's just…"

I laughed silently and held up my fingers, my hand bent backward at the knuckles. "It's okay. I am leaving for a reason." A good reason, but that didn't make this any easier. I lowered my fingers and sighed. "They say Earth was lovely once."

"Before pollution, war, and the climate made it harder to live there," he said as though reading from a vidscreen. "I came top of my class in history." He puffed out his chest and for the first time I really noticed the bulge of muscle under his shirt. From what I've heard, the training with the IF was rigorous.

"Where are you headed?" he asked.

I glanced down at my watch. "I'm making a stop at the Moon Station for a night, then on to Agus."

Danec's face lit up. "Me too. Are you joining the GASP?" The

Galactic Armed Space Force.

I hesitated. "I don't think I'm military material. I trained as a nurse, but my knowledge of alien—I mean, non-human biology is limited. I've heard the medical training facility on Agus is the best in the IF. After that, I'm not sure what I'll do."

"It is the best," Danec agreed. "I might see you around then." He looked hopeful. The expression made him even hotter, if that was possible.

"I'd like that," I said softly. "Can I ask you a question?"

"I…" He blinked and his shyness returned. "I suppose so."

I chewed my lip for a moment. "Is everyone from Freytauri blue?"

"Oh," he looked relieved. What had he expected me to ask? "Yes, we are. Although some tend toward purple. Some confuse us with the Agusians because we look similar, but they tend toward green. We share a common ancestor with them and the people of Earth—" He stopped, eyes wide. "I'm babbling again."

"Not at all," I said. "It's nice to see someone so passionate about things."

He blushed again. "My friends called me a gwarp, because I like to read and learn."

I bit back a laugh, in case he thought it was directed at him. "A gwarp? Is that like a nerd or a geek?"

"Or a dork," he said. "Human slang is fascinating."

"Oh I don't know, Freytaurian is pretty interesting too, by the sound of it."

He cocked his head. "We have fewer words for toilet and penis than humans do." He said 'penis' like he'd said 'arm' or 'leg.' Just another body part, nothing to be embarrassed about.

I liked that.

"I'm not even slightly surprised," I said ruefully. "Humans have long been obsessed with both of those things." Not that I could talk. I enjoyed toilet humour and cocks as much as the next girl.

"We have many words for stars and hard work." The side of his mouth quirked up. "I suppose our culture has different priorities."

I laughed again. "You could say that." Apparently ours was all about the groin area. No wonder the planet was a mess.

I looked out the window and sighed, as did several other humans who sat in the seats behind me. The shuttle was small, only big enough for a hundred people, but it moved fast enough that I could already see almost the whole side of Earth. Mostly blue, the continents stood out as the only landmasses still above water. The rest were gone some fifty years ago, before I was born. Old footage shows islands dotting the ocean, full of life and odd trees called palms. Agus had islands. With any luck, I'd get to see one.

"I remember the first time I left Freytauri," Danec said softly. "I was nervous too. I was worried I would never return."

Without looking away from the window, I asked, "Did you?"

"A few months later, yes, for the equinox festival. It's an old tradition on Frey-T, as we call it. Some think it's silly to keep celebrating it. It goes back to times when we believed in gods and demons."

I glanced over to him and nodded. "Some humans still believe in those things, but we have celebrations that go back a long time, too. Christmas, for example."

"Ah. Turkey and a man in red who fits down a—" He paused and looked uncertain. "Chimney?"

I smiled. "Something like that. Don't tell me, you didn't ace Earth ceremonies."

"Uh." He rubbed his smooth chin. "Earth ceremonies only takes up half a page in the book about galactic traditions."

I sniffed. "I think I should be offended we're not considered more interesting."

"Oh, microns," he swore under his breath. If you can call that swearing. "I didn't mean to offend you. The IF knows comparatively little about your culture and it takes a while for them to start to teach them. They spend m-more time talking more about updating the syllabus than doing it. Or s-so my teachers say."

"It's okay." Without thinking, I took his hand and gave it a squeeze. "I'm not really upset. Everywhere else seems more interesting than Earth."

He looked down at our hands until I felt uncomfortable and drew mine back.

"Please tell me that didn't mean something rude on Frey-T," I said tentatively.

He looked surprised. "Not at all. It's considered intimate."

"As in sexual?" I felt my face heat.

"Oh no," he said quickly. "Like two people who care for each other. If you had laced your little finger into mine, that might be construed as, um…"

"Yes?" I prompted. "As what?"

"As you wishing to have sex with me." He blushed.

"Oh, I see. that's good to know." It really was. A girl didn't want to get herself into trouble accidentally. On purpose, well that was another story, but we had just met. He seemed cute and sweet. Okay, a little hot too, but ten minutes was too soon to jump into anything with someone, no matter the size of his biceps.

"I'll be sure to keep my hands to myself from now on," I said. "Just in case I do something wrong."

"Yes." He grimaced. "I don't mind. Most people understand—well, have misunderstandings, but some get offended easily."

I knitted my brows slightly. "You seem to be referring to something in particular."

He exhaled and lowered his voice. "Some of the folk from Parvora 12 can be cranky. A few of the trainers on Agus are from there and they..." He inhaled through his nose. "Most of the cadets and ensigns are terrified of them."

"So they're assholes?" I suggested.

Danec looked confused. "Oh, you mean they aren't very nice. You used body parts to say that?"

I grinned. "Like I said, we're obsessed with that area of the human body. Dickhead, asshole, butthead, wanker..."

Danec looked even more confused. "Isn't that last one another word for masturbation?" Just as he spoke, silence fell across the shuttle and his words seemed to echo through the cabin.

Several dozen eyes turned to Danec and several people snickered.

"Yes, it is," I said, my voice softer than his. "It's considered something people don't talk about in the open. Is it different on Frey-T?"

He shrugged. "It is as talked about as any other act of sex, which is to say not much. It's not considered strange or shameful."

"Right. But you wouldn't do it in public?" Wonderful, now I

was imagining him doing just that, his hand wrapped around his throbbing…

Gods, stop it, Edie, before you leave a puddle on the seat.

Danec turned darker blue than ever. "Oh, microns no. It's an intimate thing."

"We really aren't so different," I said. I couldn't help but wonder what our similarities were, biologically speaking. I eyed his groin. He did seem to have a bulge there, like a human guy, but that didn't necessarily mean it resembled a human cock.

"So, um… Do they feed us on board the shuttle?" I was hungry now, but not necessarily for food. Although, I could eat if it was offered. If, that was, my stomach would stop with the acrobatics.

"Uh." He tongue slid over his lips and I suspected he was thinking along the same lines as I was. Not about food, about other things, like intimacy. "The ride is short and the shuttle has no galley. But Moon Station has a large mess."

"I'm sure it does." I chuckled. 'Large mess' sounded like anywhere I stayed for more than a few days. I saved cleanliness for work.

Danec cleared his throat. "Would you like to ha-have…" He looked frustrated at his own stammer. "Have dinner with me?"

"I'd like that." When I'd stepped onto the shuttle, I hadn't expected to make a friend, much less dinner plans, but why not embrace it? My old life was disappearing in the window at the back of the shuttle, I should grab the new one by the balls and enjoy the fuck out of it.

That didn't stop another sigh from escaping my lips as the Earth turned and Australia passed under us. It too had islands around it once.

2

"CAN YOU BELIEVE THIS PLACE?" The voice who spoke was female, but it took me a few moments to realise she was talking to me.

I turned from staring out the Moon Station window. "I suppose I can't."

She was shorter than me, but more slender. Her pale hair was swept back in a neat ponytail, with no strands escaping from anywhere. Absently I patted my own hair, but my dark curls wouldn't be tamed, no matter how hard I tried. I have the kind of hair people claim they wish they had, but those of us who did, spent hours detangling it with a hairbrush and a straightener.

"It's mind-blowing," she declared. "We can see the whole Earth from here. Well, the bit that's facing us. Look, North America. I'm Brinley Grant."

She slipped in her name so quickly I almost missed it.

"Hi. Edie." I put down my cup of coffee onto the table in

front of me and offered my hand.

She shook it and slipped into the seat opposite me.

"Where are you from?" she asked. "Obviously Earth. Me too. I'm from the south of England."

I had figured that from her accent. "Australia," I said while she took a breath. "Sydney, specifically."

"Oh, fabulous. I watched that go past on the last rotation. It's amazing to see water where there wasn't water for hundreds of years." She must have seen the expression on my face, because she stopped speaking.

"I'm terribly sorry. My mouth runs away from me at times. A lot of the time, actually."

"It's okay," I said quickly. "We need to think of ourselves as citizens of the IF now, not just Earth." It was a simple thing to say, but to do, that was something else.

"Yes. Or Agus. You're going there too, aren't you?" Brinley asked. "I checked the manifest. Oh, don't worry, I wasn't spying. I'm training to fly the shuttles. I'm hoping to fly the bigger space transports." She smiled like a child whose dreams had all come true. Or were about to.

"That sounds like fun." I tried to seem enthusiastic, but I'd never had much affinity with machinery.

"Doesn't it?" she agreed. "There's nothing like flying. I started with small planes when I was younger and—" She rattled on while I watched the world go by.

"So, why are you going to Agus?" she asked.

When I told her, she all but bounced in her chair. "It's good to know I would be in good hands if I got sick," she said.

"You might be," I replied modestly. "I mean, I do my best." I loved my job and knew I did it well, but I might be out of my depth dealing with other species.

I watched two women walk past the table. One, who I assumed was from Frey-T, had skin lighter than Danec and dark, pin-straight hair. The green-skinned woman from Agus had antennas and scales across her chest and up the sides of her neck. Both were slender and taller than me.

"They're beautiful, aren't they?" Brinley said softly. "I wish I was that tall. And thin."

I pursed my lips. Even the prettiest amongst us was unhappy about some aspect of ourselves. Did the aliens feel the same way? Was 'alien' even the right word? We were as alien as they were.

IF, I reminded myself. *We're all IF.*

"From what I know of their physiology, they have narrower, longer bones," I said. "We couldn't look like that if we tried. Besides, if you were too tall, you wouldn't fit into the cockpit." I was guessing, but cockpits always seemed small to me.

Apparently it was the right thing to say, because she smiled.

"That's true, but if I was any shorter, I wouldn't touch the floor while sitting in a pilot's chair either."

"I'm sure you would find a way," I assured her. She didn't seem like the kind of woman who let a thing like height stop her from doing what she wanted.

"Yes, I suppose I would," she said thoughtfully. "Did you know there isn't any meat on the Moon Station? Apart from human meat, that is."

I wasn't sure if I should feel whiplashed from the sudden change of topic, or sickened at the idea of people being meat. Maybe both.

I shook my head. "I suppose it's hard to farm up here, apart from grains and vegetables."

"Exactly. The amount of oxygen it would take to support a herd of cattle would be prohibitively expensive. That also means the milk in your coffee is plant based."

"Most of the IF doesn't farm animals," I said. "Most other worlds find the eating of flesh to be…"

"Yucky?" she suggested.

"Yes, yucky. Luckily they like coffee and chocolate as much as we do." The introduction of those two things to the IF might be Earth's greatest contribution, which was kinda lame. At least we contributed *something*.

"I'm not sure I would have left Earth if there wasn't chocolate out there," Brinley said with a cheeky smile.

I chuckled. "Me either." A girl had to have some vices and I had several, but chocolate was the biggest one.

"Maybe we can share a cabin on the ship to Agus?" Brinley suggested.

"That would be nice," I said. I didn't want to be the kind of person who left home and only congregated with my own kind, but leaving Earth was a huge deal and having another human close by would help ease us both into this new life.

"Great, I'll sort it out." She glanced at something behind me. "In the meantime, that guy from Frey-T. I don't think he's taken his eyes off you since I sat down."

I swivelled in my seat in time to see Danec look away, his cheeks flushed.

"Oh. We met on the shuttle up," I said. He really was pretty adorable. He looked back for a second and blushed darker.

"We're supposed to go out to dinner tonight." I offered him a smile and turned back to Brinley.

"But?" she prompted.

"But there are so many women on the station who are more interesting than I am," I finished with a sigh. "And prettier." Slimmer. Taller.

I would understand if he changed his mind.

"Bollocks," Brinley said loudly. "You're very interesting. If you weren't, he wouldn't have asked you, would he?"

I gaped for a moment, surprised at the force of her reply. "I suppose not."

"Exactly, and look, he's coming over here."

I just took a sip of coffee and now I almost choked on it. I coughed and swallowed as hastily as I could and put my cup back down.

"Watch where you're going." A human man, a scowl on his features, all but pushed Danec out of the way as he made his way past.

"I-I'm sorry," Danec stammered. "I-I didn't—"

"Stupid prick," the man muttered, loud enough for me to hear.

"Prick," Danec said loudly, his eyes bright. "That's another word for penis, isn't it? You humans really are obsessed with the groin area."

The man, a badge on his chest read 'Jones,' glared at Danec and stomped away.

I put a hand over my mouth as he passed, to stifle a laugh.

Danec watched him leave, confusion on his face. "Was it something I said.?"

I couldn't hold back any longer. I laughed until tears leaked down my cheeks.

Danec looked bewildered all the while.

"It's all right." I wiped my eyes with my sleeve and rose to pat him on the shoulder. "Some humans don't like to be reminded of our obsession."

"And some people are just cranky," Brinley said. "I met him on the shuttle up. He really didn't want to leave Earth."

I immediately felt bad for laughing at him. We were all in this together, or at least we should be. Later, I might seek him out, to see if he was okay, but I would give him time to calm down first.

"Do you still want to have dinner with me?" Danec asked. He gave me a shy, uncertain smile.

Those backflips in my stomach were back. I'm sure it was a coincidence they happened whenever he spoke to me.

My mouth was suddenly dry, but I managed to say, "Yes. I'm looking forward to it." I moistened my lips with my tongue and added, "I feel like maybe I should tell you all the groin-related words and when to avoid using them."

"I would welcome any education you could give me." He nodded vigorously, eyes wide with excitement.

"Lucky girl," Brinley murmured.

I glanced at her and blushed. I didn't think that was what he meant. At least, I was *almost* sure.

"Um, so I'll meet you back here in..." I pulled up my sleeve so I could see the face of my watch. "Two hours?"

"Yes." He checked his own watch, a newer version of mine. He must have some credits if he could afford it. Not that I cared about his credit account balance. He was sweet and seemed genuine. And the trapeze in my belly must mean *something*.

"I should go," he said regretfully. "I have to catch up on my studies."

"Three cheers for free, intergalactic internet," I said, if only to keep him there a few moments longer. The internet was still used for the same things it had always been used for: studying, cat videos, and porn. These days the cats were more interesting, like the Parvoran cheetah, with its two tails and distinctive purr. And the Blarvian Watercat, with their gills and fishlike tail.

The porn, well I'd never been one to partake. I preferred to make my own experiences. Which brought me back to the present moment.

Danec's eyes lingered on mine before he smiled and turned away.

"He has a cute ass and everything." Brinley sighed. "Can you ask if he has a brother?"

"I'm sure there will be plenty of guys on Agus," I assured her. "Or girls. Or whatever you're into." The IF was diverse in ways humans wouldn't have imagined a hundred years ago. Some worlds had multiple genders. Some, like Blarvius, had the reproductive abilities of males and females, so they could have their own children if they wanted to. A handy skill, I guess.

"I'm into people with brains," Brinley replied firmly. "And a sense of humour. It wouldn't hurt if they just happen to be cute as well. Danec certainly is."

"That he is," I agreed. And he wanted to share dinner with me. *Me.*

"I suppose I should shower and start getting ready," I said uncertainly. How seriously should I take this? Fancy hair, makeup, and everything, or casual and without too many expectations? Oh, who was I kidding, it would take me two hours to untangle my hair. I should start on that right now.

And think about what to wear.

And—

"Do you want some company while you get ready?" Brinley asked. "I just got the latest episodes of *Darker Side of Parvora* on IF-View."

I managed to hold back a squeal. "That's my favourite show. Right along with *The Real Domewives of Garvi-3.*"

Brinley snorted and offered me her arm. "You know none of that is real, right?"

"Of course, but that's half the fun." Really, if I had that many credits in my account, I'd probably find more useful things to do with my time, but it was just a Vid show.

"It's definitely better than *Keeping Up With the Centaurians.*" Did people really believe what went on on that show?

"That's true," Brinley agreed. "Can you believe some people dyed their skin yellow, just to look like them? Folks do the strangest things."

I laughed and walked out of the mess hall with her. Just outside, the station opened out into a large space that led to the hangar. Across on the other side, a sulky figure stood alone. Jones turned and looked at me as though his eyes might pierce a hole. Nothing about him suggested he'd welcome a chat from me, even if I was just being nice.

I looked back, my gaze unwavering, until we moved into the corridor which led to the living quarters. I put him out of my mind as best I could, but I felt as though his gaze was bored into my skin.

3

"IF WE WERE ON EARTH, I would ask you where you wanted to go," Danec said. "Or what you wanted to eat. There's not much to choose from here. It's the mess or the mess."

"Hmmm, let me think about that for a moment." I twirled a curl around my finger. "How about the mess?"

He laughed, awkward and high. "Great idea." He drew his shoulders in like a shy schoolboy, and added, "You look lovely, by the way."

"You too," I replied. "I mean, handsome." Trust me to put my foot in my mouth. Not literally, of course, these were my favourite heels. Okay, my only heels. The luggage weight limit meant I had to leave the other dozen pairs behind. My parents promised to take care of them and send them on when I was settled, along with my collection of earrings shaped like food. What? Who doesn't need earrings shaped like purple gummy bears, or vodka bottles?

He really was handsome though. His blue skin had a subtle

sheen in the station's lights. His short hair was damp around the edges and he smelled clean, like he'd just come from the shower. His uniform was neat and fit like it was cut just for him, firm across his chest and biceps. I was tempted to ask him to do a twirl, just so I could see how it fit his ass. What I saw was pretty damned good.

"The mess it is then," he said. "I heard they're thawing pizza tonight."

I wrinkled my nose. "Mmm, thawed pizza." The resources here on the station were limited and the galley was relatively small, even if the mess could seat a few hundred people. So frozen food it was, much of the time, usually prepared on Earth.

"It's better than fish sticks." He stuck out his tongue in disgust. "I had that on the way through. I don't think it was real fish."

"They can put a station on the moon, but they still can't make decent fish sticks," I said.

Danec chuckled. "Yes. Um." He looked toward his booted feet.

"Shall we start walking?" I suggested. "Otherwise the mess might close before we get there."

"Right!" he said so quickly he seemed to startle himself. "I mean yes, good idea." He sighed. "I'm sorry, I don't mean to be awkward." He walked beside me. "My mother hoped being an ensign might make me more, um..."

"Confident?" I suggested.

"Exactly. Even with the uniform on, I feel as though I'm going to fall over my own feet."

"I'm sure you're not," I assured him. "You look very dashing. That shade of grey suits you."

I supposed I would have to wear a uniform too, once I boarded the ship to Agus. All the more reason to enjoy wearing a black skater skirt and a pale pink top. Both would probably look better on Brinley, but I felt cute in them.

"Thank you. You're very sweet."

Sweet? That sounded like a friend zone word right there. For some reason, my heart sank a little, but it was okay, really. Who couldn't use more friends? Especially when travelling to a whole new planet? If he just wanted friendship, then that's what we'd do.

"I try," I said, suddenly as awkward as he was. "There's an empty table, over near the window." If we ran out of things to talk about, we could always watch the world go by.

"Yes, great." He barrelled toward it like a man on a mission, almost leaving me standing at the entrance.

I raised my eyebrows at his back and hurried to catch up. At least I got a good view of his ass. It was everything I hoped it would be.

"We got it." He smiled like a little boy who rode his bike alone for the first time. If little boys had muscles and a dimple in their chin. I hadn't noticed that before, but now I did, I found it endearing.

Friends, Edie, friends, I reminded myself. It's okay to think your friends are hot, right? Awkward or not, he was a pretty sexy guy. Of course, leave it to me to meet an adorable guy who wanted to be friends. I suck at this love thing.

I shook off my self pity and smiled. "Good work. We beat another couple of people to it as well."

A woman with a tray had headed straight for it, but she slumped down at another table instead.

Danec's face fell. "I hope we didn't upset anyone." He pulled out a chair and gestured for me to sit. "I read in etiquette class that human women always like someone to pull out a chair for them."

It was a gesture all but abandoned on Earth, in favour of equality and all that, but I didn't have the heart to tell Danec that. Instead, I smiled and slid into the seat.

"Thank you, that's very gentlemanly of you."

He furrowed his brow. "Gentlemanly? You have some words which aren't related to the groin."

I snorted so loud the people at the next tables turned and stared. I ignored them.

"Yes, one or two," I agreed. "Some countries have lots of words for snow."

"Interesting," he said. He pulled out his own chair and went to sit, but caught himself at the last moment. "I should get us food." He shot back up so fast, he knocked into his chair. It skidded back into the one behind him, earning him a glare from its occupant.

"Um, sorry." He retrieved the chair, tucked it back under the table and hurried away. Eyes and chuckles followed him.

My gaze followed his ass. Brinley was right, it was as perfect an ass as I had ever seen.

Friends, friends, I reminded myself again. I focused my attention out the window at the twinkling lights of some city below. I couldn't tell where it was and truthfully I wasn't trying very hard. If I did, I might cry. I hadn't expected to feel homesick, but it crept up in me while I sat alone at the table. I almost gave in to tears when Danec plonked a plate in front of me, startling me out of my thoughts.

"I'm sorry, the plate got hot." Danec placed his down opposite me and blew on his fingertips.

"Did you burn yourself?" I asked. "Here, let me see." I held out my hand.

I examined his fingers closely, partly because it's my job and partly because I hadn't seen blue skin up this close before. Like humans, he had fingerprints, but they all looked like arches, rather than whorls or loops. Lines crossed his palms the same as they did mine. That was a no brainer. without those, he couldn't open and close them. Still, it intrigued me.

Without thinking, I traced the lifeline across his palm with my fingertip.

"Is it all right?" he asked. "Did I damage myself?"

"Hmmm? Oh." I almost dropped his hand when I realised what I was doing. "Yes. I mean no, everything seems fine. No burns that I can see." I hadn't expected to find any, or he would have been more distressed.

"That's great," he said. "Thank you, I feel much better having you look at it."

"Even if I'm not familiar with your physiology?" I asked. "You might have nerves in the skin I can't see."

He flexed his hand, then picked up a piece of pizza—for some reason they were cut into squares—and shrugged with his opposite shoulder. "It feels fine. I might even be able to play the, what do you call it, piano, some day."

"Oh, you play?" The pizza looked as though it was made out of spare sheets of cardboard, but it tasted okay.

"No, I've never been any good at music." He grinned.

I chuckled. "Being uninjured doesn't give you magical powers, my friend."

He seemed disappointed at something, but he didn't say anything other than to flash a vague smile and went on eating.

We ate in silence for the next few minutes. Every so often I glanced out the window. Clusters of light were interspersed with great expanses of blackness. Oceans, I supposed, or places too small to be visible from space.

"It's so dark compared to Frey-T," Danec said softly. "Everything is run on solar power, water and all of that, but there are more lights at night. Even the oceans are dotted with floating cities."

"It sounds pretty," I said.

"It is," he agreed. "Our population is a lot more spread out, so everyone has privacy and room to— I'm babbling, aren't I?"

I smiled. "Not at all. I like to hear about other planets. I've only seen them on my vidscreen."

"Same, until I came here." He waved toward Earth. "Seeing it from the station, or a screen, and being there, are two different things."

"I suppose that's true." Seeing Earth from here made it look like any other planet. That thought sat so heavily on my chest it became difficult to breathe. I grabbed a cup from the tray in the centre of the table and poured myself a drink of water. I gulped it down so fast I almost choked.

"We call it The Yearning," Danec said softly. "When you're missing home. Do you have a groin related word for it?"

His joke took me by surprise. I started to laugh, but ended up snorting water out my nose.

"Shit," I said under my breath. I pulled a tissue out of my

pocket and wiped my nose. "I'm sorry." He must have thought I was an absolute dork by now. No wonder he only wanted to be friends.

He sat with his head cocked, eyes wide. "Fascinating. Your nose leaked. Are you unwell?"

I held back another laugh. "I'm fine. It's a human thing I guess. My eyes leak too, sometimes." I felt like they might right now.

"Oh, ours too. It keeps our eyes from becoming dry."

"You don't cry?" I asked. "With tears?" I leaned in and peered more closely. He had tear ducts, more or less like mine.

"We cry, but no excess water comes out."

"Oh, I see." I sat back and went on eating. I'd always felt like men came from another planet, this one actually did.

"I—"

I let out a squeak as an alarm pounded through the mess. I dropped my piece of pizza and looked around, frantically.

"All IF personnel report to their stations," a robotic voice said over the speakers. A trill sounded, following the announcement.

"A drill?" Danec said. "Now?" He sagged back in his chair and made a face.

My heart sank. "I suppose they want to keep everyone on their toes," I said. The timing sucked. Our date, if you can call it that, was awkward, but I was enjoying myself.

"I suppose so," he said. He shoved a mouthful of pizza into his mouth and washed it down with water, while the people around us scrambled to their feet.

"That includes you, ensign." A cold voice was followed by a shadow which fell over the table.

Eyes colder than his voice regarded Danec and me. Deep red eyes, almost black, narrowed as I stared back. His skin was a shade lighter than his eyes. No, I realised, it wasn't skin, he was covered in a fine layer of fur. At least, his face was. The rest was obscured by a uniform like Danec's, but somehow neater and with the rank insignia of commander on his chest.

Danec leapt to his feet. "Yes, sir. Sorry, sir." He saluted sharply. "At once, Commander J'avet." He shot me an apologetic look, which lingered a nanosecond longer that was necessary, before he hurried away at a trot.

J'avet's eyes locked on me like a heat seeking missile. Or a heat giving one. My heart raced and I might have smiled if I didn't get the sense he loathed me on sight. Okay, two can play at that game.

I didn't move, I didn't blink even though I needed to. I sat perfectly still like scared prey. Except the scared part. I wasn't scared at all, no way. Well, maybe a little bit. He was clearly the kind of man used to giving orders and having others jump at them.

Right when I was about to look away, he did first.

"If you're heading for Agus, you're also IF personnel. You should get to your station."

"Uh, yes, sir," I said without thinking.

Shit, he turned back and stared at me again, this time with a raised eyebrow. Technically, I didn't report to him, unless he was the head of the station, which I was sure he wasn't.

"Commander is adequate," he said in a voice deep enough to make me wonder where else he had fur.

I shook myself out of my silly thoughts and stood. It was unlikely I would find out, unless he was sick or injured. I wouldn't wish that on anyone, no matter their attitude toward me.

I gave him a nod. "Commander then," I said, and hurried away to the infirmary.

4

"What was that all about?" Brinley set down her mug and flipped her plait over her shoulder.

"What was what about?" I sipped my coffee with its not-quite milk and wrinkled my nose. The more I drank, the more I could taste it. I shouldn't be drinking caffeine this close to bedtime anyway, but I hoped to bump into Danec, Brinley or even Commander J'avet. What can I say, I'm a glutton for punishment.

"The drill." She flopped into a chair and pulled her plait back to the front of her shoulder. "I got to the hangar, but it was over before we could even step foot on the shuttle. It was almost as though..."

"Someone just wanted to interrupt things?" I suggested. For some reason, my mind went to J'avet. I dismissed the thought immediately. For one thing, why would he bother? For another, he undoubtedly had better things to do with his time.

I shrugged. "Maybe it's just a thing they do in the IF. Get

everyone to jump up to see how fast they can get to their stations."

Brinley snapped her fingers. "That's probably it. I wonder how we did."

I remembered how slow Danec and I had been, and grimaced. "I would expect they'll test us all again soon." Next time we wouldn't let anyone else down.

Brinley placed her elbow on the table and leaned her head on her fist. "At least life won't be boring."

"That's true," I agreed, "but I hope they don't decide to run drills in the middle of the night."

I've done my share of night shifts, like any other nurse, but I hadn't slept much the night before. We'd had to turn up at the launch site yesterday morning. They'd put us through a health test and information sessions about what to expect on the shuttle and on Agus. We'd each had an individual assessment of our mental health as well. Most people saw a psychologist these days, for one thing or another, and no one so much as blinked. Mental health doesn't have the stigma it once did.

After the interviews, we were housed in a long building, with a small room each. A handful of couples shared, or people who were friends already. The rest of us had a room to ourselves. Of course, the rooms were uncomfortable and sterile and the thrum of air conditioning kept me awake half the night. The couple in the next room kept me awake for the other half. Whoever 'babe' and 'sweet cheeks' were, they were vigorous and energetic. Lucky them.

"So, how was your date?" Brinley gave me a sly smile.

"Short and sweet," I said ruefully. Much like my last sexual encounter. "He just wants to be friends. I guess that's for the best. We'll both be busy for a long time." I debated whether or not I should mention the commander, when the man himself strode past. My eyes locked on him so hard I wasn't sure I could look away if I wanted to. Damn, the guy would make any woman wet.

Shit. He turned and his gaze fell on me. I would have called it smouldering, until he curled his lip at me.

Asshole.

"Who is that?" Brinley whispered loudly.

"No one," I replied firmly. I looked away and picked up my cup as if it was the most interesting thing in the world. I wanted to look back and see if he'd gone, but I didn't dare.

"No one is hot," Brinley said.

"I think he thinks he is." I sipped my coffee and tucked a stray curl behind my ear. It popped straight back out again.

I heard someone laugh and thought it came from J'avet's direction, but I ignored it.

"He either doesn't like humans or he doesn't like me," I said. Either way, I had no time for him, even if I could imagine his hands on my—

No, I told myself. Leave the attraction to jerks behind on Earth, where it belongs.

There, that was great advice I gave myself. I should start one of those blogs where people ask for advice on their love lives. Oh, who was I kidding? I'd make theirs worse and get tossed out an airlock.

"Jerks are everywhere," Brinley said with a nod.

"Yeah, all over the galaxy," I agreed. Our galaxy at least.

I finished my coffee and stretched my arms over my head. "I might turn in. We have a big day ahead of us."

"Right. Assuming the ship is on time, it should dock around nine am, station time," Brinley said. "It'll be refuelled, cleaned, and ready to head back by two pm."

I was expected to board shortly after docking, to help clean the infirmary and to get my rosters. This was no free trip across the galaxy here. I was expected to work, as least as much as I could with unfamiliar species, for full shifts.

A flutter of nerves tickled the inside of my belly. Not the kind I felt when I spoke to Danec. Those were the size of Earth. This was the size of the moon. Maybe two moons. The possibility of messing up too badly was minimal, I would be watched closely every shift, but I was still going to be on an alien spaceship, headed for a whole new planet. It was the adventure of a lifetime, but it was terrifying.

"You'll be fine," Brinley said, as though she read my mind. She probably felt the same way I did. She seemed as nervous. "We'll take care of each other."

I nodded. "I'm glad we're traveling at the same time."

"Me too." She smiled softly. "I'm going to finish my coffee, then turn in."

"Night." I rose and covered a yawn as I dropped my cup in a bucket outside the galley and made my way out of the mess.

"You can't mean to consort with them?"

I hadn't seen Jones until he spoke. He stepped out of the shadows near the sleeping quarters, his eyes on me.

"Huh?" I was too tired for pleasantries right now. "Did you want something?"

He took his time to answer. "I want the aliens to back off Earth," he said finally. His voice was rough, gravelly.

I rubbed my forehead. "You're on a station on the moon. Aren't you headed to Agus too?"

He huffed. "Because I want to learn more about their power systems. They're better for the environment. I'm going to take that back to Earth. To make it better."

"That's admirable—" I started.

"Yeah. Then we won't need them anymore. Earth can stand on its own. They can fuck off where they came from."

A knot of anger stirred in my chest. "Is that what this is about? Good, old fashioned racism? I thought they'd stamped that out decades ago."

"I don't care what colour they are," he hissed. "I just want them gone from Earth. We don't need 'em, and here you are, having dinner with one, making eyes at another." He wore his dark hair in a low ponytail. He gripped it now and clenched his teeth until his face turned red.

"Are you stalking me?" I asked. That, unfortunately, hadn't been stamped out. Even with better mental health care, people slipped through the cracks, as they say.

He sighed and dropped his hands to his sides. "No, I just happened to see. You can't want Earth to become a colony of some other planet. We'll all end up slaves." He didn't sound delusional, just scared.

"The IF would never let that happen," I said.

"Let?" he echoed with a bitter laugh. "Once our minerals are gone, they won't care. They'll abandon us to..." He shook his head. "We can't let that happen."

"We won't," I said firmly. "Humans are badass, and other planets will help—"

"At what price?" he asked. "No one ever does anything for free. Ever."

That was true, but I wasn't going to be dragged into a debate right now. "Look, I'm tired."

"Just watch yourself," he hissed. "Don't trust any of the aliens. Be careful. Promise?"

I didn't owe him a thing. Perhaps he was unhinged after all. How had he passed the psych test?

"I promise I'll be careful," I said. That was an easy promise to make. I had no intention of getting injured, or anything else for that matter.

"Good." He nodded. "If you need help getting away from them, you only have to ask. I'll... I'll do something."

I didn't know what he might do, and I suspected he didn't either. I made a mental note to check his assessment when I boarded the ship in the morning. If anything strange stood out, I would speak to my supervisor. Before the ship left with Jones on board. He wouldn't thank me for getting him kicked off, but if he needed help, he should go back to Earth and get it.

"Thank you," I said awkwardly. "I'm sure I'll be fine. It's nice to, um, have someone watching my back."

He nodded, flashed me a smile which might have been charming at some other time, and turned and walked away.

I watched him through narrowed, confused eyes and gave my head a shake. Some of what he said made a lot of sense. Earth *could* use some more sustainable energy, and shouldn't become too reliant on other worlds. On the other hand, places like Agus and Frey-T had benefited from IF membership for over eighty years now. It wasn't perfect, no organisation was, but it did seem to help its member worlds more than it hindered them.

Unless, of course, he knew more about it than I did. That was entirely possible. I had spent the last few years studying and paying little attention to galactic politics.

"I should keep doing that," I said to myself. A couple walking past stopped to stare, but I flashed them a smile and kept on walking toward my accomodation. With any luck, I wouldn't be next to 'babe' and 'sweet cheeks' tonight. Or the walls here would be nice and thick. Very thick.

I found room seventy-one and slid the card into the slot beside it. Humanity had yet to find a better way to unlock doors. The door slid aside and I stepped in.

The room contained one wide bed, a small wardrobe, and a table. No scope for more than a night or two. I guess the moon didn't want too many people to overstay.

I stripped down to my underwear and tossed my clothes in the direction of the table. I preferred to sleep naked, but in the case of a sudden drill, I decided it would be better if I didn't. Running around the station naked was something I didn't want to do, if I could help it.

I slipped into bed, pulled the covers over myself, and let my mind wander. If I dreamed tonight, it would consist of red fur, blue skin, and conspiracy theories. Preferably the first two. Maybe separately, maybe not.

A girl could dream, right?

5

THE INFIRMARY onboard the *Infinity* was bigger than the one on the Moon Station. Unlike the station, this was designed for a few hundred people. I didn't want to think about what might cause it to be at capacity. Space battles *had* happened in the past. With any luck, they would stay in the past, but ships were still made fully equipped for just about anything.

In one corner, a curtain was closed around a bed, obscuring a patient. I craned my neck and tried to peer through a gap, but before I could, another medic entered.

She saw what I was doing and cleared her throat.

I jumped to attention, my face pink. "I'm sorry, um, Doctor." Her badge read, 'Kalvix'. I groaned to myself. Of course I'd make a fool of myself in front of the senior medic on the ship.

Kalvix was slightly taller than me. Her skin was the soft green of new leaves. Her dark hair was cut short, like a pixie. Her green eyes added to the effect of an ethereal forest creature, as did the line of scales which ran down her neck and disappeared under her IF tunic. Her antennae twitched, one in my direction, the other toward the curtain.

"Mmmm." Her lips pursed disapprovingly, but she didn't appear to be angry. "Nurse Wright, I assume."

"Yes," I said quickly. "It's nice to meet you." I wasn't sure if shaking hands was something done on Agus, so I kept them by my side. "I mean, reporting for duty."

What would she think of my intention to dig into Jones' file? I suspected she wouldn't be pleased if she caught me. I better not let her catch me then.

She nodded. "You've been assigned a supervisor, but they aren't on board currently. I urge you to familiarise yourself with the infirmary as best you can until then. Take extreme care and avoid anything you're not familiar with."

I got her message loud and clear. Look, but don't touch.

"Um, I see we have a patient already, Doctor. Perhaps I could see if they need anything."

For a moment, I thought she might refuse. Instead, she nodded and almost looked approving, and for some reason, relieved.

"Yes, do that," she said hastily. "I need to complete the inventory check."

Before I could offer to help with that, she bustled away, out the door.

"Okay then," I said under my breath. I put on my best smile and approached the cubicle. I drew the curtain aside slowly, just enough to step inside.

On the bed, a figure lay still, covered in a layer of blankets. Only his head was uncovered and that was enough to make me stare. His skin reminded me of Danec's, but with a distinctive purple hue. A Freytaurian, I assumed. A wide bandage was wrapped around his forehead.

As I approached, he turned his face and frowned.

"Have you come to poke and prod at me too?" he asked coolly. His eyes raked me up and down, and my neat blue uniform. It was tight here and there, but it would do until I could find one that fit better.

"No," I replied cheerfully. I had met his kind a hundred times before. The type who hated to be flat on their backs, in hospital or an infirmary. Honestly, that was most people, no matter what planet they're from. Lying in a hospital bed was boring, so I didn't blame him for being grumpy. It was my job to cheer him up, if I could.

"I came to see if there's anything you need." I tugged a corner of the blanket over to straighten it.

He responded with a lazy smirk. "My cock is itchy. Care to scratch it for me?"

I raised my eyebrows at him, as if I was offended. "I'm pretty sure you can scratch it yourself."

"You can see through all of those blankets?" he asked. "I didn't know Earthians had that ability."

Earthians?

I shook my head. "We don't, I just—"

"You assumed." There was that smirk again. "Do you think you should check?"

I wasn't falling for what he wanted. He obviously thought I'd peel back the blankets and look at his—presumably—naked body. As tempting as it might be, it was also unprofessional.

Instead, I clicked on the screen beside his bed.

"It says here you fell off the railing above the engine. Hit your head, broke both... Oh. Both arms."

"Yeah, Oh." There was that smirk again. "So, about my itchy balls?"

I frowned at him over my shoulder. "I thought it was your cock that was itchy?"

He shrugged with one shoulder, then winced. "They're both itchy. I keep telling the other medics, but they ignore me. I'm thinking of filing a complaint."

I held back laughter. It wasn't nice to laugh at a patient, especially one who couldn't do things for himself. He struck me as independent, as well as arrogant.

"I suppose I could apply some lotion to stop the itch," I said. Even for a different species, a simple cream should be harmless. I had seen a bottle on a shelf near a desk, so I hurried to grab some and slipped back into the cubicle.

I snapped on a pair of gloves and started to peel back the blankets. The skin of his body was slightly lighter than his face. On the left side of his chest he sported a tattoo in the shape of a whorl. His chest and torso looked so firm I could have broken diamonds on him. Or licked him for an hour or two. Damn.

I swallowed back the thought. I had seen plenty of bodies before, enough to simply think of them clinically, as just a patient. But there was something about him...

I forced the idea away. Nursing rule number one, never get intimate with a patient.

I exposed his cock and wasn't surprised to see it was big and slightly hard. Lines of small bumps covered him from balls to tip. They protruded further when he became slightly more erect. I was tempted to touch them, to see how they felt. Professional curiosity, that was all. Or so I told myself.

"So, um, how did you fall?" I asked, determined to be all business. I poured lotion on an applicator and began to slather it over his length.

"Would you believe I was dared to stand on the railing?" he asked.

"Actually, yes," I said. "I believe it, but I have a feeling that wasn't what really happened."

I glanced at his face. His eyes were half closed. He was obviously enjoying the attention a bit too much.

"I reached for a conduit and missed," he said with a scowl. "I should have used a longer ladder, but I figured..."

"Accidents happen," I said graciously. He made a mistake and he was being punished for it. There didn't seem much point in rubbing it in. So to speak.

"Yeah." He shifted his arms and grimaced. Both were encased in bone knitters, which would heal them fully in around a week. That must seem like a long time for an active guy.

"You know, if you put on too much of that, you'll have to lick it off." He gave me a boyish smile, which I responded to with a roll of my eyes.

"And to think, I was worried you'd be different from human men," I said. "In the end, you all think with your dicks."

"Haha, ow." He sucked in a breath. "If we didn't have dicks, you women wouldn't talk to us."

I pouted at him. "That's not true. I'm talking to you, aren't I?"

"While you're creaming up my dick," he shot back.

"What's your name?" I asked.

"Slek," he replied, "son of Arron."

"I'm Edie," I said. "Has anyone told you you're incorrigible?"

"Hmmm, hot, sexy, great in bed, irresistible... No, I don't think they have."

"Consider yourself told then," I said tartly. Tentatively I touched the applicator to his balls and slathered quickly.

"Your bedside manner could use some work," he said.

"At least you won't be itchy anymore," I said.

"In a few days I'll be out of here and you'll be begging me to nail you so hard you scream," he said with such certainty I raised my eyebrows at him.

He looked back at me intently. His gaze didn't waver. He didn't even blink.

I usually didn't go for guys as self assured as him, but my mouth went dry. When he wasn't a patient, maybe, but for now...

"There, that'll do," I said quickly, my attention firmly on work. "That should keep you moist for a day or two."

He grinned. "Ah, you can play the flirting game too. I was starting to think they'd sent another dull human. There's enough of those on the *Infinity* at the best of times."

"I'm pretty sure there are dull people from every planet," I said, trying not to take offence at the dig at my home-world.

"That's true." Slek sighed. "Take Kalvix for example." He wriggled his brows. "I tried to. Take her, I mean. She wouldn't play. She's all work and no fun. You, on the other hand, seem like the kind of girl who likes to have a good time." He nodded toward his groin. "Now I'm all moist, why don't you climb on board and go for a ride?"

"I'm starting to think," I pulled the blanket back over his cock, "that you didn't fall, but instead were pushed."

He feigned hurt. "Only if they're jealous of my prowess. Come on, I can keep a secret."

I pulled the blanket higher. "I can't begin to tell you how much trouble I would be in if I did," I said. "I'd be on the first cargo carrier back to Earth and never work as a nurse again."

"That really matters to you, doesn't it?" For a few moments at least, he was serious.

"Very much so," I said firmly.

"Would you fuck me if it wasn't against the rules?"

I frowned. "We've just met."

"That's never stopped me before," he said.

"Well, it's stopped me," I said firmly. "I like to get to know a guy first."

"Fine." He sighed loudly and shifted his rear to get more comfortable. "When I'm out of here, can I ask you out?"

"That depends, "I replied. "Are you sure no one pushed you?"

Now Slek frowned. "I'm sure, Why?"

"Because I don't want to go out with you if someone wants to hurt you. Or worse." I was only half joking.

He grinned. "I knew you'd say yes."

"You're a cocky bastard, aren't you?" I asked.

"I've been called worse," he said. "For the record, no one wants me hurt. I was a victim of my own arrogance."

"Why do I feel as though I should get that in writing?" I teased.

"Because I don't go around making admissions like that," he said. "This is a one time thing."

I shook my head. "I figured. Now, I should put this away and update your file."

"Thanks," he said. He seemed genuine.

"For what?" I asked. "I was just doing my job."

"Yeah, but my balls really *were* itchy. They were driving me crazy."

"Well, we can't have crazy patients, can we now?" I backed out of the cubicle and let the curtain fall back into place.

Speaking of crazy...

I tossed the gloves down the chute, and the applicator down another and returned the lotion to the shelf. I washed my hands thoroughly and, with several glances over my shoulder, sat at the desk.

I brought up Slek's file and Jones' and sat them side by side. If anyone came, I could hide Jones' before anyone saw.

I started there though, and read quickly. As far as I could tell, Jones had a normal childhood. The usual broken bone from falling off a hoverboard. Childhood fevers, ear infections, a cochlear implant to improve his hearing. Treatment for depression and anxiety. That had stopped a year before, after at least five years of steady treatment. The last letter from his doctor stated she had suggested more visits, but nothing in the file stood out. Nothing to suggest he was anything out of the ordinary.

I shrugged to myself and closed the file just as Kalvix walked back into the infirmary.

"How is our patient?" she asked in a tone that suggested she didn't think I'd been capable of handling him.

"He's fine, thank you, Doctor," I replied as I typed in updates. "His needs were—" I cast a sly glance toward the cubicle, "small."

"Small, my ass," Slek called out.

I chuckled.

Kalvix smiled. "You might do well here yet. He's been troubling us all over several—small issues."

"I feel ganged up on," Slek said.

I grinned. "He seems to be healing well at least. He won't be a big problem for too much longer."

"That's better." Slek sounded smug. "I can't wait to get out of here."

Kalvix smiled wryly. "No one will be happier than I will."

I wondered if he had asked her out too. It was his business, his and hers, but I couldn't help but be curious. He seemed like the kind of guy to grab every opportunity he could as often as he could. I usually avoided players, but it was only one date. How could it hurt, right?

I clicked save on his file and closed it. Thankfully Kalvix hadn't seemed to have noticed my slightly guilty look, or my distraction. I forced myself to focus, but the matter of Jones stuck in the back of my mind.

6

"I THOUGHT I might f-find you here." Danec offered me a shy smile, which I replied to with one of my own.

"I can't resist the last view of Earth before we're too far away to see it." I gestured for him to sit beside me and scooted over on the bench to make room.

"It's a bittersweet sight," he said. "I'll miss the...the ducks."

For a moment I thought I'd misheard. "Ducks?" I asked.

"Yes, ducks. They're my favourite Earth animal, apart from humans. I like their quack and the paddle of their feet under water." He mimed the action with his hands.

I smiled. "They are pretty cute. People used to eat them once." I regretted my words when his face fell. "They don't anymore," I added quickly. "At least as far as I know." I decided against telling him what humans did to chickens.

"Oh, great." He sat sideways and rested his elbow on the back of the bench. "I'm sorry about last night. I came back to look for you, but I couldn't find you. And then, well,

Commander J'avet saw me and ordered me to turn in for the night." Danec looked rueful. "I don't think he likes me."

"From what I've seen of him, he doesn't like much of anyone." I swivelled to face Danec and tucked one foot behind the other. "It probably didn't help that we didn't move fast enough during the drill." I half expected to hear the alarm sound the moment the words left my lips, but it didn't.

"Yeah, I guess so." He glanced down at his lap. "Have you seen the, um, recreation centre?"

From the way he spoke, I wondered what kind of recreation he was referring to, but I decided he meant the innocent kind.

"I haven't. Is it… nice?" Really? Nice? Was that the best word I could come up with? I wanted to sink into the bench, but I smiled instead and tried to look as though I didn't feel like an idiot.

Danec nodded. If he thought anything was off, he gave no sign. "It's g-great."

I noticed he used that word a lot. He must have noticed it too, because now he looked embarrassed.

"Can I show it to you?"

If someone like Slek had asked, he would have meant something else entirely, but Danec was different. Sweeter. I didn't mind flirting, of course, but it was nice to have a friend on board. Two friends, but I hadn't seen Brinley since we boarded. I suspected her days would be spent on the bridge, or flying one of the small pods which belonged to the ship.

"I'd like that," I said.

"Great," he said. His eyes widened. "I mean good. I mean—" He stopped. "Unless you'd prefer to stay longer?" He nodded toward the window.

I exhaled through my nose. "I'll see it again some day." There wasn't much point in spending the rest of the day with my nose pressed against the glass, watching Earth become a dot in the rearview mirror, so to speak.

"I'm sure you will," he assured me, then smiled softly. "So will I."

"You're thinking of the ducks, aren't you?" I asked, half teasing.

He looked sheepish. "Yes. they remind me of the dorva bird from back home."

"Do they have paddling feet too?" I mimed the action.

"They do," he confirmed, "but they honk, rather than quack, and they have teeth." He bared his.

I grimaced. "They sound…adorable."

He chuckled. "They're mostly harmless. Unless you go too close to their burrows."

"I'll remember that if I ever visit Frey-T," I assured him. "Now, you were going to show me the rec room?"

"Right, yes," he said quickly. He rose and stepped away from the bench to let me out. "I'm sorry, I can't pull the chair out this time."

I laughed, because as far as I could tell, every bit of furniture was bolted to the deck.

"Not without getting into trouble anyway. You don't want to get thrown out the airlock."

He looked confused for a moment. "Oh, that's a reference to Earth science fiction movies, right?"

"Right," I said. "I've seen, like, every one ever made. Even the bad ones."

Danec frowned. "Why would anyone make a bad movie?"

I snorted. "That's a very good question. I don't know why. I guess they didn't realise it was bad at the time."

"Oh, I see. I suppose it's a matter of opinion as well."

"That too." I followed him to the ship's elevator bank.

He pressed the 'up' button and we waited. After a minute or two, one of the doors slid open silently and we stepped inside.

"It's on level five." He pressed the second button from the top.

I knew there was a level above that as well, which was only accessible from a secure part of level six. What was up there, I could only guess. I considered asking Danec, but I doubted anyone would tell a lowly ensign, any more than they'd tell a lowly nurse. I wondered if Slek knew. As an engineer, he should have intimate knowledge of every part of the ship. I made a mental note to ask him the next time I saw him.

The elevator door slid open to a corridor. On one side were several closed doors. On the other, was a single open one. From that doorway came the sounds of laughter and something that might be a computer game.

I stepped into the doorway to see a room full of long couches, tables and chairs and a wide screen on the opposite wall.

In front of that stood several people, a human or two, a woman from Frey-T, two from Agus and a yellow skinned Centauri man. They all had controllers in their hands and were moving avatars inside some kind of game. As far as I could work out, they were exploring a damaged spaceship and shooting androids whenever one appeared.

Space Invaders, present day version. It was certainly more advanced than anything I had played. The ship on the screen looked real enough to put my hand in and touch it.

"There's a library room in the back," Danec said. "It's quieter there than in here. The computer bank holds copies of almost every book ever published."

"I hope the authors get royalties," I remarked.

"Of course. The IF believes in fostering the arts," Danec said.

I nodded and scanned the room. "Is that a chess set?"

"Yes, do you play?"

"No, I've just never seen one that wasn't on a screen." I walked over and picked up a pawn. It was carved from wood, with a base covered in a circle of black felt. Such craftsmanship hadn't been seen on Earth for a couple of generations. I certainly hadn't expected to see it here.

"Chess is a game of subtlety. It takes an intelligent mind to grasp it properly."

I knew that voice before I turned around to see the disapproving look on J'avet's face. He stood with another Parvoran who had the same disdain on his features.

"Is that so?" I tossed the pawn into the air and caught it on my palm. "Seems like just a game to me."

J'avet looked as if he wanted to snatch the piece out of my hand. "I wouldn't expect you to understand."

"Interesting." I tossed the piece again. "Because you know nothing about me."

This time he grabbed the pawn out of the air and put it back in place on the board. "I know your kind. Flighty, thoughtless, disrespectful."

"Sir—" Danec started.

He was silenced with a look from J'avet.

"You would do better to stay away from her, ensign," J'avet said coldly.

"Sir, I—"

"We're friends." I managed a good bit of frost in my tone as well. "Do you actually have the authority to make those kinds of decisions for him?"

J'avet stepped closer to me, until his nose was a handspan from mine. "I have the authority to have you put you on night shifts, and him on days until we reach Agus. I have the authority to order you both to refrain from fraternising. I have the authority to throw you both in the brig."

I swallowed. Not because I was scared of him, but because his proximity threatened to set my blood on fire.

"Commander," Danec began.

I interrupted him. "We're doing nothing wrong," I said coldly. After all, it was him who had approached us and insulted my intelligence, literally. I was furious, but I managed to contain myself, at least for now.

"See you don't," J'avet said. "One toe out of line and you will be in the brig until we reach Agus. Upon our arrival there, you'll be placed on the first ship back to Earth."

I had never wanted to punch someone more than I wanted to punch him. If I didn't believe his threat, I might have. Unfortunately I did believe it. I would have to watch myself, especially when he was around.

"We'll both be... be model passengers, sir," Danec stammered.

"See you are," J'avet said without taking his eyes off me. "I'd hate it if you shared her fate because of your poor taste in... friends." He glanced toward Danec and nodded.

"I'm sure both of you have somewhere else to be." Apparently he wasn't going to order us to avoid each other, at least not yet.

"Yes, Commander." I actually managed to keep sarcasm out of my voice. Gold star for me.

"Yes, sir." Danec put a hand on my shoulder and steered me toward the door.

It wasn't until the elevator doors closed that I let my anger show.

"Who does he think he is?" I snapped. "Surely the rec room is there for everyone?"

Danec sighed. "It is. I think I angered him when I didn't respond to the drill fast enough. He thinks I'm incompetent." He looked so sad, my heart went out to him.

I put an arm around him and gave him a hug.

He looked at me in surprise and his eyes lingered on mine for a moment. He swallowed audibly, then looked down at his feet.

"I don't think it's you," I assured him. "It's me he doesn't like." I had no idea what I had done, but his attitude pissed me off. At least let me screw up before you decide you don't like me. Then it might be justified.

"They said Parvorians are difficult," Danec said.

"They were right." I tucked a curl behind my ear, then did it again after it popped straight out. "From now on, I'll do my best to avoid him."

"Good idea," Danec said. "Is he what you humans would call an asshole or a dickhead? Or a prick?"

I laughed. Leave it to Danec to turn this into a learning

experience. "I'd say he's all three. And a few more words as well."

Danec nodded. "Asshole-dickhead-prick. That's quite a mouthful."

"I recommend you don't call him that to his face," I said. Although I would dearly love to.

Danec laughed, but cut it off when the doors slid open. "We shouldn't allow ourselves to be overheard," he said softly.

"Right." We would have to watch our backs until we reached Agus. I wasn't going to let any asshole-dickhead-prick get the better of me. No way. Whatever his problem was, it was his problem, not mine. He could carry around his groundless grudge, if that's what made him happy. I would forget all about him and get on with my life and my work.

If only I could forget how it felt to be that close to him. Perhaps a nice cold shower would help. Or a workout session with my trusty vibrator. We couldn't get to Agus soon enough, as far as I was concerned.

7

I'M sure it's a complete coincidence that I had night shifts every night for the next week. Kalvix and the other medics kept me so busy I had no time for more than a few words with Slek. I stumbled into my cabin just as Brinley was heading out for her shift. I would mutter tired words and she'd respond with sleepy ones. At least I didn't see J'avet, but I didn't see Danec either.

"Our patient's bone knitters come off today," Kalvix said as she walked into the infirmary right at seven am. "I trust you'll have no problem staying on for a while longer."

I suppressed a groan. "Yes, Doctor, of course." Truthfully, the night shift had been a long one.

A human woman had cut her finger and needed a couple of stitches.

A man from Garvi-3 had a kink in his tentacles, which I didn't know how to deal with. The doctor on duty had connected him to a machine that seemed to administer some kind of electric shock. The man had jerked, and his tentacles shot out like an angry puffer fish.

For a moment I thought he was in pain, but he smiled.

"That was exactly what I needed, thanks doc." He gave me a nod and made his way out the door.

"That was interesting," I remarked.

The doctor smiled. "Garvians are interesting folk." He was an older man, who spoke with a low, warm rumble. "They're technically blind, as we understand vision, but they use electric impulses to guide them around. When they've overdone it, they need a brief recharge."

"So their tentacles flop when they're tired?" I said.

The doctor chuckled. "In a manner of speaking, yes. Ordinarily they'd plug themselves in while they sleep, but sometimes that's not enough."

"That's cool," I said. Strange, but cool.

"Very." The doctor nodded and went back to his desk.

I went back to mine and opened the file on Garvi-3 so I could read more. With Slek asleep, and every surface spotlessly clean, there was little else for me to do. No nurse wished for a busy shift, but this was slower than I preferred. By the time it was over, I was ready to eat and sleep.

Until Kalvix arrived.

I followed her to Slek's bed and slipped in behind the curtain.

The purple guy from Frey-T was already awake and waiting for us. He'd managed to work himself up so he was sitting, but his arms stuck out uncomfortably.

"Oh good, you're both here." He grinned. "Time for a sponge bath and maybe a quick blow job?"

"It's time to remove those." Kalvix nodded toward the bone knitter closest to her. "You'll be able to wash and pleasure yourself soon enough."

Slek pouted. "But it's so much more fun when someone else does it. Wouldn't you agree, Edie?" He quirked an eyebrow at me.

"Sure," I said with a shrug, "but it's time you scratched your own itches."

From the deadpan look on Kalvix's face, she had read the file.

"She's spent too much time with you," Slek told the doctor. "She's become a spoilsport already." He raised a finger at me. "Don't forget we have a date planned after I get out of here. That," he paused for emphasis, "is imminent."

Kalvix shot me a look.

I suppose, unlike J'avet, she didn't care who her subordinates fraternised with outside their work hours. Maybe she thought I had dubious taste. Either way, she said nothing.

"I haven't forgotten," I assured Slek.

"Have you removed bone knitters before?" Kalvix asked.

"Yes, Doctor." I nodded.

"Very well." She waved at me to take off the left one, while she unwound the bandage from Slek's head.

He winced at her, then at me while I undid the clasps which held the knitters shut. Carefully, because the newly healed bone was still tender, I worked the knitter apart as wide as the hinges would allow.

"Can you lift your arm?" I asked.

Gingerly, Slek raised his arm so I could slide the knitter out from underneath it.

"It feels so light now," he said.

"Of course it does," I replied. "And look how puny your arm is." It was anything but. He was all muscle from his shoulder to the tips of his long, thick fingers.

He grinned and laughed. "You're a hard woman, Nurse Wright." He winced as Kalvix eased the gauze from his head wound. "Not as hard as you though, Doctor."

"Keep still," Kalvix said.

I didn't blame him for wincing. His head was a mess of fading bruises and a healing gash that must have hurt like a bitch.

I slipped out between the curtains to grab an X-ray wand and came back as Kalvix was applying some kind of blue substance to Slek's wound.

I passed the X-ray wand over Slek's arm and watched the small screen.

"I'm seeing a newly healed bone," I said. "It looks straight."

Kalvix nodded. As the doctor, she would double check, but I was confident she'd agree.

"Remove the other knitter, please," she instructed.

I stepped around to the other side of the bed and did as she asked.

"Another puny arm," I teased. What did he do for exercise, lift shuttles? I didn't ask him that, though. He seemed to have a healthy enough ego as it was. Besides, I knew my expression spoke volumes.

"This bone looks good too," I said.

"All my bones are impressive," Slek said with a sly smile. "Especially my cock."

"A penis is not a bone," I said dryly.

"Not right now it's not," he agreed, "but with a little encouragement— Ouch!"

"Sorry." Kalvix didn't sound sorry. "We can heal bones, but bruises need time. Perhaps don't land on your head."

"Thanks, I'll remember that next time I fall," Slek said sarcastically.

"Make sure you do." Kalvix took the X-ray wand when I offered it to her and waved it over his arms. "You're fit to leave, but I need to see you every morning to have that head wound assessed."

"Yes ma'am." He gave her a cheeky salute and swung his legs off the bed. The blankets fell aside, revealing his still naked body, ridiculous muscles and all.

"Nurse, bring him some clothes, please," Kalvix said. She averted her eyes, I suspected out of respect for her patient rather than because his nudity made her uncomfortable. She was too professional to behave otherwise. She stepped out of the cubicle with a shake of her head.

"No need, I'm not modest," Slek stood fully upright. He stood over a head taller than me.

"You might not be," I said, "but the rest of the ship doesn't need to be subjected to your—"

"Puny muscles?" he finished with a smirk.

"Exactly," I said. "There's no cure for that kind of trauma."

He chuckled. "So, about that date. Should we go now, or can I bend you over the bed and pound you silly?"

"If you harass my staff, I'll have to report you to your superior officer," Kalvix said from outside the curtain.

"*Now* you object," Slek said, loud enough for her to hear. "I think she likes me, deep down."

A snort and the sound of footsteps moving away was the only response his comment got.

"Wait there, I'll see what I can find." I slipped out without a glance over my shoulder and headed for the wardrobe where spare clothes were kept for times like this. I found a shirt and a pair of trousers in IF grey which should fit well enough, and took them back in. I handed them both to him and stood back while he dressed.

"I was serious about the date," he said. He winced a little while he pulled the shirt over his shoulders. "I know just the place."

"I'm sure you do, but it's breakfast time and I probably look a mess." I didn't need to consult a mirror to know much of my hair had exploded out of my hair-tie and sat around my head like a crown of fuzz.

"You look beautiful," he said firmly. "I don't offer to nail every girl I see, you know."

"Mmmhmm," I said, disbelieving.

"It's true," he protested. "Just the cute ones."

I might have stood up a bit taller. "You think I'm cute?"

"You're adorable," he said. "You must have guys chasing you right and left."

"Not exactly, no," I replied. "Some even hate my guts." I debated telling him about J'avet, but it didn't seem fair to get him involved in the situation, especially if he had to work with the man.

"Their loss." He buttoned up his shirt and leaned against the bed to pull on his pants.

"That's true," I agreed. Unless the asshole-dickhead-prick made Danec's life more difficult.

"What about tonight?" Slek zipped up his fly, after making a show of trying to tuck his cock in, as if it might be too big to fit. Maybe it was. "I can't work for a few more days, so I know I'm free."

"I'm on two days off after this," I replied.

He grinned. "Perfect, we can have dinner and then spend the next two days in bed."

"You're very sure I'll sleep with you," I said.

"I'm an eternal optimist," he said unapologetically. His expression turned serious for a moment. "I'm also a shameless flirt, in case you hadn't guessed, but I will respect you if you say no. Although, you've seen my dick, who wouldn't want to—"

"Engineer Slek," Kalvix's warning tone came from just outside the curtain.

"Oops, she's using my job title. She must be really pissed," Slek said loudly.

"Can you blame her?" I teased.

While he pretended to be hurt, Kalvix didn't bother to suppress a bark of laughter.

"See, she does like me," Slek said. He stuck his head out the curtain, then tugged it aside on the rail.

"Interesting theory," Kalvix said from the sink where she stood, washing her hands. Her antennas turned toward us, as if keeping an extra set of eyes on him.

Slek scratched his forehead. "So, no threesome then?"

"If you don't leave, I'll call security," Kalvix said, but she didn't look too serious. Yet.

"All right, all right, I'm going." He held his hands out to either side.

"Me too," I said. "Unless you need me for anything further?"

Kalvix waved me out the door with the cloth she used to dry her hands. "Enjoy your days off."

"I will. Thank you, Doctor." I could have skipped, but I walked out the door, weary and hungry. To Slek I said, "I'm in room seventy-seven. I'll see you at seven."

He saluted with a smile. "I'll be right on time." He turned smartly on a heel and winced as his bare foot squeaked on the floor. "That would have worked much better with boots on," he said over his shoulder.

I chuckled and started toward my room. Before I took a handful of steps, I spotted Jones, hands holding something to his chest. His eyes shifted this way and that, as though he was searching for someone, or hoping not to be seen. A Centaurian passed him and he looked down at the floor until he was past.

He drew himself up and strode down the corridor, but my suspicion was already piqued. He was up to something and I wanted to know what. I should probably call security and let them deal with it, but they might only scare him away. For whatever reason, he seemed to think he could talk to me. He might do that now, but I didn't want to confront him directly.

I changed direction and followed him at a distance

Jones ducked around a corner and into another section of the corridor. I stopped at a discreet distance and waited, but he didn't come back out. A sign on the wall next to the corridor was in English and a few other alien languages. It read, 'Communications and navigation.'

Nothing suspicious about him going in there. Maybe.

I hurried across and peered down into the corridor. A woman from Agus stepped out of a doorway and gave me a funny look.

Now who seemed suspicious?

I flashed her a smile. "I think this is the right place. This ship is a maze, don't you think?"

"Uh, indeed." She hurried away without a backwards glance.

I made a face to myself and moved carefully in the direction Jones had gone.

The room the woman had stepped out of was wall to wall vidscreens and about half a dozen occupants from different planets. All calling home, I presumed. I would have to do the same at some point, but until now I'd been too busy to give it much thought. My mother would be wondering how I was doing. My siblings too, if they took a moment from their busy lives to think about me.

Yeah, none of us would win the prize for keeping in touch.

I straightened my back and marched past the doorway as though I belonged in that part of the ship, and kept walking. If that was communications, then navigation must be—

"Why are you following me?" Jones hissed.

He appeared in front of me so suddenly it took a moment to register.

"Where did you come from?" I asked. "What makes you think I'm following you?" I crossed my arms over my chest and tried to stare him down. He was only the same age as me, maybe even a little younger, but his eyes were blue chips of bitterness and ice.

"Navigation," he said icily. "I wanted to see how long until we reach Agus."

I narrowed my eyes. "You know as well as I do how long the journey is." I noticed then that whatever he'd held to his chest, he no longer had it. His arms hung by his sides, hands curled half into fists. "What are you really doing here?"

"I could ask you the same thing," he said, "if you weren't following me."

I exhaled in frustration. "Fine, I was following you, but only because you looked suspicious."

He frowned, then shrugged. "If I did, it's because I don't trust *anyone* on board."

I didn't miss the emphasis. "I thought humans were okay, as far as you were concerned?"

"Until they start following me," he retorted.

"Touché. You still haven't said why you're really here."

"Like I said, I wanted to know—"

I interrupted. "I don't buy it."

He growled in the back of his throat. "I get caught up in studying. I lose track of time. I thought it was the third day of the week, but it's the fourth. I assumed my watch was faulty." He held up his wrist. Around it, he wore a watch the same as mine.

"That's what you were holding?" I asked.

He looked confused for a moment, then nodded. "I was ready to throw it at a wall if it was that off. Turns out, it was me who was off." He gave an awkward laugh, but there was something in his eyes that suggested he wasn't telling the whole story, and that he wouldn't, even if I pushed.

I considered my next words, and went with a gentle tease, in the hope it might defuse the situation somewhat.

"That's really dorky. Maybe you should take a break once in a while."

He snorted. "Yeah, that's what my father used to say before he worked himself to death."

"Oh." So much for making things better. "I'm sorry. That must have been difficult."

He rubbed the bridge of his nose with one finger. "I guess. I hardly saw him, so it's no great loss, I guess."

"I don't know, it hurts to lose someone you love." I spoke from experience, but only older, frail and not well known aunts and uncles. It still stung each time.

"Yeah, I guess. Do you want to get a coffee?" His expression was so guarded, I couldn't tell if he hoped I'd say no or yes.

"I really can't," I said regretfully. "It's been a long shift and I need to grab a sandwich and some sleep."

He seemed indifferent to my response, but at least he didn't get angry again.

"Fine. Another time maybe."

"Sure. I need a coffee quite often. If I see you in the mess, I'll say hi. Or, you know, if I see you skulking around the corridors."

Anger flashed in his eyes for a moment. "I wasn't—" He must have realised I was teasing because he stopped and sucked in a breath. "You're joking. Sorry, sometimes I just…"

"It's okay." I put a hand lightly on his shoulder, but drew it back when he frowned at it. "If you ever need to talk, I'm here for you. Or one of the doctors."

"I don't need their help," he snapped. He rubbed the bridge of his nose again. "I should go."

"Yeah." I stepped back away from him and let him stalk past me, back down the corridor. "I'll see you later."

"Yeah," he said over his shoulder. "Later."

He disappeared around the corner and was gone.

It wasn't until I turned back in the direction of my room that I realised his file hadn't said anything about his father dying.

8

"ARE you sure we're allowed up here?" I gripped the railing in both hands and peered over the edge into the near darkness. The only light below came from a bank of controls on the far side of the lower level, near a door.

"Of course we're not," Slek said. He turned the light on his watch. "That's half the fun." He must have seen my expression because he grinned, white teeth flashing in the dark.

"Don't worry, we won't get caught. No one comes here, especially at night. Except to do maintenance, and no one's rostered for that right now. I checked."

"If you're wrong, you'll be in the brig right beside me," I said in a playful growl. I assumed they wouldn't send an engineer back to his home world in disgrace, but he could still get in a lot of trouble.

"I'll happily share a cell with you," he said, his smile lopsided. "Imagine the things we could get up to in there."

"Nothing, they'd have security watching us all the time," I said dryly.

He made a dismissive sound. "A minor inconvenience. Besides, I would soon make you forget all about them." His hand brushed across my ass and I jumped.

He chuckled. "Come on, I have everything set up over here."

'Everything' consisted of a blanket spread out on the floor near the wall, and a picnic basket, made of metal. Okay, it was a maintenance bucket, but I appreciated the look he was going for.

He knelt on the blanket and switched on a small light which sat to one side.

The light flashed frantically, like an emergency light.

I held up my hand in front of my eyes and squinted against the sudden, pulsating glare.

"Oops, wrong setting." He flicked a switch on the side and the light settled to a single, soft glow.

I lowered my hand and took in the sight of him on his knees on the blanket. He wore casual clothes. Black trousers and a black shirt which was so tight around his enormous biceps that I didn't know how the seams held together. On his feet he wore boots which looked well worn. Also black.

In comparison, my aqua t-shirt and black pants looked like a riot of colour.

"This is romantic," I said. Honestly, I was surprised. I wasn't used to guys doing sweet things like this. Usually it was a fast food meal and an action movie. Both awesome things, but not very intimate. Perhaps I had misjudged his flirty nature. There was clearly more to him than I had suspected. I reminded myself to keep an open mind from now on.

I sat on the blanket with my back to the wall. My hand tingled from where it touched his. It was a different feeling to Danec's touch, but just as heady. The butterflies in my stomach moved around in lazy spirals.

"We're not allowed alcohol on board, so we have water or synth milk." Slek reached into the bucket and pulled out a bottle of each.

"Water is fine, thank you." I accepted the metal cup, full to the brim when he handed it to me and quickly sipped to keep from spilling it. "Delicious."

Recycled umpteen times, it didn't exactly taste fresh, but it was drinkable.

"I looked for champagne glasses, but for some reason the *Infinity* doesn't have any." He made a face. "Something about wasting space and not being a priority. Blah, blah. Anyway, we also have sandwiches." He drew out a plate. "Vegetables, garu nut butter, synthcheese, or honey?"

"Honey?" I echoed, unable to keep the excitement from my voice. "Is it real?"

Slek tried to look insulted, but he ruined it with his smile. "Yes, a friend brought a few jars from Earth. I managed to score a couple." He handed me a honey sandwich on brown bread.

"By score do you mean your friend doesn't know you have them?" I asked. A smile tugged at the corners of my mouth. Being around him made it hard not to smile and laugh. He was fun to be around. What was the old saying? Never a dull moment.

Slek laughed. "No, he knows. I might have over exaggerated the amount of pain my injuries caused, so he'd take pity, but it was voluntary on his part."

"More or less," I said.

"Well, yes," he agreed, without a hint of shame or regret. "I owe him now though."

I bit into my sandwich and savoured the sweetness of genuine, sticky honey. It tasted like home and deliciousness.

"Mmmm, totally worth it. So, do you come here often?" *Geez, Edie, why don't you say the corniest line in the book?* I mentally cringed at myself.

"All the time," he replied around a mouthful. "I fell over the railing right beside you."

"Ah." I glanced at it as though it might give way at any moment. "That's very... romantic." It was certainly an interesting location for a date.

"Isn't it though?" he agreed. "Scene of the crime and all."

"I thought you fell?"

"Scene of the accident, then. Actually," he looked serious for a moment, "I was nervous about coming up here. I thought if I had a good memory, it might help me when I have to get back to work. Is that weird?" The side of his mouth drew back as if he expected me to laugh.

"It's sweet," I told him. "I'm glad I could help in some way."

He blinked in surprise, then fist pumped the air. "I've never been called sweet before."

I laughed. "Don't let it go to your head too much."

"Which head?" he shot back immediately.

"Either," I replied firmly. Silence fell for a moment before I said, "Can I ask you a question?"

"Anything," he said. "If you're going to ask if you can suck my cock, the answer is yes."

"I wasn't," I replied. I ignored his pout and said, "I know a guy, a friend, who is also from Frey-T. He seems a lot more, uh, innocent than you. His knowledge of humans comes from a vidscreen."

"Mine comes from being on the *Infinity* for a few years," Slek replied easily. "And fucking a number of them."

"I see." I should have known what his response would be. "You've been with a few of us?"

"Well..." He drew out the word.

"One or two?" I cocked my head.

"Um..."

"Slek?" I raised my eyebrows.

"What? Zero is a number," he said sheepishly. "I have interacted with a lot of humans and tried to sleep with the pretty ones, okay?"

I shrugged. "Okay, but why not be honest about it?"

"I have a reputation to uphold. What would people think?"

"I don't know, does it really matter what they think?" I creased my brow and watched him intently.

He hesitated. "I guess not." He paused again before he added, "I care what you think."

"Because you want to sleep with me?" I finished my last bite of sandwich and washed it down.

"No," he said firmly. "I mean yes, I do, but I care what you think because I like you. Most humans are kinda dull and..." he grinned, "puny. But you're cute and funny and smart. And—"

"Yes?" Did I really want to know what he had to add?

"No one on Frey-T, or most of the planets I know, have curly hair. It's..." He cocked his head. "It's special."

I put a hand to my hair and blushed furiously. "You think so?"

"I *know* so," he said. "What a fascinating shade of pink your skin has become. Are you part Parvoran, by any chance? Wait, no, you don't seem furry enough. Not in any places I've seen yet, anyway."

I blushed harder. "I'm one hundred percent human," I muttered. "And not furry, except where I'm meant to have fur. I mean my eyebrows," I added quickly.

"Of course you did." He laughed. "So, why don't you tell me more about yourself."

"What do you want to know?" I asked. I hoped the blush would fade quickly.

"Everything." He reclined on his elbow and toasted me with a cup of synthmilk. "Start with where you were born."

He listened intently while I told him about my childhood, my parents, my tendency to nurse my siblings while they were sick, which led me to go into the profession. I told him why I left Earth and how much I loved chocolate.

"I'll have to remember that," he said. "I think I'm going to have to work hard if I'm going to impress you."

"Yes, you do," I said, only half joking. "What about you?"

"What about me?" He leaned back against the wall, a lazy smile on his lips. "I'm already impressed with myself."

I swatted him on the arm. When I touched his skin, my fingers burned like I'd swiped my hand across a hot stove. More electricity than the jolt the Garvian had received, shot through me, to the last drop of blood which now pounded in every vein like a hammer.

Slek's lips dropped apart and I knew he felt it too. It was more than desire. It was a yearning to be close to him, to find out everything. To understand the man behind the flirtation. Okay, it was desire as well, I'm only human.

"I told you everything about myself," I said softly. "Now I want to know about you."

"I have a feeling," he said, his voice the same pitch, "that I've only started to scratch the surface." He sucked in a breath and his usual boyishness was back. "I was born in the capital of Frey-T. My father was a teacher, my mother is an engineer. She designs ships like this." He gestured around the room with his cup. "So guys like me can complain about the bad design when we have to repair things. Before you ask, no, she never listens to my suggestions. If she had, there would be Blarviun ale running through the pipes instead of water."

"I don't fancy the idea of showering in ale." I wrinkled my nose.

"That's what she said. In your case, I would happily lick it all off." He stuck out his tongue and licked the air a couple of times. The end split in two, like a snake's.

A shiver passed through me. I could imagine him doing a few things with that tongue...

I cleared my throat, but it did little to suppress the throb in my body.

"That wouldn't work for everyone on board," I said, my voice higher than usual. "Commander J'avet, for one." I meant it as a joke, but the image of the Parvoran sucking ale off my breasts popped into my head. Just the thought made me wet as hell. Okay, more wet.

"It might do him some good," Slek said. "He might lighten up a little."

"Yeah." I really needed to change the subject before I made a total mess of my panties. "So you went into engineering because your mother did it, or just to get ale into the pipes?"

He chuckled. "I had an aptitude for it. My father was disappointed." His expression turned rueful. "Teaching is a traditionally male job on Frey-T. He wanted me to follow him. Can you imagine me teaching university?"

"I can imagine you getting into trouble with every pretty student who came your way," I replied.

"Yeah, I probably wouldn't have lasted very long. It's safer to work with machines. They don't mind if you get intimate with them." A frown crossed his features. "I don't mean like *that*. That would be weird. I mean you touch them and they don't complain. Unless they're androids. Some of those really hate being repaired. I met one once who swore it tickled every time I tried to unscrew a bolt." He shook his head and furrowed his brow, but looked amused.

"Is that even possible?" I asked. My knowledge of androids and robots was limited to the ones in factories, which put together vehicles and technology. I'd never actually seen one.

"Yes and no," he replied. "Technically, machines can't feel anything, but their creators can make them think they can. I'm not sure if they want to make them like living beings, or if they're just smart asses."

"Both?" I suggested.

He scratched his forehead. "Possibly. Personally, I don't see the point. Imagine if the *Infinity* was more alive. She might throw us off if we touch her the wrong way."

"Perhaps that was what happened." I waved at the healing wound on his head.

"Now you mention it, that makes sense." He looked thoughtful. "I should be more careful how I handle the old girl from now on."

I shook my head at him and smiled. I couldn't picture him being rough with the ship. After all, if he broke it, he'd have to fix it.

"Siblings?" I asked.

"Two sisters, both older," he replied. "They liked to play with me like I was a doll."

"I can see you in a dress and a pretty pink wig," I teased.

He put his empty cup in the bucket and took mine from my fingers when I nodded that I was done.

"The funny thing is, that's exactly what I would put myself in." He leaned back against the wall again and cupped his hands behind his head. "A curly pink wig and yellow dress stuffed full so I had big boobs." He wiggled his eyebrows at me and grinned.

"I'm sure you were very pretty," I said, trying not to laugh. He would have looked adorable and I had no issue with people of any gender or species dressing however they liked.

"The prettiest," he agreed. "But not as pretty as you." He leaned in to catch a curl around his finger. He twirled it slowly and stared in fascination as though he'd never touched hair before. "You're so soft." His voice broke on the last word. "I had no idea."

I blushed.

He smiled and moved his hand to the back of my head, feather light, stroking in wonder. He caught up a handful and gently pulled me to him.

My eyes locked on his. I had never seen that shade of blue before. They looked as if they should crackle with electricity.

"Edie." His breath brushed my cheek, warm and scented with honey. Sweet and hot, all at the same time.

"Mmmhmm?" I couldn't be trusted with actual words right now.

"Can I kiss you?"

"Mmmhmm." My eyes half closed, stomach fluttered with nervous anticipation.

When his lips met mine, I wanted to explode and implode all at once. Fire danced through my veins like flames on tinder dry wood.

He kissed me gently, softy, barely more than a brush before he pulled away.

"I want so much more," he said, his voice husky, "but I don't want to spoil this. I don't want to rush."

I nodded. Part of me wanted him to pin me beneath him and pound me until I screamed, but I wanted more with him than just sex.

"Agreed," I said reluctantly. "No rushing. We have—" I was going to say, 'all the time in the world' but in truth, we had this journey. Once we reached Agus, I would get off the *Infinity* and he wouldn't. My heart sank a little, but if there was anything to this, we would make it work.

"I—"

His words were interrupted by an enormous bang and the deck shifted under us.

9

"WHAT THE—" The deck slanted and I was thrown painfully against the rail. Tears of pain sprang to my eyes. I blinked and cleared them as the bucket and lights slid through a gap and were gone.

We were plunged into darkness.

Slek said something which sounded like, "Not again," and grunted. He reached for my hands and pulled me to him. His arms went around me and he held me while the ship canted the other way.

"Fuck." I gasped as we hit the wall, although he shielded me from the worst of the impact. "Your bones are still—"

"I'm fine. We need to get out of here."

An alarm sounded once, twice. A voice thundered out speakers a metre or two overhead.

"All personnel and passengers, make your way to the pod bay, immediately. This is not a drill. I repeat, make your way to the pod bay and prepare to evacuate the ship. This is *not* a drill."

"Getting out of here is a good idea," I said. Blood slammed through my ears, which rang from the volume of the warning. The silence which followed was almost as loud.

"Yeah." Slek grabbed my hand and pulled me to my feet.

I turned the light on my watch and he did the same with his.

"Don't let go," he said.

He didn't need to tell me twice. Truthfully I wasn't sure I could release my grip on him if I wanted to. The warmth of his skin helped keep my fear at bay.

He tugged me back toward the hatch which led out of the engine room. Thank goodness we didn't have to climb a ladder to get down, although the hatch was small. Designed only for maintenance and not regular traffic, we both had to duck while we stepped over the threshold. My heart hammered all the way, sure that with one more cant in the wrong direction, we'd be flung off the railing and into the engine.

We stepped out of the hatch and into the chaos of confused passengers and ship personnel.

"It must be bad if they aren't calling for you to fix it," I said, breathless with fear and adrenaline.

"All the more reason we should hurry." He pulled me between two dazed looking Centaurians, who seemed to have been woken from a deep sleep by the alarm.

"Brinley," I said quickly. "And Danec. What if they're asleep?" I couldn't leave them.

The alarm sounded again, even louder out here than in the engine room.

I winced at the noise. "On second thought, I doubt they would sleep through that." Still, I scanned the corridor ahead for a sign of either of them.

"Slek," I said after a few moments.

"Yes, Edie?"

My tongue darted over my lips. "Please tell me there's enough pods for everyone."

The woman in front of me turned and gave me a horrified look before she hurried on.

"More than enough," Slek assured me. "Frey-T learnt that lesson after the first ship needed to be evacuated."

"Was it called Titanic?" I asked ironically.

He gave me a funny look. "No. *Dreevam*, after our first president."

"Ah. Ow." A man from Agus stepped on my toe in his attempt to push past us. "We'll all get there."

No sooner had I said that than the ship rocked again. We were thrown against each other, and the wall.

Someone screamed and I realised it was me.

Slek's hand gripped mine tighter than ever. "We need to reach the end of this corridor, then—"

"Then what?" I asked, my voice high.

"We take an elevator or service shaft."

"If the power goes out while we're on an elevator—"

"We're fucked," he finished for me. "Service shaft it is." He pulled me so hard I almost had to run to keep up. We skidded to a stop at the end of the line which led to a hole in the wall. A security officer with the tentacles of a Garvian directed people one by one into a dark hole in the side of the wall.

"One at a time in an orderly manner," he said calmly. "One at a time."

In spite of that, the crowd pushed and jostled as people pressed to reach the chute first.

Someone else stepped on my foot, but at this point I was too scared to growl at them.

Slek squeezed my hand. "It's okay. We'll be fine."

The ship rocked and I squealed. "Are you sure?" Right now, I didn't feel very certain. Anything but.

"I'm absolutely sure. Look, we're next." He nodded toward the chute. How he or the Garvian could be so calm, I didn't know, but I drew on my training for emergencies and forced myself to breathe.

The voice over the loudspeaker repeated the warning to evacuate the ship.

"We're trying to," I muttered. Then I was face to face with the deep, dark hole. And the chute which disappeared around a bend and out of sight.

"Ladies first." Slek said. "It's just a big slide. It's usually used for dirty laundry."

"Wonderful," I muttered. "For the record, that isn't the kind of dirty talk I like." I let him help me through the hole, so I was sitting at the top of the chute.

He chuckled. "You have your watch and I'm right on your ass," he said. "I'll be thinking dirty thoughts all the way down."

All the innuendos and no time to enjoy them.

I sucked in a breath and might have hesitated, but he gave me a shove and I started to slide. With nothing to hold on to and no way to slow myself, I gritted my teeth and tried not to scream. I felt as though I was in free-fall, with no net and no end, just round and round in a loop, faster and faster.

I let out a whimper which bubbled up in my chest. It bubbled harder and harder until I wasn't sure I could stop myself from screaming and screaming.

Just before I did, I slid out the end of the long tube and into the arms of someone who thrust me aside the moment I regained my feet. They turned to do the same for Slek, but he flew out of the chute with a grin and landed like a cat.

"You've done that before," I said.

"A time or two." He reclaimed my hand and we made our way with the throng toward the rear of the ship. A lot of people were dressed in IF regulation pyjamas, but some were naked. I guess when a disembodied voice tells you to leave immediately, you do just that.

I thought I caught a glimpse of Kalvix, but she was swept away before I could be sure.

The push and jostle resumed at the entrance to the pod bay, which was wide enough for four or five people, but not the eight or nine which were trying to get through all at once.

Slek and I stopped and waited along with the rest, taking only small steps every few moments.

I was so focused on the doorway I didn't see anyone approach until I was almost knocked off my feet.

"Edie!" Brinley almost shouted in my ear. She hugged me so hard I could barely breathe. "You're all right!"

"Yes." I drew my head away from her and winced. "You too. Do you know what happened?"

Brinley shook her head. "Something about an explosion in or near the navigation array. They're worried whatever caused it will spread."

The ship rocked again and a bang sounded, followed by another.

"Shit," I muttered.

"Yes, come on." Brinley grabbed my spare hand and pulled.

"I've been assigned to pod twelve. I was on my way there when I saw you." She blinked at Slek, who was still attached to my other hand. "You can come too."

"Thanks," he said dryly, but let himself be pulled through the crowds to the doorway.

"Pilot coming through," Brinley said, her voice brisk, businesslike.

The crowd muttered, but they parted to let us pass. I ignored the glares. They would all get on a pod, but without a pilot, they wouldn't leave. Without a nurse, their injuries would go untreated. I made every justification I could think of, but I still felt guilty for pushing in.

I forgot about it a moment later when Danec, with a worried look on his face, spotted me. His face split in a broad smile. My heart promptly flipped, because it has no idea about appropriate timing.

"You're okay," he said happily.

"Have you been assigned a pod?" Brinley asked. When he shook his head, she nodded. "You're with us then, ensign." She nodded up ahead. "Pod twelve. It will be up to you to make sure we have no more than fifty on board. That's more than I'd like and we'll have to recycle the oxygen more quickly, but any less and we won't all get off this ship."

"Yes, ma'am," Danec said. "I can do that." He drew himself up taller and made his face look stern. He looked a bit like he needed to pee, but when it came down to it, he would do as she asked. All of our lives depended on it.

We pushed through to our pod and Brinley keyed in a code on the pad beside the door. Silently, it slid open and we stepped inside.

"Stay by the door," Brinley told Danec. "Count them all."

"Don't forget to count us," Slek said helpfully.

Danec gave him a funny look, but nodded.

A shout came from outside, followed by the sound of people eager to board.

"Five. Six."

While Danec counted, I moved further into the small vessel. Really just a shuttle, the pod consisted of a cockpit, storage bay and a section for seating. Off to one side was a small room full of bunks, perhaps enough for twenty to sleep. We'd have to sleep in shifts if we were here that long.

Brinley hurried into the cockpit.

Slek followed. "The pod should be ship shape, but just in case—"

I settled into a spot at the front, near the window and sat facing the door. On a small craft like this, we'd have little more than a first aid kit, but I would be ready if I was needed. Okay, *when* I was needed.

"One at a time," a voice roared from outside the door. "Ensign, how many passengers are in this pod?"

I squashed down in my seat and grimaced. With any luck, he would keep moving.

"Forty-six, sir," Danec replied.

"Three more over here. No, I said three. No more."

Three evacuees, two women and a man, hurried inside and took the last of the seats. When the door slid shut, I grimaced. It deepened when I saw Commander J'avet firmly on *this* side of the door, followed by Danec, who looked like he wished the floor would swallow him up.

"Fuck," I said under my breath.

The pod's engine started up. J'avet strode between the seats to the cockpit. He stopped when he reached me and scowled, but he marched inside.

The pod rose and glided toward the outer door. It slid first into a small section, where we stopped. A door slid closed behind us and the space doors opened.

"See, no being thrown out the airlock." Danec slipped into the seat beside me and put a hand on my knee.

"No, we're just flying out of it instead." I watched the side of the ship glide by before we moved out into space.

"The IF will send help." Danec sounded so sure.

"And if they don't?" I asked. I hadn't planned to die on a pod, out in space, with Commander J'avet present.

Danec shook his head. "Then we'll find a moon and wait."

"Oh good." That didn't sound much better.

"At least we both made it." Did he move his hand further up my thigh on purpose?

"Yes, thank goodness for that," I agreed.

Infinity grew smaller in the window. Once in a while, another pod would shoot out, or what looked like debris would float past.

I put my hand over Danec's and we sat there like that for a while, in silence.

10

"ANY IDEA WHAT HAPPENED?" Slek flopped into a chair and propped his booted feet on the one in front of him. He spoke softly, so as to not wake the twenty or so sleeping passengers in the bunk room and the dozen who curled up on the floor.

J'avet rubbed his hands over his face and pinched the bridge of his nose. "Sensors suggest an explosion. Cause unknown."

"There's nothing in that part of the ship to cause something catastrophic." Slek frowned. "Just a few conduits, computer banks... They should have been isolated automatically as soon as something went wrong."

"Assuming it was accidental," J'avet said. He lowered his hand and exhaled. "We won't know until IF can get out and tow her to port."

"The closest port is Dendra," Slek said. "But it will take weeks for IF to get around to sending anyone."

J'avet nodded, then scowled at me as if he'd just realised I was there.

I ignored the look and aimed a question at Slek. "Is there any chance it was sabotage?"

In the corner of my eye, J'avet twitched.

"What?" he snapped.

Slek's brow furrowed deeper in confusion. "What do you mean?"

I tried not to wilt under the scrutiny of them and Danec, who sat beside me still, his hands on his lap.

I told them about my encounter with Jones in the corridor and his claim to have needed to check his watch. It had seemed halfway plausible then. Now it sounded ludicrous.

If J'avet's face wasn't already red, I think he would have turned maroon. His eyes flashed, literally. I swear I saw sparks of electricity erupt in his irises.

"You were aware of a potentially dangerous dissenter on board and you said nothing?" he growled.

Part of me wanted to shrink back from his anger, but I didn't. Fuck him, I wasn't going to let him think I was weak.

I lifted my chin. "If I told security every time someone was angry at someone else for no apparent reason, I would waste a lot of their time."

J'avet's eyes narrowed. "Not everyone, just the ones who plan to destroy a ship and everyone on it."

I clenched my jaw. "I'm not telepathic," I said coolly. "Besides, Jones wouldn't be the first human who thought we should take better care of Earth and stand on our own two feet."

J'avet poked a thick finger in my direction. "And that's why Earth isn't ready to join the IF."

I wanted to swat his finger away. "That's not up to you."

"No. If it was, you'd be out, and all spacefaring craft ordered to stay away."

Slek looked as if he wanted to say something, but he closed his mouth. I guess he figured I could stick up for myself. He didn't seem to find J'avet intimidating in the least.

"You sound just like Jones," I told J'avet curtly. "Closed minded, just because people are different."

He spluttered for a moment before his expression turned cold. "I have no issue with people being different. I take exception to those who harbour resentment because other worlds are far more advanced."

"I wouldn't say far more," Slek said. Apparently he couldn't keep silent anymore.

J'avet glanced at him, then back at me. "If the IF finds an explosive device planted on *Infinity*, in the area of communications and navigation, with any trace of your friend on it, I will consider you complicit in the destruction of the ship."

Before I could do more than gape, he rose and stalked away, as far as he could go in such a small space.

"He's not my friend," I said to J'avet's back.

"Asshole-dickhead-prick," Danec whispered.

I held back a snort. The situation was bad enough without J'avet knowing we were laughing at him.

"Yeah," I muttered, then cursed softly to myself. "Is that even possible?"

"Finding you complicit?" Slek asked. He lowered his feet and leaned over to put a hand on my knee. "We'll be sure it doesn't happen."

"Yes, we will." Danec shifted closer and put an arm around my shoulders.

With both men so close, I was both confused and hot at the same time. Danec wanted to be friends, Slek wanted to take it slowly, and we were on a pod full of people. That didn't stop my mind from going into overdrive, fuelled by heated, pounding blood.

I swallowed and forced a half smile. "Thanks, guys. I suppose I should have said something, but Jones just seemed angry, not destructive. He wanted to go to Agus to make Earth a better place. Or so he said." Maybe I was so naive, I bought every word. I didn't want to think the worst of people. Well, most people.

I glanced toward J'avet, who now stood in the cockpit, speaking to Brinley in a low voice. I heard the name 'Jones' mentioned and Brinley nodded. No doubt J'avet put the word out to find the man. That was fair enough. With any luck, they would find him and he'd tell them I had nothing to do with what happened. Then J'avet could apologise—

Okay, I'm not that naive.

"We should try to get some rest," I said.

"Right. That reminds me." Slek pulled a screwdriver out of his pocket, rose, and crouched beside me. He undid the screws which held the row of seats in place and pushed it back as quietly as he could.

"If we're going to be here a while, we might as well get comfortable." He put the screwdriver away while Danec pulled out three spare pillows from the bunk room.

He tossed them into the empty space, then blushed. "Ummm."

"I'll sleep in the middle," I said, lying down.

Eyes wide, Danec lay down on one side, while Slek lay on

the other. I faced Danec, who blushed even harder, before he placed a hand lightly on one of mine.

I gave him a soft smile, which he returned and made my heart flip.

Slek placed a hand on my hip, which made the *rest* of me flip.

"Good night," Danec whispered. His eyes flicked down to my lips. If I didn't know he wanted to be friends, I would think he wanted to kiss me. Instead, he swallowed hard and closed his eyes.

"Night," I said. Why was I so disappointed that he didn't kiss me? I was okay with being friends, wasn't I? Plus Slek's hand had moved to my ass. He cupped a cheek and gave it a squeeze.

Oh my goodness.

I closed my eyes and tried to sleep, while wishing Slek would move his hand down between my legs.

I fell asleep and dreamed of Slek, Danec, and J'avet, their hands all over me, mouths licking and sucking—

"Attention everyone."

I woke with a jolt. The pod's lights were on, suggesting it was morning, at least by someone's calculations. Considering the timing, I would guess J'avet's. Damn, dream him had been about to slide into—

"Pilot Brinley has informed me we don't have enough fuel to reach Denara." J'avet spoke from the front of the ship.

The evacuees let out a collective groan.

J'avet scowled at me as though the whole thing was my fault.

I hadn't even groaned. Except in my dream. I groaned a lot there. And moaned. Oh crap, had I moaned in my sleep? I glanced at Danec and Slek. They were sitting up, intent on what J'avet was saying.

I rubbed my eyes and tried to wake up more. I finally registered what J'avet said.

"We'll have to put down on Calig," J'avet said. "As most of you will know—" Again he glared at me, "Calig is unpopulated. The atmosphere is conducive to life, but resources are minimal. We will have to ration our food until the IF can reach us."

Danec raised a shaking hand. "Sir, will all the pods land there?"

J'avet nodded. "Each pod was allocated the same amount of fuel. We will all make our way there and wait." He nodded and went to sit beside Brinley, who looked exhausted. He said something about taking a break and she nodded.

She rose and came to flop down beside Danec.

"I'm sorry, I tried to be sparing, but the pod really wasn't designed for so many people, so far from a port."

"We'll be sure to evacuate somewhere more convenient next time." Slek grinned.

Brinley snorted and lay down on his abandoned pillow. "Do that," she said with a smile. "The pod is on autopilot. I should sleep for a few hours. We won't reach Calig until tomorrow morning."

"Just enough time for J'avet to decide I should take a space-walk," I said, with a frustrated sigh. "I wish I knew why he hates me so much."

"Because you're adorable and have people who care about you?" Slek suggested. He leaned down to give me a lingering kiss on my mouth.

"Right," Danec agreed. "He's just a grumble pants."

Slek and Brinley laughed and I made a face, but managed to smile at Slek.

"Thank you for thinking I'm adorable," I told him.

"I think you are t-t-too," Danec stammered. "Adorable, I mean, not a-a grumble pants."

"I can be both," I admitted. "I'm only human."

"Hey." Slek caught my chin with his finger and lifted it so I looked him in the eyes. "There's no such thing as 'just a human.' Humans are amazing."

"Even if a human might have been responsible for this?" I asked.

When Brinley gave me a questioning look, I told her about Jones.

"Oh," she said slowly. "He's odd and angry, but to do something like this? It seems extreme."

"Yes, well, tell J'avet that." I jerked an elbow in his direction. "After you sleep," I added, when she looked like she might get up and tell him off right now.

"If he wants me to fly this pod, then he better be nice," she declared.

"Are you planning to stop?" Slek asked, his expression somewhere between teasing and genuine curiosity.

Brinley barked a throaty laugh. "Of course not. I want to get us off this pod safely as much as everyone else." She sighed loudly. "Still, I wish we could make it further. Calig is off any shipping routes. Uninhabited, deserted."

"It sounds like paradise," I said. "Jones will love it." Assuming he made it off *Infinity* alive.

"There's no internet," Brinley groaned.

"What?" I feigned outrage. "No cat videos?"

"Not one," she agreed. "No online shopping either. Or chatting to friends. No social media."

"This is sounding better and better," I said. "But we won't be there for long."

"Right," Slek agreed. "The IF will have a ship on the way there already. They might even arrive before we do."

"That's right," Danec agreed. "Just in time for a hot shower and warm food."

Brinley groaned. "I hadn't even thought about showers."

"I guess you never camped as a kid?" I asked.

"Hell no." She grimaced, her tongue stuck out between her teeth. "I'm a city girl through and through."

"You're in for a treat then," I said, "if IF doesn't arrive first."

"Oh, you've camped?" Slek asked.

"No," I replied, "but how bad can it be?"

The side of Brinley's mouth drew back. "Let's hope the IF is there, waiting."

I agreed, but silently I was worried. What if they found Jones, but he claimed I was his accomplice? Nothing anyone said to J'avet would change his mind about me, I was sure of that. He'd send me straight back to Earth and that would be that.

It might come to that, but I would fight before it did. For some reason I couldn't explain, some tiny part of the back of my mind wanted to change his mind about me. The fact he hated me hurt, although it shouldn't. No part of me should care what an asshole thinks, especially with Danec and Slek on either side of me.

Who needs you, J'avet? I thought.

Want, well, that was another thing.

11

WE PASSED through the atmosphere of Calig without more than a bump. Still, a few gasped and exhaled loudly. Most aboard were awake now, huddled in groups with blankets around them, or nibbling on the dry ration bars and instant noodles which were all the pod was stocked with. Thankfully the pod was also stocked with enough clothes that no one was naked. Some still wore their pyjamas, but didn't seem too worried. At least they were alive.

"I'm looking for a place to land," Brinley said over her shoulder. "Everyone strap in."

She looked worried about something, but I couldn't ask right now, especially with J'avet sitting in the copilot's seat beside her.

Instead, I sat in what was my usual spot now, between Danec and Slek. Slek had screwed the seats back in and checked on the rest of them, and the strapping. If we crashed, no one would get thrown through a window. Small mercy considering we'd probably die anyway. Of course, I had every faith in Brinley that wouldn't happen.

"Are you all right?" Slek ran a thumb over the back of my hand.

"I'm fine," I said. "We're about to land on a strange, alien world. What could go wrong?"

We hadn't seen any sign of the IF. If J'avet had received word from them, he wasn't sharing that information, at least not with me. I certainly didn't see a big ship in orbit, nor were we heading for a safe little ole pod bay. Nope, we were heading for a world that looked to have less water than Earth, approximately eighty percent if I guessed right, green continents, and huge frozen poles.

"From what I've read, Calig is like Earth was before industrialisation," Danec said.

I was coming to realise that. "Why hasn't it been colonised?"

"Few natural metals," Danec replied. "And it's out of the way from everywhere."

"Right. If you tell me there are dragons on this planet..."

He gave me a funny look. "Dragons?"

I shook my head. "It doesn't matter." Old sci-fi books from Earth's archives were a hobby of mine, but one they apparently didn't share. I would have to work on that.

One hand in Slek's, the other in Danec's, I watched out the window as the ground got closer and closer. Patches of green became trees, bushes and wide expanses of grassland. It was to the last that we headed.

"That's strange." Slek's forehead all but touched the window.

"What is?" I leaned over until my chest was pressed against his bicep.

"There should be other pods out there," he said.

I blinked. He was right. Pods had left *Infinity* after us, but we hadn't been the first off.

"They must be on some other part of the planet," I said.

"I suppose so." But he didn't look convinced.

I peered into the cockpit, but saw nothing but the back of Brinley and J'avet's heads.

"If they got eaten by dragons or space spores, I'm out of here," I muttered. Who knew where I would go, because I didn't have a clue.

"It'll be okay," Danec said. "The pod is equipped with laser rifles and I know how to use one."

He puffed out his chest until Slek said, "You point and shoot. Nothing to it."

"You have to…to aim as well," Danec said, obviously rattled.

"I'm sure it's not that simple," I said, addressing them both. Danec was trying hard and Slek didn't need to make him feel bad about it. We were all on edge, but we didn't need to take it out on each other.

Slek shrugged. "I guess, but if you really want a challenge, try a sonic bow."

"I w-won second place with a sonic bow when I was six," Danec said softly.

Slek looked impressed. "We should hunt some Parvoran boar some time. Good eating, but a bitch to shoot."

"That would be great," Danec said. "I've always wanted to try hunting those, but a permit is so hard to get."

"I have one. I use it when—"

I sighed to myself. We were about to land on a mysterious planet and they were talking about hunting pigs?

"Can I come?" I asked. If you can't beat 'em, join 'em.

"Absolutely. Wait until you see the sunset over—"

Something thudded against the side of the pod, hard enough to throw it sideways a kilometre or two.

"Hang on!" Brinley shouted.

The pod banked hard to the right and I was thrown against Danec. At least this time I wasn't thrown far. The harness held me for the most part.

Out the window I caught sight of a deluge of hail. No, not hail; rocks.

My heart stopped. Not rocks. Pieces of ship. My stomach twisted.

"The other pods," I said, my voice choked.

"There's too much debris for that." Slek's face was so pale he was almost lavender. "That looks like a whole ship."

"And the first of the pods," Danec said softly. "If they docked already."

"Oh no," I whispered. Tears sprang to my eyes. The IF must have been waiting and the first few pods had reached the ship. And then—

"What could have done this?" My eyes widened. And could it happen to us?

J'avet turned in his seat and looked in my direction. "Your friend Jones is on a pod behind us. Whatever did that—"

"Isn't him," I finished. "Then what?"

J'avet shook his head and turned back. That was probably the closest to an apology I would get from him. That didn't much matter now.

"I'm taking us in to land," Brinley said loudly.

"Everyone get ready for landing," J'avet said.

The pod banked the other way and headed for an expanse of grass. Chunks of debris rained around us, but only small pieces hit the pod.

When we landed, we did it in a skid. We slid across the ground for a hundred metres or more, then came to a stop just short of slamming into a trunk.

"Everyone out and make for the trees," J'avet ordered. He had already undone his harness and now threw himself at the door controller. It slid open silently and he stood to one side and waved everyone out ahead of him.

Someone took my hand, I couldn't even register who, and we ran.

The world around me became a blur of green until we reached a section of forest that was deep enough, the canopy thick enough, that we came to a stop.

"Trees aren't going to be much protection against space junk." Slek peered upward.

A crash sounded through the trees, followed by a rumble, then an explosion large enough to make the ground tremble under my feet.

"Neither was the pod," a Freytaurian woman remarked.

I grimaced in agreement. Had debris done that, or whoever had destroyed the IF ship? I shook my head and gulped. "We should find a bush to hide under."

"Or a cave," Danec said. "I've read about those."

"Yeah." I ducked down and peered through the trees. "Do you think Brinley—"

"She's fine," Slek said. "I saw her get off the pod. She won't be far behind us." I wish he looked as sure as he sounded.

"We should wait," I said. The forest had fallen into near

silence, apart from the occasional shout, or thud. A tree a few metres away exploded into splinters when something hit it, but I couldn't see a cause, apart from more debris.

"We should find a cave," Slek said.

"Well fuck," I replied, "I forgot my map." I was also trembling so hard my hair bounced around my head.

Danec crouched beside me and wound his arms around me. "It's okay," he said softly. "I won't let any harm come to you."

"Who's going to protect you?" I asked with a sniff.

"You will," he said firmly. "And Slek. We'll look after each other."

Slek gave him an 'I can take care of myself, thanks dude,' look, but said nothing.

"We shouldn't stay here," Danec said. "Just in case."

I didn't ask 'just in case what?' Truthfully, I didn't want to think too hard about it. Not now.

"We should find some of the others," Slek said. "Commander J'avet, even."

"What about Commander J'avet?"

I never expected to be happy to see him, but when he stepped around a trunk and stopped a few metres away, Brinley beside him, I wanted to hug them both.

Instead, I rose and hugged her.

"Uh, we're craving leadership, sir," Slek said with both respect and irony.

"I'm certain you are." J'avet looked me up and down and, for the first time, I didn't see loathing in his expression. I saw no kindness either, but indifference was better than hate, at least in these circumstances.

"Or a map," I said.

J'avet rolled his eyes at me and I thought he might snap. He spoke coolly instead. "This is an uninhabited planet, Nurse Wright."

"Edie," I said. "And uninhabited doesn't necessarily mean uncharted." I glanced at Brinley for support and she nodded.

"There might be maps, but unless we can access communication from a remaining pod—"

She didn't need to finish the sentence, we all knew what she was going to say. We might be alone here.

"We'll gather everyone and stay together," J'avet said. He pressed his watch and sent the location to each evacuee. If we couldn't communicate with the rest of the universe, at least we could communicate with each other. Until our watches died. Each only held enough power for a month, two at the most, before they needed to be recharged.

J'avet leaned against a tree, arms crossed over his burly chest. This was the first time I got a good, long look at him. His jaw was wide and stern. The fur on his face was so fine it could easily be mistaken for skin. His lips were thin but his mouth wide. His brow was heavy right now, in an impatient frown.

"Why would someone attack the IF?" I asked before I had any idea I was about to speak.

His frown deepened. "Apart from your friend, I can only guess." He pushed himself off the trunk. "Not everyone is in favour of the IF. There are those without and within who would end the alliance altogether."

"Apart from humans?" I asked.

He stiffened. "There are others, yes." He turned away then and I knew that was all I was going to get out of him, for now.

Brinley was busy tapping away at her watch. She looked up

and said, "I'm trying to warn the other pods. Two more landed about thirty kilometres east. They saw nothing but the tail end of the debris."

J'avet turned back. "It's possible whatever attacked the ship thought all the pods were aboard."

"Or they couldn't wait," Slek said.

"Or the pods weren't a target at all," I said. "Just an unlucky coincidence."

"Yes, that could be it." Danec seemed as eager to cling to a shred of hope as I was. "Just in the wrong place at the wrong time."

"Nevertheless, we'll be careful," J'avet said. "As soon as everyone is here, we'll go."

"Go where?" I asked.

"East," he replied simply.

Thirty kilometres through an alien forest, to meet up with the other shuttles, with who knows who or what possibly after us. Nothing could possibly go wrong, right?

I stepped closer to Danec and Slek moved to my other side, next to Brinley. In silence, we followed J'avet deeper into the trees.

12

WE SKIRTED the edge of the forest, alert for hazards amongst the trees and in the sky. Once in a while, in the corner of my eye, I saw movement. When I looked straight on, it was gone. Or maybe I imagined it.

"There's no such thing as invisibility cloaking devices, are there?" I asked Brinley.

She shook her head. "Not that I know of."

"Me either," Slek said. He seemed weary, his eyelids heavy. His head injury must be wearing on him more than I had suspected. He could use a doctor to assess him, or better yet, an infirmary.

"Are you all right?" I put a hand on his bicep as we walked. The muscles under my hand screamed 'invincible alien badass.' The lines on his face suggested mortal still recovering from an injury which might have killed him had he been far from medical help.

He covered my hand with his large one. "I'm okay. I could use a big chunk of Parvoran boar steak right about now."

J'avet glanced back over his shoulder at him. "Don't start thinking about food. We have a long way to go."

"Can't a pod come and get us?" asked an evacuee who walked behind us. He was tall and lean, with the yellow skin of a Centauri. He had given his name as Humar, but he seemed anything but funny.

"Not without drawing attention to whatever destroyed the ship and other pods," J'avet snapped.

"That could get us all killed," Slek said.

"So will starving to death," Humar said. "Are you sure we're going the right way?"

"Absolutely certain," Brinley said. "It's not that far. We've covered four kilometres already."

Humar groaned. "Only four?"

"You could always sit here and wait until someone comes for you," I snapped. "None of us are having fun here."

Danec murmured his agreement.

Humar grumbled something but fell silent.

I breathed out through pursed lips. "We could probably do with a break. Just five minutes. It's been traumatic for everyone."

I thought J'avet would refuse, but he stopped for a moment, then nodded. "Five minutes. Under the trees. Keep your eyes open."

"For what, sir?" Danec asked.

"Anything," J'avet replied smoothly. While most of us sat under the shelter of some tall trees, whose lowest branches were too high to reach, J'avet leaned against a trunk.

"Does he ever rest?" I whispered to Danec. I hadn't seen J'avet sleep on the pod either. An exhausted leader wasn't a good thing.

"I think he lay down for a little while," Danec whispered back. "On the pod, as we were going to sleep."

"Maybe he's an android." Slek grinned. "I bet he's the kind programmed to do any function required of him."

"Any?" I blushed.

Slek chuckled.

"He seems humanoid enough to me," Brinley mused. "Some people don't need much sleep."

"Others do." I nodded to where Humar lay beside a bush, eyes closed, breathing softly.

"Centaurians sleep more than they're awake," Slek said.

"That is incorrect," Humar said, without opening his eyes. "I am merely tired from a long shift and sudden evacuation."

"Right," Slek drawled.

"That's enough rest," J'avet said suddenly.

It was only four and a half minutes, but I didn't bother to say so. I pushed myself to my feet. A blur of movement caught my eye. This time I managed to focus for a second or two before it disappeared behind a tree.

"Please tell me someone else saw that." I pointed.

"I did," Danec said. "It looked like a sphere of..." He shook his head.

"Of stone," I said. "Black stone."

"Stone doesn't fly," Slek said. "It was probably some kind of metal."

"Oh good," I said sarcastically. "Are you sure this planet is uninhabited, because things like that don't just float around by themselves."

"No, they don't," J'avet said, his voice tight. "Do you think it saw us?"

I frowned in thought. "It did seem as though it stopped to check us out."

"We should hurry." J'avet gave the order to resume walking, but faster now.

"Do you think that's what happened to the ship?" I asked, my voice low so only Danec could hear.

"It's possible," he replied, "but whatever that was, it didn't seem aggressive. It looked like it was scared of us, or something."

"I am pretty scary," I agreed. I gave him a cheeky smile.

He smiled back, but his eyes were laced with worry. "If that was a scout of some kind..."

"Then they've been watching us for hours," I finished for him. "That's the first time I got a good look, but I'm sure I've seen something floating around before now. I wasn't sure if I imagined it, or maybe it was a bird or a bat, or..." Some other alien species I was unfamiliar with.

"Me too," Brinley said. "Whatever they are, they're trying to avoid being seen."

"Until now," I said.

"Or you seeing it was a coincidence," she said.

"I suppose it could be," I conceded. I had the niggling feeling it wasn't.

"Maybe we shouldn't be going this way," I said loud enough for J'avet to hear.

He stopped and turned around, his customary scowl in

place. "What do you suggest?" he asked in a tone which clearly indicated he didn't much want to hear it.

I chewed my lip. "I don't know. Deeper into the forest?"

He sighed. "Unless that's a couple of bags of rations under your shirt?" He looked about ready to grab one of my breasts and find out.

I crossed an arm over them. "I have half a ration bar in my pocket."

"Then we continue this way, but stay alert," he said curtly. "Although, some of us could stand to miss a meal or two." He gave me a pointed look, then turned and stalked away.

My jaw dropped, and I know my face turned bright red.

"Why you fucking—" I started forward, but Danec and Slek each grabbed one of my arms and held me back.

"Don't, Edie, it's not worth it," Slek said.

"Yeah," Danec agreed. "You'll be in trouble when we get off this planet."

"If we do." I strained against them for a moment, then sagged. "You're right. he's not worth it." Asshole-dickehead-prick didn't cut it. He was a stone cold bully. I would be happy when I never had to see him again.

"We should keep going," I said.

The guys hesitated for a moment, then let go of my arms.

"It's not okay." I stomped in J'avet's boot tracks, which gave me some satisfaction, small and petty though it was.

"No, it's not," Brinley agreed. "You could always file a complaint later."

"With who?" I spread my hands. "Management is a bit scarce out here."

She giggled and almost forced a smile out of me. Almost.

"He has a commanding officer out there somewhere," she replied.

"General Taffin," Danec said. "She's the only human of that rank in the IF."

"Let me guess, he resents her?" I asked bitterly.

"I-I don't know," Danec admitted. His eyes widened. "Sh-she's pretty intimidating."

"Men and their fucking egos," I muttered. I didn't care what his reasoning was. His bruised ego was his problem, not mine.

"You know what," I declared, my voice a bit louder. "I'm not sharing any of my half-a-ration bar with him."

"Good for you," Slek said. His voice sounded strange enough for me to glance at him. He looked back, a deep frown on his handsome face.

"What is it?" I asked.

"I think we're being followed," he said softly.

"There are other evacuees—" Danec started.

"No," Slek said abruptly. "Something else. Something... I don't know."

"Evil?" I suggested.

He glanced at me and a small smile flashed across his face. "Hopefully not. Excuse me." He trotted forward to J'avet, but his movement seemed forced, tired. "I think we're being hunted," he said, loud enough to be overheard.

J'avet scowled and gave a curt nod in response. "Ensign Danec, Engineer Slek, you and Ensign Humar make your way parallel to our position. Try to get around whatever is behind us."

"And then what?" I demanded.

J'avet ignored me. "Assess the threat and report back," he said to Danec.

"Yes, sir." Danec's eyes were wide and full of regret as he glanced at me, then hurried away to the north.

Slek grimaced, but followed, a surly Humar on their tail.

"Continue on," J'avet ordered, without so much as a glance at the rest of us.

I gave Brinley a worried look. We linked arms and stepped as quickly as we could behind the commander. I hated the idea of being anywhere near him, but if something came at us, maybe I could duck fast enough that it would eat him first. That thought felt so good, I found myself smiling.

"Having fun?" Brinley asked, clearly not sure if she should tease or be concerned.

"No." I shook my head. My mouth moved, but I couldn't explain without J'avet hearing and getting pissed off even more. "It doesn't matter."

"If you say so," she replied.

"Quiet," J'avet snapped. "Unless you want what's tracking us to find us."

Us? No. Him? Right now, I wouldn't mind if it bit off his head and licked his bones clean.

I fell silent anyway.

If I hadn't, I might have missed the crack of a twig behind us.

I tapped J'avet on the shoulder to tell him and had the petty satisfaction of seeing him jump.

He glared at me, but I jerked a thumb behind me.

He peered toward the trees and squinted, then waved us toward a clump of bushes. "Get down," he hissed. He all but shoved us over and pushed himself down so close to me his arm was pressed against mine. I wanted to jerk away, but I stayed perfectly still, frozen except the pounding of my heart.

Another crack sounded, closer this time. Whatever it was, they were trying to be careful, trying not to to make a sound. If it wasn't for the dry twigs, I wouldn't have known anything was there at all.

I swallowed hard to push down rising panic and ducked down further.

Leaves in front of us rustled. At first I thought it might be the wind. The second time, I knew there was something there.

Beside me, Brinley trembled, and knew I did the same. Did J'avet tremble too, or did I imagine that?

The leaves rustled again, closer still and a voice swore.

"Slek?" I started to stand, but J'avet pulled me down so hard I landed on my ass. I exhaled out my nose at the pain and glared at him.

He mouthed, "Do you want to get us killed?"

I glared, but shook my head. Of course I didn't, but I could have sworn...

"Where did they go?"

That was definitely Danec's voice, whispering loudly.

J'avet blew out a breath and rose. "We're over here," he said, his voice only slightly louder than Danec's.

"Oh." Slek stepped into view now and rubbed his forehead. "There was nothing there. No sign of anything either."

"You must have been hearing things," J'avet said accusingly.

"I guess so." Slek looked around carefully. "I could have sworn..."

"You were mistaken. We've wasted enough time on this. We'll walk for two more hours, then find a place to make camp."

I shivered at the idea of spending a night here, but the look on Slek's face made my blood run cold. He frowned at the trees back the way we'd come and shook his head, obviously not convinced we weren't still being hunted.

13

THE SUNSET WAS STUNNING, but night fell rapidly. Without flashing computers or corridor lights, the darkness was unsettling.

"There's no way I'm going to imagine a monster creeping up on us," I said sarcastically.

"The moon should rise soon, according to Brinley," Danec said. "Oh. Do you see that?"

I jumped. "Where?" I glanced around and listened, but heard no enormous footsteps, no ominous sound of a giant alien slug sliding toward us, no buzz of people-eating bees. What? I've seen a lot of science fiction movies, okay?

"Over there." If he pointed, I couldn't see it. I could barely make him out as it was.

"Please say it's an underground bunker full of cheese," I pleaded. I ate a bite of my ration bar, but it wasn't close to enough. "Above ground would be good, too."

"Um, no, I don't think so. Look over there, on the lake."

Before dark, we had stumbled across the small body of water, nestled half in and half out of the trees. When I say stumbled, I mean one of our party had stepped out of a clump of bushes, right onto the bank. Only the quick-thinking companion who grabbed her arm kept her from falling in.

J'avet crouched beside the water and tested it with his watch before he declared it safe to drink. He wasn't the first to try it, but neither was I. That dubious honour went to Danec, who J'avet waved forward as he stepped aside.

I might have told him to fuck off, but Danec knelt, drank, and lived to tell about it.

I squinted at the water. "The plants floating on the surface are phosphorescent." In daylight, they looked like some kind of waterlily. In the gloom, they glowed a soft green. "It's so pretty."

The slowly rising moon cast a silvery glow, which illuminated his face. He looked right at me. "Beautiful," he said softly. Surely he was only talking about the plants.

In spite of myself, my mouth went dry and I had to swallow. "Should we go and take a closer look?"

"Hmmm? Uh, yes." I couldn't see him blush, but for some reason I was sure he was. "I'd like that."

I followed him around the edge, keeping a safe distance from the water, and watching for fallen logs and mutant slugs.

I stepped around a patch of grass and slid on muddy ground. I windmilled my arms, but Danec grabbed my hand before I fell and kept me upright.

"Thank you." My heart pounded so hard it left me breathless.

"You're welcome." His voice was rough. He didn't let my hand go again. Instead, we walked like that, close together and hand in hand, to the other side of the lake.

Here, the leaves glowed brighter, but still soft on the eyes. In the centre of each plant, the lilies glowed as well, each a different shade of pink, purples, blue, and yellow. Even white here and there.

The glow increased as the flowers, closed at first, gradually opened their petals out to embrace the night air and the ever brightening moon.

"Oh my goodness." I inhaled the scent of the blooms which grew stronger the wider they spread their petals. The smell was warm and heady, intoxicating. "We should go for a swim."

I took half a step before Danec pulled me back to him.

I didn't realise he was going to kiss me until his mouth was on mine. His lips were soft, but hungry, as though he wanted to devour me in one mouthful. His tongue went searching and I opened my mouth to him. He licked my lips and his tongue felt rough, unlike any other I had tasted. No, not rough, textured.

In the next moment, it was gone and him with it. He stepped away and rubbed a hand over his face.

"I'm sorry. I'm s-so-sorry," he stammered. "I shouldn't have done that. I-I—"

I closed the gap between us and put a hand on his muscular forearm. He felt like rock under my fingers.

"It's all right," I said. "I liked it." I more than liked it; I wanted more. What I couldn't understand was what he wanted. He had my head spinning this way and that and I didn't want to do that anymore. Whatever he had to say, I needed to know.

"Are you sorry because you just want to be friends?" My tone was more blunt than I intended, but the words were out there. Regardless of the outcome, I had made the first step.

He gazed toward the lake. "No," he said finally. "It's because I thought you wanted that. I mean, you called me friend. I'm all right with that, I just..."

"I only called you that because that's what I thought you wanted," I said. Right now, my body throbbed like crazy and my mind buzzed. Was he saying he also wanted more?

"From the first moment I saw you, I hungered for you," he said, his voice low and rough. "I was prepared to respect whatever you wished, even if it was friendship, just so I could be near you. Every time you let me hold your hand, I was happy just to do that. That sounds so pathetic." He exhaled loudly

"No," I told him, "that sounds sweet. You've helped me get through the last day or two. Hell, only a few minutes ago, you stopped me from falling into the water." I didn't want to think of the glare I would get from J'avet if I returned to camp, my clothes soaking wet.

"I would do anything for you." He took my hand again and drew me to his hard, warm body.

"You were even the first to drink the water," I pointed out.

His body shook with laughter. "Even that. If I died, well..." He paused and inhaled through his nose in a way that suggested he was about to broach a difficult topic. "Slek—"

Ah. That certainly was difficult. "I like him too," I admitted, even as I pressed my head against Danec's chest. "I know that's not—"

Normal?

Sane?

Sensible?

"Ideal."

"It's a-all right," Danec said. "I'll be here when you figure out what, or who, you need. As long as it takes. But I hope you choose me." His arms closed around me and squeezed, gentle but firm.

"I make no guarantees." The scent of him was more heady than the flowers. I leaned back and looked up at him.

His blue face was a riot of different shades in the light from the flowers. Slowly, he lowered his mouth to mine and kissed me gently. This was nothing like the first kiss, but the fire it sent through me was hotter than ever. I wanted to throw him down into the darkness, tear off his clothes, and feel him sink deep into me.

We broke apart and I nestled my face into his chest again.

"I feel safe with you," I said. More than physically safe. He was sweet and kind and I knew if he broke my heart, it wouldn't be intentional. He probably didn't have a mean bone in his body.

Unlike— No, I wouldn't think about J'avet just now. He didn't deserve to spend a moment inside my head. Not even a nano-moment. Was a nano-moment even a thing? Whatever, he could stay out.

"Good, I want you to feel safe. We'll get off this planet and make it to Agus, no matter what."

"And if we don't, we'll have to colonise and populate Calig," I said more lightly than I felt.

He chuckled. "Yes." A couple of heartbeats later, his body stiffened. "Edie, I don't think we're alone"

"There's about forty-eight other people beside the lake," I said.

"Not them," Danec said. "Behind you."

I turned slowly. There, in the bushes, were several sets of

shining eyes. Every so often, they blinked both lower and upper lids at the same time.

"Hello?" I said tentatively. "We mean you no harm." With any luck, they meant us none too.

The response was a rustle of leaves and one individual rose. The multiple pack of abs and broad arms suggested he was male. His skin shone silver in the glow from the flowers, although interspersed with other other colours.

Another form rose beside him, this one with bare breasts and hair which fell past her waist.

"Harm," the woman said as if feeling out the word.

"No harm," I said quickly. "Peace. Um." I looked to Danec for help, but she seemed to understand.

"Peace," she echoed.

"So much for uninhabited," I muttered. To the pair I asked, "So you live here?"

"Here." It was the man who spoke this time, his voice a pleasant rumble.

"Yes, here, Calig." I pointed to the ground.

He cocked his head. Long silver hair fell to one side, almost as long as the woman's. He said a word I didn't understand.

"Dirt?" I guessed. "Uh, the ground is dirt," I agreed. "The whole planet is." I had no idea where to go from here, or if they understood a word I said.

"Iritauri," Danec said suddenly.

Both the man and woman's head jerked to look at him. The woman nodded excitedly and pointed toward herself. "Iritauri. Selvia." She pointed to the man, "Landu."

Danec pointed to himself, "Danec." Then to me, "Edie."

"Eeedee," the woman drew out my name and nodded.

I smiled, then out of the corner of my mouth, I asked, "Who are these people?"

"The Iritauri," he said. "Or Iri. They were a race of people who shared Freytauri."

Landu spat on the ground.

I wrinkled my nose. "Past tense?" I asked.

"They were persecuted. Many left. Those who didn't..." His voice was laced with regret for an event which had probably happened before he was born.

"And here they are," I finished. No wonder they hid from us. They probably thought we'd come to finish the job.

"I'm sorry your people were treated badly," I said. "Can they understand me?"

"Your watch should have a translator on it," Danec said. "Turn on Iritaurian and it'll do the rest."

I did as he said. "Testing." The word spoke the word again, but this time in a different language.

Landu chuckled and repeated the word.

My watch responded. "Testing."

This would be slow and clunky, but better than nothing.

"So, you live here, on this planet?" I asked again.

"Yes, yes." Salvia nodded. "We crashed here. Calig is home now. For three generations."

"Oh." I hoped we wouldn't be here for that long. "I suppose that means there's food around."

"Lots of vegetables and fish." Landu pointed toward the lake. "There's good eating when the moon flowers bloom."

That was good to know. Food was that close, we just had to catch it. Of course, my knowledge of how to do that was limited to not at all.

"Maybe we can trade," I suggested. "Food for... Well, we must have something you'd want."

Salvia gave a curt nod. "Trade."

"Great," Danec said. "Maybe you could teach us to fish in return for my watch?"

Before he could slip it off his wrist, Slek spoke loudly from a few metres away.

"Who are you speaking to?"

I put my hand up as a sign to wait, but Selvia and Landu, eyes wide, ducked back down and all of the eyes melted away.

"Oops, sorry," Slek said. "I didn't realise there was anyone here." He peered toward the bushes, but they fell still. The Iri were well and truly gone.

I sighed and told him about the encounter.

"Iritauri," he said in wonder. "I thought they were extinct. Bare breasts, did you say? That's a local clothing tradition I could get behind." He eyed me speculatively.

I rolled my eyes at him. "I would say you first, but you'd have your shirt off before I could blink."

"If you did it too, I would," he replied. "I thought you two had come over here to go skinny dipping." He didn't seem bothered that I might swim naked with another man.

"We came to see the flowers," Danec said. "Do you think we should follow them?"

I peered into the darkness. "I hate to say it, but I think we need to tell J'avet."

"After we skinny dip?" Slek asked.

"Instead of that," I said regretfully.

Slek and Danec both sighed. I did the same a moment later. Here I was, beside a stunning lake, on an alien world, with two guys hotter than the nearest sun, both of whom wanted to get naked with me, and I was going to report to the leader of our group instead.

I must be crazy, at least a bit. At this point, I might come if one of them looked at me the right way.

"Come on, we should get back," I said. "Before he thinks we deserted and decides to have us all arrested." Good luck with that, since we had no security officers with us, but once we got off Calig, that would change. There was no point in giving him another excuse to be an asshole.

Slek slipped his hand into one of mine and Danec took the other. They shared a look, which seemed to be an under-standing of some kind. They would respect me and my wishes until I decided between them.

If I did. That might be harder than getting off this planet. How could I possibly make a choice between two guys I was falling for?

14

J'AVET MASSAGED the bridge of his nose with his fingertips. "Tell me again what you saw? Iritauri?"

"If you've never heard of them—" Slek started.

J'avet glared at Slek past his hand. "I've heard of them," he snapped. "Their genocide is a source of shame for the people of Freytauri, and the IF itself. Had they intervened sooner..." He waved a hand. "And you claim they're alive and well and living on Calig?"

"We don't claim anything," I said coldly. "We saw them. Spoke to them. They're as real as you." But a lot more friendly.

"Near blooming moon flowers." His tone matched mine. "A known hallucinogen."

I wanted to slap the smug look off his face. Instead, I shrugged. "We're just telling you what we saw. Believe it or don't believe it, that's up to you. Now, if you'll excuse me, it's late and I'm tired."

If I had a shred of sympathy for him, I might admit he

looked tired too, but I didn't. I gave him a glare through narrowed eyes and stalked away to the tree where Brinley sat.

I threw myself to the ground. "He's such a motherfucking twatbag."

"I assume that's a bad thing?" Danec lowered himself down beside me.

I half snorted, half choked a laugh. "Yeah, it is."

"You'd let him near your mother?" Slek asked. Clearly he understood the irony in the comment, because he smiled and one eyebrow twitched upward.

"Over my dead body," I muttered. I lay down on my side and sighed. "We really should get some sleep."

Brinley nodded. "Yes, we should." She put her hand over a yawn.

The guys got comfortable on either side of me. Danec, who lay in front of me, gave me a smile before he closed his eyes.

Slek rested a hand on my hip.

I closed my own eyes and, for a long while, I stayed like that, but my mind spun faster than light.

What if J'avet was right, and we had imagined the Iri? It wasn't the first time I've pictured muscular, alien men. I might be horny enough to imagine bare breasted alien women too, although my taste didn't usually run that way.

I shifted my hip to get more comfortable.

"Are you all right?" Slek said right beside my ear.

I rolled over to face him. "I can't sleep," I whispered. The only sounds around us were Danec snoring softly and Brinley murmuring what sounded like coordinates in her sleep.

"Need some help?" Slek's hand slid down my hip, to my thigh.

I bit back a moan. After a moment, I bent my knee to let him slip his hand between my legs.

He moved, slow and feather-light, to brush against the front of my pants. He rubbed again, firmer this time, and tickled my neck with his tongue. Like Danec's, it was textured, enough to drive me wild.

His teeth grazed my skin, up to my chin before he claimed my mouth with his. His lips fastened on my lower lip. He sucked it gently, then gripped the skin between his teeth and bit down lightly.

He pulled away long enough to whisper, "I could eat you up." With one hand, he undid the front of my pants and pushed his fingers inside. He was a tight fit, but he found the front of my panties and rubbed with a firm, confident touch.

In a heartbeat, I was wet as hell and rocking against his fingers. I had to press my lips together to keep from screaming, or begging him for more. We lay on the edge of the group of evacuees, but still so many slept close by.

With his other hand, Slek pushed up the front of my shirt, just to the bottom of my bra. He reached in and cupped a breast. My nipple hardened against his palm.

I wanted more. So much more.

He tugged the side of my panties aside and slid the tip of his finger against my folds.

I quivered.

He pulled his hand out of my pants and wiggled them down my hips, just enough so they were out of the way. He left my panties, except to again pull one side out of the way. He grazed the whole of his hand over my clit, from the tips of his fingers to the heel.

I let out a tiny whimper.

He pressed one finger gently inside me. At the same time, he peeled back my bra cup and massaged my nipple with his thumb and forefinger.

My breath was coming in tiny pants now. For a guy from another planet, he knew his way around a human woman's body. I knew the physiology of many different species had similarities, but sexual pleasure wasn't something they taught in nursing school.

He slid another finger inside and another, until I felt almost full. The heel of his hand rubbed my clit while his fingers massaged my insides.

I bucked against him, faster and faster.

He leaned over to slide the tip of his tongue over my nipple. His tongue split in two and each side went over and around my sensitive peak. Double the fun.

Just that small touch drove me close to the edge.

He caught my nipple in his lips and suckled for a moment before biting down gently.

I quivered and whimpered again.

"Slek," I whispered.

"Mmm?" he said while his teeth grazed across my breast, nibbling here and there. He bit hard enough to leave a mark and I had to bite back a scream of pleasure.

"You like that." He moved to another place and bit again.

"Please—" I didn't know what I was asking for, until he exposed my other breast and nibbled on it too. "Yes."

The next time he bit me, I came, hard and fast against his hand. "Yes... Slek..."

I rocked, eyes squeezed shut until he milked every bit of

orgasm out of me. Only when I was finally still and panting, did he still his hand and raise his mouth from my breasts.

"There. That might help you sleep." He worked my bra cups back into place and tugged my shirt down. He drew his hand out of me last, brought his fingers to his nose and sniffed.

"I didn't know human women were so scented." He stuck his fingers into his mouth and sucked. "And delicious," he said around them.

My hand hovered near his groin. "Do you—"

He pulled his fingers from his mouth and shook his head. "I'll keep. We agreed not to rush."

"Okay." I pulled my pants back up and did them up. "Thank you." I was slightly disappointed. I had seen his cock and looked forward to playing with it. On the other hand, exhaustion started to seep into my body, down into my bones.

Anticipation never killed anyone, right?

He hooked an arm around me and drew me closer, him the big spoon, me the smaller one.

I wiggled against him for a moment, then nestled down, safe and warm in his strong arms.

"Do you believe we saw them?" I asked sleepily.

"Do you?" he asked. He sounded equally weary.

I thought for a moment. "Yes, I'm certain we did. If I was going to hallucinate, I would see a big pile of chocolate. Or pizza, wine, and a movie."

Slek chuckled. "Hunger will do that."

"Yes, it will," I sighed. I looked forward to a good meal after this. At least we had plenty of water from the lake to sustain us tonight and tomorrow morning.

"If you had imagined it, you wouldn't have seen the same thing," Slek pointed out.

I stiffened for a moment before I forced myself to relax again. "You're right, we wouldn't." Part of me wanted to march up to J'avet and tell him that, but the other ninety-nine percent of me was perfectly comfortable here. Besides, picking a fight now wouldn't achieve anything.

I squeezed my eyes tight and let my mind wander. The lake, the flowers, Danec's kiss, the Iri... It was all real, I was certain of it. That led me to wonder what it was about the Iri that the Freytauri felt the need to eradicate them. Race? Language? Disputes over land?

I was about to ask Slek when he started to snore loudly. I moved my ear further away from his mouth and exhaled through my nose. My last thought before I slipped off to sleep was that I must be the last person awake in camp.

I wasn't the first to awaken when dawn broke over this part of Calig. That honour went to Humar, who woke the rest of us with his shout.

"We're surrounded!"

15

"I TOLD him the Iri were real," I muttered. I sat up, pulled my hairband from my wrist and tugged my curls into a hasty ponytail.

"We believed you," Brinley assured me.

I flashed her a quick smile and got to my feet.

Humar's declaration about being surrounded was a slight exaggeration, but there were quite a few Iri standing around our camp. Each was armed with a long, slender bow. None were nocked, but the Iri all had a quiver of arrows on their backs. I would bet J'avet's pension they could have them ready to shoot in a heartbeat or less.

"We want to speak to your leader." Selvia's words came through my watch, translated for those close enough to hear.

Those who couldn't, muttered amongst themselves. "What did they say?"

"I don't know, I think we might be breakfast."

"Shit."

I rolled my eyes and stepped forward.

"Hi, Selvia, it's me, Edie." My watch spat my words out in Iritauri.

She turned toward me with a proud tilt of her head. "You are the leader?"

"No, I am." J'avet stepped forward. Judging by the way his watch translated his words too, he cottoned on quickly.

I had to give him some credit for that.

"What do you want?" he asked warily.

"We want to trade," Selvia replied.

I took my eyes off her long enough to look around at the rest of the Iri. A few metres from Selvia stood Landu. He gave me a nod, then went back to scanning the encampment, his whole body tensed, ready.

Right. Just because Danec and I were harmless didn't mean the rest of the evacuees were.

"We don't have much," J'avet said. "We had to evacuate our ship. Our escape pod was destroyed."

Selvia tilted her head at him. "My symbiont says you have access to resources not of this world."

Symbiont?

J'avet's brow jerked upward.

I glanced back toward Slek and Danec. Neither looked surprised in the least. Was this the reason their people hunted the Iri? What form did this symbiont take?

J'avet's reply tugged my mind back to the moment.

"We have access," he said carefully, "but only when we can reach the other pods, safely."

Selvia nodded. "We will be your escort and guides. We brought food." She half turned and waved toward the trees.

From between the trunks came a handful of men and women. Each carried a basket. Every one was laden with loaves of bread and fruit.

My eyes widened and my stomach rumbled so loudly I was sure J'avet would hear.

"That's very good of you," he said, his tone still wary.

I could almost see him thinking, wondering what they really wanted. I wondered the same thing, but maybe they were just being nice. Surely that was possible? If not, then what did they want in the way of off-world resources? It may be nothing more than wine or chocolate. Truthfully, it wasn't really my problem. The IF would deal with them and give them whatever they needed once we were safe. And we got to eat. That sounded like a win-win to me.

"Help them distribute the food." J'avet waved at Danec and Humar. Danec nodded, but Humar looked horrified at the idea of going anywhere near them. Hunger, or the need to follow orders, won in the end, and he took a basket of rolls and took them around the evacuees.

I grabbed one, still wonderfully warm and soft, and bit into it. While I chewed, I caught J'avet watching me. Then everyone else. I deliberately swallowed and took another bite.

When I didn't die, the others started to eat.

If Selvia and the others noticed, I saw no sign, their expressions were closed doors. That in itself made me uneasy, but the bread was so tasty I put the reservations aside for now.

I finished my roll in about three seconds and grabbed a piece of fruit from the basket Danec had passed around, but which now sat at his feet. It looked like an apple, but with bright orange skin.

"Any idea what this is?" I asked.

Danec had one of his own on the palm of his hand and was examining it with careful curiosity. "I have no idea. It must be native to Calig."

Landu still stood back from us, but he had one of the strange fruit as well. He bit into it and chewed happily.

"If it's safe for him," Danec said, "it should be safe for me." He bit into his and nodded his appreciation of the taste.

Before I tried mine, I asked, "What did they mean about the symbiont?"

Danec swallowed in a hurry and coughed a couple of times.

I patted him on the back and waited for him to regain his breath.

"Some of our people chose to accept a symbiont to be their host," he said finally. "Others of our people..."

"Didn't like the idea?" I finished for him. I wasn't sure I blamed them. I wouldn't want to be a host for, well, anything. "So there's a parasite of some kind living inside them?" I whispered.

"Something like that, yes," he agreed.

I eyed the closest Iri, a woman around my own age. Like the others, her breasts were bare, but her hair was shorter, the ends cut ragged. I suppose they didn't have access to a hairdresser down here. Maybe all they needed from the IF was a few good pairs of scissors. Somehow, I thought there might be a bit more to it than that.

I bit into the fruit. Juice flooded into my mouth like a bite of honey, but not as sweet. While I chewed, I watched the Iri woman for some sign, any sign, of a worm, or slug, or whatever might share her body. Nothing rippled under skin, or burst out to announce itself. She looked like an ordinary alien, with silvery skin.

"This fruit is good," I said. I ate it down to its core and tossed the remains in the direction of the trees. It wasn't chocolate, but I could happily live on that and bread for a few days.

"Yes," Danec looked like he might say something, but he just tossed his core in the same direction as mine and grabbed another.

"Are you all right?" I asked.

His eyes widened, but he looked toward the ground. "Um…"

"Okay." I crossed my arms over my chest. "Out with it."

"I…You and Slek—"

I grimaced. "You heard that?" When he nodded, I grimaced harder. "Sorry, I thought you were asleep."

"I was. And then I wasn't."

"We didn't mean to wake you." Especially like that. We should have crept off into the bushes or something.

"You didn't," he said quickly. "It's okay, it's not about that." He blinked slowly. "Did you choose him?"

My breath came out in a rush. "No," I said quickly. "I would have told you if I had." I understood where he was coming from though. If I'd woken to find him with his hands down the pants of another woman, I'd assume he'd made up his mind too.

I licked my lips. "It's just… I needed… And wanted… I still want to see where we go." I put a hand on his arm. "I'll understand if you don't feel the same way. If you want to find someone else."

"I don't want anyone else," he said in a hoarse whisper. I had noticed he'd hardly glanced at the Iri's bare breasts, at which some of the evacuees hadn't stopped staring.

"If I have to share you with him, I'll do it. But—"

"But what?" I asked.

"If you choose him, please tell me. And if you need... Want... I'm here too. I might not be as experienced as Slek," he blushed, "but I can learn."

My heart melted a little more. I grabbed his hand and pulled him in to kiss his cheek. At the last moment, he turned his face and my lips grazed lightly over his.

"If J'avet sees—" I started.

"If he doesn't like it, I'll quit," Danec growled. "You're more important to me than the GASP."

Now I blushed. "Don't throw your career away because of me," I told him. "What would you do anyway?"

He shrugged. "I could work cataloguing the IF database of books. Don't worry about me, I'll work out something."

"In the meantime, we should hand out more fruit." I leaned to pick up the basket and we walked around the group of evacuees until it was empty. Once or twice I caught J'avet watching me, but I pretended not to notice. We'd be off this planet and away from him soon enough.

I hoped.

"All right," J'avet called out suddenly. "Finish stuffing your faces and prepare to make your way out of camp in an orderly fashion. Follow the Iritauri leader." He said the words like they left a bitter taste in his mouth. Was he still angry with me because he'd said we hadn't seen the Iri, only to be proven very wrong? If so, then he would have to get over himself, whether he liked it or not.

16

"I DON'T THINK we're going the right way," Brinley whispered.

We'd been walking for two hours now, but I began to wonder the same thing.

"It's east-ish," I said, unconvinced.

"It's north-east," Danec said. He walked beside me. The worry on his face was a look I hadn't seen on him before.

I wanted to ask where we might end up if we kept going, but any reply would only be a guess.

"Should we speak to J'avet, or ask the Iri?" Brinley asked. Her expression matched Danec's.

I chewed my lip. I wasn't going to speak to J'avet if I didn't have to.

"I'll ask Landu," I said finally. "He seems nice enough."

"I'll come with you," Slek said. "I haven't spoken to an Iri up close."

I hesitated, then nodded. "All right, come on then."

He grabbed my hand and we hurried to catch up with the silver skinned alien.

"Landu," I greeted when we were close enough. I smiled and looked as friendly as I could, which didn't look suspicious *at all.*

"Eeedee," Landu replied. He gave me a nod without slowing and shot Slek a speculative look.

Slek's grip on my hand tightened and he drew me closer.

I raised my eyebrows at him, but he was looking at Landu with undisguised wariness.

I cleared my throat. "Um, so. We thought we were going east. This is, um, not east."

Landu frowned until my watch translated. "Not east," he agreed.

"Why?" Slek asked. "We need to go to the pods."

"Selvia said we're going this way," Landu replied in a tone which suggested we shouldn't argue.

That might have worked on his people, but not on me.

I stopped and planted my fists on my hips. "Why? What is this way?"

Landu stopped too and cocked his head. "That is for Selvia to say."

"I'm asking you," I insisted.

He hesitated for a moment, his face expressionless. "Shardu is this way," he said and kept on walking.

"Wait." I grunted in exasperation and dragged Slek along to catch up. "What the hell is Shardu?"

"Shardu," Landu said, "is where we live."

"But we need to go to the pods," Slek said. "You're supposed to take us that way." He looked like he might be tempted to punch Landu in the face if we didn't get some straight answers soon.

"I have no more answers," Landu said simply. "We will be in Shardu soon."

"Then will we get answers?" I asked.

"If Selvia wishes to give them," Landu agreed.

Slek swore under his breath. "Not good enough," he snapped.

"I can do no more," Landu replied indifferently. "Selvia will say no more until we arrive in Shardu."

Now I swore, because asking her was exactly what I was planning to do next.

"And what if we don't want to go to your city, or whatever it is?" Slek asked. "We might just continue east by ourselves."

Without a word, Landu put a hand on his bow.

"Or we could just go with you to Shardu," I said quickly.

Landu lowered his hand and nodded.

"So much for friendly," I muttered. "Beware of aliens bearing gifts." We should have known them giving us food was a part of some kind of plan. Okay, I think we did know, but we were too hungry to care at the time. I could blame J'avet for letting us fall into this trap, but then I'd have to think about the asshole. My day had already taken a turn for the worst without that.

"I won't let any harm come to you," Slek promised. "If they so much as touch a hair on your head, I'll—" His face turned dark purple and eyes flashed with anger.

"You won't do anything which might get you killed," I said firmly. "We've come this far, we can deal with this."

He looked like he might argue, but he nodded and the anger faded from his features. "You're right. Danec and I and the other

Freytauri will need to be especially careful. The need for vengeance can last for generations."

I hadn't thought of that. Now I did, the fruit soured in my stomach. "I hope that's not what this is about."

"If it is, we'll handle it. Just make sure you and the others get off safely."

"I always like to be safe when I get off," I assured him.

He chuckled. "Good girl. Me too." He sighed. "I hope I don't regret not asking you to suck my cock last night."

"Priorities," I teased.

He grinned. "What can I say? I've waited a long time to feel your mouth on me."

"We only met a couple of weeks ago," I pointed out.

"Did we?" he asked. "I feel as though I've known you all my life." He slung an arm over my shoulder, and didn't remove it until Brinley and Danec caught up.

We told them what Landu said, and they both frowned.

"So we're prisoners?" Brinley asked.

"In a manner of speaking, yes," I said. "They're outnumbered, but we're unarmed. So far they don't seem to want to do anything to us." If they wanted us dead, we'd be dead. "If we just go along with what they say, we might be okay."

We might also be lunch, but I didn't think that was the case. I personally didn't think I would be that tasty, but that was a matter of opinion, I suppose.

I glanced around at the weary faces around me, some looking concerned, others oblivious. Past the closest handful, I caught the look on J'avet's face. His mouth was a tight line, eyes narrowed and snapping with their usual bad temper. There was something more though. He understood the situation. If I didn't know better, I would think he had always been aware of it. I suppose he had; he was an asshole, not an idiot.

That idea made me angry. He knew, but he'd let us all walk into this anyway?

I huffed a breath through my nose. Not two minutes earlier, I pointed out we weren't armed. He'd had no choice. That realisation did nothing to make me feel better.

I shivered.

Danec put an arm around me. "It'll be all right. I won't let them do anything to you."

I gave him a watery smile for making the same promise Slek had.

"Thank you. I'll make sure nothing bad happens to you too," I told him. "Or Slek, or Brinley."

She gave no sign that she was bothered by me getting the attention of two guys. In fact, she seemed happy for me. Once in a while, I caught her smiling when one of the guys held my hand, or said something sweet. A lot of girls would get jealous, even bitchy, but not her. That made me like her all the more.

Brinley grinned. "Yeah, take care of the one who can fly us off this rock."

"You're not the only pilot," Slek said, speaking as though he was teasing a younger sister.

"Just the best," she said tartly. She even stuck out her tongue at him.

He stuck out his in return.

I stared in fascination as he spilt the tip of his tongue in two, until it looked like a fork. Both sides curled upward, so he looked like he was sticking up two fingers at her.

I laughed.

He grinned, then rejoined the sides of his tongue together before drawing it back into his mouth.

"Do you think we should be more mature?" Danec suggested.

"*Pfft*, maturity is overrated," Slek said. "So I've heard anyway."

"Who do you know who is mature?" Brinley asked. "Apart from Danec. And maybe J'avet."

Slek rubbed his chin. "No one I can think of," he admitted.

"Exactly," Brinley said.

"Shhh," Danec said suddenly.

"What—" I stopped to listen.

"There's nothing—" Slek started.

"Yes there is," I said quickly. In the distance, engines thrummed. They rapidly grew closer.

"Friend or foe?" Brinley wondered out loud.

I shook my head. I didn't know. At least until a pod appeared over the trees, followed by another. And another.

They passed overhead and kept on in the direction we were going. My eyes followed them the entire way over and my heart followed them down to the ground.

"Keep walking," Selvia ordered. Her expression offered nothing, no hint of her thoughts on seeing the pods.

For some reason, that gave me chills. I rubbed my hands up and down my arms and stomped on behind Landu. If my eyes could bore a hole in the back of his head, they would.

"Shardu," he said after about another twenty minutes of walking.

"I figured," I muttered. Shardu was a collection of buildings made from sheets of metal. Some bore signs of having been a ship of some kind. Others looked like flooring or walls. Several buildings had two stories and balconies made from catwalks.

"Reduce, reuse, recycle," I muttered. "Is that why you destroyed the IF ship?" I directed the question to Landu. "For housing parts?"

He half turned his head toward me. "We destroyed nothing."

"Right." Then why did I sense a 'yet' at the end of his sentence?

"This way." Selvia waved to the open field beside the town where the pods were neatly parked, side by side. Six of them. Their passengers stepped out into the sunshine, followed by several Iri armed with bows and even a knife here and there.

"This can't be good," Brinley said softly.

Silently, I agreed.

The passengers were directed to sit in a spot under the shade of a wide tree with white flowers dotted here and there. Under other circumstances I might have appreciated its beauty. Now though, I sat where I was told and searched the gathered crowd.

There. Scared and angry, but alive, Jones sat near the edge of the group, apart by choice or because no one would sit closer, I don't know.

"What do you want with us?" a Garvian woman called out. Her tentacles dropped with obvious exhaustion.

Selvia ignored her and spoke in low tones to two or three other Iri. They nodded and bustled off, presumably to do as she'd asked.

"Food will be provided," she said. "Do as you're told and no one will be harmed."

"Right," someone said, disbelievingly.

If Selvia heard, she ignored it. She nodded to another Iri and disappeared into one of the buildings.

I started to look for J'avet, but soon found him sitting directly behind me. I caught his eye and nodded toward Jones.

J'avet followed my gaze and nodded. "Your accomplice," he said, but sensed he didn't believe it anymore.

I snorted anyway. "Hardly. You can ask him yourself."

"I will," J'avet agreed. He glanced at the Iri closest to us, rose and kept low as he made his way over to Jones.

Acting on instinct, I followed. I didn't need to look over my shoulder to know Danec, Slek, or Brinley followed. Possibly all three.

"Jones." J'avet plopped down beside him. "Did you plant a bomb on *Infinity?*"

That was blunt.

Jones blinked, the confusion genuine. I didn't need to hear his answer to know he hadn't.

"Of course not," he hissed. He nodded toward me, cold fury on his face. "Did she tell you I did?"

"She suggested you were acting strangely in the part of the ship which later exploded," J'avet said.

Thanks for throwing me right under the shuttle. I glared at him, then at Jones.

"You were acting funny and you hate aliens," I pointed out.

"Not enough to potentially kill myself," Jones retorted. "And certainly not if I knew we'd end up here." He shot daggers at the Iri with his eyes. his mouth was set in a line so tight his lips turned white. "What do they want with us anyway?"

"Hostages," Danec said. He had followed and now sat on the

other side of me. Slek and Brinley were on the other side of him.

"Obviously," Jones snapped. "But why?"

"I think we're about to find out." J'avet nodded toward the closest building.

"Shit."

17

My curse was followed by the sound of dozens of nocked bows, all pointed toward the gathered evacuees.

The Iri moved amongst us, directing some toward the building Selvia had gone into, and others to the one beside it. Still others were pointed toward a third building.

Selvia herself reappeared in front of us, a long, slender tube held in one hand.

I was no expert, but I knew a weapon when I saw one.

"Laser hand cannon," Slek muttered. "An oldie but a baddie."

That didn't sound good.

"You are their leader," she said to J'avet.

He nodded and rode steadily to his feet. "I am."

"You, a pilot and these Freytaurians," she shot Danec and Slek a disgusted look, like they smelled of something nasty, "will come with me."

Before I could twitch, much less argue, she waved her cannon at me and Jones. "These two as well," she stated.

Jones shot to his feet. "I'm not going anywhere with you."

Calm to the point of coldness, Selvia raised her cannon toward him. A beam of orange light shot out the end. It struck him in the chest, then enveloped him entirely. He threw his head back to scream, but then disappeared as if he'd never existed.

My breath caught in my throat. I'd seen people die before, but never like that, with no warning at all.

"Shit," I whispered.

"Now you understand," Selvia said. "Obey and no one else will be harmed."

A thousand questions tumbled around in my head, but for once I kept my mouth shut. Selvia's demonstration was more than enough to convince me to contain my patience.

J'avet looked furious, but when Selvia gestured us toward the closest pod, he nodded for us to walk that way too.

As if I had planned to do otherwise.

"If you have further thoughts of escape," Selvia said, "we have other weapons, all trained on the others in your landing party. Their continued existence depends on all of you."

I thought that might be the point in separating us all. Divided, it would be harder to rise up against them.

"I'm not sure there's enough fuel to get far," Brinley said as we stepped into the pod.

"My people have worked to drain the others. The combined fuel is on board."

"Oh." Brinley nodded. "That would work."

I wouldn't even pretend to be surprised they knew how. The Iri were clearly more advanced than they let on. The bare chests must be a life choice, not a lack of resources. Good for them, I suppose.

Selvia nodded. "Fly us up into orbit."

"There's the small matter of someone up there taking aim at ships above this planet," J'avet pointed out.

"They are of no concern," Selvia replied.

I frowned at her and caught Danec and Slek with identical looks of disbelief on their faces.

"We'll be concerned when they shoot at us," Slek muttered.

Selvia waved us toward the seats and sat behind us.

"Does anyone else think this is a bad idea?" I whispered.

"I have a bad feeling about it," Slek agreed.

A dozen Iri stepped onto the pod, along with Humar, an Agusian woman, and four more Freytaurians.

The doors slid shut behind us and Brinley turned on the ship's engines.

"They sound healthy enough," Slek said after a moment. "I saw no sign of damage to the exterior."

"That's good to know," I said.

Danec was quiet, his skin pale.

I took his hand. "Are you all right?" I asked.

"I'm sorry," he whispered. "I should have done some-something."

"You would be dead too if you tried," I reminded him. "At least this way we have a chance." How, I didn't know, but we'd come up with something.

The pod jolted and rose off the ground. Out the window I watched the last of the refugees ushered inside the buildings. Some stopped to stare, but were soon hurried on. Was Kalvix amongst them? I hadn't seen her, but I had been busy with

Jones. I hope she was all right. I hated to think the doctor had died on *Infinity*, or one of the pods.

"Uh, Iritauri leader," Brinley said awkwardly. "There's a ship in orbit. I'm pretty sure they've seen us. They aren't IF."

Selvia nodded and rose. She pointed her cannon at Slek and Danec.

"You two, into the cockpit," she ordered.

I opened my mouth to argue, but when she aimed her cannon at me, I shut it so hard my teeth clicked. I raised my hands and slumped in my seat.

"Contact them," Selvia said. She gestured for Slek to sit beside Brinley and Danec stood beside him, in front of Selvia.

"Tell them we're a Freytauri pod," she ordered. "Liberated from the IF."

Slek gave her a funny look, but cleared his throat and did as she asked.

The closer we got to orbit, the bigger the ship became.

"IF design," J'avet muttered. "But an older one."

"Older as in supposed to be scrap, but currently flown by pirates?" I asked.

He glanced toward me as though he'd forgotten I was there. "Pirates, or those who don't believe in IF ideals," he said.

"Like Jones?"

J'avet looked grim. "Far worse, if I'm guessing correctly."

I thought quickly. Why would Selvia want the ship to think we were Freytauri and not IF? Unless...

"Rogue Freytaurians?" I guessed. "Ones who want to finish off the genocide, but the IF won't let them?"

"Possibly." His eyes unfocused and he thought aloud. "Their plan may have been to slow us down, to keep us busy fixing

Infinity so they might get it done before we reached orbit. *Infinity* was evacuated more quickly than they anticipated."

"Is it possible they tried to sabotage the engines first?" I asked. Maybe Slek was pushed after all. "If that's the case, then..." The blood drained from my face.

"There's a Freytaurian or two willing to kill us to finish their job, and they may be on this pod." J'avet looked toward the cockpit.

"It's neither of them," I said firmly.

He looked like he might say something more, but the communicator in the cockpit crackled.

I leaned forward to hear the rogue's response.

"Nice work," I couldn't see them, but their accents sounded like Danec and Slek. "Can you prove it?"

"We're both Freytaurian, aren't we?" Slek spread his arms. I was sure he was grinning, but could only see his back.

"Who else would be bold enough to steal a pod right from under IF noses? As a bonus, we have hostages. More on the planet and a colony of Iritaurians, ripe for the slaughter."

Did he have to sound so convincing?

Apparently J'avet thought so too, because he gave me a side-long glance.

I didn't want to draw Selvia's attention, so I refrained from giving him a one finger salute.

The comms went silent for a moment.

My heart stopped. I was sure the ship had cut contact and was about to open fire. We would be the proverbial sitting ducks.

This was the moment my father would say to kiss my ass goodbye, but I wasn't ready to do that yet.

My hand in my lap, I pressed a couple of buttons on my watch.

I looked up to see J'avet's eyes on me. He nodded, then turned back to the cockpit.

The comms crackled. "You're cleared for boarding in pod bay three. We'll send a contingent to meet you."

In other words, 'come on board, but we don't trust you as far as we can spit you, yet.' Fine, whatever got us on board. Once there, I'd figure out a way to prevent us from getting killed.

"Thank you." Slek cut the comms.

"Back to your seats," Selvia ordered. "Don't get too comfortable, You'll be needed soon enough."

Visibly troubled, both guys rose and flopped back into place next to me.

"Out of the frying pan, into the fire," I said.

"I wish we *had* hallucinated them," Danec said. "Or better yet, run."

"We might have, if we'd been believed," I said to the back of J'avet's head.

He turned and scowled at me. "Save your 'I told you so' for when we get out of this."

"I prefer to say it now," I said easily. "We might not live long enough for me to do it later."

He rolled his eyes and turned away.

"Fine. If we live through this, you can tell me why you hate me so much."

The ship loomed closer in the windows, especially the gaping hole in the side that must be the pod bay door. It sat open like a giant maw, ready to eat us whole and crunch our bones.

With that cheery thought in my head, I gripped Danec's hand and braced myself.

The pod slipped neatly through the door and into a long, well lit tunnel that led deeper into the ship.

The space door closed behind us and I immediately felt a bit heavier. Presumably the ship's gravitation was heavier than the pod's. I felt stuck down to the floor.

Danec grunted and shifted uncomfortably. Evidently he felt it too.

I looked past him to Slek, who seemed uneasy for different reasons. My tongue darted over my lips. "Those things you said—"

He set his mouth in a line. "I didn't like it any more than you did. I'll say whatever I have to to keep us alive."

"I know," I said quickly. "But you knew what they wanted to hear. You don't seem too surprised to find Freytaurians out here who—"

He cut me off. "I'm not. They usually stay away from IF space, but I knew they existed."

Danec looked at him in surprise. "I had no idea."

Slek smirked. "No offence, but you're barely off your mother's tit. Figuratively speaking. If you were any more innocent, you'd still be back in school, playing mathematics games on your tablet."

"I'm not that innocent," Danec muttered angrily.

"We shouldn't fight with each other," I snapped. "Slek, what are these Freytaurians capable of?"

"Besides running around the galaxy, destroying IF ships, and hunting Iri to kill? Just about anything, I'd say."

"They wouldn't hesitate to kill you," Selvia said. She'd walked back and forth through the seats and evidently heard at least the last bit of our conversation. "They would likely have their pleasure with you first." She cast an eye around the pod. "Anyone who isn't a Freytaurian. Perhaps even those who are, but who disagree with their ideals."

My stomach turned at the idea of any of us being violated like that. Even J'avet.

"I will die before I let him touch me," Humar declared loudly.

Selvia turned a cold smile on him. "You may get that chance."

She would kill as easily as any Frey-T rogue.

The pod bumped to a stop beside another couple, both a lot older and more battered this one. The rogues would probably welcome it with open arms, if not its passengers.

"We're here." Brinley sounded relieved, but anxious. If all Selvia needed was a pilot, she may have no further need for my friend.

Selvia nodded and waved for Brinley to step out of the cockpit.

"Close the door," she ordered, waving her cannon at Brinley.

Brinley nodded and hurried to comply.

"You two, to the pod's door." Selvia gestured to Danec and Slek. "You as well," she said to the other Freytaurians. "Everyone else, in front of me."

I hated the idea of turning my back on her, but I complied.

Brinley, her pretty face creased in the kind of frown my mother would have told me off for, stood beside me. She grabbed my hand and moved in close.

"It'll be all right," I said softly. "We'll get through this."

"I know," she replied. She didn't seem convinced.

I gave her a small smile as the pod door opened.

Six, maybe eight Freytaurians, skin ranging from pale blue to deepest purple, stood with weapons raised at us. Every one, man and woman, wore clothes that had seen better decades, with patches here and there to cover the multitude of holes.

They certainly looked like a bunch of pirates. Hungry ones, from the way they eyed us all.

A cold shudder passed through me. For the first time, I really wasn't sure we'd survive this.

"Step down slowly," one ordered. Evidently he didn't notice Selvia until she stepped off the pod last. When he did, his eyes widened and he raised his blaster.

Before he could fire, Selvia pulled a tube out of her pocket and tossed it onto the floor. When it hit, the tube shattered. Hundreds of tiny, glittering particles were dashed across the floor.

"Oh, shit," Slek muttered.

1 8

"WHAT THE—"

The particles drew together like a swarm of bees. Then, as though on some unseen signal, rose like a wave toward the rogues.

One aimed their blaster and fired. The shot hit the centre of the wave and made a hole, but it closed over again a moment later.

"Nanobots," Danec said.

His word took a moment to sink in.

Nanobots.

The symbionts.

The Iri didn't have slugs or bugs inside them, they had nanobots.

The wave lurched toward the Freytauri, who hurried back, blasters still aimed, although they must know the futility of them now.

The tail end of the swarm broke off when the swarm

stretched too far. The new pack headed in the other direction, toward Danec and Slek.

"No!" I cried out.

Someone grabbed my arm and tugged me back toward the pod. In the back of my mind, I registered J'avet.

"We can't leave them behind!"

The swarm caught up with a rogue who almost slipped in his haste. They crawled up his body like ants on a honey pot, until they reached his face. His eyes went wide. They slid into his ears and up his nose. His whole body stiffened. His arms flew out to either side and his back arched. The striking shade of blue faded out of his face and became a softly mottled silver.

He relaxed.

He smiled. His blaster dropped from his fingers.

My blood went cold. "Danec! Slek!"

J'avet pulled me hard and Brinley was right behind him. Selvia stood aside now, the other Iri arrayed behind her. Her expression was one of triumph. Her smile grew when the swarm engulfed another man.

I caught sight of Humar. He backed away from the swarm. His face was a mask of terror. He all but shoved a fellow evacuee in front of the swarm in his haste to reach the pod.

The evacuee, a Freytaurian woman named Kaeran, almost fell into the swarm from the force of his shove.

Danec reached for her, but missed her hand by a hair.

She staggered and kept her feet, but disappeared from view behind the silvery mass. She squeaked out a choked scream, then fell silent like the others.

A section of the swarm broke off and headed toward Humar. Just when I thought it would engulf him too, it split in two and went around him and hovered in the air before it headed right for Slek.

"It just wants Freytaurians," J'avet guessed. "Everyone, back in the pod! Ensign, Engineer—" He broke off as another evacuee was swallowed up.

"No!" Selvia growled. She aimed her cannon at Danec. "All Freytaurians will accept a symbiont."

"Personally, I'd rather die," Slek remarked.

She swung the cannon toward him. "You will be a host."

I held my breath. What I was about to do, could have me full of symbiont, or dead, or—

Without stopping to think for a moment longer, I broke away from J'avet and threw myself at Selvia. With her attention on Slek, she didn't see me coming. I barrelled into her hard enough to knock her back a few steps.

I grabbed for the hand cannon and tried to pull it from her.

Of course, someone full of nanobots and used to manual labour was a lot stronger than me, but it gave Brinley time to act. While Selvia and I wrestled, the small pilot darted past Slek and Danec and scooped up the rogue's dropped blaster. With no hesitation, she turned and aimed at Selvia.

The shot hit her full in the arm, a fingertip away from my hand. The force sheared through her wrist, severing her hand.

The smell of burnt flesh in my nostrils made me gag.

While Selvia stared in horror at her stump, I dove for the cannon and grabbed it before the other Iri could blink.

I waved it at them. "Move away from the pod. Everyone, get inside." I had an idle thought and aimed the cannon at the nanobots who were closing in on Danec.

"No," Selvia groaned.

That was all I needed to hear. I fired the cannon toward them. The blast cut a swathe through them.

For a moment they paused and I started to think they were out of commission. Slowly, gradually, they moved toward each other, closing the gap and re-forming. Their numbers were fewer, but I suspected just as dangerous.

The cannon on them and the Iri, I hurried toward the pod, waving everyone inside with my spare hand.

I fired another shot at the swarm which made a last lunge at Slek before the door closed behind us. A second before it did, I caught sight of the rogues. They were all Iritauri now. The smiles on their faces chilled my bones. They and the swarm turned and headed deeper into the ship.

"We need to get out of here," I said.

Brinley gave a sharp nod and hurried into the cockpit.

"A weapon doesn't make you the leader," J'avet said, but his tone wasn't as cold as it had been.

"Are you sure?" I asked, but I let my hand drop and the cannon with it. To aim it at anyone, even as a joke, wasn't funny.

"Certain." He took the cannon from my hand and patted my shoulder. Without another word, he retreated to the cockpit and left me to tremble before Slek and Danec gathered me in their arms and led me to a seat.

"I don't know if I should be happy to see you, or angry you didn't tell me anything about nanobots," I growled, but I was glad to be alive.

"I wasn't certain," Danec said. "The history books were never precise."

"No one has used nano technology for a long time," Slek added. "It was banned over fifty years ago."

"I wonder why," I said sarcastically. "I suppose that's the reason your people tried to kill the Iri. It wasn't because of the people, but because of the nanobots."

"I assume so, yes," Danec agreed. He cupped my cheek and leaned in to kiss my mouth lightly. "That was the bravest thing I've ever seen."

"Yes, you saved my ass," Slek agreed.

"I acted without thinking," I admitted. "I couldn't let her kill you, or let you be assimilated."

"Either way," Slek looked sly, "I owe you a lifetime of orgasms."

I laughed softly. "Totally worth it then."

"Strap in!" Brinley shouted.

The pod lifted off, turned in a slow circle and headed back the way we'd come.

We moved slowly, or at least it felt like it. We approached the first set of doors and stopped. A lifetime passed, but it wasn't even a minute before the door slid open.

"It's there to keep pods out, not in," Slek said.

"Oh." I still watched the door carefully until it was fully open, then left out a soft breath when it closed behind us. "One to go."

I didn't know if it was the ship or us which shook for a moment.

"Slek?" I asked slowly.

"Yes, Edie?" He quirked an eyebrow at me.

"Do ships of this age have a self-destruct?"

"Ummm. Yes. Yes they do."

"Shit."

The pod shook again, but this time I was sure it was only us.

"I, once again, have a bad feeling about this," I said.

"Me too," Danec agreed.

We approached the space doors and stopped. Like the last time, they took their time in opening. The longer it took, the more convinced I was we'd have an army of newly minted Iri chasing us.

"Danec, are the Iri dead?" I asked.

"No, they're under the control of the nanobots. From what I've read, they can still think for themselves, they just can't go against the nanotbot's programming."

"I see," I said. "I would hate to be at the start of the zombie apocalypse."

Slek gave me a funny look, but Danec smiled briefly. Apparently I needed to educate Slek on movies from Earth.

The space doors finally slid open on the beautiful expanse of space and the glittering stars.

The relief was short lived.

Between us and the glittering stars, something else glittered. It trickled down the side of the window, then moved to the edge as though seeking a way in.

"We have company," I said loudly. I shoved Danec and Slek toward the middle of the pod and faced the window. "I guess they won't suffocate in space?"

"No," Slek replied. "But we will need to get them off somehow."

"An interstellar car wash isn't a thing, I suppose?" I asked.

"No," Danec replied. "And we can't fly too close to the sun and burn them off. And we can't—"

Together we said, "Throw them out the airlock."

I would have laughed. Maybe later I will. Not now.

"What kills them?" I asked.

"Time," Slek replied slowly. "They'll power down if they don't find a host."

"How long?" Danec asked.

"Uhhh. About three weeks," Slek said regretfully.

"We don't have three weeks." J'avet had stepped out of the cockpit to listen. "We have maybe five days of oxygen. No more."

"I said *about* three," Slek muttered, "It could be less."

"Less than five days?" I asked.

"No," he admitted.

"Unless you have a solution..." J'avet stared him down.

Slek frowned. "The cannon Selvia had might do it."

"It's in *here*," I said. "The nanobots are out *there*."

Slek rubbed the side of his nose. "Unless we can rig that up to the forward array and..." He wandered off toward the cockpit, talking under his breath about numbers and technical specifications.

"In the meantime, stay away from—" J'avet's eyes widened at what he saw in the opposite window, behind my shoulder.

I turned and gaped.

The rogue's ship flashed with warning lights. I braced myself for the wake from the explosion if the Freytauri had engaged the self-destruct.

From one breath to the next, the lights turned off and the ship began to move away.

I creased my brow. "Either the Freytauri kept control, or—"

"Or the Iritauri are leaving orbit," J'avet finished.

Barely a minute later, another ship appeared in the window. This one was more distant, but coming fast. It was followed by another and another.

"It's about time," I muttered.

J'avet smirked.

"What?" I asked. "I sent the distress signal hours ago."

"They got here as soon as they could," he said.

Before I could respond, he turned away.

He was right, but the nanobots were quickly increasing in number. I didn't want to think about how. They didn't seem to feed on each other, and there was no material floating around, except the pod. They would either eat their way in, or they would eat the pod around us, until we were sucked out into the vacuum.

Maybe now I should kiss my ass goodbye. Instead, I moved to lace my arm around Danec's.

"It'll be all right," I said. I wasn't sure if I was trying to convince him or myself.

The pod shuddered as the nanobot swarm started to tap at the windows.

"Yes, it will," Danec said. He sounded as terrified as I felt.

The IF ships drew closer, but they seemed slow, too slow. The rogue ship increased speed.

"If we get out of this," I started.

"We will," Danec said. "We'll be fine. The IF is here. Slek is working. We'll be okay. We'll be okay."

The tapping became more insistent. I felt the overwhelming need to pee.

"We're going to die!" Humar shouted. His voice was raw

with stone cold fear, the likes of which I had never heard before. It accurately summed up what I was feeling myself.

"We'll be fine," I snapped, in spite of myself. "Keep calm."

Tap.

Tap.

Tap

Crack.

Oh shit.

I squeezed my eyes shut and leaned into Danec. At least my life would end beside someone I cared about.

"When this is over, I want to watch movies and eat popcorn," Danec said.

"You like popcorn?" I asked.

"I've never had it, but I've heard about it," he admitted.

"Okay, we can make that happen," I said.

A moment later, the engine stopped dead and silence fell over the pod. Silence deeper than the universe itself.

Then the tapping increased and the window went black, covered entirely with tiny nanobots.

"Shit," I muttered.

19

THE LIGHTS in the pod went out. We were plunged into darkness.

I waited for my eyes to adjust, to find some hint of light to see by. They didn't. The darkness was absolute.

My heart raced. Panic rose inside me, along with a scream which threatened to tear from my throat.

Danec held me closer and whispered something.

I couldn't hear it over the pounding of blood in my ears and the ringing from the utter silence.

"What?" I asked.

"I said I like you," he repeated. "A lot."

"I like you too." Was now really the time for this? I supposed it was, we might never get another chance. "Very much."

Before he could respond, the lights came back on so bright I blinked hard and shook my head.

"There," Slek said. "I've rigged the cannon to..." He shook his head. "It doesn't matter. What does matter is that we have one chance at this. And..."

"And what?" J'avet asked, eyes narrowed at Slek.

"And it could backfire and blow us all up," Slek said lightly. "But if this doesn't work, we're probably screwed anyway, so I say we give it a shot."

"That's your professional opinion?" J'avet asked.

"Professional. Personal. Guy who doesn't want to end up infested with nanobots." Slek sounded indifferent, almost sarcastic, but fear flashed in his eyes.

"I say we do it," I said.

J'avet glanced back at me, quirked a brow, then nodded at Slek.

"Do it." To the rest of us, he said, "Sit down and strap in. This could get rough."

"It isn't already?" I asked under my breath.

Danec snorted his agreement, but strapped in beside me and draped an arm over my shoulder.

"In three," Slek said loudly.

Beside him, Brinley's face was pale with anxiety, but she looked hopeful. If anyone would understand what Slek had rigged up, she would. Her expression gave me hope too. Maybe we'd be okay.

"Two."

J'avet's eyes were on the window. The odd lights in his irises flashed briefly. Maybe he was part machine too, I mused, but I was almost certain he wasn't.

Humar squeaked with fear, but I had no sympathy for him. The nanobots wouldn't have touched him. He hadn't needed to push the Freytauri woman into their path. If he hadn't, she might be here with us.

I sighed softly. He wasn't to know, I suppose.

"One." Slek slammed the heel of his hand down onto a button.

The cannon, attached to a cable of some kind, lit up. Or at least, a series of buttons down the side did.

For several heartbeats, I was sure it was about to explode and kill us all.

Something outside the pod flashed and Slek let out a whoop of joy.

The flash was followed by another flash, further down the ship, then another. The swarm on the window thinned.

Thinned further.

With the fifth flash, the last of the nanobots fell away and floated off into space.

"If they don't bump into any ships, they'll deactivate and become harmless," Slek said.

With any luck, that would be exactly what happened.

"We've taken a lot of damage," Brinley said. "Those nanobots were hungry."

I shivered.

J'avet nodded and pressed a button in front of him. After a crackle, a face appeared on the comm screen.

"Commander J'avet, you're alive." Did the Centaurian woman on the comms from one of the IF ships sound disappointed or did I imagine that?

"So it would seem," he said dryly. "You need to go after the other ship before they get too far for interception."

An Agusian man looked over the woman's shoulder. He bore

the same rank insignia as J'avet. His antennas twitched toward the screen. "Thanks for the tip, commander. We're already in pursuit."

As he said that, two of the IF ships broke away from the other, which remained on a course straight toward us.

"Did someone chew on the pod?" the commander asked.

"Yes, Zarex. I got hungry waiting for you," J'avet said sarcastically.

Zarex grinned. His eyes were warm with humour.

"You always were impatient," Zarex said.

"You were always late," J'avet retorted.

"Not this time," Zarex said. "We got here just in time to see you blow nanobots off your pod with an old-fashioned laser hand cannon. I didn't think those things existed anymore, after they were, you know, banned." Zarex cocked his head and looked slightly accusing.

"It wasn't ours," Slek said helpfully. "We were just using it to save our asses."

"I'll brief you when I'm on board." J'avet looked like a man who had used up his last fuck. I didn't blame him. I was running short on them myself.

"Copy that." Zarex moved out of view.

The Centauri woman nodded at the screen. "The pod bay is ready, Commander J'avet. Please proceed."

"I hope this old girl has enough left in her to make it that far," Brinley said. She leaned over to press a few buttons and we slipped through space, toward the welcome sight of the open space door.

A moment before we slid inside, I caught a glimpse of an explosion in the distance. I couldn't be certain, but I assumed the IF ships had caught up to the rogues and blew them out of space. Freytauri or Iri, they were a threat to the IF either way, but the idea of all those deaths made me shudder.

I swallowed hard. "It looks like you get popcorn after all." I tried to speak lightly when all I wanted to do was drink a bottle of some kind of alcohol and eat a whole pizza while hiding in a blanket fort. I mean, we've all felt like that, right? I felt like that several times in the last twenty-four hours.

"I'm just happy we're safe," Danec replied.

I exhaled through my nose as the space doors closed behind us. "So am I," I said. "That's all that matters right now."

Slek stepped out of the cockpit and slipped into the seat beside me.

"If it wasn't for you, we'd be bare-chested and silver skinned by now," he said.

"If it wasn't for you, we'd be dead," Danec told him.

"That's true," Slek said, with no humility whatsoever. "Just an old engineer's trick."

"Does that mean you're an old engineer?" I teased.

"Ouch," he laughed. "I'm just a boy. Not as young as Danec, of course."

Danec looked annoyed. "I'm not that young."

Slek leaned over to slap him on the shoulder. "No, I just hope you're old enough to deal with it when Edie chooses me."

"Who said I'm choosing you?" I asked.

Slek's confidence didn't slip an iota. "You will. Why wouldn't you, I'm adorable."

"Danec is pretty cute too," I said.

Danec looked embarrassed, but pleased. "You think I'm cute?" He shot Slek a triumphant look.

"You *are* cute," Slek said. "So are kittens. Edie needs a wildcat to keep up with her." He made a gesture with his hand, like a cat batting the air.

The pod slid through the second set of doors and landed in the pod bay with a bump which might have thrown me off my seat if not for the harness.

Slek grabbed the seat in front of him to stay in place.

"Sorry," Brinley called over her shoulder.

"At least we're alive," Slek said.

"Yes, everyone out," J'avet ordered. "The IF will want to look over the pod. Engineer, stay with the pod. They'll be sure to have questions."

Slek looked disappointed, but nodded. Before I could step toward the door, he grabbed me to his firm body and planted a searing kiss on my mouth. His tongue split and one side slid over my lips, while the other slipped inside my mouth.

I melted a little before he pulled away.

"Just something to keep you warm for a while." He gave Danec a challenging glance which clearly said, 'game on' before he pushed me gently toward the door.

I stepped outside and gasped. The outside of the pod really did look like it had been chewed.

Chunks of metal were gouged here and there. In more than one place, it seemed so thin I don't know how it hadn't ruptured.

"I didn't realise how close we came," I said in a whisper.

"Too close," Danec agreed. His eyes were huge.

"Oh my goodness." Brinley stood beside us. Her face was pale with exhaustion and horror. "I'm not sure I want to fly a pod again." After a pause, she added, "At least not today."

I smiled softly and gave her a quick hug. "I'm glad you did fly us. You did an amazing job."

"Awww, thank you." She looked pleased. "I need to find where I can clock my hours. They all count toward my qualifications."

"Ah, the intrepid pod crew." A door at the end of the bay slid open and Commander Zarex stepped through, followed by a contingent of security and a couple of engineers.

Zarex's gaze scanned us all. I probably imagined his eyes lingered on me for a moment longer.

"J'avet, I'm sure this will be an interesting debriefing," Zarex said.

"I would imagine so," J'avet agreed. "We should start by sending pods to rescue the other refugees from Calig." His voice lowered and he and Zarex stepped slowly around the pod, talking with their heads close together.

"I suppose we're dismissed," Danec said uncertainly.

"I hope so," I said, "because I really need a shower and change of clothes. And a hairbrush." My hair must look like a bird's nest had an argument with a squirrel.

"We'll show you to your quarters," one of the security officers said. The way he looked at me suggested we weren't trusted yet. I was too tired to think why, or what it might mean. I just nodded, took Danec's hand, and followed them out the door.

Before it closed behind us, I glanced back to see Zarex's eyes squarely at me. He looked away the moment he saw me notice.

I shrugged it off as nothing. To Slek, I gave a smile and a wave, then the door closed between us.

"It's not far." Both of the security officers were Parvoran. In spite of their lack of smiles, they both seemed friendlier than J'avet. It must be just him then, who was a grumpy pants.

I rubbed my weary brow with the tip of my fingers and said, "I've never seen a female Parvoran. Are there any?" That sounded rude, even to my ears, but I was tired and my diplomacy needed a polish as much as I did.

"There are many," one of them said. He had a pleasant face, like he smiled often. "They remain on Parvora."

"All of them?" I asked in surprise.

"Yes indeed." He had clearly fielded this question before. "As is their place."

"Oh. I see." Was that why J'avet didn't like me? Because I hadn't stayed home? I smirked to myself. If that was the case, he was shit out of luck. I still planned to go to Agus and continue my study. Nothing he said or did could change that.

"They prefer it that way," the other guard added. "Fewer men to inconvenience them."

"Right." I was sure some of them would agree. Goodness knows plenty of human women have wanted just that since the dawn of time, but plenty didn't. Men, after all, have cocks. Those come in handy from time to time.

The security officers exchanged glances, but neither seemed bothered by my response. It was their culture, they could live it however they wanted, but I wasn't my cup of tea.

We stopped in front of a set of doors which slid open at the press of a button on the wall.

"You're free to come and go, but we'll accompany you until the captain says otherwise," one of the officers said. "It's just a precaution after what happened with *Infinity* and *Artemis*."

Was that the name of the ship the rogues destroyed, which

sent chunks raining down on Calig? I spared a thought for her crew, caught up in an old war that had nothing to do with them.

I nodded. "Fine. We only plan to rest."

The officer nodded. "I'll have food sent."

We stepped inside and the door closed behind us.

The room we were in was as small as one might expect on a ship. Down one side were cubicles, each containing a bed and set of drawers. Down the other was a table and a long bench under the wide window. A door to the rear led to a bathroom, with four shower stalls and four unisex toilets. Two sinks occupied a space in the corner. Beside that was a set of shelves full of clothing, with the size marked on each shelf.

A quick glance showed they even had my size.

"I'm going to have a shower," I said. I hesitated for a moment before I added, "Do you want to join me?" With a trembling hand, I laced my little finger in his.

Danec's eyes lit up like all of his festive celebrations had come as once. "Yes," he said immediately. His face turned darker blue. "I mean, that would be great."

"Great," I said too. Suddenly shy, I turned my back, stepped into a shower cubicle and stripped off my clothes.

He followed me in and closed and locked the door behind us.

I heard him undress and saw his clothes join mine in a pile on the floor. Without turning around, I waved my palm over the sensor to start the water.

Always warm straight away, the spray on my skin made me sigh.

"That feels so good," I said.

"You look so good," Danec said.

I turned slowly then, to face him.

He was trim and lean in the waist and hips. His stomach was flat under the washboard lines of his abs. A perfect V slanted down toward a cock bigger than I had expected.

"Wow." I grabbed the bar of soap and started to wash my arm.

"Wow?" He took the soap and turned me gently so he could run it over my back.

"Yes." I pulled my hair up out of the way. "You're hot. Mmmm, and you have great hands."

"Thank you." He leaned in and kissed the back of my neck. He kissed around to the side and let his tongue flick across the point just under my jaw. "You taste good."

He wound a hand around me and ran the soap over my breasts, first one, then the other. From there, he moved down my belly.

I shivered with the deliciousness of his touch. This felt so decadent and right. His touch was light, gentle, but erotic at the same time. My exhaustion wasn't gone, but I put it aside in favour of quickly growing desire.

"It's my turn." I took the soap from him and turned him so I could lather his back. I started at his muscular shoulders and worked down slowly. I took my time with the firm cheeks of his ass.

He gave it a playful wiggle.

I giggled and moved the soap over his hips and around to his rock hard belly.

"All right, turn around." I soaped up my hands and placed the bar back on the shelf.

Danec turned, but I saw him swallow. He knew what was coming and so did his cock, which was half erect already.

I gripped it carefully in my hands and rubbed my fingers up and down until his length was slick with lather. I worked it a bit more firmly, as his cock hardened more. The water washed the soap away until there was nothing under my hands but wet cock.

The more I worked him, the more individual bumps rose on his cock. Those bumps became nodules the size of a pebble, like a handheld massager, or pearls.

Holy fuck, how would he feel inside me?

While I worked, his hands wandered all over my body, caressing here and stroking there. He brushed over my nipples, down my belly to my other curls.

His hand slid between my legs and grazed against the front of my folds.

I shifted one foot enough to part my legs a little more.

He slipped his hand in further and brushed against my clit.

I whimpered as even that small touch sent bolts of desire arcing through me.

"Danec," I said breathlessly. "I want you."

He silenced me with a kiss as sweet as it was wet with water from the shower.

He pulled back and spoke with a husky voice, "I want you too."

I worked his cock until his eyelids fluttered shut and his hips bucked against my hand.

Before he could come, he drew himself out of my hands and knelt down in front of me. Gently, he parted my legs and pressed his face between them.

I propped my foot on the seat to the side of the shower to give him better access.

His tongue, split in two, flicked lightly against my folds. Then firmer as his confidence grew. Both sides licked my clit, tickling and teasing. He must have pulled both sides of his tongue together, because in the next moment his touch was firm, hard, the texture licking insistently while his lips sucked all around me.

I arched my back and let the water wash down over me, while an orgasm built inside me. Every flick, every lick, every suck drove me higher and higher, closer and closer. This was more than just pleasure, it was intimacy between two people who cared for each other. Who had been through an ordeal and survived.

Every moment showed how we felt about each other. I trusted him with all of my intimate places, inside and out.

"Danec," I breathed. I moaned so loudly the whole ship might hear, if the walls weren't thick enough to keep in the sound. "Yes..." I cried out as I came, hard and fast, my body rocking, grinding against his mouth.

He licked me until every last drop of orgasm drained out of my body and washed down the drain. Then he stood.

I caught my breath, but didn't hesitate to pull him to me, so his cock was against my entrance, bumps and all. I pushed my hips forward, onto his tip.

"Oh." His tongue darted over his lips. "Are you sure?"

I wasn't sure how much more I could do to declare my certainty, but I whispered, "Yes. Please."

He blew out a breath and eased his cock inside me. His bumps rubbed against my clit as he slid in and slowly out again. The friction felt incredible and made me horny all over again.

I quivered and tilted my hips forward to take him in deeper.

The nodules on his cock rubbed their way up my insides. They created a flood of sensation like pops of electricity that sent pleasure all the way up to my belly.

"Oh my goodness," I breathed.

He froze. "Are you all right?"

"Better than all right," I said. So, so all right.

"Great," he exhaled a ragged breath.

I fought back a smile and reached around to cup his hard ass. Damn, how did I get so lucky?

He drew out, then slid back in deeper. Each thrust massaged me inside and out. Another orgasm grew faster than I ever would have thought possible. I may never get enough of this, enough of him.

He placed his hands on the wall to either side of me and closed his eyes as he thrust harder and harder.

"You feel great," he said softly. "I mean, amazing."

I smiled. "You feel pretty amazing yourself." The last word trailed off into a moan. My fingernails dug into his ass.

He leaned down to graze his teeth over my shoulder, then bit hard enough to leave a mark.

I groaned louder.

He bit harder. Not enough to draw blood, but enough to drive me wild. His teeth would leave marks to match the ones on my breasts from Slek.

The thought pushed me to the edge and over, into an orgasm so intense it bordered on painful, but in the best way possible.

Danec grunted and paused mid-thrust to grunt again as he came, buried deep inside me. He ground his hips against me, his breath in ragged pants. Just when I thought he would sag, he grunted again, louder this time and ground harder still. He bit down on my shoulder and cried out against my flesh as he came again.

Oh my.

Finally, he gasped and his body sagged, his face pressed against my shoulder. His weight bore us both down to the seat, where we half sat, half leaned, still entangled, his cock still deep inside me.

"Wow," I said.

"Wow is right." He pulled out of me and we got more comfortable. He put his arms around me and held me close.

We stayed like that until my eyes started to close.

"We should get dry," I said reluctantly.

"Let me," Danec said. He rose, turned off the water, and reached for the towel, which hung on a hook on the back of the door. He tugged me gently to my feet and started to dry me, first my face and hair, then moving down slowly. He lingered at my breasts and ass, but soon worked his way down to my feet.

"Thank you." I took the towel from him as he rose and wrapped it around my hair before I grabbed a dry one and started on him.

"Hey, where are you guys? There's food here." Slek's voice startled me.

"Coming," I called out. I shared a smile with Danec. We had both done our share of coming already, but this time involved food. I was okay with that.

I wrapped one towel around Danec's hips and pulled the one

off my hair to pull around myself.

Danec opened the door and stepped outside. I followed a moment later.

Slek, who stood in the bedroom, a sandwich halfway to his mouth, gave Danec a look of envy, but he was clearly impressed. "There you two are. I see you missed me." He grinned.

I rolled my eyes and found some clean clothes to pull on. I chose a big t-shirt and some soft shorts.

Danec only grabbed some track pants.

"So what did the IF want?" I stepped into the bedroom and started to work my hair dry.

"They wanted to see how I rigged the cannon to the pod, and asked what I knew about *Infinity*. They think..." Slek paused for effect, "I was pushed."

"I keep telling you that's what happened," I said, only half joking.

Slek shrugged. "The problem is, there are more rogues out there. More Iri too. They aren't going to stop trying to kill each other, and other people are going to get caught in the middle."

I walked to the tray of food on the table and snagged a sandwich and a cup of water.

"There's more," Slek said. "IF is sending me to Agus to teach other engineers my cannon trick."

I stopped, mid-chew. "You're coming to Agus too?" I swallowed hastily and grinned.

He grinned too. "Yes, we're all going. And with any luck, coming."

I laughed.

Danec blushed, but managed a laugh as well. "That's great,

we can take care of each other."

"Yes, us and Brinley," I said tired but happy. "We make a good team."

Slek raised his cup at me. "A very good team.

Danec added his cup to the toast. "A great team."

I laughed and threw a piece of sandwich at him.

He caught it and when I thought he might eat it, he placed it into my mouth instead.

I smiled around it while I chewed.

"An awesome team," Danec said softly. "Will that make it harder to choose?"

I grimaced. That might make it impossible to choose, but I had a feeling I was going to have a good time, in the meantime. I eyed Slek's groin speculatively. I was satisfied for now, but I was curious how he would feel. Some ridiculous part of me was still curious how J'avet would feel. It was probably professional curiosity. I was supposed to learn about alien physiology after all. Maybe I could write a book. Or I could focus on getting to know the two incredible guys right in front of me.

The future was going to be interesting.

THE PARTICLES FLOATED THROUGH SPACE. Some nanobots found others and they joined up, like their programming dictated. They floated past debris, crawled over it and cannibalised as much material as they could use.

The swarm grew.

Floated on.

Toward the shipping lanes.

STAR DEFENDERS

MY ALIEN MATES BOOK 2

"THE IF HAS CONCLUDED—" J'avet's eyes scanned the room. His gaze settled on me and the sides of his mouth drew back. He looked away before I could flick him the finger.

He continued as though he hadn't paused. "The attack on the *Infinity* intended to slow the ship. The explosives were intended to incite panic, not destruction."

"It would have been good to know that before we evacuated," I muttered.

Beside me, Slek murmured his agreement and his hand tightened in mine. As a ship's engineer, he hadn't been called upon to assess the damage before we piled into pods and fled. His admittedly large ego survived that slightly, but the encounter with the Iri and their nanobot symbionts who had tried to inhabit him and Danec, could have ended badly for us all, especially them.

"However," J'avet continued, "the perpetrator, or perpetrators, remain unknown and at large. We suspect they were a member of a group of rogue Freytaurians, but that's all we know. Consider everyone on *Infinity* at that time to be a suspect."

I expected him to look at me and the Freytaurians who sat to either side of me, but he didn't.

Evidently, Danec expected the same, because he exhaled loudly out his nose when J'avet turned away.

"Commander." Slek stuck his arm up in the air like a schoolboy. "I assume I'm exempt from suspicion, because I was, you know, pushed."

J'avet turned around slowly. "That was only speculation, Engineer. We have proof of nothing."

Slek lowered his hand, and his expression went with it.

I patted his knee. "We know you did nothing wrong," I said loud enough for J'avet to hear.

Typically, the Parvoran ignored me. That was probably just as well. I was done listening to him and I might be tempted to tell him that. While technically he wasn't in charge of me, he could make my life difficult if he wanted to.

"Those of you still going to Agus, the *Halcyon* leaves Dendra Station in two days' time, at fifteen hundred hours precisely." J'avet's eyes swept over the room and settled on me again.

"I'll be on time," I said sweetly.

Before I even finished my sentence, his gaze moved to Danec, and then to someone behind us.

Asshole.

"Dismissed," J'avet said finally. He strode out of the room, full of his own importance, leaving the rest of us to file out of the debriefing in small, quiet groups.

"Someone went to a lot of trouble to keep *Infinity* from

protecting the Iri," Brinley said. My friend, and the best pilot in the galaxy—okay, I'm biased, but she is amazing at her job—frowned. Not even a scowl could mar her pretty features. She flicked her hair over her shoulder. "And *Artemis*."

Of the two, we fared better. The *Artemis* was completely destroyed.

"What if it wasn't the rogues which attacked *Infinity*?" Danec asked softly.

"What do you mean?" I asked.

He shrugged. "I-I don't know. Maybe someone wanted us to go to Calig." Colour crept up his already blue face.

"Like an Iri spy, sent to force us to go there to become nanobot hosts?" Slek asked.

"S-something like that," Danec stammered slightly, as he did when nervous or anxious.

"That would mean there's someone ready to throw every Freytaurian to the nanobots." I shivered. "Who would do that?"

"I don't know," Danec said. "Someone who doesn't like Frey-taurians?"

"How could anyone not like us?" Slek asked. As a Freytaurian himself, his skin tended toward purple, rather than blue, and he was more street smart than Danec, but they both shared the same vulnerability to the nanobots.

"I can't think of a single reason," I said lightly. "But this would cast suspicion on everyone on board the *Infinity*." I hated to agree with J'avet, but he was right about that.

I stopped beside a window which looked out over Dendra Station. *Infinity* floated beside a dock she shared with a dozen other ships of various sizes. From this angle, she looked whole, undamaged. I knew she was crawling with engineers who worked quickly to fix the IF vessel and press her back into service. I also knew Slek itched to be one of them. He requested to help, but that was denied. It seemed the IF wasn't allowing any passengers from her last voyage to board for any reason. I took that to mean they still searched for tampering or explosives. They wouldn't want us to remove evidence which might implicate us.

Surely since the IF was letting us leave Dendra, they had determined our innocence? That, or they hadn't found proof of guilt. Nor would they. I wouldn't even know how to tamper with a spaceship if I wanted to. Which I didn't. I was a nurse. Of the four of us, Slek and perhaps Brinley were the only ones with that kind of knowledge.

"So, two more nights here, hmmm?" Slek said. He slung an arm over my shoulder and toyed with my hair. He was fascinated with my crazy curls. I was fascinated with his ridiculously enormous muscles, amongst other things.

"So J'avet said," I agreed. "Why, what do you have in mind?"

His hand trailed down my back to cup my ass. "I can think of a few things."

"Oh?" I asked teasingly. His touch made my blood hot and the butterflies in my tummy were doing flips. They did that around Slek and Danec. In the couple of months I'd known them, they hadn't diminished in the slightest. If anything, they'd increased.

"Can you cure the Iri?" Danec asked. His expression suggested he'd been thinking hard and didn't realise he was going to speak until he did.

"Cure?" I echoed. "As in, get rid of the nanobots?"

Danec nodded vigorously. Damn, he was cute when he got

all excited.

"They could potentially be switched off," Slek said thoughtfully. "But there's a long list of problems with that."

"Like what?" Brinley asked.

Slek counted them off his fingers. "We'd have to switch them all off at once, or more would infest the host. We'd have to find a way to do that, which would require IF support. Then there's the issue of consent."

"Right," I sighed. "The Iri might like being hosts."

"What if they don't?" Danec asked insistently. "They might want to be free."

"If we ever meet another one, you can ask them." Slek patted him on the shoulder.

Danec looked disappointed, but he didn't press the matter. Still, I knew he was thinking about it. He had that look in his eye, like cogs and wheels were turning in his mind.

"In the meantime," I said as brightly as I could. "Who's up for popcorn and some movies?"

"If by movies, do you mean, long, slow foreplay?" Slek asked.

"No. By movies, I mean movies," I replied.

Now he looked disappointed, but nodded anyway. "Sure, I guess I could watch one or two before bedtime." Now his mischievous smile was back.

"I have a training flight," Brinley said regretfully. "Apparently my evasive manoeuvres weren't up to par." She made a face.

"You saved our asses," I pointed out, offended on her behalf.

She raised her hands to either side, palms up. "A pilot can never know too much."

"That's true." I gave her a quick hug. "I'll never stop learning either."

I turned to the guys as she trotted off.

"I have some things I need to do," Danec said reluctantly. "I have classes I have to catch up on."

"Why do I have a feeling you'll never finish learning either?" I asked.

He smiled briefly. "There's always something else to discover about something." He didn't quite meet my eyes.

"I suppose there is," I agreed. I gave him a sidelong look, but he flashed me a smile and turned to disappear down the corridor.

"Now that was odd," I said.

"Really?" Slek asked. "I didn't think it was that odd. I mean, he obviously wants to give us some time alone together."

I watched Danec's perfect ass round a corner and shook my head. "I don't think that's it."

"No," Slek said lightly. "He's probably going to look up nano —" He cut off mid-sentence. "Commander Zarex," he greeted with a smile. "I didn't see you coming."

Neither had I. The green-skinned commander appeared almost out of nowhere. With scales on the side of his neck resembling a reptile, he might have the ability to slink. Or I hadn't been paying attention, distracted as I was by Danec's ass... I mean, sudden departure.

I smiled. "Good afternoon."

"Good afternoon Nurse Wright, Engineer Slek." Zarex's voice was smoother than a chocolate fountain and almost as delicious. His slow smile was the kind you might call panty dropping. His antennas, the same shade as the rest of him, bent toward me like a bow, or an attentive listener. Yeah, okay, he was hot.

"What can we do for you?" I found myself asking.

"I need some of your time," Zarex replied. His tone was self-assured, a man accustomed to giving orders and having them followed. Not in the same way J'avet insisted on obedience. People obeyed Zarex because he made people *want* to obey him.

"Uh." I swallowed. "Me?" I, on the other hand, am not so self-assured.

Zarex smiled, a slow, almost lazy smile that made my panties want to twist under my trousers.

"Yes, you, Nurse Wright. Unless you're too busy?"

"Oh, I'm not," I said quickly. I glanced toward Slek, who was watching me, one eyebrow raised. "I mean, we were just going to watch movies, but we can do that later if it's important."

"Oh, it absolutely is," Zarex replied. "It shouldn't take too long, though. I have you back to your...movies in no time." Did he wink at Slek, or did his eye twitch?

Either way, I blushed.

"All right then, Commander. Um..." I shot Slek a glance.

Slek held up both hands. "Go ahead. I'll hunt down some popcorn and warm up the vidscreen."

I nodded. "Okay, sounds good. And don't forget, not so much salt this time."

"And more butter," Slek added.

"Yes, and that," I agreed. Popcorn was always better when it was oozing so much butter it covered my fingers and trickled down my wrist. Okay, it's not the healthiest option, but it was movie night. I could indulge this once.

"This way." Zarex gestured down the corridor, toward the command section of the station. It was generally a place someone like me wasn't allowed to go, except in the company of someone like him.

"Can you tell me what this is about?" I asked. "Am I in trouble?" Just being beside him gave me goosebumps.

"Should you be?" He gave me a slow, sly smile, his eyes half lidded.

I swallowed.

Oh yes, I should be spanked, I thought.

"No, not that I know of." My voice was slightly higher than usual. Hopefully he didn't notice my blush. More than that, I hoped he couldn't read my mind. That would be a touch embarrassing, to say the least. Although, just in case, I thought about what he could do with his tongue between my legs. "There's a first time for everything," I added. Um, what were we talking about again?

He chuckled, deep in the back of his throat. His antennas quivered with what I assumed was laughter.

"So they say," he agreed. "Often the first time can be the most memorable."

I was sure he meant it to be a completely innocent remark, but my mind took it to a whole new place. I watched him in the corner of my eye and decided his remark wasn't so innocent after all. His smile certainly wasn't.

"Um." Damn, my ability to speak seemed to have fled for a moment. "I guess so," I said finally. *Lame, Edie, lame.*

"Come this way." He waved toward an open door.

Okay, I knew his words were no accident this time. He was flirting, but with more subtlety than Slek. So subtle, in fact, he could easily claim he meant nothing by it at all. I would have to keep my wits about me when he was around.

I stepped into a room with a stunning view of the side of the station, the docks and a hint of Dendra far below us.

Almost entirely green, it was hard to tell the land from the oceans. Truthfully, it looked inhospitable, but was home for a few billion Dendrans and other species.

I turned as Zarex closed the door behind us. I couldn't shake the feeling I was prey, but his expression was benign. For now.

"So." I crossed my arms over my ample chest. "What is this about?"

Zarex circled around the room and stopped at the window. "You saw some of the passengers from Frey-T," the shortened name for Freytauri, "turned into hosts for the Iri nanobots."

"Is that a question?" I asked. "Because you know I did." He had attended the first debriefing on the IF ship which had rescued us from our pod above Calig.

"Yes, I do." He pulled a chair out from behind a desk and propped a booted foot on the seat.

Evidently he didn't plan to offer me a chair.

"I want to hear it again, slowly, and from the perspective of a medic," he said.

"Okay." I pictured the moment in my head before I spoke. "The nanobots looked like a swarm of glitter. I'd hate to get it on the carpet. You'd be vacuuming it up for years."

He cleared his throat.

"Right. Well, they crawled up the bodies of the Freytauri and crawled up their noses and into their mouths." I shuddered.

"They didn't enter anywhere else?" he asked.

I thought for a moment, then shook my head. "I don't think so. If they did, they went under clothes, so it would be difficult to see."

He nodded. "Why the nose and mouth?"

"I don't know, I didn't know nanobots existed until then." What was he getting at?

"In your opinion," he said slowly.

"Because they're holes?" I suggested. "A way into the brain."

He snapped his fingers so suddenly I jumped. Where J'avet would have found it amusing, Zarex looked apologetic.

"Into the brain," he repeated. He lowered his leg and looked out the window. "All the better to control thoughts and movements."

"I suppose so," I agreed. Now I thought about it, it made perfect sense. They wouldn't be efficient if they congregated in one elbow.

"Did you get any sense of who or what was giving them orders?" He turned and gave me a piercing look.

"No," I said slowly, "but I wasn't looking. A bunch of Iri had weapons on us. I was trying to survive."

"Of course, of course." He waved a hand. "As you should."

"Right. Did they find anything on Calig when they went down to free the other evacuees?" A few hundred had been held hostage so the rest of us behaved when the Iri attacked the Freytauri rogues.

"Signs of recent habitation, but not much else," he replied, which was more than J'avet told us. "It's as if they melted into the trees, but their life signs went with them. They found none."

"Do they have them?" I asked dryly.

He did a double take. "I beg your pardon?" He seemed shocked. For some reason, I found that fascinating. He seemed more—well, not human. Vulnerable.

I replied slowly. "Danec said the Iri aren't dead, but what if the nanobots suppress their life signs? Do their hearts still beat naturally?"

His eyes widened. "Did you see any children?"

My lips dropped apart. "No. Do you think—"

He toyed with one of his antennas.

I wondered what it felt like. Skin? Scaly?

"They have an outpost somewhere," he mused.

"I was going to suggest they're immortal, but that works better," I admitted.

He smiled briefly. "It's possible the nanobots suppress our ability to detect them."

"That would explain why everyone thought Calig was uninhabited," I said.

He looked surprised again. "That's true." He lowered his hand from his antenna and dropped it to his side. "Thank you, Nurse Wright."

"Edie," I corrected.

"Edie." My name sounded nice rolling off his tongue. "I look forward to working with you further on the journey to Agus."

"You're coming too?" I asked, confused. I thought he had a command on the rescue ship.

He smiled. "Someone has to help the captain with the *Halcyon*, and keep Commander J'avet on his toes."

"He'll love that," I said sarcastically. From what I had seen, the pair didn't much like each other. I understood that; J'avet was pretty unlikeable.

"Yes he will, won't he?" Zarex looked completely unruffled by the fact. If anything, he seemed to find it amusing.

I shook my head. This was going to be an interesting journey.

2

"So, what movie are we watching?" I flopped down beside Slek on the wide armchair in front of the big vidscreen.

Dendra Station housed a permanent population of personnel. As such, they accommodated residents and visitors in relative luxury. More luxurious than Moon Station or *Infinity* at least. Both of those were built for function, not fun. With resources sourced from the planet below, the food was better too.

"I found one called *Attack of the Killer Tomatoes*," Slek said. He looked part amused and part confused.

"Oh, a classic," I said approvingly. "And popcorn." Thank goodness corn grew just about everywhere, although it tasted slightly different from planet to planet. Something about soil composition, but I don't know. I'm no farmer. I just eat tons of the stuff, especially on movie night.

"With lots of butter, just as the lady asked." He balanced the bowl on his lap and put an arm around me.

"Start movie," he said.

The vidscreen flickered to life and the movie, bad special effects and all, began.

"What did Zarex want?" Slek asked after a few minutes.

"He wanted to hear about the nanobots again." I told him about the conversation as briefly as I could, with one eye on the vidscreen.

"Masking their life signs, hmmm?" he mused.

"Is it possible?"

He shifted his ass on the seat. "In theory. If we could get our hands on any nanobots, we could find out."

"Whatever could go wrong with that?" I asked sarcastically.

"I didn't mean I would literally touch them," he replied. "But point taken. If someone other than a Freytaurian, or anyone else the nanobots could choose as a host, got their hands on them…"

"Anyone else?" I echoed. "They avoided the rest of us."

"Human, Centauri and Parvoran," Slek said slowly. "We had no one from any other planet with us. For all we know, they'd like Argusians. Or they're currently programmed to seek out Freytaurians, but could be reprogrammed."

"Oh. I hadn't thought of that." I shivered. "Would there be information in the databases that might be helpful?"

"Probably," he agreed, "but if there is, Danec will find it." He smiled slyly.

I swatted his arm. "You're letting him do all the work?"

Slek rubbed his arm and shrugged. "Why not, he's eager. Besides, it means we finally get time alone."

"Things have been hectic, haven't they?" I sighed. "With any luck, the next two days will be as boring as hell."

"Not a chance of that." Slek leaned over to press his mouth to mine. His tongue slid over my lower lip, then the tip split into a fork.

I'd have to remember to ask him later how he did that. Right now though, I kissed him back and opened my mouth to his.

When he pressed his tongue inside my mouth, I sucked on both slender tips. The texture reminded me of a pair of sugar coated sour worms, but there was nothing sour about him.

His hand went to my hip and he gently pushed me until I lay on my back on the couch.

I pulled my face back and asked, "What if someone comes in?"

He chuckled. "Then they'll get an eyeful."

I wasn't sure how I felt about that. On one hand, a thrill of excitement passed through me. On the other, I hadn't been with Slek before and this seemed, well, not special.

When he kissed his way down my neck and started to peel off my shirt, caution evaporated in place of desire.

My shirt ended up on the floor somewhere, then Slek paused. He looked at me in confusion. Or specifically, my bra.

"How does *that* work?"

I chuckled. "The fastener is in the back."

"Oh." He nodded as if he'd known that all along. "Roll over then."

I did as he asked and grinned over my shoulder while he tried to work out the hooks and eyes.

"Ah-ha!" He tugged it out from under me and held it up triumphantly. He tossed it aside and straddled my legs.

While I lay and closed my eyes, he kissed and licked his way from my left hip to my shoulder, then all the way down the right side to the top of my pants. He teased them down and ran the tip of his tongue over my ass.

I wriggled with the deliciousness of the sensation.

"You like that, hmmm?" He tugged at my pants. "You might need to help me out here."

I lifted my stomach and undid the front of my trousers.

"That's better." He tugged them down and threw them aside as well, then did the same with my panties.

"You're a cute shade of pink," he remarked.

"I try," I said while blushing.

He settled himself beside me and traced circles around my bare ass with his tongue. "You taste good too."

He parted my legs gently and flicked his tongue from my rear hole to my folds and around my clit.

I moaned softly.

He flicked again, then ran a hand up my legs, up between my thighs. He rubbed his fingers against my clit and already wet entrance, while his tongue circled my rear hole.

When my whole body started to ache for him, he pressed a finger inside me, then another.

I arched my back. I wanted more, needed more.

He pumped his hand in and out of me, then pressed a finger lightly into my ass.

"You're so soft and warm," he marvelled.

I groaned. "Please," I breathed.

He bent my knee and opened me out to him further. With fingers and mouth, he went to work on my clit.

In moments, I was gasping and grinding my hips against the chair.

On the vidscreen, a woman screamed. I understood how she felt. I wanted to scream the station down.

"Slek," I moaned.

"Yes, Edie?" His voice was muffled.

"Don't stop," I pleaded.

"I had no intention of it."

"Good. Mmmm." I pressed my palms to the chair on either side of my head and closed my eyes.

He paused for a moment, then his fingers were replaced with something bigger, harder. Slowly, he slid his cock into me and sank down deep.

"Oh. My. Stars," he breathed. He kissed the back of my neck, then began to thrust like a man starved of food. Every pound let the massager-like bumps on his cock rub against my clit and all the way through the bottom of my belly.

I was on the verge of coming, but I didn't want to, not yet.

"I want to look at you," I said. "Please."

He thrust another time, then pulled out and helped me to roll onto my back. No sooner was I settled than his mouth descended on my breasts, licking, sucking and biting hard enough to leave marks on my tender skin. Between him and Danec, I was covered in them.

I tugged up the hem of his shirt and helped him out of it. His purple skin covered a rock hard chest with abs to match.

I blinked a couple of times, still unable to believe a guy like him would care about a girl like me, much less want to fuck me.

"What?" He turned his head and looked at me with one eye.

"You're hot," I said.

He grinned. "Yes, but so are you."

I wasn't sure if I should sock his arm or blush. In the end, I did both, but he just laughed and went back to leaving love bites all over my breasts.

I ran the tips of my fingers over his skin, from his shoulders to his belly. I had seen the size of the weights he lifted. They were twice as heavy as me. No wonder he looked like he did.

I reached down to grip his cock, still slick with my juices. The nodules on his length started at his balls—which looked human, only more purple—and continued, stopping under his head. They massaged my fingers and palm as I worked him with slow, firm strokes.

His hand ghosted over my clit, his touch feather-light, but enough to drive me wild.

I let go of his cock and hooked a leg over his so his tip was poised at my entrance.

We locked eyes in a fierce, intense gaze more intimate than any touch or embrace. In that glance, I saw the depth of his feelings and I know he saw mine.

He licked his lips and slid back into me. This time his thrusts were slower, more deliberate. He wanted, needed to take his time, to let us enjoy each other.

I wasn't sure I could last much longer, but I closed my eyes and savoured the feeling of him sliding out and pounding back in.

The pressure built like a volcano, hot and wet, threatening to blow.

"I'm going to come," I panted.

"So am I." He sounded barely able to speak coherently, like making words was a struggle.

With a cry, I gave in to the whirlpool of desire which

whipped me around in a frenzy of pounding blood and pleasure.

He gave his own cry, lower than mine, and thrust furiously. He stilled and I felt his heat rush through me. The warmth made my orgasm last longer and linger in my belly and toes.

I opened my eyes a crack and looked at his face, his mouth opened as he came. A rictus of pleasure and pain, I wanted to capture this moment forever.

He let out a gasp, then resumed thrusting. Just as I wondered if he would come twice, like Danec had when we were intimate, he froze and grunted again.

I thought I was spent, but between his expression and the sensation of his bumps on my clit, I came again too. I had to bite my lip to keep from crying out so loud they heard it on Dendra.

I tasted blood, but it was lost in the cacophony of blood in my ears and the pure fire of my orgasm as it burnt through me without a hint of mercy. Every bit of me throbbed and tingled, ground and bucked to make it last as long as possible.

When finally it faded, it took my energy with it. I sagged like a rag doll onto the couch and Slek sagged beside me.

"Well then," he half panted, half laughed.

"I hope your first human didn't disappoint," I said, my eyes heavy.

He chuckled, low in the back of his throat. "Quite the opposite. But you would never disappoint me anyway."

"That's sweet," I murmured. "Same to you."

"Of course not," he joked. "I'm awesome."

Now it was my turn to laugh. "Yes. Yes you are," I agreed. "We should probably get up from here."

"Yes." He pulled me closer and nestled down further.

"That's the opposite of getting up," I pointed out.

"Yep," he agreed. "What are you gonna do?"

Before I could respond, the sound of Danec clearing his throat came from near the door.

I flinched and raised my head.

"Um." My face heated hotter than lava. Okay, maybe not that hot, but I had hoped to dress before anyone found us. Thank all of the stars above it was him and not someone like J'avet.

"Oh, hello," Slek said brightly. "Did you find anything interesting about the nanobots?"

I blinked. He spoke like we weren't lying naked on a couch in the middle of the room.

Danec, his face blushed brighter blue, stepped closer.

"No. I mean, yes. Um…" He licked his lips. I could almost see him wondering if he should turn away or not. We were seeing each other, and sleeping together too, but this whole situation was new to all of us.

I saved him the confusion by sitting up and grabbing my shirt. I pulled it over my head and tugged it down to my thighs. It would do for now.

Slek sat up and crossed his arms.

"What did you find?" I asked finally.

"Nothing," Danec said. "That's just it."

I creased my brow.

"There should be *something*," Slek said. "Did you check the histories?"

Danec shook his head. "Even in there, there's nothing. Not even the word nanobot. I tried a translation, in case the word has changed, and still nothing."

Slek scratched his head. "That is strange."

"Could someone have wiped the information?" I asked.

Slek considered for a moment. "More likely they've hidden it behind a higher level of security. Danec wouldn't have the rank to access it."

When Danec opened his mouth to argue, Slek said, "Neither do I. Given time, we could hack in, but the chance of being caught…"

I sat back against the cushions. "We could ask. Zarex seems to like me."

"Given his questions, it would probably be him who hid it," Slek said. "Or J'avet. Or someone with higher rank than either of them."

"Or…" I paused.

"Or?" Slek prompted.

"Or there's someone on board working with the Iri and they don't want us to find that information."

"Doubtful," Slek said. "The rank they would need to do it would be high. To think someone got in that deep…"

"Stranger things have happened," I pointed out.

"Unfortunately that's true," Slek admitted. To Danec, he said, "You should be careful. If they know you were looking, things might not end well. For any of us."

3

"Behold, the *Halcyon*." Slek's grand declaration made me smile. "She's something, isn't she?"

I glanced at Danec, who stood to one side of me as I watched the ship's approach through the station window.

He shrugged and half smiled.

Slek didn't seem to notice Danec's apparent disinterest. "State of the art," he enthused. "Out of dry dock only three months."

"She's sleek." I didn't know Zarex was nearby until he spoke. "I'm expecting a smooth ride from her."

Slek managed to tear his eyes away from the ship for long enough to flash a smile. "Finally, someone else who appreciates a fine woman."

Zarex eyed me. "Yes, I do indeed," he said.

I blushed and turned my gaze back to the window

Danec made a face. "I appreciate a fine ship," he said. Evidently the innuendo went over his head. Or he chose to ignore it. "An hour ago, Slek said new ships always have teething problems because the engineer who designed them doesn't fly them, or see to their maintenance."

I glanced toward Slek. "Is that your mother?" I asked.

"It's more than likely," Slek replied lightly. "I've tried to tell her, but she's always off in an orbit of her own."

"The challenge of an intelligent woman, eh?" Zarex said, but he quirked an eyebrow at me.

"Right?" Slek drew the word out, as though he was long suffering. "Can't live with 'em, can't suck your own cock." He placed an arm around me and gave me a squeeze.

"Not unless you're a Centaurian," Zarex said.

Slek did a double take. "Really? I didn't know that about them." He cocked his head. "Hmmm, how about that?"

I cleared my throat. "As fascinating as this is, shouldn't we get ready to board?"

"Yes, we should," Danec said, obviously uncomfortable at the subject of the conversation, and how friendly we were being with Zarex.

I understood Danec's reluctance to trust the Agusian. He was likeable, but he wasn't above suspicion.

Speaking of guys who were not above suspicion, J'avet stepped up behind us wearing his customary scowl. His dark red eyes focused on Zarex, as if the rest of us weren't there. Maybe to him, we weren't. Undoubtedly he was wondering why another commander would bother with the likes of us.

"Ah, J'avet," Zarex spoke before he even opened his mouth. "I was wondering when you'd slink out from wherever you're hiding."

J'avet narrowed his eyes. "Your people are the ones with reptilian ancestors. I'll leave the slinking to you."

"But Parvorans are catlike," Zarex said easily. "I would think slinking is more of a feline thing." He turned to me and added, "Wouldn't you say?"

I ignored J'avet's glare and raised my hands. "Sorry, I'm staying out of this."

"Oh come now," Zarex said. "You're the nurse. In your professional opinion—"

"Enough," J'avet growled. "Are you planning to be insufferable during the whole journey?"

Zarex smiled. "I never plan that far ahead. I merely seize the moment as it comes."

"Then I'll stay in my cabin, just to be sure." J'avet seemed to regret having left it.

For some reason, I actually felt sorry for him. To Zarex, I said, "Maybe we could all be nice to each other and get along?" I gave him a meaningful look.

"Perhaps you should mind your own business," J'avet snapped. He turned on a booted heel and left me to gape after him.

"He's so charming," Slek remarked.

"That's one word for him," I said.

Danec opened his mouth and closed it again.

I suspected he was about to use our nickname for J'avet—asshole-dickhead-prick—but thought better of saying it in front of Zarex. Seeing the two commanders at odds with each other was one thing. Getting in the middle of it, and insulting J'avet, was another. One which might get him thrown in the brig until the *Halcyon* left without him.

"J'avet is a good commander," Zarex said, confirming my suspicion that while he ribbed the other man, he didn't approve of others doing so.

"Did you know the *Halcyon* is the fastest ship of its kind?" Slek said suddenly. "With a smaller, more efficient engine."

"She'll get us to Agus two days sooner than another ship would," Danec said.

Relieved at the change of topic, I added, "I've heard she has a pretty good infirmary too."

"A full body scanner was installed before she left dry dock," Zarex said.

Did I imagine his eyes raked my body as he spoke? I stood between Slek and Danec, with Slek's arm around my shoulders and Danec's hand touching mine, and Zarex was still looking at me? Yes, I was sure I imagined it. I already had my hands full.

So why did I want him to look again?

"Um. Really? That's… Fabulous." *Very eloquent*, I told myself. It was a shame Kalvix would never see it. The Agusian doctor Slek had flirted mercilessly with was a passenger on a pod destroyed by the rogues. Or so J'avet said. I had no reason to think he lied. He was an asshole, but he was honest to a fault.

"We can scan Danec and see when his balls will drop," Slek said with a laugh.

Danec took a step toward him, outrage on his face. He must have realised Slek was teasing, because he stopped and said, "We can see if Slek has a brain."

Slek looked surprised, then burst out laughing. "Good one. You wouldn't be the first to wonder."

"Because you think with your cock most of the time?" I asked.

"Exactly," he said, with no hint of annoyance.

Zarex shook his head. "I expect to see you all ready to board in two hours." He gave me another look, then nodded to the guys before he walked away.

"Looks like Danec and I have some competition," Slek remarked.

"I beg your pardon?" I frowned at him.

"He's obviously interested," Slek said. "You saw it too, didn't you Danec?"

Danec hesitated before saying, "Now you mention it, yes, I did."

My mouth formed an O. "But I'm so... You two are..."

"We're big boys," Slek said. "A little competition never hurt anyone. I already know you're going to choose me." He puffed out his chest. "If you want to spend time with Zarex before then, I'm okay with it."

"So am I," Danec said softly. "But she'll choose me."

Slek clapped him on the shoulder. "As long as Edie is happy."

"Right," Danec agreed. "We really should be ready to board."

"Yes. Yes, we should." I shook my head to clear it. What the hells? The guys just gave me their blessing to see a third guy if I wanted to. Did I want to? Truthfully, I wasn't sure I could trust Zarex, but I did want to. Then there was the small matter of my physical attraction to J'avet. Yeah, okay, that made no sense to me either, but sexual attraction rarely does.

"At least it won't take long to pack," I said. I had managed to retrieve most of my belongings from the cabin I shared with Brinley on *Infinity*. The clothes I wore when we evacuated were destroyed, just in case a nanobot hitched a ride. Shame, that was my favourite skirt.

"I packed last night," Danec said.

"Um, pack?" Slek said.

I turned my face and looked at him sideways. "Unless, you're only going in what you're wearing?"

He glanced down at himself. As usual, when he wasn't dressed for work, he wore black from head to toe. "I look good like this," he said. "But I'll need my work clothes, I suppose."

"Is this where I offer to help you pack?" I asked.

He raised his head and smiled brightly. "Would you? That would be *great*."

Evidently he'd picked up the word from Danec, who snorted. "I'll help too, to make sure we're not late. The ship won't wait for us."

"It might," Slek said. "I mean, it's us." He gestured, hands straight, toward himself, then to Danec and me.

"If J'avet has any say, they wouldn't wait *because* it's us," I said dryly. "Come on." I took a step, then stopped and pointed at Slek. "We're just packing, though, nothing else."

He held up his hands in surrender, then frowned and jerked his head at Danec. "Why aren't you telling him that?"

"He can think with the head on his shoulders," I said tartly.

"Ah." Slek nodded. "Fair point. Lead on then."

I bit back a smile and slipped my hand into Danec's.

"Are you all right?" I asked him. "We haven't had much time to talk since…" I jerked my head back, toward Slek.

Danec gave my hand a squeeze. "It's a…a new situation. Not something I planned or…or expected." He was clearly uncomfortable at expressing himself. He swallowed visibly. "I meant it when I said I want you to be happy. If that means sharing forever, I'll do it." He nodded several times, then smiled.

Forever. I hadn't even thought about that. The idea was both daunting and intriguing. The guys got along, in spite of the ribbing they gave each other. They were like brothers, in a way.

"And the other thing?" I asked carefully. "The thing you were researching. Has anyone asked questions?"

Danec glanced over his shoulder. If he was looking to see if anyone could overhear, he was about as subtle as shuttle landing on your foot. His innocence was endearing, although sometimes I worried about what the big, bad galaxy might do to him. He had seen people killed in front of him, and almost became an Iri host, and those hadn't changed him too much. He seemed a bit more worldly, but not bitter, not yet. I hoped he never did.

"I had the feeling I was followed this morning," he said softly. "On the way to the shower. When I turned around, no one was there." He frowned. "I suppose it was in my head because I'm expecting something, someone."

"Or they hid before you saw them," I said. "They could have been admiring your cute little ass." I leaned back and peered at it while he blushed bright blue.

"It's not that great," he murmured.

"Nah, she's right," Slek said. "Your ass is adorable. I'm jealous." He gave Danec a lopsided grin.

"Your ass is pretty amazing too," I said before I realised Slek was fishing for compliments. I took the bait, line and all.

His grinned widened. "That's true. Not as perfect as yours though." He slapped my ass lightly.

Now *I* blushed. I turned away to press the buttons on the keypad which would open the door. It slid open without a sound and we stepped inside.

I frowned. "Has someone else been in here?"

"No," Slek replied, "it's just as messy as I left it."

Clothes dotted the floor. A drawer hung half open. The sheets were half on, half off the bed. A dirty plate and cup sat on the table.

"I don't know, I don't remember it looking this bad." I shrugged.

"How do you live like this?" Danec grimaced in disgust.

"How do you not?" Slek asked easily. "I bet your rooms are always spotlessly clean."

"They have to be, I'm in GASP."

The military arm of the IF was as meticulous as any military, one speck of dust and he'd probably be made to do a million pushups, or something like that.

"Well, I'm not." Slek crouched to pick up a pair of underpants and a shirt.

I pulled his case out from under the bed and opened it so he could toss it inside.

"Do you own any clothes that aren't black?" I asked after he threw in several socks and more underpants.

"I have a white shirt somewhere," he replied. "Not much goes with purple."

"Oh. I hadn't thought of that."

He grinned and I realised he was joking.

"Remind me to swat you on the arm later." I checked my watch. "We need to hurry or we'll run out of time."

"That's the last thing, I think. Oh, wait." Slek grabbed a sock from under the bed and threw it toward the case. He missed by a metre.

Danec scooped it up and tossed it just before I shut the case and clicked it tight.

"If there's anything else, they'll have to send it on," I said.

"Yes." Danec checked his own watch. "We'll have to run. Literally." His eyes were wide with worry.

Slek grabbed his bag and swung it onto his shoulder.

"Come on then, less talking, more running."

I bolted out ahead of him and started down the corridor at a trot.

"How long do we have?" Slek asked.

"Ten minutes," Danec replied.

"Shit." I skidded to a stop outside the room I shared with Brinley. The pilot was waiting outside with my bag and a frantic expression on her face.

"Eight minutes," Danec said.

We dashed to his room, where he grabbed his own bag in about thirty seconds.

"Five minutes," Slek said.

I shook my head. I was already puffing, but I gave up trotting and headed to the *Halcyon's* dock at a dead run. My bag hit me painfully with every step.

I faltered and started to slow. By now, I could barely catch my breath.

Danec grabbed my hand and silently encouraged me to keep going.

"I can carry you if you need me to," Slek said. How was he not out of breath?

"I'm not arriving slung over your shoulder," I wheezed.

Slek chuckled.

We were forced to stop at the door to the docks and wait while Danec pressed his palm against the palm pad beside it.

The palm pad beeped and flashed red. The door remained closed.

"What the—" Danec frowned.

"Here let me," Slek said. When Danec stepped aside, he pressed his palm against the pad. It flashed green and the door slid open.

"See, nothing to it."

"I don't understand," Danec said.

Neither did I. All of our palm prints were on file, as was that of everyone else with legitimate business on the station.

"Worry about it later," Brinley said. "They're boarding everyone."

She was right. A handful of people with bags stood in line at the door. The rest must be on the *Halcyon* already. Beside the door, Zarex and J'avet stood, watching closely.

"Come on," Brinley said.

Resuming our running pace, we bolted to the door as the last of our fellow passengers stepped over the threshold.

"Cutting it close," Zarex remarked.

"Another minute and you would be too late," J'avet said darkly.

"Looks like we got lucky," Slek said easily.

J'avet muttered something and waved us inside.

Zarex's eyes followed me the entire way; I saw him in the corner of my eye.

He followed us in and J'avet came behind him.

The door shut with a soft whoosh, locking us in.

4

"Is it everything you thought it would be?" I trailed a finger down the back of Slek's hand.

"You always are," he replied smoothly. He gave me a lopsided smile which didn't waver when I poked him hard in the back of the hand, fingernail and all.

"I meant the ship, smart ass," I said. "You've practically been drooling since we boarded."

"Who says that has anything to do with the ship?" he asked. He added a brow wiggle to his playful expression.

I cocked my head until he held up a hand in surrender.

"Fine. She's a beauty. Part of me wishes I could stay on her longer." He sighed, then his boyish grin was back. "But then I remember I'd rather stay on you."

I was about to respond when Danec swore at the nearby beverage dispenser.

"Bloody microns," he growled. "Come on."

"We really need to teach that boy to swear properly," Slek remarked.

I chuckled and got to my feet.

"Is everything okay?" I put a hand on Danec's shoulder and startled when he jumped in surprise.

"Oh, s-s-sorry," he stammered, more pronounced than usual.

I hadn't heard him do that in a while. That he did so now was concerning. What had him so anxious?

"Nothing on this ship will work for me," he said. "It's like I don't exist. It doesn't know my palm print, fingerprints or retinas."

"It's a new ship," I said. "It's probably a glitch. It could be that you need to be added into the system again." That was odd though. We had all been scanned and added to the system while on Dendra Station. Yeah, computers still weren't infallible.

I glanced over my shoulder. "Slek, can you do it?"

"Of course I can. Anywhere, any time," Slek replied.

I rolled my eyes. "I meant can you add Danec into the system?"

"Sure, but get the boy a drink first." Slek rose to his feet.

"Oh, right." I looked questioningly at Danec.

"I only wanted a drink of water." He gave the dispenser a dirty look.

"Okay." I put my palm on the pad beside the machine. "Glass of water, please."

A green light blinked. In the front of the machine, a claw lowered a glass and water trickled into it.

I picked up the glass and handed it to Danec, who accepted with a smile and nod.

"All that technology and I can't get a drink of water without help." He looked more embarrassed than annoyed.

"We'll get that fixed," Slek assured him. He jerked his head towards the door before starting off in that direction. "It shouldn't take more than a few minutes."

"Is this a usual problem?" I asked.

"I haven't seen it before," Slek admitted. "New ship, new glitches. They'll probably start to pop up all over the place now."

"As long as the captain and pilots can still operate the ship, then I don't suppose it's a big deal," I said.

"Yeah." Slek frowned at Danec. He seemed troubled, but he didn't say anything. Instead, he led us into a room full of screens and flashing lights and waved toward a stool. "Sit down, Danny."

"Danny?" I choked back a laugh at the expression on Danec's face.

"Sure. You're Edie, so it makes sense that he'd be Danny—"

"Slekie?" Danec suggested sarcastically.

Slek grinned. "Absolutely. Why not?"

I shook my head at them both. "Let's get on with this?"

Slek glanced around. "It's a bit public, but all right." He grabbed the hem of his shirt.

"Not that," I said, putting my fingers on his hand to stop him.

"Spoilsport." He pouted. "Fine, let's do it." He leaned past Danec and pressed a series of buttons beside a screen. The screen lit up with a series of shapes I recognised as letters and numbers from one of the IF species. Parvoran perhaps.

Slek tapped the screen and it changed to another language.

"Freytaurian," Slek said.

I nodded. I recognised some of the letters and words, but not enough to really read it.

Slek pressed another button and lines of English appeared under the Freytaurian.

"Thank you." I rested my hands on Danec's shoulders.

"Let's see here." Slek keyed in a code and the words 'security recognition' flashed up on the screen. That was followed by a menu. 'Check' and 'New'. Slek pressed 'New'.

The screen narrowed to a circle, with Danec's image in the centre. He twitched.

"Keep still," Slek said.

Danec licked his lips. "S-sorry." He glanced down at his lap, then back at the screen.

Beside his image, his name appeared. 'Danec, son of Jaek.'

Under that came the word 'Unknown.'

A moment later his name came back on screen, then 'unknown' again. They alternated for several moments.

I gasped, "What is going on?"

"I don't know." Slek tapped the screen and it returned to the option to start over. "Sit as still as you can. Edie, move over here, so the computer can't sense you at all."

I moved around behind him and watched around his shoulder.

Danec swallowed audibly, but froze as still as a statue.

Danec, son of Jaek.

Unknown.

Danec, son of Jaek.

Unknown.

Danec…

"What the fuck?" Slek muttered. "It's as if the computer can recognise you, then it can't. You do exist, right?" The side of his mouth turned up, but he sounded worried.

Danec shot him a dark look, but he didn't seem certain himself. "I think I do," he replied. "If I don't, you're talking to yourself."

I snorted.

Slek grinned. "Good point. I might be a little crazy, but I'm not *that* crazy. Yet." He blew out a short breath through pursed lips. "I have no idea why the computer is acting like this. I've never seen anything like it. I'll speak to the computer gwarps and see if they have a solution. In the meantime, you might need help getting food and drinks."

"I can help," I said immediately. "Until we can get this worked out." I chewed my lip. "This can't just be happening to him, right?"

"Probably not," Slek agreed. "If it's a glitch, there will be several. It might even spread during the journey."

"That's something to look forward to." I grimaced.

Slek shrugged. "The gwarps will be all over it as soon as they can. We can't let Danny here go thirsty." He clapped Danec hard on the shoulder.

Danec winced. "Ouch."

"Sorry." Slek patted him more gently.

"Do you think the scanner would recognise him?" I asked suddenly.

When they both looked at me in confusion, I added, "The new one in the infirmary. It does full body scans. If it doesn't work for him and he gets injured…"

Danec's eyes widened.

"Don't worry," I said quickly, "there's plenty of old fashioned ways to diagnose injury."

"Like you bitching about it," Slek said. "Just remember if you break your arms, Edie is really good at moistening cocks."

I swatted his arm. "I was doing my job."

"I'll keep that in mind," Danec said. "What if I don't break my arms?"

"I'm sure if you asked nicely..." Slek said.

"So anyway," I interrupted, "let's go and do that scan."

"Fine." Danec stood, but his pants bulged. "Then I need to get some study done."

"I'm sure Edie will help you with that too," Slek said as he shut down the computer.

Danec blushed.

I just rolled my eyes at Slek and took Danec's hand as we left the room. "I'm sure we'll figure this out," I said softly. "They'll reboot the computer or something, and it'll be sorted." A ship's computer was probably quite different to a personal one and a reboot in space sounded like a bad idea, but I could be wrong.

"Yes, I know," Danec said. "It's just f-frustrating. If I can't access the computer properly, I'll h-have trouble with my studies. I don't want to fail because of a glitch."

I squeezed his hand. "I'm sure they would understand." I wasn't certain of that, to be honest. If someone like J'avet was in charge, he would get angry, if only for the sake of it.

"We'll let Zarex know and he can send word if necessary," I assured him.

"If I fall behind, I'll have to repeat my classes," Danec said with a sigh.

"You're such a gwarp," Slek said fondly.

"You're pretty gwarpy yourself," I told him.

"Hey," he protested. He paused, frowned and said, "You're right. Don't tell anyone."

I snorted. "Our lips are sealed." I glanced at Danec, who nodded and mimed sealing his lips.

"I think everyone knows though," Danec said. "You are an engineer after all."

Slek pouted. "Hey, I have a reputation to uphold. Player, lover, fighter, badass."

I patted his bulging bicep. "Keep telling yourself that. Meanwhile, we're all gwarps, so you might as well accept that."

"Gwarps and proud of it," Danec declared.

A Centauri man in the uniform of a cook gave us a funny look and hurried past.

I bit back a laugh, but Slek slapped himself on the forehead.

"So much for my reputation. It'll be around the whole ship in an hour." His eyes smiled from around his arm.

"They've seen you with us more than once," I said. "It's likely not news to anyone."

We reached the infirmary and the door opened automatically.

"At least that's working," Danec muttered.

Slek opened his mouth to say something, but closed it when I gave him a glance. The last thing Danec needed right now was ribbing. Whatever was causing the glitch, it had him worried, or at least frustrated. That was understandable. I would be pissed too if it was me.

I nodded to the doctor on duty and waved toward a bed to the side of the infirmary.

"Lie down and I'll turn the machine on."

"I'm already turned on," Slek said.

I shook my head and ignored his comment.

Danec frowned at him, but climbed onto the bed and stared at the ceiling.

I caught sight of his face in the bright infirmary lights and blinked.

What the fuck?

I glanced at Slek, but if he'd noticed anything strange he gave no sign. He wouldn't have held back if he had seen anything odd. I must have imagined it.

I swallowed back my misgiving and swung the scanner over Danec's feet.

"This will move slowly all the way up to your head." I pressed the buttons on the side.

"The good news is, it can see you," I said happily, trying to mask my real concern.

"That's great." Danec gave me a grin which made my heart flutter and flip. He always had that impact on me. Slek too, but they were both different guys. Slek was a jokester and seemed to think about sex ninety-nine percent of the time. Danec was sweet, smart and probably thought about sex just as often, but he kept quiet about it.

The scanner gave a soft whir and began to slowly move up Danec's body.

Half way up, I stopped it and stared.

"What the absolute, everloving fuck?"

5

SLEK FROWNED. "Is that—"

"What?" Danec looked panicked.

"It..." I sucked in a deep breath. "It looks like a couple of nanobots."

"What—" Danec tried to sit up, but the scanner blocked the way. "You must be imagining it."

"I hope I am," I replied. "There's definitely something moving around in your bloodstream. Two. Three of them."

That would explain the slight silver sheen I had seen on his face. It was gone now, replaced by a paler version of his usual steel blue.

"It's...it's not a computer glitch, is it?" Danec's voice was soft with fear. "It might be them, trying to take over."

Slek took a step back. "No offence, buddy, but those things are contagious."

"Yes, stay back." I waved at him. "But I don't think they're powerful enough to take you over. It took dozens, hundreds even to make the rogues into Iritauri. I suspect three isn't enough."

"Until they make more of themselves," Danec said.

I reached for his hand and squeezed it. "We won't let them do that," I promised. "We'll get them out of you."

"What if you can't?" he asked.

I waited for Slek to suggest he'd be thrown out the airlock, but he didn't speak.

I glanced over my shoulder and saw his expression was almost as scared at Danec's.

"We will," I said to them both. "In the meantime, we should tell Zarex or J'avet." I didn't relish either conversation.

"I should be isolated," Danec said softly.

I hesitated, then nodded. "The infirmary has a room for patients with contagious viruses. It should keep them from spreading into the ship." It wouldn't stop them from cannibalising the metal around them until enough existed to claim Danec as their host. With any luck, it wouldn't get to that.

"Edie." Slek put a hand on my arm and drew me away. "I don't think those things are contagious. From what we've seen, they could eat their way out."

My eyes on Danec, I nodded. "I know, but what else can we do? We need to get them out of him. Until then, all we can do is isolate him until we're commanded to do otherwise."

Slek gave a quick nod. "I suppose so. It's just…"

"I know. You're vulnerable to those things too. For all we know, the whole ship is, if they're programmed to—"

He startled me by snapping his fingers. "That's it." He headed for the door and was gone before I could even ask what 'it' was.

I sighed and turned back to Danec. "I'll finish the scan. It might tell us something useful." I didn't add that something might not be good. I didn't need to, I saw it in Danec's expression.

"Go ahead." He turned his face to the ceiling and closed his eyes.

I restarted the scanner as the doctor approached.

A Garvian, the tentacles on her head stood almost straight up. She must have just started her shift. By the end, they would droop almost to her shoulders.

"Is everything all right?" she asked, her voice high but soft. If she shouted, she would be ear piercing.

I explained the situation as briefly as I could and hoped like hells she didn't panic.

To my relief, she nodded. "The isolation room is the best option, yes. We will work to remove the parasitic invaders from our young friend here." The way she spoke was melodic, like she was reciting a poem, not talking about a terrible threat.

She rubbed a tentacle thoughtfully. "Do you know which metal they cannibalise?"

I frowned. "They seem to like the exterior of escape pods. Apart from that, I'm not sure."

"Ah." She nodded. "Let us follow that line of questioning with the engineers. But first, the scanner is finished."

"Oh, yes." While we'd talked, it had scanned Danec's chest and head. "Everything seems to be normal."

"What does that tell you?" the doctor asked.

I thought back to the conversation with Zarex. "They aren't in his brain. They must need greater numbers for that."

"Possibly," she agreed. "Escort your patient to the isolation room, then inform the ship's command of the situation. I will speak to the engineering team."

"Yes, Doctor." I offered my hand to Danec. For the first time since we met, he didn't take it. Instead he pushed himself off the bed and followed me to the Iso room.

"We can't risk them jumping from me to you." He sounded despairing.

"If they wanted to jump, they would." But I wouldn't press the matter. For one thing, I might be wrong.

I punched in the code to open the isolation room and the door slid open. "I'll put some sheets on the bed and make things—"

"I'll do it," Danec said. "You shouldn't be in here with me. No one should."

I wanted to argue. I tried to think up the right words, but they wouldn't come. In the end, I had to give up and concede he was right. "At least let me get you an extra pillow. Maybe a nicer blanket."

I thought he might refuse, but he nodded.

"Fine. I might as well be comfortable in the time I have left."

"You're not dying," I protested.

He sank onto the bed and tucked his feet up. "I might as well be."

"Hey." I fixed him with a stern look. "We will figure this out. Okay?"

"And if we don't?" he asked.

"I hear Calig is nice this time of year," I said lightly. "I wouldn't mind seeing the moon flowers again."

"You would go with me?" He stared at me in surprise.

"Where you go, I go," I said. "But it won't come to that." I wanted to promise, but I couldn't. I honestly didn't know how this would end, and that made my heart ache.

I tossed him a pillow and said, "I love you, Danec, son of Jaek."

He caught it by the corner and drew it to him. "I love you too, Edie Wright."

I smiled. "Thank you," I said.

"For what?"

"For not calling me Edith." I grimaced.

"It's such a pretty name though," he said. "For a pretty girl."

"We'll have to agree to disagree on those counts." I leaned against the doorframe. "You have a vidscreen in there, with all the latest shows and movies. If it doesn't work, we can operate it from out here. If you need anything else, food, blankets, anything, you only have to ask."

"Right." He squeezed the pillow tighter. "I just want to know I'm not a risk to the whole ship."

I brushed a tear from my cheek and realised I was crying. "Of course. We'll do everything we can to make sure you're not, and that you're not at risk. There are only three, how hard can they be to deal with?"

There might have been one at first. In the time we'd spent on Dendra Station, that one became three.

"Yes, I suppose." He didn't look like he believed a word of it, but he was trying not to give in to his darkest fears. "You should close the door."

I should, but damn it, I didn't want to. He didn't deserve to be shut away from the rest of the ship, alone with three tiny parasitic nanobots which would invade his brain and change him if we let them.

We *wouldn't* let them. Whatever it took, we'd purge them.

Regretfully, I stepped back and watched the door slide shut, blocking him from view. I could watch him on a screen on the wall, but instead I turned to the doctor.

"Doctor—"

"Mazic," she supplied.

"Doctor Mazic, is there a chance the nanobots could be surgically removed?"

"Judging by the scan, they move quickly," she said after a few moments of thought. "We may damage him if we were to chase them about his body. However, in the absence of another option, we may have to consider it."

I nodded. "I understand." The only ways I knew to neutralise them was time outside the body and a laser hand cannon. The cannon would do more damage to Danec than the nanobots, so that didn't even factor on the 'maybe' list.

"You are close to him?" the doctor asked. Her expression gave away nothing of her thoughts. She might be curious, or she may wonder why a hot guy like him would care about someone like me.

"Very close." I ran a hand through my ragged ponytail of curls. "He has to be okay." I wasn't prepared to face any other option, not yet. I would cling to hope with an iron grip and not let go unless there was no choice. Even then, they'd have to drag it out of my fingers.

I turned to look at the screen. Danec lay on the bed, his back to the camera. From the look of it, he still held the pillow in his arms. He was very still. So still I glanced at the monitor which showed his life signs.

Like the one Slek used to recognise him, it flicked between living and not existing.

Limbo.

I swallowed back the choked feeling in my throat before emotion overcame me entirely. I wanted to curl myself into a ball and cry, or better yet, wind myself around Danec and not let go until Doctor Mazic, and whoever else, rid him of the parasites.

I schooled myself into taking long, slow breaths and calmed myself. Hysterics wouldn't help Danec. Only cool heads would.

"Go and tell the ship's command," Mazic said, soft but firm. "Remember your training. Remain focused."

Right. But my training included not getting attached to patients. It was far too late for that. Well then, I would have to fake it, or they wouldn't let me near him. That would break the last of my resolve into a thousand tiny pieces.

I drew myself up. "Yes, Doctor. I won't be too long." I gave a perfectly professional nod, straightened my back and walked from the infirmary so quickly my skirt swished with each step.

A chunk of my heart stayed behind.

6

Technically non-command personnel and passengers weren't allowed in the command area, but fuck that. This was important.

I flashed a dazzling smile at a pair of security guards and swept my palm past the identification pad beside them. It beeped and flashed yellow.

"What is your business here?" one of the guards asked. Their badge read, 'Farnx' and I wasn't sure what species or sex they might be. Their skin looked like it was carved from a lump of jade and they had no hair anywhere I could see. A Dendran, they must have come on board at the station too.

"I need to speak to one of the commanders," I replied. I almost added, 'or the captain' but better she hear about Danec from a commander than lowly little me.

"About?" Farnx asked.

"It's a medical matter," I replied. "It's important."

Farnx and their companion shared a look and Farnx nodded.

"Very well. Go on in. We'll send word you're coming."

I nodded and marched past.

I only made it a few steps when Zarex stuck his head out a doorway and beckoned me over.

"Edie, is everything all right?" His antennas bent toward me as though they too wanted to check up on me.

I waited until I'd stepped into his office and the door closed behind us. Only then did I sag a little and tell him everything. His eyes widened, but he listened without saying a word.

When I finished, I moved toward the window and stood looking out at the stars. They shone and twinkled like nothing in the universe was wrong. Like Danec wasn't stuck alone in a room hoping to keep control of his own mind. Like the galaxy would go on without him. Like—

I wasn't aware I was crying until I sobbed.

I felt the warmth of Zarex's body before he slipped his arms around me and pulled my back to his chest. He felt so strong, so comforting.

I leaned back into him and let the tears tumble down my cheeks.

"It's okay," he said in my ear. "It's okay. Cry it out. We'll make this right, I swear."

I sobbed for a few minutes, until I gradually began to regain control of my emotions. Or maybe I just cried all the tears I had.

"Shhh. There you go." He smoothed a hand over my hair, down my cheek and stopped at the side of my neck.

His touch made my pulse race.

Fuck, Edie, Danec is in an isolation room and you're getting all hot for Zarex. He and Slek had given me their blessing to explore my attraction to the commander, but the timing sucked.

"I—" I pulled myself from his arms and walked a few steps before turning around to face him. "Danec said there's no mention of Iri in the ships databases. Did you hide it?"

Zarex quirked an antenna at me and an eyebrow to match. "That's a specific accusation." His eyes held a hint of warning.

I stared him down until he lowered his brow and the antenna moved back beside the other one.

"No, I didn't remove or hide any information. In fact, I went looking myself and found nothing. I suspect we really know why."

He pulled a handkerchief out of a desk drawer and handed it to me.

"We do?" I wiped my cheeks and under my nose.

"Who else would have a vested interest in hiding information about the Iri?" He leaned his hip against his desk.

"Other Iri?" It took me a moment to grasp what he suggested. "You think Danec did it himself?"

"Not him, as such, but the entities deep inside him."

Why did I hear innuendos in just about everything he said? Maybe because, in spite of myself, I wanted him badly. Stupid libido.

I cleared my throat. "You think they have that much control over him?"

"What is your professional opinion?" He crossed his arms over his chest and watched me like I was the only other person in the known galaxy.

I shook my head slowly. "We found none in his brain. That doesn't mean they haven't been in there at some point. I'm guessing they don't have the strength to force him to be the host for a swarm of them." I sounded bitter, even to my own ears.

"I can think of three possibilities." He lowered his arms and counted them off on his fingers. "One: they took control for just long enough to wipe or hide the information. Two: they've been ordered to stay out of sight until needed."

"They failed in that, if that was their mission," I said. I gestured for him to continue.

"Lastly, someone else is responsible for removing the data." He crossed his arms again. "Is that why you thought it might be me?"

I shrugged. "You have the rank."

"So do several others," he pointed out.

"You're the one most interested in the Iri, as far as I can tell," I said.

He looked contemplative for a moment. "It wasn't me. There is something else I'm interested in though. Or someone else."

He locked his gaze on mine and stalked toward me.

I couldn't move or look away. Didn't want to. Everything else melted away except him and I.

He slid his palms across my cheeks and around to the back of my head. Slowly, as though time stopped, he drew me to him and pressed his mouth to mine.

Where Danec's kisses were sweet and Slek's were smoking hot, Zarex's felt possessive. As if by locking his lips on mine, he might claim me as his own. His tongue probed my lips, delving with greater persistence until I opened my mouth to let him inside.

Triumphantly, he slipped inside and thrust while I sucked on the soft thickness of his tongue.

His hands moved slowly, but gradually down my back until they cupped my ass. He pulled me to him until the length of my body was pressed against his rock hard one.

I let out a muffled moan. Hells help me, I wanted to climb up him and ride him like a wild horse.

Instead, I forced myself to tear away from him.

"We should… We need to…"

"Right, Danec." Zarex blinked a few times. I guess he wasn't the only one who needed to clear his head. "I'll inform the captain. She'll be the one who needs to make any decisions about him. Her and Doctor Mazic. Uh, and Gaffid, the Chief Engineer."

I nodded. "Yes. Right." My heart pounded and my panties were already as wet as fuck.

Without the fuck.

He walked to his desk and tapped at the keyboard for a couple of minutes.

"The captain will consult with the doctor and keep me informed," he said finally.

"Okay." I exhaled through my nostrils. "What can I do in the meantime?"

He smiled.

"While Danec's whole existence is up in the air—"

"Of course," he said smoothly. "When it isn't, I fully intend to finish what we started."

"I might even let you," I said tartly.

He gave me a look that said he expected nothing less, then said, "Didn't you say your other lover, Slek, said something about nanobot programming?"

"I don't know what he meant by that," I said.

"Then let's find out." He leaned in and kissed me on the mouth, quick, tender, but just as possessive. He meant for me to be his, I was sure of that.

No, my life wasn't complicated. At. All.

"Right. Lead on then," I said. Before we stepped out the door, I glanced back at the screen. "Shouldn't the captain be raising hells about this by now?"

He smiled with one side of his mouth. "Who said she isn't?"

I paused, mouth open for a while, then shrugged. "I suppose I wouldn't know if she was, would I?"

"Exactly," he agreed. "The whole ship will know when she deems it necessary."

I thought he was about to add, 'If she does', but he gestured me out and closed the door behind us.

I caught a glimpse of J'avet hurrying down the corridor in front of us. He didn't slow or glance back. No doubt he was doing something important.

Or something he *thought* was important, I added cynically. I should probably not think that way. He might be one of those who the captain assigned to look into the nanobots. He could be on his way to the infirmary right now to interrogate Danec. Part of me wanted to follow and stop him from being an asshole to my lover. Truthfully, if Zarex wasn't with me, I would have.

But if there was a chance Slek had some answers, I wanted to find out. Needed to find out. Danec was a big boy anyway, he could handle himself with J'avet. Well, as much as anyone could.

Why then, did my eyes follow his ass all the way to the corner? Why did I feel even a shred of disappointment when he disappeared from view? Okay, I knew why. Crazy, stupid lust. In spite of myself, I found him hot. Even with an equally hot and clearly interested guy right beside me and two more who seemed to feel the same way about me that I felt about them.

I shook my head to myself mentally and exhaled through my nose. I needed to focus on one thing right now: Danec and the nanobots. All right, that was two things, but they were intertwined.

"The IF boasts the resources of over a dozen worlds," Zarex said, as if he could read my mind. "We will draw on whatever is necessary to stop the bots."

That sounded so much like a political slogan I had to smother a laugh.

"I know we will," I said. "Danec just looked so...so vulnerable." For a big, muscly dude, he could still break.

"Then, we'll do all we can to ensure he doesn't need to feel that way," Zarex said smoothly. "Especially because you care about him."

"That doesn't bother you?" I asked carefully.

Zarex smiled like the cat who knew the cream was coming. "Quite the opposite. A woman like you has complex needs. I can't possibly meet them all. You need Danec and Slek to satisfy you in the ways I can't. Particularly when I'm busy working."

He stopped and lowered his voice. "A woman like you shouldn't spend a moment unsatisfied, mentally as well as physically."

I blushed so bright I swore my face would catch alight. "It sounds like you have it all figured out." I wasn't sure if I should be flattered, or cranky at him for being presumptuous. Maybe both.

"From the moment I saw you," he said. "I know you felt it too."

"And if I didn't?" I asked.

He smiled as though there was little possibility of that. "Then I would have to relentlessly pursue you until I changed your mind. Or," he added after a moment, "back off and respect your choices." He brushed stray hair off my cheek. "I won't pressure you. There's an attraction there. If you prefer not to explore it, then so be it."

My tongue darted over my lips. I wanted to see where this would go. I wanted to tell him that. Now, however, was not the time.

"I'm sorry," I said softly. When his face fell, I quickly added, "I can't think about this right now. We need to help Danec. After that—"

Zarex looked relieved and nodded. "Of course. He should be our priority. *Is* our priority. And the ship as well."

"Absolutely," I agreed. The nanobots were a risk to everyone on board, not just Danec. He knew that. I knew it too, deep down.

"Promise me something," I said, my tone firm, gaze locked on his.

"That depends on what it is," he said carefully, a smile on the corners of his mouth.

"Promise me you won't jettison Danec unless it's a last resort."

His lips dropped apart in surprise. "I wouldn't even consider it, unless there was no other way," he said. Something in his eyes made me wonder if he was being entirely honest. I realised ultimately it was the captain's call, not his. He could make me all the promises in the world, but they may come to nothing.

"Let's hope it doesn't come to that." He resumed walking and I had to trot a few steps to catch up.

"It better not," I growled. "Or you might have to jettison me with him."

Zarex snorted a laugh, but he said nothing, just hurried his steps.

7

"WHAT DID YOU FIND?" Zarex spoke before I could give Slek a greeting, or warn him we were there.

His face was obscured by some kind of machine which looked like an alcove full of lights. He went to stand too quickly.

"Ouch." He stepped back slowly and rubbed the back of his head. "Warn a guy next time." He gestured at the screen. "I managed to pull the data from the medscanner to analyse the nanobots. I suspect they've been in there for longer than we thought."

My breath caught in my throat.

I gaped at him. "Longer? How much longer? Long enough for him to be the one to push you?" I thought for a moment. "He can't be. He was on Moon Station with me when that happened."

"Yes, he was," Slek agreed. He gave me and then Zarex an appraising look. An eyebrow twitched, but he said nothing.

"How long then?" Zarex asked impatiently.

"Before Calig," Slek said. "If I had to guess, I'd say not long before the explosion that crippled *Infinity*. If that's the case, there was another Freytaurian aboard who let him get infected."

"Or did it on purpose," I said.

Slek nodded. "That too. The good news is, they seem to have minimal programming beyond existing and trying to replicate. The bad news is, that could change and I can't see how to predict when that might be. Or how."

"Can you switch them off?" I asked eagerly.

My heart sank when Slek shook his head.

"If I could get my hands on one, I might. As it is, I'm really only making extremely educated and highly intelligent guesses." He grinned.

I rolled my eyes.

"See, that's a level of arrogance I cannot give you," Zarex said, his expression completely deadpan.

I hesitated for a moment, then said, "Yes, you can."

A smile broke across his face. "Fine, I can, but I prefer subtlety."

"Hey, I can be subtle," Slek protested.

"When?" I asked, then shook my head. "It doesn't matter. Let's save this conversation for later."

"Good idea." Slek turned back to the machine. "As long as they stay more or less dormant, they won't do him much harm. However, they will seek out metal to make into more bots. With only three of them, that will be a lot harder. Many bots make for light work, and all that."

Zarex tapped a finger against his lips. "We need to find whoever infected him. They may have more nanobots."

"They could have infected more than just Danec," I said.

Zarex blinked. "Correct. We'll have everyone use the medscanner. That will at least rule out everyone on the *Halcyon*. Starting with you." He nodded toward Slek.

"I don't *feel* infected," Slek said.

"That doesn't mean you aren't," Zarex said. "Whoever pushed you might have infected you at the same time."

"Assholes," Slek declared.

"They would be, yes," Zarex agreed. "If you're infected, then everything you told us might be untrue."

Slek looked offended for a moment, but then sighed. "In a way, I hope that's true. Who knows what Danec got up to without knowing it."

"It might be nothing," I argued. "They could have been swimming in there this whole time and nothing more."

"Possibly," Zarex agreed. "Engineer, infirmary. Edie can run the scan on you."

"Someone is going to need to scan me," I pointed out.

They both opened their mouths, but instead of innuendos, Slek said, "I'll scan you after you find nothing inside me."

I nodded and didn't rise to the bait. "You should be scanned too, Commander."

"And Doctor Mazic wanted me to analyse the metal in the isolation room," Slek said. He grabbed up a small tablet from a table. "We need to ascertain its suitability to be nanobot food, then assess it daily for bite marks."

I shuddered.

"You seem competent," Zarex remarked.

"I am," Slek said with no hint of modesty. "I'm sure you are too."

"I am," Zarex agreed.

I sighed. "Is this one of those, 'my dick is bigger than yours' things?"

"He would win," Slek said ruefully. "He has two."

I blinked and shook my head. "I beg your pardon? Did you say Zarex has two cocks?"

"I do," Zarex said, "but Slek's might be bigger than each of them."

I clapped my hand on my forehead. "Two cocks," I muttered. "We really need to concentrate on Danec." But *two* cocks? Holy hells. I glanced at Zarex's groin, but couldn't make out two bulges. "I think I should have boned up on alien anatomy a lot more before I left Earth."

Slek chuckled. "Boned up."

Zarex grinned, but waved us toward the door. "Enough of this, you'll make me blush."

"Like hells we will," I told him. "You might make Danec blush, though."

"She's not wrong about that," Slek said. "I've never met a guy who needed corrupting—" He stopped and looked regretful for a moment before he added, "I mean, leading astray, than him."

"Yeah." I hurried my pace and walked ahead of them. If I discovered who infected Danec, I was going to punch them in the face. If they had a face. Otherwise I'd punch them in the dick. Or—somewhere it would hurt. No one deserved this, especially Danec. He was the sweetest, kindest, most loyal, with the best ass…

"Hey, Edie." Slek hurried and slipped his hand into mine. "I'm sorry, it was a bad choice of words."

"It really was." I let my hand slide out of his and crossed my arms. "This is not a joke."

"I know. I just deal with things like with, well, inappropriate humour. It's who I am."

I glanced sidelong at him. "I know. Any other time, I might laugh. Not while Danec is all alone, uncertain, scared…"

"Him, or you?" Slek asked softly.

"I…" I looked down at the floor as I walked. "All of those things, I suppose. I care about him. I don't want to lose him. Or you." I dropped my arms and accepted his hand back. "He has to be all right. We all do, you know?"

"I do know," he agreed. "Danec is the gwarpy younger brother I never had." He glanced over his shoulder. "Maybe Zarex is the big brother I never had."

"Only if you remember big brother always knows best," Zarex said lightly.

Slek snorted. "Hardly. Anyway, the point is, we're a family now. Your worries are mine. You're not alone. If I have anything to say about it, you never will be."

"Unless I want to be alone," I said firmly.

"Yes, unless that," Slek agreed. "Everyone needs some me time once in a while."

"Right." It was strange to think a few months ago, I had nothing but work and me time. I had friends, but we mostly spoke for a few minutes via vidscreen when they weren't too busy with their own work, partners and children. Now I had three hot guys who were into me. I might take the time later to wonder why. In the meantime, I opened the infirmary door and waved the guys inside.

"You know the drill," I told Slek.

Doctor Mazic was off to the side, tending to a woman with a deep cut across the palm of her hand. Another nurse hovered at her shoulder, ready with bandages to help stem the flow of blood.

This was the kind of thing I expected to face day to day in my job, not nanobots and murderous alien species. At least life was never dull.

I turned on the scanner and let it do its thing. Slek lay on his back, hands under his head, eyes toward the ceiling. He whistled off-key as though he wasn't even slightly scared. The hint of fear in his eyes said otherwise.

"I was right," Zarex remarked.

I twitched at the sudden sound of his voice. "Right about what?" My heart pounded so hard it hurt.

"His single cock is bigger than mine."

I rolled my eyes, but I couldn't contain a slight smile at his attempt to lighten the moment.

"Men," I said under my breath. I glanced toward the screen which showed Danec apparently asleep. He looked so peaceful like that, so untroubled. His leg jerked and he shifted. Dreaming, I assumed. I hoped it was a sweet dream. He jerked again and lay still.

"So, what's the verdict?" Slek asked. "Am I bot-free?"

My attention shot back to the scanner in front of me. "It's not seeing any," I said, relieved. "Just some bones which have been broken, but have healed." I knew about his arms, but his ribs had taken a battering in the past, as had one leg.

"Reckless youth," he said. "Lucky I have you now to save me from myself."

"Luckily she has me to save her from you," Zarex quipped.

Slek stuck out his tongue at Zarex.

"Is that any way to treat a superior officer?" Zarex asked.

Slek grinned. "I wouldn't do that to my superior, but I'm not in GASP."

"Just as well, or I'll have to have you court martialed ."

I gestured for Zarex to lie down when Slek vacated the scanner bed.

The scanner restarted.

I will not look at his cocks, I told myself. *I will not look at his—*

My eyes widened. He didn't so much have two, as one which split above the base, like Slek and Danec's tongues. Individually, they weren't as thick as Slek's, they were right there, but it still looked like a ton of fun.

I blushed bright red when I realised both guys were watching me.

"I can't see anything so far," I said. I cleared my throat and tried to push my professional face into place. Considering how hot my face felt, I wasn't sure I succeeded.

I caught a glimpse of something on the screen and stopped the scanner to check again.

"You have a pacemaker," I remarked.

"Reckless youth." He gave Slek a smile. "Actually, it's genetic. My family all have bad hearts. I've had that, or a variation of it, since I was three."

"Oh. Well, it's better than nanobots," I said.

"There are certainly better things to have inside you than those," Zarex remarked.

Slek chuckled. "I like this guy."

I gave him a sidelong look. "Me too. He seems to be clean."

After a moment, I added, "Of nanobots." He was definitely dirty in other ways. All the right ways.

"Okay, you can get off now," I said.

"Promises, promises," Zarex said.

"Is everything about sex?" I asked, half exasperated.

"Yes," both guys said together.

I shook my head and climbed up on the scanner bed. "Press the green button and it will start again," I said.

Slek did as I asked and stood back, his hands crossed over his chest.

"I'm worried you'll think I can't be romantic," he said.

"I know you can be," I assured him. "I remember that picnic. Right before we had to evacuate *Infinity*. In the place where you nearly died. That's totally romantic."

"You took her to a place where you almost died?" Zarex asked, his brows raised.

Slek shrugged. "It was the service catwalk above the ship's engines. What could be more romantic?"

Zarex regarded him for a moment. "Just about anywhere. When we're done here, I'll take you to a place I—"

"Wait." Slek pressed the scanned and it stopped just over my belly. "What the fuck?"

I half sat up. "What? What is it?" As hard as I tried, I couldn't see the screen from my angle.

Neither answered. Both stood with their eyes glued to the screen, brows in matching furrows.

"That's strange," Zarex said.

"Very," Slek agreed.

"Would you tell me what the fuck you can see?" I growled.

They looked confused and worried. Neither expression filled me with much confidence.

Slek straightened up and looked directly at me. "I don't know how to say this, but—" He looked like a doctor about to deliver a terrible diagnosis.

"Just say it," I said. "I'm a big girl, I can take it." At least, I hoped I could.

I held my breath.

8

"You have nanobots," Slek said finally.

I jerked. "I have..." The scan was supposed to be a precaution. I never expected they'd find anything. "But they ignored me."

"That's the strange thing," Slek said. "They appear to be dead."

I exhaled through pursed lips. This got more and more bizarre.

"Can they come back to life?" I asked tentatively.

Slek shook his head slowly. "I think they're dead-dead, but if we can extract one or two, I can get a better idea." He cast me a sidelong look, wide eyes and all.

I could just about read what he was thinking. What if the nanobots had been alive and jumped from me to him? There were plenty of opportunities for them to do that.

"I can extract them," Doctor Mazic said.

I hadn't seen her approach, but she now stood behind Zarex.

"It should only take a keyhole and tube to suction them out."

"Can we do it now?" I said eagerly. I wanted these things gone. The sooner the better.

"I have time now, yes," she replied. "Engineer Slek, please assess the isolation room. Commander Zarex, I will inform you when the procedure is over."

He looked as though he might protest, and truthfully I wanted him to stay and hold my hand. However, I knew he was a busy guy. He'd taken enough time for me as it was.

"All right, Doctor." He was all business now. "Inform me and I'll inform the Captain. Engineer, take the dead bots to engineering and begin your assessment. If you find anything of note, let me know immediately."

Slek stopped with his hand on the keypad beside the iso room door. "Sure thing, Commander," he said with just the slightest hint of respect. Enough not to be rude, but lacking enough to make Zarex snort.

"Nurse Wright," Mazic said in that way people did to let others know they were dismissed and she was taking the conversation back again. "I'll need you to move to the operating room. Luuvor will administer a mild, local anaesthetic."

I grimaced to myself, but rolled off the scanner bed and changed into one of those delightful operating gowns everyone loves so much. I held the back together and climbed onto the operating table, hoping I didn't flash everyone present with a view of my lacy, black panties.

Luuvor, a Centauri who rarely spoke, lifted my gown— flashing everyone anyway— and pressed anaesthetic into my belly with a needle.

I looked up at the ceiling and tried to ignore the sting with each injection. Like most people, I can think of many things I'd rather have stuck into me than a needle. Like—just about anything. I cheered myself with thoughts of thick cocks and double ones, split tongues and hungry mouths. By the time Luuvor was finished, I was ready for a good probing, but not what the doctor had in mind.

She inserted another needle into my belly, this one attached to a long tube and a machine I hadn't seen before. I presumed it supplied the suction.

That assumption was confirmed when she switched it on. The machine hummed for a moment, then made a grinding, sucking sound. Not disconcerting. At. All. Okay, a bit.

Her eyes on a screen, Mazic pressed the needle to my torso and inserted the tip.

"If they are indeed dead, as Engineer Slek suggested, they won't fight their removal," she said. "If that's the case, this shouldn't take too long."

I didn't ask what would happen if Slek was wrong. The tip of the needle was metal. The nanobots would probably munch on it the moment it got close. That idea was discomfiting, to say the least.

"First time dealing with nanobots?" I asked conversationally.

"Indeed. Unlikely to be the last," she said.

"Yeah, I suppose not." Well fuck, that was a cheery thought.

"They're responding to the suction," she said, her tone lacking any expression.

I held back a reflexive flinch. "Responding?"

One eye on the screen, the other on me, she said, "Moving, but not under their own power. They are not resisting the suction." She removed the needle and tapped it on a dish beside her. A lump of black goo slithered out the end.

"That's... more than three," I said.

"Several hundred," Mazic replied. "That's approximately half."

I swallowed back the sick feeling in my stomach. "How many— Never mind." I didn't need to know the total number. "Can you tell how long they've been there?"

"I would suggest they've been in your bloodstream for several weeks." She frowned. "Your body should have purged them by now. Have you felt unwell?"

"No, I've felt fine," I replied.

"I see. They must be designed to have some compatibility with their host, so the body doesn't reject them. However, yours can't give them what they truly needed. Perhaps humans have lower iron in their bodies than Freytaurians, but I am guessing."

That made sense. Something else didn't. "Why not leave me and search for what they *did* need?"

Mazic tapped out a second lump of goo and turned off the suction.

"I cannot answer that. It seems logical to assume they would seek a Freytauri for their host." She rose and snapped off her gloves while Luuvor placed a bandage over the tiny incision.

"Right," I said softly. I nodded my thanks to Luuvor and rose as Slek appeared to take the dish of dead nanobots.

"Do you want me to carry those?" I offered. I eyed the screen, which now showed Danec awake and looking wistfully at the door.

"I'll be all right as long as they stay dead," Slek said lightly. "Doctor, the isolation room walls are a highly compressed plastic, not metal at all. It might be best to swap out the bed with a plastic or timber one, but he's safe enough while the bots are dormant."

Mazic nodded. "I'll see to that at once, thank you, Engineer." The relief on her face was clear.

"He'll be safe then," I said. "No metal for them to eat."

"Exactly." Slek smiled sideways at my gown. "I like this new look. Especially the back." He tried to peer around while I grabbed hold of the sides.

"I'll get changed and come with you to engineering," I said.

"Or come with me *in* engineering," he said with a sly smile.

"You want to take the risk of there maybe being a live nanobot in there?" I asked. "It might crawl up your cock and live in your balls."

His eyes widened in horror. "I'm sure Doctor Mazic got them all." He squared his shoulders.

"I could get scanned again, just to be sure," I said.

He brightened. "Would you? I've always been in favour of safe sex. And not having ball bots."

"Ball bots bad," I agreed. "Let me get changed first."

I hurried off to do that, before the infirmary got inundated with passengers and crew wanted to assure themselves they were nanobot-free. Hopefully it wouldn't take long. It would be all too easy for hysteria to take hold. When it did, people might start to watch for strange behaviour and point fingers at each other. That would turn ugly fast.

"Okay," I stepped out of the cubicle I'd used to get changed. "Let's do it."

I tried to ignore the dish in Slek's hand as I climbed back onto the scanner bed.

This time, the scanner found nothing out of place.

"Not even a healed bone," Slek remarked.

"What can I say, I didn't start living until recently," I said. That wasn't untrue. I felt as though I lived in a cocoon until I stepped foot on the shuttle and left Earth. I thought I enjoyed life, but now I knew what that really meant.

"That doesn't mean I aim to break a bone," I added quickly.

"But you will abseil the underground caverns of Blarvius with me, won't you?" he asked.

"Abseil?" I shot him a doubtful look. "That sounds more like something Zarex or Danec would be into."

"We would keep you safe," he promised. "After that, we can free-glide off the peaks of Frey-T, and swim in the thermal lakes."

"Now thermal lakes sound like my jam," I replied. I didn't know what free-gliding was, but it sounded terrifying. Not as scary as the clumps of dead nanobots. I didn't know much about them, but I knew broken tech could be fixed. If that was the case, then...

I shuddered.

"Maybe I should carry those," I offered. "Just in case."

Slek had the dish up to his face and was eyeing the clumps with a mixture of fascination and caution. Mostly the former, which was worrying.

"To think, no one has studied nanobots for fifty years since the IF banned them," he said.

"Except whoever made those," I said.

"Well, yeah, but that doesn't count. They did it illegally." He handed me the dish.

I held it at the end of my arm and grimaced. "They're a powerful weapon."

"In the wrong hands, they are. Imagine what we could do with them if they let us."

I arched an eyebrow at him. "Like what?"

"I don't know. Maybe they could break down old ships and rebuild them from scratch. Or crawl into tight spaces to fix engines. Or... Things like that."

"I can see their value there," I agreed. "But I think I prefer they stay banned."

"I guess so," he said reluctantly. "I might be out of a job if they do any of that anyway."

"Yeah, that would suck."

"In the worst way." His gaze settled on my mouth and he smiled.

I was about to say something when the clump slid a millimetre across the dish.

I stopped mid step. "I must have let the dish slip a little." Yes, that must be it.

Why then, did it move a bit more while I stood perfectly still?

"I thought you said these things were dead?" My voice sounded high to my own ears.

"I did. They are." Slek sounded just as worried. "The dish is glass, the lid is on tight. They should be contained in there."

That should fill me with confidence, but in truth I was terrified.

"Engineering or airlock?" I asked. I dared not move a muscle.

"I don't know. We should be able to keep them contained in engineering, but..."

"Yes, it's the *but* I'm worried about," I said.

Slek marched past my vision. The clump moved as if to follow. He pressed a button on the wall and waited.

"Just keep as still as you can, help is coming."

I licked my lips and nodded. "I hope they hurry."

Not a minute passed before the sound of booted feet approached from behind.

"What's the nature of the emergency?" I didn't recognise the voice of the security officer who spoke, I knew the one who followed.

"I should have known," J'avet drawled. "Whenever there's trouble, Edie isn't too far behind."

"Fuck you too," I muttered. "None of this is my doing."

"And yet, you're always right in the middle." He moved around in front of me and peered at the dish. "Activated nanobots."

"It would seem so," I replied. They moved around the dish more freely now. "You're welcome to take them from me if you like. I'm not too attached to them." My hand started to ache with the effort of holding still. No matter how much it hurt, I wouldn't drop them. Not for all the credits in the IF.

"Sir, what are your orders?" The security officer also stepped around me and stared at the dish with curiosity.

"We might never get another chance to study them," J'avet said thoughtfully.

"With all due respect," I said ironically, "if they escape, they'll chew their way through *Halcyon* and enslave every Freytaurian on board."

"I'm not an idiot," J'avet said coldly.

I arched an eyebrow.

"They will be contained in engineering," he said. "Take them there."

"I'm happy to let you do the honours," I said.

"You have them, you can carry them." That was the first hint J'avet was as scared of the robotic critters as I was.

"Your chivalry is touching," I muttered. "Fine, let's go there before my arm gets too tired." I glanced up in time to see a flash of fear on J'avet's face. It gave me no comfort whatsoever.

I took a breath and resumed walking slowly.

9

"FOR THE RECORD, I think this is a stupid idea." I wanted to march the dish to the nearest window and toss it out. If we weren't on a spaceship, with windows that didn't open, and if I wouldn't be sucked out into space, I would. I suspected J'avet would have the security officers stop me if I tried. I might spend the rest of the journey in the brig, while Slek got stuck studying the nanobots anyway. The suspense alone would probably kill me.

Still, I couldn't let it go without giving J'avet my professional opinion.

"For the record, your opinion doesn't interest me," he said coldly.

"I wasn't under the illusion it did," I said, my tone matching his. "But it had to be said. I bet these good security folk agree."

They said nothing, of course, because he was their commanding officer.

Slek, on the other hand, had no such reservations. "On

behalf of Freytauri everywhere, this really is a risk I'd prefer we not take."

"Noted," J'avet said.

"How about that?" I remarked. "He's interested in what another man has to say, but not me."

"I saw that too," Slek said. "The fact you're carrying a dish of live nanobots is a good reason to treat you with respect. One of many reasons."

"Enough," J'avet snapped. "Focus on walking and keeping your hand steady. We don't want any accidents."

"Exactly my point," I muttered. The nanobots were moving quicker now, swirling around the dish like a group of drunk people trying to find the door. "We should move faster. I have a really bad feeling…"

The nanobots tapped at the lid of the dish. They dashed away to the side, gathered into a ball and swept back, tapping harder.

My hand trembled. "I don't think I can hold them."

"Just a few more steps," Slek said.

They slammed again and I swear the lid shifted.

"In here," Slek placed a hand on my back and steered me through a doorway. "We'll put them in the deep freeze."

"Will that hold them?" I asked.

"I fucking hope so," Slek said. "Here, place the dish inside." He opened a hatch on the wall.

I did as he asked and stepped back quickly as he slammed the door shut and hit a button beside it.

The screen showed the dish snap frozen. The glass cracked and the nanobots slid a centimetre or two before they stopped entirely.

I sagged against Slek. "Will that hold them for long?"

"Space is colder and they live there," Slek said. "I think they're stunned. We'll have to work quickly."

"What could go wrong?" I gave J'avet a dark look.

"Fortunately we can jettison them the moment they pose an increased risk," Slek said.

A handful of engineers gathered around to peer at the screen attached to the freezer unit. They muttered amongst themselves, but moved aside when a woman in an IF uniform strode into the room. Taller than me by at least a head, she held herself like someone accustomed to being obeyed.

"Captain Uval," J'avet greeted with more respect than I had ever heard from him. I sensed he still held something back, even now.

Sexist pig, I thought.

She turned eyes as green as her skin, and slender antennas toward him.

"Commander J'avet. I hear you're responsible for securing a cluster of nanobots for my engineers to observe."

"Yes, ma'am," he replied smartly. He gave me a look as though he wanted me to keep my mouth shut. Fat chance, asshole.

"Engineer Slek and I found them," I said. "With Doctor Mazic's help. He—" I jerked a thumb toward J'avet, "told us to bring them here."

"It was a team effort," Slek said, much more kindly than anything I would have said.

"I see." Uval gave J'avet a speculative look and turned toward the screen. "Curious little machines."

J'avet shot daggers at me with his eyes behind Uval's back

and said, "Indeed they are. I understand they were dormant inside Nurse Wright, until they were removed. Perhaps with too much haste."

"Perhaps," Uval said. "They are here now." She glanced at me. "Dormant?"

"I thought they were dead," Slek said. "Either Edie's system suppressed them in some way, or their programming caused them to reactivate."

"Curious. Well, I won't order them to be placed back inside you." Uval smiled faintly.

"I appreciate that," I said dryly.

"Yes. Well, you might donate some blood for Engineer Slek to test on the nanobots," she suggested. If she wore glasses, I'm sure she would have looked at me over them.

"I'm happy to," I said firmly. "I'll go back to the—" I stopped and felt the blood drain from my face. "The infirmary. Danec! What if—"

"Shit," Slek said softly. "You go, I need to get started on these."

I nodded and started toward the door.

"Commander J'avet, accompany her."

I'm sure he was as happy to hear the captain's orders as I was, but I didn't stop to check. I barrelled out the door and bolted down the corridor as fast as my short legs would pump.

"It won't make a difference if you get there a moment later," J'avet called out to my back.

"I don't care," I panted. "You might not give a shit about him, but I do."

Somehow he caught up to me. It might have been his much

longer legs and higher level of fitness, but I was only guessing here.

"Who says I don't care?" How was he not even puffing? "He's my subordinate, and he's a good kid."

"He's not a kid," I snapped. "He's a better man than you will ever be."

"That's probably true, yes. You won't do him any good if you're winded." He made a grab for my arm, but I swerved to avoid him.

"Don't touch me," I hissed, but I slowed down. "What the fuck?"

"If you can't control yourself, how are you going to be any use to anyone else?" He trotted beside me, his breathing a little heavier now.

"I can control myself just fine," I snapped. Maybe he had a point. I was supposed to be the one who was cool and calm in an emergency. Now here I was, bouncing around like a rabbit in a trap. A cute rabbit, but still...

"Of course," he said. "Is that why I had to tell your pilot friend to get herself scanned after nanobots were found inside you?"

I almost choked on air. I had been so wrapped up in myself, I'd forgotten all about Brinley. I was a crap friend.

"She had none," he said after a moment.

"I knew that," I lied.

He snorted.

"Fine, but I would have told her." When though? When I finally pulled my head out of my ass? When I stopped swapping innuendos with the three guys? I couldn't reason it away. I should have told her first.

"Why do you care anyway?" I asked.

"I don't." He shrugged.

"Sure. You were probably looking for the chance to point out what a horrible person I am."

"As much pleasure as that would give me," he said, "I have better things to do."

"Sure you do," I said sarcastically. "Do you have friends? I've never seen you with anyone." I snapped my fingers. "Except that time on *Infinity* when you told me I was too dumb to play chess. You had someone with you then."

"It's nice to know I'm so memorable," he remarked.

"For all the wrong reasons." Why were we even having this conversation? Or any conversation? What he thought of me was clear enough. "Maybe you should lighten up."

"I'll keep that in mind," he said.

I shot him a confused look. "Right. Okay." He made even less sense than most people. That was saying something.

A shout sounded from up ahead, in the direction of the infirmary. That was followed by a crash. A heavy silence was followed by another crash and another.

"Please, no," I whispered.

"Stay calm," J'avet urged.

For once his words were soothing.

I nodded. "I'm calm." Scared, but calm.

We stopped in the infirmary doorway.

"Bloody hells," I murmured.

Danec was still inside the isolation room, but on the screen, his skin shone silver. In his hand he held the thick wooden leg of what must have been a bed. He pounded the leg on the door over and over. The leg cracked and splintered. With a roar of rage, he slammed what was left of the bed against the wall and tore off another leg.

With this new leg, he resumed his pounding on the door. I saw no sign the door was giving, even slightly, but he kept on until the second leg fell into splinters.

Fuck. The nanobots inside him were evidently not dormant anymore. Had the ones inside me triggered them off somehow, or were they removed in time?

"Can he be sedated?" J'avet asked.

Doctor Mazic, who stood to the side of the door, frowned. "We can flood the isolation room, yes," she said, her tone as clinical as ever.

"Do it," J'avet said.

"You're not a—" I started.

"The security of the ship is what matters at the moment," he said curtly. He nodded to Mazic who nodded and moved to do as he said.

"Shut the door," J'avet said to a security officer who must have followed us from engineering.

"What the—" I started.

He rounded on me. "Think," he hissed.

I actually took a step back and swallowed. "If the nanobots are active in him, they might be… active in others." And those others might come here.

He waved a hand in my face. "Exactly."

"We don't know if there's anyone else on board with any inside them," I pointed out.

"We don't know there *aren't*," he said. "We're safer here than anywhere, but we need the infirmary intact."

I nodded and my training kicked in. "Doctor, can we scan

Danec again when he's out cold?" I resisted looking at the screen. "That's a lot of control for three which seemed all but dormant."

"There's minimal metal in the isolation room," Mazic said, not looking up from the buttons she was pressing.

"Minimal, but not none?" J'avet growled.

"This is a spaceship, there is always metal," Mazic said. "The door handle for one."

"Fuck," I muttered. "He probably had metal on his boots, around the lace holes." Whatever those things were called. Did they even have a name?

"Right," J'avet nodded. "What else? Earrings, rings, pierced dick?"

"No, no and sadly no," I replied. "Zipper. Watch."

"He isn't wearing a watch," J'avet said.

I glanced at the screen. "Not now, no. Why did we not—"

"Berate yourself later," he snapped. "What else?"

"I think that's it. Um, he's wearing pants."

J'avet frowned at me.

"His zip must be intact. The button too. There's more metal in with him they haven't eaten."

"Good. As soon as he's asleep, we'll remove it and scan him."

"What could go wrong?" I muttered.

"Everything," he agreed.

My heart stopped. "How far are you prepared to go if this goes badly?"

The expression on his face made my blood run cold.

10

"HE'S ASLEEP," Mazic declared.

"Are you certain?" J'avet asked.

Mazic hesitated.

"Be sure," J'avet warned.

"He is unconscious," Mazic said firmly. "He'll stay that way if he's left where he is, so we need to hurry."

J'avet nodded and unlocked the door to the isolation room. Danec had slumped against the door and now flopped to the floor.

"Grab his boots." J'avet crouched and started undoing Danec's trousers. "Hurry."

I crouched and grabbed Danec's boots. I tugged them off and shoved them into a plastic box Luuvor held. I slid my hand under his ankle and helped J'avet slide his pants off, one leg at a time.

"That should be it," I said.

"Everyone out then." J'avet dropped the trousers into the box and Luuvor snapped the lid shut.

I gave Danec's sleeping face a quick, regretful look and followed the others out.

J'avet closed the door behind us.

Mazic started the scanner which would read the entire isolation room.

"This will take some time," she said. "It's not as specific as the new body scanner, but should give us a good idea of the situation."

J'avet nodded. "Body scans for everyone else. No one leaves the infirmary until they're clear of nanobots." He paused for a moment, then added, "Scan that box first."

I stood beside Mazic, rocking on my feet with a mixture of impatience and fear.

"There are certainly more parasites than before, and more active." She could have been talking about the menu for the night's meal, she sounded so bland. "If we could freeze them, we might remove them."

"If we do that, we might kill him," I said with a sniff.

"We might not have a choice," J'avet said over my shoulder.

I turned to glare at him. "I'll go in there with him and try to extract them myself, if I have to," I said. "I won't give up on him."

"If it's him or the ship…" J'avet said.

"It's not there yet." I paused. "You would really destroy the ship if you had to, wouldn't you?"

"To save the IF, I would," he agreed. "You should be ready to make that call if necessary."

"Me?"

"You." His hand swept across the room. "Doctor Mazic, all of us. If we have to make the sacrifice, we will."

I stared at him until he frowned.

"What?"

"Would blowing the ship up kill the nanobots?" I asked.

"Technically, they're not alive—"

I scowled.

"I don't know," he admitted.

"Seems we should find out before we kill ourselves then," I said bluntly.

J'avet looked thoughtful and nodded. He walked to the comms panel on the wall and spoke to someone in engineering.

"Controlled experiment. Small explosion. Yes. As quickly as you can."

I only caught snatches of the conversation, enough to understand. Slek's voice on the other end was soothing.

I jumped at a sudden banging on the door. I backed away, half expecting it to crash open. An army of Iri, with silver faces and glazed eyes, would pour in and eat our brains—

Oh wait, that's zombies. Iri have a normal diet of fruit, vegetables and fish. Still, when the pounding came again, I looked around for something to use to defend myself.

"Let me in," a voice came from the other side of the door. Specifically, the comms beside the door, which delivered the sound into the infirmary.

"Zarex," I said with some relief.

J'avet scowled. The two men seemed to hate each other with a passion, although I didn't know why. Maybe because Zarex was nice.

"What is your status?" J'avet replied. He hadn't moved from the comm panel.

"Nanobot free, as of the last scan," Zarex said. "I have someone here who requires medical assistance."

I thought J'avet might refuse, but he nodded to the security officer who opened the door.

Zarex stepped inside, his arm around Brinley, who looked dazed. Blood covered her forehead, but it had already begun to dry.

I hurried forward, but J'avet waved me back.

"Scans first, then we decide if you're welcome or not," he said coolly.

"It's good to see you too, J'avet." Zarex smiled. It broadened when he saw me, but then his attention was on helping Brinley onto the scanner bed.

"What happened?" I asked from a safe distance.

"We met an Iri," she said weekly. "He tried to get onto the bridge. We managed to push him into an escape pod and eject it, but…"

"They have a whole pod to devour," J'avet said darkly.

"With any luck, they'll deactivate before they meet anyone," Zarex said, but he didn't seem confident of that.

"No nanobots," I reported when the scan was finished. I helped Brinley off and gave her a hug before Zarex climbed up in her place.

"We really need a handheld version," I said. I led Brinley over to a cubicle and started to clean up the gash in her head. "How are you feeling?"

"A bit wobbly," she replied. "I didn't lose consciousness and I don't feel like vomiting."

"Good. Those would have been my next questions." I smiled briefly and wiped away the last of the blood. "That sounds like it was scary."

She shivered. "It was. He was nothing like the relatively nice Iri on Calig."

"You mean the ones who wanted to turn every Freytaurian into one of them?" I asked ironically.

She snorted softly. "Yes, them. At least they weren't violent. Except Selvia."

"I didn't see any of her companions try to stop her," I said. That made them just as bad, in my book. "I know what you mean though. Danec tried to break the door down."

For the first time, she noticed him out cold in the isolation room. Her mouth formed an O.

"Shit, this has all gotten out of hand, hasn't it?" She frowned and winced. "Ouch."

"Sorry." I finished a last swipe and reached for a bandage. "You'll need to lie down and rest for a while."

"That might teach her not to be too heroic next time." Zarex placed a hand on my shoulder.

When I glanced at him, he smiled. "Still bot-free."

"That's good. What do you mean by heroic?" I asked.

"She did the shoving while I held the door open," Zarex said.

"Pfft," Brinley replied. "We both shoved."

"Yes, but only one of us got hit by a chair leg," Zarex said.

"I should have ducked faster," Brinley said.

"You distracted him long enough for a last shove into the pod," Zarex said.

"It sounds like you both deserve a medal," I told them.

Brinley beamed.

Zarex simply shrugged. "All in a day's work. Now here we all are."

"Except Slek."

The moment I said his name, the comms buzzed.

"Engineer Slek here. A single nanobot can be destroyed by explosion. A cluster, however, is harder."

"Define harder," J'avet snapped into the comm panel.

"The ones on the outside protect the ones on the inside," Slek said calmly. "If I had to guess, I'd say they cannibalise and re-assimilate the metal, if they can reach it. A laser will destroy a cluster."

We knew that already, but lasers weren't recommended to be taken internally.

"So we can't destroy the ship," I said. "Unless we laser the whole thing."

"That would take a shit load of laser power," Slek said.

"Or a laser cannon hooked up to the weapons array," J'avet said.

"Which will only work if it's on another ship," Slek said.

"Wonderful," I muttered. "We can't self destruct, but someone can do it for us."

"Only as a last resort," Zarex said. He put an arm around me and drew me close.

"What do we do with Danec?" I asked. "We can't laser him." I glared at J'avet, in case he planned to suggest such a thing.

"They were dormant inside you," Zarex said slowly. "Was that you, or a coincidence?"

"If anyone can put someone to sleep, it's me," I said, trying to joke but falling flat.

"Has anyone tested your blood to see if it has some impact on them?" Zarex asked.

"Not yet," I said. "But I'm not sure how that will help Danec."

"Let's figure that out when we get to it," Zarex said firmly. "We need a vial of your blood and a vial of Freytauri. And some nanobots."

"That can be arranged." I nodded. I went to step away.

"Wait," Zarex said. "And a vial of Brinley's blood. To see if it's a human thing."

"It might be a programming thing," I warned him.

"At least we can rule out another angle," he said. "That will get us closer to an answer."

I nodded and beckoned to Luuvor to take my blood and Brinley's.

"We'll need a vial of Slek's as well," I said, the precious blood held in my fingertips. "Don't tell me, we have to go back to engineering."

Zarex tapped a finger against his lips while J'avet glared at him.

"The medical equipment is here," Zarex said finally. "Engineer Slek will have to bring himself and a dish here. We'll need some equipment." He crouched and started to look through cupboards. Finally he pulled out a few glass dishes, some beakers and a microscope.

"It has metal on it, but that can't be helped." Zarex looked toward the door. "Where is Engineer Slek? He should be here by now."

I jerked. "You're right. That's odd."

J'avet tapped the comm panel, but got no response. He shook his head. "I'll try engineering. Perhaps he hasn't left yet."

We waited, collective breath held.

Nothing.

"I'll try the bridge." J'avet looked impatient now. "Come in. Captain? Anyone? Any personnel aboard *Halcyon*, respond."

The silence made my ears ring.

"I guess the comms are down," Brinley said uneasily.

"That could be it," I replied. I hoped to hells that was all it was. "What do we do now?"

"Same as we already planned," Zarex said. "We'll need to take live nanobots out of Danec and test them."

"Have you lost your mind?" J'avet snarled. "Bringing them in here at all would be sheer insanity, but at least if they arrive frozen—"

"What else do you suggest?" Zarex asked pleasantly.

"We get ourselves a few laser guns from the weapons store and fight our way to a pod, then wait for the IF to laser *Halcyon* out of the sky," J'avet snapped.

"And leave Danec to die?" I asked, furious.

"Better him than all of us," J'avet replied.

"Coward," I hissed.

For a moment, I thought he might hit me, but he growled and turned away instead.

Heart racing, I curled my lip at his back and took a deep breath.

"Doctor Mazic, can we safely remove a nanobot or two from Danec?" I asked.

"Safely?" She looked doubtful. "We can try, but we'll have to stay in the isolation room while we work. Including studying them under the microscope."

I nodded and held up the vials. "Let's do it." My back

straight, I grabbed a mask so the gas which lingered in the iso room wouldn't put me to sleep too, and marched to the isolation room door. Mazic and Zarex were right behind me, each with a mask of their own.

"You don't have to come," I said to Zarex.

"Oh, but I want to," he said smoothly.

I glanced past him. J'avet paced across the room and back again, muttering to himself. "If this doesn't work, we'll try your way," I said.

He glared daggers at me. "If that doesn't work, it will probably be too late."

I nodded. He was probably right, but if human blood could do anything...

The door slid shut behind us.

Mazic held a small hand scanner and a long needle. "We can't risk the suction machine," she said.

I wasn't sure we could risk the needle or scanner, but we had little choice at this point.

Mazic crouched beside Danec and waved the scanner over his middle. "I'll be guessing here and we'll have to work fast."

She slid the needle into his middle and drew back blood and hopefully bots. She smeared a few drops on a microscope slide and handed it to me.

I slid it under the microscope and put my eye to it.

"What the fuck?"

11

_____

"WHAT IS IT?" Zarex asked.

Before I could answer, I took another long look. "I've never seen anything like it." For some reason I had expected to see a microbe, like a virus particle. What I saw instead was a robot—no, an android—in microscopic detail. I would almost swear they looked back at me.

"So long, sucker." I undid the vial containing my blood and let a drop fall onto the slide. I closed the vial and put my eye back to the microscope. At first, I didn't think anything was going to happen. Then the nanobot jerked and tiny limbs stretched out before they retracted and it fell over and lay still.

"Yawned, stretched and fell asleep," I muttered.

"Not just its programming then," Zarex said.

I jumped. I hadn't realised he'd moved and his face was right beside mine.

"I suppose not." I gave him a watery smile and moved aside to let him look.

"Here's another." Mazic shoved a slide toward me. "Try the pilot's blood."

I slid out the first slide and repeated the experiment. As with mine, the nanobot became dormant with Brinley's blood.

"Let's try with Danec's," I said. I was well aware we were running out of time. Even as the doctor inserted the needle, he twitched violently.

She handed me a vial with only a few drops.

I smeared some on a slide and checked it before I added it to one with nanobots. No point in adding them if they were already there.

As I expected, they didn't fall dormant when they were doused in Danec's blood. If anything, they became more animated, like a child splashing around in water on a hot day.

Just for shits and giggles, I added some of my own blood. The response was slower this time, but they eventually shut down like the others.

"This is great," I said, "but we don't know if adding human blood to Freytauri bloodstreams might kill them."

"I'm not sure we have a choice," Zarex said.

I looked to Mazic, who nodded.

"It's never been done that I'm aware of, but if we can make the bots dormant, I can extract them."

I nodded. "All right then." I handed the vials of human blood to Mazic and took the scanner she held out to me.

"Show me where and I'll inject him," she said.

I licked my lips and held the scanner over Danec's middle. For all we knew, they could be all over his system, but we had to start somewhere.

Mazic prepared a fresh needle and inserted it into Danec,

just below the scanner. The moment she finished depressing the plunger, his back arched. She managed to pull the needle free before he kicked out. She rolled out of the way, eyes wide.

Danec's back arched again and he let out a piercing scream which sliced my nerves in half. He kicked out with both legs and his arms flailed. He narrowly missed hitting me in the face with a hand.

"We need to hold him down, for his own safety," Mazic said. "The gas isn't sufficient to contain him."

Zarex scooted over to grab both of Danec's ankles, while Mazic and I gripped a wrist each.

I held on with everything I had, my eyes focused on Danec's face. For approximately a century, he didn't look like one of the guys I cared about. He looked like a wild beast. Eyes white, mouth frothing, jaw clenched with the effort of fighting us, or fighting the nanobots.

"Come on, babe," I said firmly. "You can do this. We can do this." *Please don't let us have killed him.*

His eyes snapped closed and the skin on his face turned entirely silver. The colour crept into his hair, bit by bit.

"Nonono." My vision blurred with tears. We must have made the nanobots fight harder to get control of him. Of *course* we had. In trying to save him, we had condemned him, turned him into a host.

I let out a sob, and managed to cling on while he gave one last furious thrash.

Then he flopped, completely still.

"Danec?" I blinked away tears.

An expression of utter calm came over his face. He smiled.

Shit.

Shit. Shit, Shit. And *fuck* for good measure.

His face went slack and his head rolled to the side. The silver colour drained out of his face and in a heartbeat it was completely blue again.

"What the—" I shook my head. Before I could say another word, or fully grasp the situation, Mazic jammed yet another needle into Danec and was busy sucking dormant nanobots out of his system.

"Nurse, scanner," she ordered. "Commander, get that glass dish over there. No, over there. Open it and hold it."

In the corner of my eyes, I saw Zarex nod. He picked up the vial of Brinley's blood and emptied the contents into the dish before he held it out to Mazic.

Good thinking. If they stayed drenched in blood, they may remain dormant indefinitely.

Clump by clump, Mazic pulled nanobots out of Danec and squirted them into the dish.

"Scan over here," Mazic ordered. She nodded toward Danec's right hip.

I did as she asked and winced at how close several bots were to his bone.

Mazic pursed her lips and moved slowly and carefully. At one point, she winced and Danec twitched. She must have grazed bone, but any pain he suffered later would be better than bots.

"Scan his head and chest." Mazic sat back and wiped her brow with her sleeve.

I did as she asked. "Clear." Anticipating her next words, I scooted down to scan his groin—no ball bots—and his legs and feet.

"Right heel," I said finally. "It's moving like crazy."

"Too far from where the blood was administered," Mazic said. "I'll have to try to isolate it."

I hoped by that she didn't mean cut off his foot.

Instead, she grabbed a tourniquet out of her bag and wound it around his ankle. She pulled it tight.

"As soon as it's out, pull that off," she said. "We don't want to cut off the blood flow for too long, just enough so the little bastard doesn't escape." Did she have to sound like she was enjoying herself quite so much?

I pursed my lips and nodded. "Yes, Doctor." Scanner in one hand, I kept the other near the tourniquet.

Brow creased in concentration, Mazic slid a new needle into Danec's heel, a smaller one this time. The others she discarded into a plastic dish.

"Come here, you little bastard," she muttered.

I moved the scanner around to follow the bot, while trying to avoid getting in the doctor's way. Several times, I had to switch position so she didn't end up in my lap.

"Gotcha!" she said suddenly and right beside my ear. She pulled the needle free and dropped the whole thing into the dish of blood.

"Take off the tourniquet."

I unclicked and whipped it clear as quickly as my trembling fingers could manage.

Mazic leaned back and rubbed her face. "He should be bot-free, but that won't be feasible to do to every single person they get inside."

"We'll figure out something." Zarex snapped the lip on the

dish. "We should get these to engineering. They can freeze them and we can go from there."

Mazic nodded. She looked tired.

I was exhausted. I leaned down to rest my head on Danec's chest. "Now we have to wait for him to wake up," I said. To go through all of that, only to lose him, would shatter my heart into a thousand pieces.

"Yes. We can move him into the infirmary now," the doctor said. "It will be easier to monitor him there."

Zarex nodded and rose. He carried the dish to the door and tapped on it.

"We've finished the procedure, you can let us out now," he called out. The isolation room had no comms panel, but doubtless J'avet was monitoring.

That was confirmed when his voice came from the speaker in the ceiling.

"How can I be certain none of you poses a risk?" he asked.

"Because I said we don't," Zarex called out pleasantly. He tapped on the door again.

"A moment," J'avet said.

Zarex frowned. He looked back toward me and shrugged.

The minutes dragged on.

Zarex knocked on the door again. He seemed increasingly uneasy.

Finally, the door slid open. J'avet stood a couple of metres back. "You ask me to put the rest of the ship at risk," he said coldly, "at least give me time to retreat all the other personnel to the far side of the infirmary."

"Good thinking," Zarex said nicely, maybe ironically. I was

too tired to tell the difference. "I come bearing nanobots. Don't talk too loudly, they're asleep."

"Your humour is as hilarious as ever," J'avet said, with no hint of mirth whatsoever.

"I thought so," Zarex agreed. "We'll need help moving the ensign into the main infirmary." He jerked his head back toward Danec.

When J'avet looked uncertain, I said, "We can use the body scanner again, if you're scared."

J'avet's eyes flashed. "Do that," he snapped.

Personally, I'd be happy if I never touched the machine again, but I nodded.

As Luuvor and the security officer moved to pick up Danec, I rose and stretched my protesting muscles. When this was over, I would sleep for a week.

I let out a soft breath. With Danec bot-free, and the nanobots off to the deep freeze, I supposed it was over. Or, it would be when he awoke.

I took a quick moment to check on Brinley, who had apparently slept through the whole thing. Lucky her.

All I needed now was to know Slek was safe.

"There's still no answer from the bridge," J'avet said as Zarex stepped toward the door.

"That's concerning," Zarex said. He didn't sound worried, but he looked it.

J'avet snorted. "We need to find out what's going on up there."

Zarex glanced down at the dish in his hand, then back up again. "Engineering first, then the bridge. We should go together."

J'avet nodded without hesitation. He gestured toward the security officer. "You're with us."

To Mazic, he said, "You're in charge here." As if she wasn't already.

Mazic looked unimpressed, but nodded. "We'll be fine here. Nurse Wright, accompany the commanders in case anyone is in need of medical attention."

My lips dropped apart. I looked toward Danec, who was being lifted from the scanner bed to one in the cubicle. Free of nanobots, just like I'd said. I didn't bother to shoot J'avet a triumphant look, that would be petty. Okay, maybe I gave him a small one.

He ignored it.

"I'll keep an eye on him," Mazic assured me. "And the pilot. Your skills are needed elsewhere."

I nodded. There was no point in arguing. She was in charge of me, so I had to follow her orders. Besides, she was right. There might be injured people on board, incapable of reaching the infirmary. I didn't want to think why that might be.

"Yes, Doctor."

J'avet looked less than pleased, but Zarex gave me a reassuring smile. He reminded me that he was hot, and later we might get to have some bot-less, clothes-less fun. That thought helped to push the tiredness away.

I followed Zarex to the door and waited while J'avet pushed the button to unlock and open the door.

The moment it slid aside, the sound of screams echoed up the corridor. Pain, rage or fear, I couldn't tell. Maybe all of them.

"Edie, walk between us," Zarex said. He stepped in beside me.

"I have a bad feeling about this," I whispered.

"Me too," Zarex said.

In silence, we started down the corridor, inching closer and closer to the source of the scream.

12

WE MADE it a handful of steps before the scream came again. Louder this time, it sounded male.

Fear crept up my spine like a spider, crawling, tickling until I had to hold back a wave of panic.

Get it together, Edie, I told myself. *You've already been through enough already and you're okay. Whatever this is, you'll be fine.*

I sucked in a breath, but squashed myself down a bit more behind J'avet.

Because of that, I almost ran into him when he stopped suddenly.

"Zarex, you and Edie go around to engineering. I'll deal with whatever is going on ahead of us."

"This is a quicker route," Zarex said. "There's no guarantee we won't meet trouble if we go the long way."

"Are there service shafts we can crawl through?" I asked.

They both looked at me funny.

"No," J'avet replied after a moment. "Only in Earth movies."

"Then how does anyone access the inner—"

J'avet put a hand over my mouth. "Quiet, or you'll get us all killed." He moved his hand and I glared at him.

I wanted to tell him that if he ever did that again, he'd find my knee in his groin. Now, however, wasn't the time.

"We're staying together," Zarex said firmly.

J'avet gave a long-suffering look and turned away.

At least I know it's not just me he hates, I thought. *He doesn't seem to like anyone, including himself. He must be lonely.* I almost felt sorry for him. Almost.

"I believe the sound came from the galley, sir," the security officer said. He was a tall man, with yellow-green skin. I couldn't tell if he was Centauri, Agusian, a combination or another species altogether.

J'avet nodded sharply.

I almost suggested a cook burnt themselves, but I bit my tongue. With any luck, that was all it was. Burns were easy to heal these days. Instinct told me it was something much worse.

We moved toward the open door to the galley, feet silent with our cautious steps.

Sweat broke out on my palms and under my arms.

Zarex put a hand on my shoulder and gave me the dish.

"Stay out here and keep this safe," he mouthed.

I nodded, although I didn't want to stand out here alone. I hugged the dish to me and hoped the nanobots would remain dormant.

The three guys stepped through the doorway. After a moment, I leaned in so I could see inside.

I held back a gasp.

Bodies lay on the floor, blood pooled around them. One, no

two, were dressed in the white uniforms of ship cooks. Both were Agusian. Two security officers, both Parvoran, held blasters. One's arm hung at his side and his sleeve was covered in blood.

What caught my eye was a woman who lay on the floor, a gaping wound in her chest. Her skin was silver. In her hand, she clutched a huge carving knife.

"Edie," Zarex said slowly, "get the dish to engineering. *Now.*" He backed toward the door, toward me.

I nodded. I didn't wait for Zarex before I trotted off. It would only be a matter of time before the nanobots inside the woman fled her in search of more bots, or Freytaurians. We didn't need them to appropriate the ones in my hand.

I made it a handful of steps before a couple of Iri came around the bend in the corridor.

I stopped dead.

Shit, fuck and more shit. My eyes widened and my grip on the dish tightened so hard I thought it might crack. I loosened it just slightly. *Don't drop it*, I told myself.

Both Iri wore IF uniforms, one of a security officer. The other from the ship's laundry. Wasn't washing other people's dirty clothes bad enough without *this* happening to them? Fuck knows I hated doing the job, and that was just my own clothes.

"Uh, hi." I raised my hand and gave a little wave. "I'm not Freytauri, as you can see, so I can't host your little friends. Sorry about that." I shrugged one shoulder and smiled sweetly. "If you don't mind, I'll just be on my way."

They looked blank, like computers waiting to boot up, or a remote control car before the operator moved the switch.

Waiting for programming? That would imply someone else

was on the end of all of this. Who or where they were, I didn't know. Couldn't guess. They could be on board, or on the other side of the galaxy for all I knew.

They stepped forward, almost in unison. I half expected them to shuffle like zombies, but they moved as naturally as they would without the nanobot infestation. Not the living dead then. More like the living infested.

I swallowed. They couldn't make me a host, but they could kill me and I was pretty sure the security officer was armed.

"I mean you no harm." I took a step back.

"You will come with us," the laundry worker said, so pleasantly they could be inviting me for a picnic, or something equally fun.

"I'd love to," I said regretfully. "But I can't. I have to meet a friend. A good friend. He'll wonder where I am if I'm late." I glanced at my watch. "Look at the time. I'm *already* late. Sorry guys."

I took a step to the side, but found a blaster in my face.

"You will come with us," the security officer said.

"On second thought, I could spare some time." I couldn't guess what they wanted with me, unless the nanobots in the dish were little snitches who told what human blood could do. I thought rude thoughts at them. Wasn't trying to take over one of my boyfriends bad enough?

Wait. Boyfriends? When did I start thinking about them that way?

Anyway, focus, Edie.

"Where are we going?" I asked.

"Turn around and walk," the security guy said reasonably. He stepped away from the laundry worker.

Rule number one, never let anyone take you to a second location. I remember my mother telling me that. I wasn't sure if it applied here, but what the hells.

I popped open the lid to the dish and tossed the contents into the security guy's face. He jerked back.

I wasn't sure what happened then, because I turned like a cute little rabbit and ran like hells.

I bolted around the bend and almost collided with J'avet. I skidded to a stop and he grabbed me before I could trip over my own feet. Or his.

"Iri," I said simply.

He shoved me behind him so fast I almost fell for the second time in as many minutes.

Zarex grabbed me this time and pulled me to him. He held me close while the three non-Iri security officers pulled their blasters and faced back down the corridor.

"The dish?" Zarex asked.

I winced. "I might have thrown it to slow them down. I figured human blood and all…"

"You're safe. That's what matters." He kissed me quickly on the mouth, then stood with a protective arm around me.

Blasters flashed and the laundry worker—it sounded like him—cried out.

J'avet shouted something and my heart skipped.

No, I totally didn't care if he was hurt. Or so I told myself. Okay, I cared, but it was only professional compassion, nothing more. Nothing to do with physical attraction. No way.

"We should see if they need help," I said. Technically, we should get as far away from here as quickly as possible, but if anyone needed my help, I'd stick around to give it.

"Keep near me," Zarex said.

That was the plan. I slipped my hand into his and we walked shoulder to shoulder.

A dozen steps and the laundry worker lay on the floor, presumably dead. Beside him, J'avet held his arm. His sleeve was torn, but I saw no blood.

"Blaster singe," he said with a grunt. "Security went after the last one."

More blaster shots and a shout sounded from a room nearby, followed by silence.

"I'll go check on that," Zarex said. "Edie, see to J'avet's arm." He trotted off before I could nod. So much for sticking close.

I frowned, but it wasn't as deep as the one on J'avet's face.

"I don't need help," he snapped.

"Let me look anyway," I said. "Medic's orders."

"That only goes for doctors." But he lowered his hand and let me get a good look. His skin was burnt as was the light fur around it, but it was shallow.

"You'll need to get that cleaned up and bandaged," I said, "but you'll live." Gently, I brushed away a corner of tattered fabric. When I did, my fingers touched his fur. A jolt of electricity passed through me, along with surprise at how soft he was.

"You're—"

He jerked away. "I'm fine, as you said," he growled. There was something in his eyes though, something which suggested he felt the jolt as much as I did.

I held my hands up in surrender and stepped away. "I'm going to see if Zarex is okay."

"You should stay here," he said. Before I might actually think he cared, he added, "You'll only get in the way and get him killed."

The second part was a good point, at least. I didn't want anything bad to happen to Zarex.

I nodded and looked away, but I was fuming. Partly because J'avet was such a jerk and partly because he was so confusing. He could be... Okay, maybe not nice, but something close to it. And then he could be a total ass a moment later. He changed so fast he gave me whiplash. Some part of me wanted him to whip me, but not like that.

I remembered what Zarex had said about the guys all giving me something different. J'avet gave me a challenge as much as he gave me a headache. Life was never dull with him around. He'd probably prefer to take a blaster shot to the head than be interested in me though.

"It's just us." Zarex's voice came out of the room before he did. He was followed by a haggard looking security officer. "And who knows how many nanobots who might search for a new home any moment now."

"We no longer need to go to engineering." J'avet gave me an accusing glance, which I ignored. "We should check the bridge." He accepted a blaster when Zarex handed him one.

Zarex nodded. "I can't guarantee that blaster is bot-free. Nor this one." He held up the weapon held in his hand. "But we might need them to save our asses. And Edie's." He offered me a warm smile.

I gave one back. "Does Edie get one?"

"You should return to the infirmary," J'avet grunted. "It's safer there."

"Safer, or out of the way?" I asked sweetly.

"Both," J'avet said coolly.

"We'll need her if anyone is injured," Zarex said in a tone which settled the matter. "Come on, we've spent enough time here."

J'avet turned on a heel, apparently done with us both, and started toward the bridge.

"Should we try to evacuate?" I asked.

Zarex looked rueful. "We could, but I can't guarantee we'd leave the Iri behind. None of the shuttles is equipped with a scanner. Not like the infirmary has at least."

I nodded. "Right, they aren't. I guess we're on our own to deal with this. Unless the IF decides to blow us up."

"Yes, unless that," he agreed. He looked rueful.

"Is...that likely?" I asked.

"If I was them, I would have lasered *Halcyon* to pieces by now," he admitted. "The threat to the IF is too great. What's a few hundred lives compared to that of every Freytaurian, or anyone the Iritauri might kill?"

"Not much, I suppose," I said. What a cheerful thought. "Still, it's my job to try to save lives until there are no other options. I prefer we do it that way first."

"Me too," Zarex agreed.

"Would you both shut up," J'avet growled over his shoulder. "You'll draw every nanobot on the ship to our location."

A rumble passed through the ship the moment he'd finished speaking, as though the words needed an exclamation mark.

"What the—" I said under my breath.

"Hurry," J'avet snapped.

I made a mental note to stay off ships once we reached Agus. If we ever did.

We reached the command area and J'avet pressed the code to open the door. It slid open with almost ominous ease.

Slowly, and with eyes and ears open, we stepped inside. Nothing moved. Nothing made a sound except blood in my ears and the usual thrum of the engines.

I startled when the door whispered shut behind us, closing us in.

I had bad feelings before, but not like this. Fear crept up my skin like smoke.

When J'avet and Zarex moved forward slowly, I followed.

13

_____

THE ONLY SOUND was my own breathing.

In.

Out.

In.

Out.

I concentrated on that to keep myself from imagining any number of things. We might have stepped into a room full of people going about their jobs as normal. The last time I was in here, it was quiet.

But... was it *this* quiet? I couldn't remember.

"The bridge is this way," J'avet whispered.

I barely heard the words, but his voice sounded loud.

I winced and nodded.

J'avet gestured for me to stay back and for Zarex to move forward with him.

Zarex nodded. He moved the blaster into his other hand. His face was drawn, brow creased in a deep frown. Worried, but not scared. Or scared, but hiding it well. He had probably faced worse than this before. What, I had no idea. I barely knew the man. When this was over, we'd have to sit down for a coffee and a nice chat. Did he even like coffee? That was another on a long list of things I wanted to find out.

I tiptoed after them, keeping what I hoped was a safe distance. I glanced into the rooms we passed, the few whose doors stood open. An administration room full of screens, another with a desk. A third held boxes piled on top of each other. Empty or full, I couldn't tell.

The corridor widened.

A shuffling sound came from somewhere up ahead.

We froze.

When no further sound came, we moved forward again. My whole body was so tense it almost hurt. Not in a good way. An orgasm wouldn't release this pressure.

"I smell blood," J'avet whispered.

My gaze swivelled to stare at him. What was he, a space vampire? That would explain why he was such a broody asshole. Luckily, only his eyes shone and not the rest of him. Well, he could stay the fuck away from my blood. My neck on the other hand...

Focus, Edie.

I sniffed. I smelt it too. A good deal of it must be spilled for it to be that strong.

"It's not blood," Zarex said. He seemed more troubled than ever. "It's the smell of acrolein."

J'avet and I both stared at him.

"Burnt fat," Zarex said. "It's the smell of bodies after—"

"Multiple blaster shots," J'avet finished.

"We should see if anyone is alive in there," I said uneasily.

Zarex nodded. His back straight, he marched toward the bridge. J'avet hurried to follow. Both men still moved with caution, but now with a new need to hurry.

I bit my lip and followed, but the smell became more pungent the closer we got. Burning flesh would have been more sickening, but this was bad enough.

We rounded a corner and I gasped out loud at the scene in front of me.

Three Iri lay dead. At least, I presume they were Iritauri. Hints of silver remained around their foreheads and on their lips. The rest of their skin was blue or purple.

The remainder of the bridge crew lay dead, slumped over consoles, or splayed on the floor. Most displayed blaster wounds, but one looked to have fallen or been pushed and hit their head hard enough to leave a fatal gash.

There was blood, but only smears here and there.

"They're all dead," Zarex said, his expression horrified.

"Who's flying this thing?" I asked softly.

J'avet's eyes widened. He hurried to a console and looked down at what looked like random letters and numbers to me.

"We're off course." He rubbed his forehead. "Headed for... Out of IF space."

"Can you put it back on course?" I asked.

He tapped a few buttons. "I'm locked out. We'd need a pilot with the right access, or the Captain." He waved toward a Centauri man on the floor. "The first officer is dead. They must have forced him to lock us out before they killed him."

"So the Iri are pirates now," I concluded. Fucking wonderful.

"We'll stop them," Zarex said. "We just need to get Brinley up here."

"Piece of cake," I muttered. "What if she's locked out too?"

"We'll cross that bridge when we get to it," Zarex said.

"I see what you did there," I said without smiling.

He looked wry and nodded. "I thought you might."

"Shhh," J'avet said.

I opened my mouth to tell him there was no one here to hear us, when I heard it.

Footsteps.

"Should we hide?" I hissed.

Zarex nodded. "Get down behind the console." He all but shoved me in that direction.

I ducked down and crouched, hands on the console a bare centimetre from its last operator. I sent them a silent apology for the disrespect of hiding near their dead body. I'm sure they wouldn't want us to end up the same way.

I squashed myself down as small as I could, while Zarex and J'avet hid behind their own consoles.

The footsteps drew closer.

I peeked around the side of the console and caught sight of a blaster. I wasn't sure if it belonged to the bridge crew or the Iri, but neither needed it now.

Without thinking, I darted out from my hiding place, grabbed the blaster and darted back before J'avet could do more than growl in annoyance.

Fuck him. Did he even care anyway?

I'd seen enough blasters to know which way to hold it, and where to press to fire it. At least I wouldn't shoot myself in the foot. Maybe.

The footsteps entered the room and stopped. They moved slowly toward the console, then moved away.

A voice swore.

"This is some fucked up shit."

I blinked.

Slek?

I was sure it was him, but I still moved slowly, peering out, blaster in hand, aimed at him. I caught sight of his hand. He too, held a blaster, ready to use.

"Who's there?" he called out.

I crab walked a step or two, looking carefully at the skin on his hand.

Finally, I sucked in a breath and rose.

The purple of his skin was the most beautiful thing I had ever seen.

"Hey," I said.

He turned suddenly and aimed at me. He lowered the blaster when he realised who he was aiming at.

"Edie, you're all right." He sagged with relief. "Um…"

"Oh." I lowered the blaster and hurried to embrace him. "Sorry. What are you doing here?"

"I could ask you the same thing." He raised an eyebrow as Zarex and J'avet stepped out from behind their hiding spot. "Just a wild guess, you weren't having a quickie back there?"

J'avet snorted.

Zarex managed a faint smile. "Not today, no. Can you unlock the controls? Hack the computer or something?"

"I can try," Slek said. "I have a reasonably high level of clearance, but not like the Captain or chief engineer, and they're both dead." He rubbed the back of his neck.

"This is starting to look like a coordinated effort," J'avet said. "There must be someone on board controlling all of this."

"Or close by," Zarex agreed. "Slek, have you got any idea of the range the nanobots can go and still receive orders or changes in their programming?"

Slek shook his head. "I would suggest a few thousand kilometres, but I'm guessing. Signals can extend a lot further, but whatever reaches them would be more complex than a simple hello, or cat video."

He gently moved a Garvi woman aside and knelt in front of her controls.

"Could we cut them off from whoever is sending the signal?" I asked. Okay, I'd probably watched too many episodes of *Star Trek*.

To my surprise, they all looked at me, mouths slightly open.

"We might," Slek replied. "But it depends where the signal is coming from." He scratched his head and looked conflicted.

"Keep trying to unlock the controls," Zarex said. "I'll see if I can hunt down the signal." He gestured for J'avet to help him move an Agusian from his chair. The man's antennae drooped like a dead plant. Zarex's drooped almost as much, in sympathy and sorrow.

They set the man to one side on the floor and Zarex slipped into his seat. He started to tap on the controls.

"I guess we'll keep watch," I said to J'avet.

He gave me a curt nod and turned toward the entrance.

I did the same, but kept the blaster by my side. If I tried to use it, I might end up hurting more than myself. Could blaster…well, blasts bounce off the walls? If so, I might kill one of the guys by accident.

Something caught my eye and looked toward the floor.

"Um, J'avet..."

"What?" he snapped. He realised what I was referring too and took a step back. He raised his blaster and shot at the swarm of nanobots which crept across the floor like an army of ants.

The blast singed the floor and blew a hole in the middle of the swarm. They closed over the breach, but there did seem to be fewer of them.

"Edie," he growled. He fired again.

"What if I hurt you?" I asked.

"Then I get hurt. I'm sure you won't cry over me," he snapped.

"I would," I replied. "I'm nice like that." I ignored his snort and aimed away from his feet. The recoil from the blaster was less than I expected. My shot also left a black scar across the floor, but fewer nanobots.

I aimed again, this time at a smaller cluster away from the rest. If I could take them out, they couldn't reform with the swarm.

Over and over again we fired, reducing the numbers even as they sought out metal to increase their numbers. It was a bit like shooting water in a drizzle. Now, there would be fewer, now more. The side of one of the consoles looked like it was chewed, or rusting quickly.

"Shoot faster," J'avet ground out.

"I'm trying," I replied. "Hey!" He shot so close to one of my feet, I had to jump sideways. A sting of pain shot through three of my toes.

"Sorry," J'avet said. "Move over further." I had barely stepped before he shot again. At least he missed me this time. Just.

I aimed and shot again and again. "My blaster is running out of juice." Each blast was weaker than the last.

"Here." Zarex tossed me his.

I almost dropped mine, but managed to catch his and throw mine to him. No sense in leaving metal around on the floor.

I pivoted with all the elegance of a brick and got off another couple of shots.

"That's almost all of them," J'avet said. He shot the console itself, holding down the trigger so the blast lasted for a minute, two minutes.

The smell of burning made me wrinkle my nose.

Finally he released the trigger and lowered the blaster.

"There's probably more, but unless they swarm like that again, we won't see them," he said.

I nodded and hoped like hells we could keep them from Slek.

"Any luck on the unlocking?" I asked.

He shook his head slowly. "I think this might be way above my pay grade."

"I've almost traced the signal," Zarex said. "It's close, very close, but I can't quite pin it down yet. I'll keep trying."

I ran a hand over my hair. It was probably as wild as ever, and then some. When this was over, I might have it all cut off. Crew cut like the guys. I would look silly, but at least it would be tame.

"You won't unlock the controls," a new voice said. "This ship belongs to the Iritauri now."

I turned and took on the sheen of silver skin, the set of now silver eyes, the blaster held in a silver hand.

My heart came to a grinding halt and I felt sick to my stomach.

"Danec?"

14

DANEC SMILED. "YOU MISSED ONE."

"So I see," I said. I surprised myself with how calm I sounded. On the inside, I was a trembling, quivering mess. The shape of his face and body were the same, but everything else was different. The way he held himself, the way he looked at me. He seemed curious, but the warmth was gone. The familiarity was gone.

No, not gone entirely; suppressed. He was still in there somewhere, I was certain of it.

"Can I ask where it hid?" I tried to see what J'avet and Slek were doing, but both were outside my peripheral vision.

Zarex hadn't moved from the console. Nor had he stopped tapping at it.

"Inside a tooth," Danec said. "Quite clever, don't you think?"

"Right." I had scanned his face. Somehow I missed that one, tiny speck of nanobot. Evidently that was all it took.

"I'm sorry."

He cocked his head in that adorable way he had. It was so… Danec, it hurt my heart.

"Danec wouldn't want this," I said. "Being a nanobot host wasn't on his bucket list."

He looked confused for a moment, then smiled. "Bucket list. List of activities to undertake before the body becomes deceased."

"Something like that, yeah." I felt the weight of the blaster in my hand. Could I use it on him? I wasn't certain I could.

"Don't be concerned," Danec said. "I'm still me, just enhanced. I have the knowledge of the Iritauri in my mind. It's like a vast library." He looked awed.

"That sounds, um, great," I said without a hint of enthusiasm. "But you don't have free will. You have to do what the nanobots say."

He blinked several times. "The relationship is symbiotic."

"Or parasitic," I muttered. "What will you do if they want you to kill me?"

"We have no desire to kill," he said.

I gestured around at all the dead bodies on the ship's bridge. "Excuse me if I find that hard to believe."

He looked toward the bodies closest to him. He seemed confused, as though the nanobots and Danec were in disagreement.

Good, keep fighting, I thought. *Fight them off.*

His head snapped up. "Only those who try to stop us will die," he said in a robotic tone. It seemed the bots won that round. "We wish no harm to the rest."

"Stop you from doing what?" I asked carefully.

Danec hesitated. "Joining the others. Making the Freytauri

hosts. Modifying our programming so we're compatible with all other species."

"So, galactic domination," I said. "I don't think the IF will like that."

"The IF will be Iritauri in time," Danec said.

"You seem sure of that," I said.

"We have waited for this for a long time." He glanced around the bridge now. "Slek, you will be a host."

"I don't think so," Slek said from somewhere behind me. "I like my independence, but thanks anyway."

"You will be a host, or you will die," Danec said.

Slek stepped into my line of sight. "Back on Calig, we established that I'd rather die than be a host." He rubbed his chin. "In fact, we established that you felt the same way. I'm a really big fan of consent, and I don't think you've given it."

"Consent is irrelevant," Danec replied.

"Bullshit," Slek snapped. "Consent is everything. Danec knows that."

Danec looked confused, but shook his head. "I am Iritauri now. This is my purpose."

"A slave to the bots," Slek said. "Or whoever is controlling them. Who is that, by the way?"

I saw what he was trying to do; throw Danec off enough to reveal the origin of the nanobots, and maybe a way to stop them.

Danec paused, frozen like a computer awaiting input.

"You will all go to the mess," he said finally. "Those left alive will gather there."

"Why?" J'avet asked.

I had all but forgotten he was there.

Danec's head snapped to look at him. "That is the order. You will comply."

"Very well then," J'avet said. "Lead the way."

"No," Danec said. "You will lead. Place your blasters on the floor and move to the door." His blaster was aimed squarely at J'avet. He would use it, I had no doubt of that. The Iri had evidently established enough control over the ship they didn't feel the need to fight further unless forced to.

"Danec," I said carefully, "is Brinley okay? And Doctor Mazic?"

"Brinley is unharmed," he said, again speaking in that robotic voice. "Doctor Mazic is deceased."

I gasped. "What?"

"She tried to stop me." Was that a hint of regret in his eyes? If it was, it was a sign the real Danec was still in there. I had no idea how we'd get him back, but we had to try.

J'avet stepped past him and crouched to place his blaster on the floor at Danec's feet. He kept his eyes on the ensign the entire time.

When he rose, I let out a soft breath. I had half expected him to shoot at Danec. He was outnumbered and technically the enemy now. On the other hand, killing him might bring a bunch of Iri who would kill us. Cooperation might be the safer option right now.

Slek followed, but kept a distance from Danec. He looked nervous and confused.

I could relate to that. I wasn't sure why he hadn't been inundated by nanobots by now. Presumably they figured they had plenty of time.

Rather than crouch, Slek tossed his blaster onto the floor and hurried after J'avet.

"Ladies first," Zarex said. He placed a hand lightly on the back of my neck.

"Thanks," I said ironically, but I was happy to have him at my back. Well, as happy as someone who was a prisoner of the Iritauri again could be. This was a habit I really would have preferred we not get into.

"It'll be all right," Zarex said softly.

I glanced over my shoulder, sure he referred to something in particular.

"I hope so," I said. The longer this went on, the more sure I was the IF would laser the *Halcyon* out of existence. Maybe I wouldn't blame them.

I added my blaster to the pile and moved to stand beside Slek. He slid his hand into mine and Zarex took the other.

Danec gave us a look. Was he jealous? Did he still think we could be together, nanobots and all?

I honestly couldn't guess what he was thinking. I wasn't sure I wanted to. I loved him, but how much of him was in there? I couldn't pretend things weren't different now. They were. Totally fucked up, and totally different. This wasn't how I anticipated my day going when I woke up this morning.

He shook his head as though dislodging a thought. "Walk," he said curtly.

"I see you've been taking diplomacy lessons from J'avet," I said lightly.

J'avet frowned at me, but said nothing.

"Too many words waste time," Danec said.

"I disagree," I said. "A good conversation is a way to get to know someone better. You want that, right? If we're all going to be Iri some day, then we might as well get along."

"The Iritauri are of one mind," Danec said.

"That's what I was afraid of," I said under my breath. "Do you mean that literally?" I asked.

"It must be difficult to control all those seperate hosts," Slek said. He looked thoughtful. "I mean, they aren't really one mind, or they would all be here, trying to make me one of them."

"Should you be reminding him?" I asked.

Slek glanced at Danec. "I have a feeling something else is going on here."

"Something bad?" I asked. My stomach fluttered with anxiety.

"Absolutely, without a doubt," he replied. "Very bad." He smiled, but the expression in his eyes spoke volumes about his fear. Every so often, he'd glance at Danec. They were like brothers, or friends. Now, I could almost put my hand on the tension between them.

The idea they might be enemies now made me want to build a blanket fort and hide inside with a teddy bear. I had no teddy, but I was sure I could find one, or something similar.

That brought my mind back to Brinley. I hoped Danec was honest when he said she was okay. I also hoped he lied about Doctor Mazic. The Danec I knew and loved would be horrified at the idea of killing anyone.

Or would he?

I reminded myself that he joined GASP. Would he join the military if he didn't expect to kill someone at some point? The logic made sense, but I still couldn't imagine Danec harming a soul.

This Danec might not have a choice.

He followed us to the mess and waved us inside.

"Is this all that's left?" I gaped.

From a crew and passengers of nearly two thousand, less than a hundred remained. The Iri numbered maybe fifty.

Slek was the only Freytauri left who hadn't been claimed as a host.

"Edie." Brinley half rose before she was waved back down again. "You're okay."

"So are you." I flopped down beside her before Danec or anyone could tell me not to. I gave her a brief hug and told her everything.

"I thought I would die," Brinley whispered. "One minute, Danec told us all our lives were forfeit. The next he told us to come here." She averted her eyes.

"Doctor Mazic refused."

"He really—" I swallowed a ball of regret.

"He shot her when she touched the comm panel. She tried to call for help." A tear slid down Brinley's cheek.

"It's not really him," I said firmly.

"It's him now," J'avet said.

I turned to glare at him. "He's—"

"He's Iritauri. Unless you have some way to change that, then you need to accept it. If you can't, you'll endanger us all."

I opened my mouth to retort, but closed it again. Fuck him, he was right.

"Fine," I said after a minute. "What do we do?"

"I found the signal," Zarex said softly. "It's coming from outside *Halcyon*, maybe from a nearby planet, but it's being relayed through the communications systems."

"If we can cut it, we might at least disconnect them from whoever is issuing orders," Slek said.

Zarex gave him a small nod. "If one of us is good with computers, they might even reprogram the nanobots." He looked meaningfully at Slek.

"I could do that, but we need to get out of here," Slek said.

"We'll need to create a distraction," J'avet said. "Something that might keep them busy for a while."

Slek rubbed his chin. "I wish I knew how much control Danec has. If I was Iri, I could—"

"No," I snapped. Sooner or later they would try, but for now I wouldn't let him sacrifice himself. If he was lost, we were screwed anyway. "I could try to *distract* Danec." I cleared my throat loudly.

"I'm sure seducing him would work on him, but that won't distract the rest of them," J'avet said dryly. "Unless you plan on distracting them all at once."

I smirked. "I'll do the men, you do the women." I said sarcastically.

"If I thought it would work, I'd do it," J'avet said. "But it won't. There are too many to keep focused all at once.

I pictured J'avet all hands, mouth and cock with a dozen Iri women and shook my head to clear the image from my head. "Do you have a better idea?" I asked.

"Not yet," he admitted. "Unless someone has an explosive in their pocket?" He looked around while we all said we didn't.

"I should have thought to carry around a bomb," I muttered.

"It was an oversight on all our parts," Slek said with a smile.

I snorted and jerked as Danec and two other Iri approached. "Edie, Slek, come with us."

"In front of everyone?" I said sweetly.

Danec actually blushed. His face turned a darker silver and he averted his eyes.

There you are, I thought. *You're still in there.*

"This way," he said coolly. His expression was robotic again.

I sighed to myself, clasped Slek's hand and followed.

15

DANEC LED us to the galley, of all places.

"Oh good, I was feeling hungry," Slek said cheerfully. "I'd love a sandwich or two." He caught my expression. "What? A guy like me has a big appetite. I could eat two sandwiches as a snack."

"I believe it," I said. I couldn't even think about food right now.

"Food will be supplied at meal time," Danec said.

I forgot the Iri ate like everyone else. Of course they did, their bodies were organic. It was only their parasites which weren't. I presumed sooner or later they would also need to pee.

"I could handle a cup of coffee or two," I said. "Danec, have you introduced the others to the joys of coffee yet?"

I thought he might answer, but another Iri grabbed my arm and pushed up my sleeve.

"Hey." I almost jerked it back, but stopped myself at the last moment. Whatever they wanted, it was best not to anger them.

"Keep still."

I recognised the woman as another nurse. I wasn't sure if that was reassuring or not.

She grabbed out a needle from a box on the bench and pressed it into my vein. She drew out enough blood for a vial, then another and finally a third.

"Leave me some," I said under my breath.

She pulled the needle free and handed me a small bandage to stem the flow of blood. Her bedside manner could use some work.

I pressed the bandage to the small needle wound and tried not to object when they took blood from Slek as well.

"Keep him Freytauri," the nurse said, her expression and tone stone cold clinical. "We'll need him to provide blood for testing."

"Testing what?" I asked. I directed the question to Danec.

He hesitated like he was asking for orders and awaiting a response.

"Testing the impact of human blood on nanobots," he said finally. "When we know why it makes them dormant, we can stop it and humans can become hosts."

I shuddered. "And Slek's blood is for comparison?" I guessed.

Again, Danec hesitated. "Yes," he said after a minute.

"Good to know." Slek rubbed his arm. "I'm happy to let you borrow as much blood as you need."

Anything to keep him from becoming a host.

"So, about that sandwich," Slek said, as though that was the only thing on his mind at the moment. "I might pass out if I don't eat, after giving all that blood."

The nurse nodded and carried six vials out of the mess. Presumably the infirmary was their lab now.

"You may eat," Danec said. He opened a fridge and gestured toward a tray of sandwiches which the cooks presumably made before they died.

The idea made me both sad and sick, but we needed to eat, or we'd end up the same way. Hunger and my smart mouth didn't go so well together.

I grabbed up a couple of synthcheese sandwiches. "About that coffee..."

"You can return to the mess and sit down," Danec said.

"But...coffee." I sighed. "What about some water at least? Or juice. Or something. I'm thirsty."

"I'll find something. Go and sit." Danec looked torn between taking care of me, and the limit of the nanobot's programming. I assume they were only programmed for a limited amount of tolerance. I could relate to that, so was I.

"Fine." I gave him a long look, then took my sandwiches and walked back to the mess, Slek right behind me with three sandwiches.

"Here." I sat beside Zarex and handed him a sandwich. I gave Slek a meaningful look before he bit into one of his.

"But—" He sighed and handed a sandwich each to Brinley and J'avet. "I would have eaten all of those."

"I'm sure you would, but we need them alive too," I said as soothingly as I could manage, in spite of my jangled nerves.

J'avet looked at me over his bread as if he thought I would make a snide comment about not needing him alive.

For once, I said nothing. I wasn't in the mood to be that petty, even as a joke. We had to rely on each other now, like it or not.

"Thank you," Zarex said.

I nodded and told him why Slek was still Freytauri.

"Good, that will buy us some time," Zarex said.

"I wish we knew how long," I said. "They must have studied nanobots for decades. They might find the answer in a matter of hours."

"Or not at all," Slek said. "You humans are pretty complicated."

"You think so?" I asked.

"Absolutely," he said firmly. "Right Zarex?"

"Definitely," Zarex agreed.

"We really are," Brinley said, "but you guys are, too."

"You'll make me blush." Slek patted his cheek.

I smiled. "Now we're full of brain food, we need a plan." Personally, even after eating, my mind was blank. No, that wasn't true, but the ideas I had were bad ones, that would result is someone's death, if not that of all of us.

"How long until the IF gets here?" J'avet asked softly.

I looked at him in surprise. His eyes were fixed firmly on Zarex.

"It's been an hour since I sent the message," Zarex said. "It depends what other ships are in the vicinity, but I'd estimate another hour. Maybe two."

I frowned. "When you were looking for the Iri signal…"

"I sent a message to the IF, outlining the situation," Zarex said. "And the solution."

I sat back. "So we have an hour or two to find a way out,

before they come and blow us all up?"

"Precisely," J'avet said.

I swung my face around toward him and asked, "How did you know?"

He shrugged. "It's what I would have done. Sometimes leading means making the tough decisions."

I wanted to retort, to yell and shout at them both. In the end, I just sagged. They were right. There may be no other option.

"Then we better work fast," Brinley said. "What if I distract them somehow and you all run off and do what you need to do?"

"They would notice four of us running off," J'avet pointed out. "And we don't need us all for this, just Slek."

Slek drew himself up and puffed out his chest. "It's nice to be appreciated," he said.

I smiled and patted his insanely big biceps. "You're very appreciated. You're also very noticeable, being a big purple dude and all."

He exhaled as though deflated slightly. "I used to like being noticeable," he said sadly.

"It's a good thing," I assured him. "Just not when sneaking."

"Could we try to talk Danec into helping us?" Brinley asked.

"If I thought it would work, we could try," I said, "but I don't think it will. There's some of him left, but the bots are in control most of the time."

"Could we trick them?" Brinley asked.

Slek looked thoughtful. "I have an idea." He stood and waved his hands over his head. "Hey, I need to pee."

Several Iri looked his way and cocked their heads.

"I don't want to pee on the floor." Slek grabbed his groin. "Come on, guys."

Finally, one of the Iri nodded and waved his blaster toward the toilets off to one side of the mess.

"Do your business," he said. "Take no more than three minutes."

"Lucky I don't need to shit," Slek said. He stepped around me and hurried to the toilet.

"I guess he does his best thinking while he pees," I said with a shrug. Fair enough. I do mine in the shower, or while half asleep. Exactly the wrong times to write anything down, but that was my brain for you.

I jumped a moment later when the ship's alarm sounded through the mess hall.

A voice came over the speaker.

"*Halcyon*. This is Commander Calderr of the IF vessel *Retribution*. All Iritauri will stand down and surrender all remaining crew, or you will be destroyed. You have five minutes to release escape pods. All Iritauri lives are henceforth forfeit."

My eyes widened. That was harsh. Was the IF not even going to attempt to save the Freytauri from the nanobots? I suppose not. Total destruction would be...well, easier. Awful, but simple and final.

The Iri gathered together in a cluster of confusion.

"Come on," Zarex pulled me to my feet and tugged me toward the door.

"Can we get to the pods in time?" I asked.

He shot me a smile over his shoulder. "We're not going to the pods."

I stared at him for a moment before I asked, "How—"

"Comm panel in the toilet and hacking skills." He shrugged.

The ship-wide alarm was deafening, but we made it to the door and into the corridor while the Iritauri milled about in confusion. It wouldn't take them long to figure out no other ship was out there.

We ran.

"Where are we going?" I panted.

"Comms," Zarex said. "We can shut ourselves in there."

Comms was just outside the command area. It felt as though it took us days to reach it, but it was only a handful of minutes. The corridor was empty except for the sound of the alarm and some Iritauri responding to the message.

"The Iritauri are all dead. It's safe to board."

Right, like anyone would buy that anyway.

"In here."

We darted into the darkened comms room. Slek skidded in behind us before J'avet closed the door.

"They're in chaos," he said gleefully. "They're trying to find a ship that isn't there."

"It is there," J'avet said. "Just not as close as they think."

"They may think it's a hoax when they really arrive," I said. I wasn't sure if that was a good thing or not.

"In the meantime, hack away." Zarex waved at the computer screens. "I'm going to keep trying to find their signal *Halcyon*."

"I'll toy with the ship's internal sensors," J'avet said. "If I can, I'll have them fool the Iri into thinking we're somewhere else."

Zarex nodded. "Good idea."

"Can we remote control a pod?" I asked.

Zarex glanced at me, eyebrows raised. "Brinley?"

"I can try," she said. She slipped into a chair. "One escape pod with five life signs, coming up."

"I'll, um, watch the door," I said. I had no other particular skills to add.

"Edie." Slek waved toward another screen. "Can you access the medical database from here?"

"I would think so," I replied.

"Good. Access that and see what information they add after they've analysed our blood. Unless they send the information directly to the mother bot, then it'll be in there."

It's possible," I said doubtfully. If nothing else, I could see what Mazic had added, if she'd had time before Danec… I was glad to be seated in a corner, so no one could see the tears which trickled down my cheeks. Part of me wondered if all of this was to keep us all busy while we waited to die. We could spend our last hours telling jokes, or talking about our lives and deepest fears.

The other part of me had to believe we would get out of here alive. If I didn't hold onto that, I might give in to despair instead. That would help no one one.

Still, a small voice in the back of my head wondered if Danec was lost to me, even if I did make it out of this.

I bit back a sob and focused on the screen.

"They've tested the nanobots in every kind of blood," I said. They had been busy, but they didn't have answers.

Yet.

16

"THIS COULD BE A PROBLEM," Brinley said.

"What is?" Zarex asked.

"The ship has increased speed. I think they must know by now there's not another ship out there." Brinley toyed with her ponytail, but her eyes never left the screen.

"They probably suspect one is coming," Zarex said.

"I think I might have tweaked the scanners to show Iri as life signs," J'avet said.

"You think?" Zarex echoed. "I'd feel better if you were sure."

"Yes, I *think*," J'avet said. "It's not foolproof, but it's picking up clusters of nanobots. The good news is, if it's picking them all up, they're centred in the mess and galley."

"What's the bed news?" Zarex asked.

"The bad news is, it might not be picking them all up," J'avet replied.

"I prefer to assume they are," Slek said.

"There!" Brinley spoke suddenly. "One pod away. They may not buy that we're on it, but—"

"A dozen clusters of bots are moving away from the mess, toward the pod bay," J'avet said. "They must think there are others down there."

"Are there?" I asked.

"As far as I can tell, only a few others made a run for it when we did," J'avet said. "They're scattered around the ship. I can't tell them to come here without drawing attention to our presence."

I sighed and nodded. We would be more help to them if we stayed hidden.

"As it is, I have our position blocked, so anyone searching will find an empty room," J'avet added.

That was good to know. My friends and lovers were all so smart. I couldn't help but be impressed.

"There, I've found it," Zarex said.

"A human woman's G spot?" Slek asked. He gave me a smug look over his shoulder.

I flashed him a smile and had to force my eyes back to the screen. I would much rather he was exploring my body than sitting here trying not to die.

"Oh, I know where to find one of those," Zarex said lightly. "I found the source of the Iritauri signal. It's on a planet not far from here—Tarathu."

"Give me the coordinates," Slek said. "I think I can cut the ones on board off from that signal." He scratched his head. "We need to do more than that though."

"Can you take control of them?" Zarex asked. He tapped the coordinates for Tarathu into a tablet and handed it to Slek.

"I— Maybe. I'll need more time." Slek leaned over the screen, his nose almost touching the glass.

"That's strange," Brinley said. "Another pod left the pod bay."

"Who's on board?" Zarex asked.

It was J'avet who responded. "Six clusters of nanobots."

"Six Iritauri," I said softly. "Are they going after the other pod?"

"They're going in the same direction, yes," Brinley said.

"Shit," Slek muttered. "I can't cut them off if they're not on board. Or take control of them."

"Focus on the others," Zarex said. He sat back and cracked his hands over his head.

Slek nodded. "I'm going to try to cut them off, then take control. If I'm too slow, they may react badly."

"By react badly, you mean..." I ventured.

"Kill the non-Iri on board," Slek said.

"Ah. That would suck," I agreed. And hard. If anyone died because of what we did, that would be difficult to live with. Assuming we lived much longer. Which I was assuming, because I wasn't nearly ready to die yet. Not even close. Nope.

"Yes, it would suck, and not in a good way," Slek said. "Ready—"

He was cut off by a banging on the door.

"Open up," a voice ordered. "We have your fellow crewmen here. For every minute you delay, one dies."

I glanced at J'avet, who cursed under his breath.

"They masked their presence," he growled. "There's five Iri and ten crew or passengers out there."

"Slek, now would be the time," Zarex said.

Slek shook his head. "I need to get a fix on them all first. Give me two minutes."

"We might not have two minutes," Zarex said.

"I'll open the door," I said. "I'll try to buy us some time while you do your magic."

"This is nowhere near my magic," Slek said without looking away from the screen. "When this is over, I'll remind you of that."

"You'd better," I replied. I hopped up from my chair and hurried across to the door controls.

"Don't shoot," I shouted. "I'm coming out."

I tapped the button by the door and stood back, arms crossed over my chest.

As J'avet said, fifteen sets of eyes looked right at me. Several Iri had blasters to the heads of a variety of species: a Garvi man, a Centauri woman, a young Agusian and and a human whose sex I couldn't tell by looking. They looked the most scared of all.

"Hi." I put my hands out to either side and smiled. "That's quite the welcoming committee for little old me." I tucked a few strands of hair behind my ear and batted my eyelashes sweetly.

"Step out of the room," one of the Iri ordered. Her skin was such a pale silver, I suspected she was a light purple to begin with. A lovely shade of lavender, no doubt. With any luck, she would be again. With even more luck, it would be soon. Like, any moment now. I resisted the urge to look back over my shoulder. I needed all of their attention to be on me right now.

I took a few steps, my eyes on Lavender. She seemed to be the leader of this group.

"There, I'm out," I said nicely. "No need for blasters, I'll come quietly. Or loudly if I ever get the chance to come agai—"

Lavender squeezed the trigger of the blaster and the young Agusian man died without a word, a shocked expression on his face.

"Hey, I said I would do as I'm told." I curled my hands into furious fists. My eyes burned with hot tears. What the absolute, everloving fuck? So much for not killing unless someone got in the way.

"That is for disobedience." Lavender placed her blaster into her other hand and slapped me hard across the face.

I reeled back, almost into the wall. My cheek stung. The urge to strike her back was so strong I literally bit my lips to keep from doing it.

"There's no need for that." That was J'avet, right behind me to catch me and keep me from falling and retaliating. "We'll comply."

That was apparently not enough for Lavender. She nodded to one of her companions, who slammed his blaster hard into J'avet's groin.

I expected the Parvoran to double over in pain.

I didn't expect the cracking sound the impact made. I certainly didn't expect to see the blaster with its nozzle bent, held in the confused Iri's hand.

J'avet looked entirely unimpressed, bored even. How was he not writhing in pain? He must have a cast iron dick, or something. Did he give new meaning to the expression 'boner'? As in literal bone?

Lavender growled. "Back to the mess. Any more insubordination and you die."

I arched my eyebrows at J'avet. "You're going to have to explain that to me at some point."

He just smiled. Actually smiled.

"Where are the others?" Lavender leaned to the side to peer into the comms room. She jerked, then froze.

"Got it," Slek declared. "I've told the nanobots to stop and await further orders."

"That is what it looks like, yes." J'avet eased the blaster out of Lavender's hand and nodded for the rest of the crew to do the same. "Assuming it was you who did it."

"If not him, then it's the biggest fucking coincidence in the history of the universe," I said. I might have exaggerated slightly, but it would be pretty big.

"What now?" Slek asked.

"Can you ask the nanobots to get the fuck out of them?" I asked.

"We'll need a place to put them," J'avet said.

"I can think of a place," I said. "Let's make it easier for the IF to destroy them."

"Um, speaking of them," Brinley said, "we have an incoming message."

"Put them through," J'avet and Zarex said at the same time.

J'avet gave Zarex his customary scowl, but turned back to keep an eye on Lavender.

"This is Pilot Brinley Grant, on board *Halcyon*. We, um, have the situation under control now."

The screen flickered and a Freytauri face appeared.

"This is Captain Yaranin of the *Chimera*. We received a curious distress signal from the *Halcyon*. Something about nanobots and destroying the ship with a laser." He looked amused and I was reminded of Slek, but with Danec's skin colouring.

"False alarm," Zarex said. "In a manner of speaking. As Pilot Brinley said, we have the situation somewhat under control. There's the small matter of some nanobots."

"Commander Zarex, it's good to see you," Yaranin said. "You're not usually given to exaggeration."

Zarex ran a hand over his forehead and up to the top of one antenna. "You and a security team should come over here. I'll explain everything and we can discuss what to do next."

"Keep an eye out for a pod or two," Slek said. "Shoot first, ask questions later."

"Noted." Yaranin looked at someone over his shoulder and nodded. "We'll be there within the hour."

"We'll keep a light on," Slek said.

Yaranin chuckled and the screen went blank.

"All right, let's try to take the nanobots out of her first." Zarex waved at Lavender. He pulled out a drawer and emptied the contents on the floor. "Make sure you tell them not to eat anything."

"Will do." Slek worked the controls in front of him and Lavender quivered.

"Gently," Zarex said.

"Moving gently," Slek confirmed.

Lavender shuddered and the silver leached from her face, bit by bit. It was slower than with Danec, but once it started, it became faster and faster. After thirty or forty seconds, her face was, as I suspected, lavender coloured. The silver faded from her hair and a cloud of darkness crept across the floor and into the drawer.

"That was so much easier than with Danec," I muttered. I moved to help J'avet grab Lavender and lower her to the ground. I felt her neck for a pulse and crouched beside her, my eyes focused in concentration.

"She's alive. Her pulse is a bit rapid, but steady. Physically, I think she'll be okay." Mentally, she'd probably need some therapy. We all would.

The rest of the nanobots started to leave the Freytauri. Another one was a dark purple and the other three were blue, like Danec. Strangely, one man's hair stayed silver around the edges.

"He might have been like that to start with," J'avet said.

"I suppose so," I said. It might also be from stress. I probably had a grey hair or two after this.

"We should go down to the mess and collect the bots from the people down there," I said. Especially Danec. My heart fluttered at the idea of seeing him again, totally bot-free. He, too, would need therapy, particularly to help him come to terms with what happened to Doctor Mazic. I couldn't bring myself to blame him for it. The parasites had done it, not him. He was just an innocent, unwilling host.

"Are you giving orders now?" J'avet snapped.

I sighed. "I don't understand you," I said. "Sometimes you're almost nice, then you're an asshole again. Can you make up your mind?"

He gave me a long, intense look that made my panties want to twist into a knot and combust. Or maybe that was my clit. Or both. Or—

"I wouldn't want anyone getting too familiar," he said finally. "They might get expectations."

I snorted. "Fine, keep everyone at arm's length. It's a lonely way to be." I was guessing, but it sounded about right.

"It's a safer way to be," he stated. He turned away before I could see his expression. "Let's head to the mess."

"Didn't I already say that?" I asked. I wasn't going to give him a centimetre of leeway. If he wanted to be a dick, then so be it.

He sighed and rose. Without a glance back, he strode away.

"We'll need to get everyone to the infirmary," I said to one of the security officers, who sat shaking her head and looking in confusion at her blue skin. "When you're ready," I added.

She nodded. "I'll see to it. Once everyone is... oriented again."

I put a hand on her shoulder. "It'll be okay now. We'll get rid of the bots and the IF will make sure they can't take control of any of you again." I knew I was making a promise the IF might not be able to keep, but she nodded and seemed comforted by the words.

"I have to go and see to the others." I rose and gave her a smile before I trotted off after J'avet. With his long legs, he was probably halfway there by now, but my desire to see Danec pushed me to trot just that much more quickly. More than anything, I wanted him back to himself before the crew of the *Chimera* arrived. I don't know why that was important, but it was. Maybe it was simply a matter of Danec's pride.

1 7

"WHERE IS HE?" I looked around the mess full of passengers and very still Iritauri. As far as I could tell, Slek's control held them, even as far from the comms room as we were.

"He can't be far." J'avet tapped the comm panel on the wall. "We're ready."

Slek's voice came through in response. "Okay, de-botting now."

As before, the nanobots slid down from their hosts and into boxes held by me and J'avet. The passengers and crew moved to catch the freed hosts before they hit the floor. Several crashed before anyone could reach them. There were simply too many at once.

I winced each time one hit the floor and groaned. At least they were under their own control now, and broken bones mended easily enough.

"I don't see him," I said, half frantic with worry for Danec.

"I'm going to check the galley." I closed my box and thrust it at J'avet, who managed to grab it before he dropped it.

I thought J'avet might argue, but I turned my back on him so I couldn't see him scowl. I didn't need his judgement right now.

I marched into the galley. "Danec?"

The place was empty except for half a tray of sandwiches which sat on the bench.

I left it there and stepped back out into the mess. Several Freytauri were sitting up now, rubbing aching heads and attempting to reorient themselves after what they'd been through. More than one looked completely confused. I wasn't sure if I hoped they remembered later what had happened, or if they were better off not knowing. Some had killed. That was something I imagine would be difficult to reconcile. I know if it was me, I would struggle with it.

I crouched beside one, a young woman in an ensign's uniform, like the one Danec wore.

"Hi," I said lightly. "Have you see Danec? Hot guy, blue skin, great ass. He should be himself again by now."

She blinked at me a couple of times and shook her head. "I think he went with the others to the pod."

My heart sank. So they did remember. Wait—the pod? Admittedly, I was part of the way to thinking that might be the case, but even now I didn't want to accept it.

I smiled. "Are you sure?"

"I— no, but I... My memory is foggy. It was like being stuck behind a curtain. I could see out a little bit, but I couldn't pull it aside. I tried, but I just—" She dissolved into tears.

I put my arms around her and held her while she cried on my shoulder.

"It's okay," I said softly. "You're safe now. We have the bots under our control. You'll be fine." I rubbed her back gently until her sobs subsided.

Fine. It was easy for me to say that. She might never be okay. I felt a flash of anger toward the Iritauri and the nanobots. Did galactic domination have to be so ugly?

I drew in a breath through my nose. I was more determined than ever to do whatever I could to help ensure they failed at that objective.

Eventually, she pulled back and rubbed her eyes.

"Thank you. This is my first time away from Frey-T and..." She sniffed.

I patted her shoulder. "This is my first time away from Earth. It's been a lot more exciting than I expected." And terrifying. And horrible. And sexy. But also awful.

"Yes. Same here." She looked like she'd happily share a blanket fort and a bottle of wine with me sometime, but for now, I needed to find Danec.

"I'll talk to you later, okay?" I gave her a reassuring smile and rose. Careful to step around dazed Freytaurians, I walked over to where J'avet stood, peering into a box o' bots.

"She thinks he's on the pod," I said, my voice low.

J'avet nodded. "All right."

I did a double take. "All right?" I echoed. "Is that all you can say?"

He looked up at me and frowned. "What else would I say? If he's on that pod, he's out of our reach."

"He might be in reach of the *Chimera*," I said bitterly.

"Possibly. If that's the case, there's nothing we can do." He sounded so blasé, so calm I could only stare.

"What about we tell them what Slek did? Maybe they can do the same?"

"I'm sure Zarex has already done that." He snapped the lid of the box shut and handed it to one of the security officers. "See this gets to the isolation room in the infirmary and that no one enters the room or touches anything inside."

"Yes, sir," the officer said smartly.

J'avet turned to me. "Hysterics won't help the ensign or anyone else," he said coldly.

"It would help me," I said, my hands on my hips. "Or better yet, some casual stabbing."

He rolled his eyes. "You ask why I keep you at arm's length. This is why."

"Because I have feelings?" I demanded. "Because I dare to care about someone other than myself?"

He grabbed my arm and pulled me into the corridor and from there into a small room. I couldn't guess the purpose of it and, to be honest, I wasn't paying much attention. I was too busy being distracted by my desire to punch him in the face and my other desire to melt into a puddle on the floor.

"Do you realise where you are and *who* you are?" he growled.

I started to glance around, but he jerked me around to face him.

"You're on the *Halcyon*," he snapped. "You're one of the people who survived the Iritauri incursion. You helped to stop them. Further," he said before I could respond, "you're a medic. You're one of the people the other survivors will need more than anyone else. If you don't pull yourself together, you'll be no use to anyone, including yourself."

"Not that you care," I retorted.

He gave me a long, long look. For a while, I thought he would hit me or kiss me. My heart thudded so fast I thought it might burst out of my chest.

Then he stepped away. "Go and see to your patients. I'll send a few people to help clean the infirmary and give you what help you need. I'll be sure they know where Danec might be." he stepped toward the door. "He might also be dead."

Before I could even think well enough to swear at him, he was gone.

I slumped against the wall and trembled. He was right, but I hated that fact. I wanted to hate him, but I understood what he tried to do. It was my job to take care of the people left on the ship, especially the former hosts. I needed to focus on them, not myself.

By the time I stepped out of the room, there was no sign of J'avet. I ran my fingers through my hair and hurried off to the infirmary. I had to put my faith in Zarex, Slek and even the chance Danec would turn up in the infirmary. Deep down though, I knew the *Chimera* was armed with lasers and every reason to use them against the pod.

The infirmary was bustling when I stepped inside. To my relief, one of the doctors stood beside a bed, speaking to a young man with wide eyes and wet cheeks.

I half expected to see Mazic or even Kalvix, but both were gone. Both victims of the Iri and the rogue Freytauri who wanted the nanobots eradicated. In retrospect, the rogues had a good point. Perhaps we should have listened to them. They didn't give us the chance, but still…

Every so often, crew would enter, carrying bodies into the morgue. That would be full soon, if it wasn't already. I thought about looking for Danec, but before I could take a step, I spotted the young woman from the mess, and Brinley, who sat by her bed. They had their heads together and were talking in low voices.

Brinley laughed and the Freytauri woman smiled.

As I approached, Brinley looked up and grinned.

"Edie! This is Harva. I was just telling her how good chocolate is."

"It really is," I agreed. "I'll have to see if I can find you some." I could do with a block or two myself, and a bottle of vodka. Not necessarily in that order.

"I should look at your head," I said to Brinley.

"I feel fine," she replied.

I arched an eyebrow at her. "Are you going to be a difficult patient?"

"Would I dare?" she asked, rising to her feet.

"Without a doubt," I teased. "Come on, let me take a quick look."

"You can take a long look," a voice said in my ear.

I turned and threw myself into Slek's arms. I told him about Danec. He held me and rubbed my back while he listened.

"We know where they're going," he said. "The IF will send people after them."

"We're people," I pointed out.

"That we are," he agreed. "See to Brinley. The *Chimera* should be here within the hour."

I nodded. I wanted to be there when it did. I nodded to know if they'd seen the pod. If they'd...

I couldn't think about that. Danec had to be okay. Whatever

happened, we'd find him and rid him of the parasites once and for all.

I waved Brinley over to a chair and checked her head. There was no sign of fresh blood, but it would take time to fully heal.

"You should rest," I said finally.

"So should you." She put a hand on my arm. "We've all been through a lot."

"Danec most of all," I said.

"I almost became a host," Slek said as he flopped into the chair beside Brinley.

"Almost doesn't count," she told him.

He pretended to be offended. "Of course it does. They took my blood, the fiends."

Brinley smiled. "You must be traumatised."

"I am," he agreed.

I rolled my eyes. "I'm sure the rest of the Freytauri on board would suggest their trauma is worse than yours."

His smile faded and he gave me a rare, serious look. "I know," he said softly. "I wanted to—"

"Make me feel better?" I suggested. "I know, I just…" Tears prickled my eyes.

"We'll find him," Slek said firmly. "We'll save his sorry little ass and get him to Agus to finish his studies. Before you know it, he'll be a commander and as bossy as J'avet and Zarex."

"Nicer than J'avet, " I growled.

"With a better ass," Brinley added.

"Oh, I don't know, J'avet has a pretty hot ass," Slek said.

I grimaced. "Yeah. Shame he is one, too."

Slek chuckled. "Yes. He certainly keeps us all on our toes."

"Yeah." That reminded me. I told Slek about how one of the

Iri had hit him hard in the groin, but all he'd achieved was to break the blaster.

"Pubic plate," Slek said.

"Come again?" I asked.

He grinned. "I'd love to." He wiggled his brows. "Parvoran men have a plate of bone over their genitals. It's like an eyelid, but hard, and over his cock."

I blinked and shook my head. "That sounds like quite the evolutionary advantage."

Slek cocked his head. "It really does, doesn't it? I'm jealous. I wonder if I could get one made." He scratched his head while I laughed softly.

"You could try staying out of trouble," I suggested.

"What would be the fun of that?" he asked, a twinkle in his eye.

The ship jolted and I froze. I pushed down the rising fear and listened to a metallic clang from somewhere else on the *Halcyon*.

For a moment I thought something else had gone wrong. Then I realised what I was hearing.

"It sounds like the *Chimera* has arrived," Slek said.

Heart in my throat, I followed him and Brinley out the door and toward the pod bay. Just let them try to keep us out. I had to find out what they knew about Danec and I had to know now.

18

"WE ATTEMPTED TO INTERCEPT THE POD," Yaranin said.

Getting in was easier than I anticipated. In fact, Zarex was waiting with an open door and outstretched hand. He drew me to his side while J'avet scowled.

Let him scowl, I thought. I drew myself up and put my professional face on. Whatever the captain had to say, I would listen and I wouldn't cry, scream or shout until I was well away from J'avet. He wouldn't see me lose control ever again.

"Attempted?" Zarex asked.

"We passed within communication distance," Yaranin said. "We had a brief conversation, but they cut and ran. They hid amongst a comet field. *Halcyon* was the priority. The IF will seek them out."

"Can we see that conversation?" Zarex asked. He gave me a sidelong look and reassuring smile. Which didn't reassure me, but I appreciated the effort.

Yaranin's eyebrows twitched, but he nodded. He glanced

over to a commander behind him, who disappeared back into their pod.

"I'll have the message relayed to the screen in here." He eyed me speculatively, as though uncertain as to why I was there, but he said nothing.

A few moments later, the large screen on the wall snapped to life.

"This is the IF vessel *Chimera*." Yaranin's voice came over the speaker.

"Sir, there are no life signs," another voice said.

"Commander Zarex said to expect that," Yaranin said. "See if you can open communications anyway."

"Yes, sir."

The vision on the screen changed from black to the dimly lit interior of a pod. Two silver-skinned figures sat in the seats in the cockpit. Four more were arrayed behind them.

My heart stopped.

Danec stood on the right side of the screen, face blank. His glazed eyes stared straight ahead. If I didn't know this was a recording, I would think he was looking at me. Watching me. Trying to communicate with me.

A breath caught in my throat.

I found Slek's hand on my shoulder. I covered it with mine.

I only half listened to the conversation. Mostly I just felt sick. I should have tried to reach Danec when he was still onboard *Halcyon*. I could have talked to him, reasoned with him, or knocked him out cold and dragged his cute little ass with us. Anything. Instead, I'd run, looking after my cute little ass instead. I sucked. I swallowed down the need to vomit. I couldn't even take pleasure from imagining puking on J'avet's boots. All of that seemed so fucking petty right now.

I licked my lips and caught the end of the communication.

"We will not surrender. Iritauri will... all will be hosts..."

The screen flickered and went black.

"They've passed out of IF space, sir. Should we pursue?"

The message ended.

"Are you okay?" Slek whispered.

I shook my head. "I'll be okay when we get him back."

"Captain Yaranin," J'avet said, "the bridge is set up for a briefing."

Cleared of the bridge crew's bodies, you mean, I thought bitterly. He spoke like their lives had no meaning at all. Like they weren't even people. I wanted to punch him in the face. I wanted to punch myself more, for not doing enough. Okay, I don't know what more I could have done, that wouldn't have ended with me dead too, but that didn't take away from my current self loathing. Survivor's guilt. Whatever.

"Engineer Slek, can you brief the *Athena's* crew on the method you used to gain control of the nanobots?" J'avet asked.

Slek shot me a lopsided grimace, but turned and nodded. "Sure. It's a skill we're all going to need to have, until they're eradicated."

"I'll ensure those who need rest get it," Zarex said. "Including me." He stifled a yawn with his fist.

"I'll speak with you later," Yaranin said. He followed J'avet from the room, accompanied by his security team and Slek.

"I'm so sorry." Zarex faced me and cupped my face in his hands. He ran a thumb over my cheek. "We'll find a way to keep him safe, I promise. You need him, so I need him. I need him to give you what I can't." He smiled slightly. "Besides, I like the guy."

"I like him too," I said softly. "The nanobots can't have him." I made what I hoped was a fierce face, but probably ended up as scary as a puppy.

Zarex smiled, but his eyes were laced with worry. "I meant what I said about getting some rest. Come on."

He wound an arm around my waist.

"Where are we going?" I asked.

"My cabin," he replied, a sly expression on his green face.

"Why do I think rest is the last thing on your mind?" I asked. Truthfully, it was the last thing on mine. His proximity and the memory of his mouth on my lips made my blood hot in spite of myself.

"It's the last thing I want to do," he replied. "After I do a lot of much more interesting things to you."

"Oh, like what?" I asked.

"I don't want to spoil the surprise."

I made a face. "I hate surprises. After the last few weeks, I'd like a bit of dull and boring in my life."

"I apologise for being neither of those," he said, but he smiled while he spoke.

I poked him in the chest. He was all hard muscle under my fingertip.

"You're right, you're not boring, but you are less of a roller-coaster than J'avet."

"Rollercoaster," Zarex repeated. "Old Earth fun park ride, right?"

"Yes," I agreed. "Too many ups and downs and then all you want to do afterward is be sick."

330

Zarex laughed. "That doesn't sound like fun."

"It doesn't, but it is." Maybe that was why I couldn't get J'avet off my mind, no matter how much of a dick he was.

He leaned in and whispered in my ear. "I'll show you a much more fun ride."

"Promises, promises," I replied. Yet the idea of him touching me everywhere was driving me wild. My skin tingled at the thought.

"How far is your cabin?" I asked. If it was any further, I might throw caution to the wind and tear his clothes off there and then in the corridor.

"Just around the bend," he said.

I half expected Iri to jump out at us, blasters in hand, but they didn't. The corridor was deserted and eerie. That was another in a long line of reasons I was relieved when he stopped in front of a door and pressed the button to open it.

Having never been in the cabin of anyone in command before, I was surprised to see it wasn't much bigger than the rest. The view was the same, of course; stars upon stars. The bed was a similar size, barely big enough for two to lie side by side. At least it wasn't a hammock.

His bed cover looked handmade and well loved. When he noticed me looking, he said, "My mother made it. I take it with me everywhere." He clapped a hand to his forehead. "That sounds pathetic."

I wound my arm around his neck. "It sounds sweet. And practical. And…like you love to have a piece of home with you. I have a small, plush bunny I keep hidden in my bag. It smells like the laundry powder my mother uses." When I felt home-sick, I'd pull it out and take a long sniff.

He smiled softly, then drew me into his arms for a searing kiss.

I felt the tension in Zarek's touch and knew it wasn't just lust for him either. We both needed to let ourselves go for a while. Let our bodies do the talking, to give our mouths and minds a break. Truthfully, I wouldn't sleep now anyway, my thoughts were too heavy. A part of me kept guard for any news, but the rest surrendered to the here and now.

Zarex slipped his hands under my shirt and pulled it off, almost without breaking off our kiss. Our lips were apart for all of about five seconds. Maybe six. Then another six while we both pulled off his shirt and tossed it aside.

Before I could take a breath, my bra was on the floor and Zarex lifted me and carried me over to the bed. He didn't even look as though he struggled. But then, he was almost as big as Slek in the muscle department. He probably lifted twice my weight before breakfast. And three times that afterward.

Zarek's mouth left mine and he kissed his way down to my breasts.

"Human women are so soft," he whispered.

"Compared to who?" I asked. My sisters from all the other species I'd met looked pretty soft too. I mean, I was no expert here, especially since I looked and didn't touch.

Zarex trailed the tip of his tongue over my nipple and smiled. "Compared to everything. Except those marshmallows they make on Earth."

"Right." I quivered under his touch. "Those are extremely soft."

"They aren't as sweet as you though." He trailed his tongue

the other way. His antennas bent toward my face, as though watching for my reaction.

"They taste better in hot chocolate than I would," I said with a nod. I would just get hot, not melt into sticky gooeyness. Although, Zarex was doing a pretty good job getting me gooey.

Zarex chuckled. "I don't know about that. I'm not sure anything would taste better than you." He captured my nipple with his mouth and suckled gently.

"I'll take your word for it." I wasn't sure how I managed to get out the words. My thoughts weren't all that coherent.

He smiled and moved to the other nipple, while his hands shed my clothes from the waist down. Then his.

I lifted my head, trying to get a good look at his two cocks, but he moved down and buried his head between my legs. Man of mystery, I guess. Fine, I could be patient. For a little while.

My head flopped back and I closed my eyes as he lapped at my folds with firm, confident strokes.

I gripped handfuls of bedcovers in either fist and breathed out my nose as he licked and suckled on my clit. Every so often, he would slip the tip of his tongue inside me, and lick around my entrance.

I saw stars, nebulas, whole galaxies as he took me closer to coming. My breath came in little pants, like a series of moans getting higher and higher.

Finally I was swept away in a rush of sensation and fluid. One rushed into me, encompassing me like a warm sea of desire and pleasure. The other rushed out like a warm river of desire and pleasure. Ummm... Oops.

"Oh." Before I even fully came down, my eyes shot open. I lifted my head to see Zarex wipe his cheek with the back of his hand. "I'm sorry, I've never... That's never happened before." Oh gods, swallow me up now.

Instead of being horrified or grossed out, Zarex smiled. "I like to see how much I turned you on. Apparently it was a lot."

I mean, he wasn't wrong.

He scooted up the bed and lay beside me. Now I got a good look at those cocks. I was right, it was one at the base, but split just above. Individually, they looked thick enough for a bunch of fun.

"So, how does this work?" I asked.

"Like this." Zarek turned me on my side, facing him and hooked my leg over his. He guided one of his cocks to my entrance and slid it inside. The other bent like a tentacle and teased my clit.

"Okay, that works," I said.

Zarex smiled and thrust into me several times, slowly and deliberately. Then he pulled his cock out all the way. It was shining, slick with my juices.

His eyes on mine, he manoeuvred so his other cock could slide into my entrance. He eased the tip of the wet cock into my rear hole.

"Then there's this," he said. Simultaneously, he slid a cock into each hole, slowly, carefully, watching for any sign of discomfort. "I have some natural lubricant of my own, but yours added a little something to smooth the journey."

"Oh my..." Holy shit, this felt amazing. It was like being with two guys at once, only...not. I had never felt so deliciously full before. It was incredible, amazing, arousing and a bunch of other superlatives I couldn't think of right now.

He drew back and thrust again. A groan slipped from his lips.

That drove me close to having another orgasm on the spot. I'd had guys in all my holes, but never more than one at a time. My ass and my pussy both wanted more.

I pushed my hips forward, driving him deeper, until it almost hurt.

He thrust harder, faster.

"Edie," he whispered. "I'm falling for you."

His words tugged me toward the edge so fast I could barely resist.

"I'm falling for you too," I said. I could certainly get used to this. He was different to the other guys. No one was better than another, but between them, I'd be satisfied. A lot. like, really a lot. If only they didn't expect me to choose at some point. Gods, I didn't want to think about that now.

Another thrust or two and I came again, this time without the squirting. If that was the new normal, I would have to get used to it, but not all at once.

Zarex grunted and his hips moved faster.

I felt both of his cocks become even stiffer as he groaned and ground hard into me. Warm heat flooded into my pussy and ass. Evidently both cocks came at once. Good to know.

He ground for a while longer, then sagged down beside me.

"Wow," he said breathlessly.

"Double wow," I said with a smile.

He chuckled and slid carefully out of me and drew me to him.

"You were everything I imagined, and more," he said softly.

"You too." I snuggled down to his chest. Even my wild imagination couldn't have conjured him. Or any guy with two dicks, let's face it.

"You should sleep." He kissed the top of my head.

"You too," I said again. I was too tired to think up new words. I closed my eyes, exhaled softly and let sleep take me.

19

"CAPTAIN YARANIN WILL BE TAKING command of the *Halcyon*,"
J'avet said. He didn't seem pleased to be saying those words.

I guessed he wanted the command for himself, but too bad. I
looked around the briefing room. No one seemed surprised or
disappointed, except J'avet himself. Yaranin seemed pleased,
even smug. *Halcyon* was at least twice the size of the *Chimera*.
To get her and such a small crew to the nearest port would be a
challenge. The post would bring him prestige. Great if you're
into that kind of thing. Me, I was happy to be alive.

J'avet—well, no wonder he was pissed.

His tone lightened, barely perceptibly. If someone didn't
know him, they'd miss it entirely. "I'll be taking command of the
Chimera."

I blinked several times in surprise. A rumble of chatter
passed through those in the room, but it died down when he
glared.

"The *Chimera* is under orders to pursue the Iritauri."

That declaration was met with another ripple of surprised chatter.

"To that end," J'avet said over the noise, "Commander Zarex will accompany me, as will Engineer Slek."

Both guys looked as shocked about that as I was.

"The *Chimera's* current crew will stay aboard, apart from several security officers who will transfer to *Halcyon*. Those already on board *Halcyon* will remain and accompany the ship to port. From there, another ship will take you to your destination."

My lips dropped apart. I knew it was possible Zarex would be posted elsewhere, but it didn't think it would be *now*. And Slek—he was supposed to accompany me to Agus. It made sense for him to go after Danec and the others, but I wasn't ready to be parted from all of the guys, not yet.

I shook my head. "That's not—"

Slek put a hand on my knee and squeezed. "We'll talk to him. You should be included in this too."

"It's J'avet's call," Zarex said uncomfortably. "You would be safer away from all of this."

I looked at him through my eyebrows. "Excuse me? Have I not proven myself to be a badass?"

He shifted in his chair. "Of course you have. I just…"

I raised an eyebrow.

"I don't want you to get hurt."

"I don't want you to get hurt either," I said. "Slek is Freytauri and he's going."

"He has certain skills." Zarex's tongue flicked over his lips. He wasn't going to win this argument and he knew it.

"I have skills," I argued. "What if you get injured?"

"The *Chimera* has medics," Zarex pointed out. "Experienced ones. And *Halcyon* has a lot of people who need you right now."

Okay, maybe he *was* going to win this argument, but it wasn't done yet. When J'avet dismissed the room, I jumped up from my seat and stalked over to him.

"I'm coming too," I said firmly.

He barely glanced at me. "No, you're not. The decision is made and is final. You can cry on Brinley's shoulder, then continue on to Agus like you're supposed to. Or better yet," he looked at me directly now, "go back to Earth where you belong."

"Fuck you," I spat.

"That attitude is precisely why you're not ready for missions like this," he said calmly. "I need clear heads, not emotional ones."

"I can be clear and calm," I told him, being calm. *See, asshole?*

"Only when you're reminded," he said. He crossed his arms over his chest and glowered. "You would be nothing but a liability and a distraction."

I narrowed my eyes at him. "Is that what this is about? My relationship with Slek and Zarex?"

"And Danec," he said cooly. "They will all need to focus. They can't do that with you there."

I gaped, then pressed my mouth in a line. "You don't have much faith in their professionalism."

"I have utmost faith that, when not distracted, they'll do their jobs," J'avet said.

I hesitated for a moment. "This isn't about them, is it? It's because *you* find me distracting."

The way his eyes flicked away gave me all the answer I needed.

"You want me to stay behind because you're finding it hard to keep it behind your pubic plate. Yeah, Slek told me all about that. Good way to hide your reaction to someone else. Someone like me."

"You're way off," he snapped. "Even if you weren't, it's irrelevant. Orders are orders and yours are to stay here."

"You're not my commanding officer," I pointed out.

"I'm captain of the *Chimera*, that's all the rank I need to keep you off my ship. Now say your goodbyes. We leave within the hour." Before I could say another word, he turned and stalked out of the room.

I hid my tears until Slek put his arms around me and drew me to his chest.

"It's not forever," he said softly. "Just while we deal with the Iri and get Danec back. As soon as that's over, we'll meet on Agus. All four of us. Um, five with Brinley. She's kind of one of us."

"Yes, she is," I sniffed. She was definitely part of the family, odd little family though it was.

"You two will have each other. You won't have to share the chocolate," he said, his tone light.

I snorted. "I'd rather have you guys around and never have chocolate again."

Wait, was I crazy? No, it was just...love

I leaned my head back and looked him in the eyes. "I love you."

He kissed me lightly on the mouth. "I love you too. Can you believe it? The biggest player in the IF, settling down."

I gave him a lopsided smile. I wasn't sure if he really was a player or just talked the talk. I knew he hadn't glanced at another woman since we met, apart from flirting with Kalvix.

"How about that," I agreed. "I guess I better help you both to pack."

"It shouldn't take long." Zarex placed a hand firmly on my ass. "I have an idea for something we can do to pass the time after that."

"Funny, I had the same idea," Slek said, a sly smile on his face.

It took me a moment to realise exactly what they proposed. When they did, I blushed.

"Both of you? At the same time?"

"I'm game," Slek said.

"I'm reasonably certain there's nothing he can give you sexually that I can't," Zarex said, a swagger in his tone. "But I'm game too."

"You can't give her three cocks all by yourself," Slek pointed out.

Zarex opened his mouth, closed it, then nodded. "That's true. Between us, we'll have that covered."

I didn't know what to say or think, because between them, I was about to melt into a puddle on the floor.

"Maybe we should start, um, packing, before we run out of time," I said around a dry throat.

"*Chimera* won't leave without us," Slek said.

"It's J'avet, anything is possible." I took his arm and Zarex on the other and we left the briefing room and headed to Zarex's. It was closer and bigger and Slek's was always a mess.

Zarex opened the door and waved us both inside.

The door barely closed behind us when they both descended

on me in the best way possible. Clothes went flying this way and that. I think they all had their seams intact, but I would make no guarantees about that. Right now, I didn't care. I was naked before I could blink more than once or twice.

These guys meant business. Good, so did I.

I don't know how we moved from the door to the bed, but the next thing I knew, we lay next to each other, Zarex's tongue teasing the insides of my thighs, while I licked the tip of Slek's cock.

Hells yeah.

I opened my mouth to take him in deeper and sucked. Zarex licked my folds more firmly.

"Awww yeah." Slek wound his fingers through my hair and held me while he thrust in as deep as I could take him. Several times he hit the back of my throat and groaned.

I would have smiled if I didn't have a mouthful of dick. Not having a gag reflex for the win.

I was so occupied with running my tongue over his tip and tasting his juices, that I almost missed my own orgasm. Yeah, I know, right? It went through me so hard and fast, I hadn't seen it coming. Pun intended.

Slek pulled out of my mouth to let me breathe, and scooted down until we were face to face. He kissed me while Zarex slipped one of his cocks into me from behind.

I groaned against Slek's mouth.

He chuckled and drew back a little. "Just out of curiosity…"

I thought he was talking to me, until I saw him look right past me.

I glanced over my shoulder and saw Zarex smile.

"Can I be inside two at once?" Zarex asked. "I can, if they're close enough together. And…into that sort of thing."

"I've always thought you were pretty hot," Slek said with a lopsided smile, which was also sideways from where I lay. "And smart."

I didn't even raise my eyebrows. Slek's comments about Danec's ass, and other things, already suggested his interest lay with men as well as women.

"Well then." Zarex manoeuvred us until my pussy was as close to Slek's rear as possible. "Lucky I can expand a bit too."

I stared over my shoulder as his cock seemed to grow longer, almost as long as my arm.

"I'm officially jealous and aroused," Slek declared.

Zarex smiled. The cock he'd slid into me, all wet with my juices and his natural lubricant, he slid carefully into Slek. The other, he slid deep into me.

Oh. My. Gods.

With a pleased smile on his face, Zarex began to thrust.

Slek groaned. At first I thought it was in discomfort, but I soon realised it was in pleasure.

I slung my arm over him and gripped his cock with my hand. With every one of Zarex's thrusts, I worked my hand up and down.

"Hells yeah," Slek groaned.

Zarex grunted. "This doesn't seem fair." He slid out of me and rolled me so I lay in front of Slek and he was behind.

"That works too," Slek muttered. As Zarex thrust into him, he slipped his cock into me.

After a moment of trying to work out the rhythm, we

managed to move in unison, thrusts and bucks, thrusts and bucks. Sweat and moans of pleasure.

The nodules on Slek's cock rubbed my insides into almost absolute delirium. I lifted my leg to let Slek in deeper and glanced over my shoulder. Seeing Zarex pounding into Slek while Slek pounded into me was hands down the hottest thing ever. The only thing missing was Danec. I slipped a finger into my mouth and pretended I was sucking on him.

That made me come again, harder than I ever had before. So hard I probably drenched Slek, but he was busy coming himself. Zarex wasn't far behind. He fit his orgasm between Slek's first and second.

"Coming twice," Zarex panted. "Now *I'm* jealous."

I laughed, but it took me a long time to come down. Partly because I was floating somewhere outside the ship, and partly because I didn't want to. I closed my eyes and enjoyed the feeling of being with two amazing guys. The three of us and Danec would be together again, whatever it took. I would make sure of that. Maybe if J'avet would lighten up...

I pushed him out of my mind, determined to appreciate the moment, and the guys, while it lasted.

EPILOGUE

I STOOD at the window beside the pod bay and stared out at the stars. The galaxy looked empty. No sign of the *Chimera*. I had hugged both guys and kissed them soundly in front of J'avet, because fuck him.

I held in tears while they waved goodbye and stepped into their pod. I choked back a sob as the door slid shut, blocking my view of their faces. I curled my hands into fists at the metallic clunk of the space doors opening.

The first tear trickled down my cheek when the pod slid out the door, toward the *Chimera*.

Brinley put an arm around me and we watched the pod become smaller and smaller.

I was almost sure I saw Slek wave and I waved back vigorously. Who knew if he saw me or not.

The tears fell freely when the pod disappeared into the *Chimera's* pod bay. The door closing, shutting them in, seemed painfully final.

"We'll see them again before we know it," Brinley said. "A week. Maybe two."

I nodded, but I wasn't sure she was right. It might be months. It might be years. It might not be at all. I had no way of knowing what they were heading into. The Iritauri might shoot them on sight. They might...

I wiped my eyes and watched the *Chimera* move away.

I watched until she was nothing but speck.

Then she was gone and my guys with her.

STAR PROTECTORS

MY ALIEN MATES BOOK 3

"CAPTAIN, there's a ship approaching. It's the *Chimera*."

"What?" I shot up straighter. "Are you sure?"

For three weeks, Brinley and I had been at Undapan Station, waiting to hear those words. Now, my heart was in my throat. My stomach twisted into knots.

Brinley laughingly referred to the station as Underpants, but I hadn't felt much like laughing since *Chimera* disappeared in the window, taking Slek and Zarex with us. J'avet forbade me from going with them to help rescue Danec. For that, I wanted to hate the commander. Honestly, I was almost as worried about him as I was about the others.

Almost.

Equally, I wanted to knee him in the groin. From what Slek told me about J'avet's pubic plate, it would hurt me more than him.

I shook my head to clear it and focused on the station's lieutenant.

Technically, I wasn't supposed to be in the station's command centre, but they hadn't stopped me from entering the day Brinley and I arrived. As long as I helped in the infirmary when I was needed, no one cared what I did with my spare time.

Honestly, I had a feeling Zarex sent word ahead to let me in if I asked. That seemed like the kind of thing he would do. The guy knew what I needed better than I did.

"I'm sure." The lieutenant barely gave me a glance. "They're giving off a distress signal."

My face jerked toward her. I wanted to ask more, but I bit my lip instead. Now was time to keep my mouth shut and let her concentrate.

See, J'avet, I have learnt some restraint, I thought. I wouldn't mind if he rolled his eyes at me right now. At least he and the others would be here with me.

The station's captain, Vaw, exchanged looks with the lieutenant. An Agusian man, he could pass for a shorter, stockier version of Zarex.

"Open communications," Vaw ordered.

"Yes, sir." The lieutenant, I think her name was Karji, nodded. She tapped buttons on the screen in front of her.

"*Chimera*, this is Undapan Station. Do you require assistance?"

I held back a smile. I suppose the name was a *bit* funny. Still, it wasn't nice to make fun of other planet's languages. Apparently 'elbow' in English translated into Blarvian as 'penis.' That might be awkward in the wrong context.

My smile faded when I realised there was no response from *Chimera*.

"Life signs?" Vaw asked.

Karji tapped her screen again.

I curled my hands into fists until my nails dug into my palms. The anticipation was painful.

No doubt Slek was currently trying to fix the communications system and turn off the distress signal. He'd have a good laugh about all of this when they arrived.

"A lot of fuss for little ol' me," he would say. He was neither little nor old. Or modest for that matter. He'd probably enjoy the fuss for a while.

Zarex—he would smile.

Danec too. He must be back to himself now, after the others purged the nanobots from his system. Right?

That fantasy was rudely blasted to smithereens when Karji replied.

"Just one, sir."

One? What the fuck?

I gaped at her.

"That can't be right," I said. "The *Chimera's* crew—" A couple of hundred people of various species should be on board. And my guys.

"—should number higher," Vaw finished for me. "Are you certain, Lieutenant?"

"That's what my screen says, sir," Karji said.

"Can you tell who?" I asked.

"No," she replied simply. "*Chimera* looks to have taken some damage."

I peered at the screen which showed her closer than the window would have. My stomach twisted tighter. The small ship showed a scorch mark down one side. Beside that was a huge dent. What the hells caused that? Road rage incident? Well, space rage. It seemed unlikely the *Chimera* hit a tree.

"Nurse, you should make your way to the docking area," Captain Vaw said gently. "Whoever is aboard might need your help."

"Sir, should they be allowed to dock?" Karji asked. "It might be a nanobot trick."

I held back an angry response.

Vaw spoke instead. "You implemented the new life sign search which can detect Iritauri?"

Slek had developed it. Apparently he'd had time to pass it on before he left to chase the nanobot hosts. Called Iritauri, or Iri, they were usually Freytaurians who were invaded by bots, their minds taken over against their wills. They turned silver and often walked around with glazed expressions and blasters.

"Yes sir," Karji said without inflection. "It detected no Iritauri, or nanobots."

"Then we will take the risk," the captain concluded. He nodded toward me. "However, if the scanner doesn't work, Nurse Wright is the best person to send, since the bots don't like human bodies."

There was no accounting for taste. In this case, it worked in my favour. The nanobots *might* now be modified so I could become a host, but the last time we met, my blood made them dormant. I could only assume that was still the case. And hope like hells.

I nodded. "On my way." I headed toward the door, then stopped. "Can you ask Pilot Brinley Grant to meet me there, please?"

Brinley should have gone on to the study facility at Agus,

but like me, she refused. She spent time in the station's pods and on the bridge of every passing ship which would let her. Right now, only a few ships were docked at the station, so I knew she could spare the time. Even if she couldn't, she would drop everything for this. The guys were her family as much as they were mine.

Vaw nodded. "I'll see to it," he said. His smile suggested he didn't mind me bossing him around, just this once.

I flashed a smile and hurried out the door.

Undapan Station was huge. At least twice the size of Moon Station. Maybe bigger than Dendra Station.

My boots clicked on the floor as I trotted toward the docking area. I kept an eye out for a transport cart, but none passed. Like a golf cart or a forklift, they carried people and supplies all over the station. It would save the walk, but hunting for one would use time I couldn't waste.

I puffed lightly as I drew to a stop outside the docking bay doors. They stood about twice my height and several times wider. Big enough to fit a lot of things through at the same time, but not enough for a pod or ship, if they were off course that badly. Of course if a ship collided with the station, the door wouldn't save us.

Hoping I hadn't just jinxed the place, I pressed my hand against the palm pad beside the door. After a moment, the pad flashed green and the doors slid open.

"Thank you," I told them as I stepped through. Just because the doors weren't alive didn't mean I shouldn't be polite. Or maybe I was a little stir crazy after the long wait for this day to arrive. Waiting for my guys.

Until I saw the *Chimera*, and looked inside, I wouldn't accept that they weren't on board. Something weird was up, for sure. Hells, something always was. I hoped it wasn't something sinister as well.

"Hey." Brinley trotted to catch up and slipped her hand into mine. "They're finally back?"

I told her what the lieutenant said. She stopped walking and frowned.

"One life sign? That's odd." Her English accent was stronger when she was worried.

"That's one word for it," I said. "Fucked up being another."

She smiled. "That too. I'm sure it's a mistake."

"I'm worried that if it is a mistake, it's because the ship is swarming with Iri," I said. "They might have figured out how to counteract Slek's Iri-finder."

Her tongue darted across her lips. I knew what she was thinking. The easiest way for them to have done that was if Slek was Iri now too. If that was the case, J'avet would be lucky if I only punched him in the head. He was the one who insisted on Slek and Zarex accompanying him on the mission.

And leaving me out.

That still rankled something fierce. If there was any chance I might have helped, he had robbed me of it. And robbed Slek of his Freytauriness.

Okay, I was being unfair. If Slek was Iri, it wouldn't be because J'avet let it happen. Someone had to go after Danec with him and Slek was an obvious choice.

One thing I knew for sure, if Slek was a host, he would be pissed off about it. He'd made his thoughts on becoming a host very clear. Although, so had Danec, and the last time I saw him, he had silver skin and glazed eyes. He was all Iri, or almost. I

354

knew the real him was still in there somewhere, I was certain of it.

Or at least…he was a month ago. He *had* to still be in there now. I wouldn't accept he was lost to me forever. Not until I knew for certain.

"If they are Iri, we just have to make sure they don't make it past the front door," Brinley said firmly. "Security is waiting." She nodded ahead.

Sure enough, there in the docking bay stood no less than six security officers, blasters already in their hands.

A woman, who I guessed was their leader, nodded to me and jerked her head toward a screen on the wall. On it, we could all see *Chimera's* slow but steady approach.

"It should only be a few minutes longer," she said.

"Great," I said, and forced a smile that likely looked like I needed to pee. I was too anxious and scared for a genuine smile. In a few minutes, with any luck, I would have a few smiles to spare.

I glanced around at the security officers. They were all intent on the screen. One or two bounced on their heels. It might be excess adrenaline, but not much happened on the station. This could be the first excitement they'd had in a while.

What did they do in the meantime? I wondered. Folks could only do so many laps of the place, or play so many games of chess.

A person couldn't read too many books, but I hadn't seen any of the officers in the library, so maybe books weren't their jam. Shame, books are the best, amiright?

I startled when, three or four minutes later, the space doors clanged open.

An hour or seven passed—okay, three or four more minutes —and they closed again.

Everything froze.

Time.

My heart.

Everyone's movement.

Every sound.

Beyond the docking bay's doors, something beeped and time started up again.

My heart remained stopped— Oh no, it started again. Now it pounded as the docking bay doors slid open.

The *Chimera*, big as she was, looked small parked inside Undapan's bay. Her long legs were splayed out to the sides, all three of them.

"There should be four," Brinley remarked. She sounded as concerned as I felt.

"Shit," I muttered. Closer up, *Chimera* looked like someone shoved a stick in her and held her over an open flame. The scorch marks were more pronounced and looked much worse. Unlike an *actual* marshmallow, she hadn't melted, but someone had certainly given it a good try.

"Stay a good distance back," the security officer said. She'd clearly heard Brinley and was concerned the ship might topple.

Not wanting to be squashed like an ant today, or indeed any day, I stepped just inside the door and stopped.

I was about to ask what happened next, when *Chimera* shuddered. A ramp began to lower out of the side of her.

I swallowed and found my mouth dry. I stood on my toes and tried to look inside the ship for the guys. All I saw was darkness. A never ending hole of nothing.

"Hello?" I called out.

I waited for the guys to answer. No response came. Not even a smartass remark from Slek. No innuendo, no flirting. Just silence.

"Should we go inside?" Brinley asked.

The security officer held up her hand and waited a moment longer. Before she said a word, a sound came from inside the ship. A shuffle, followed by a groan.

"It sounds like they need help," I said. I wasn't ready to accept it might not be *any* of the guys. That they might be—

No, they *had* to be alive. If they weren't, I would find them in whatever came after life and kick their asses.

"Something is coming out," one of the other security officers said.

"Or someone," Brinley said firmly.

A figure appeared in the doorway. He staggered down the gangway, hand pressed to a bandage on his head.

J'avet pressed something into my hand before he collapsed at my feet.

2

I ADMIT IT, my first instinct was to drop whatever he handed me, and run. Explosive devices didn't tick anymore, but neither would a handful of nanobots.

Once I'd resisted the urge, I opened my palm and glanced down. It looked like a computer chip.

I thought about handing it to the security officers, but their eyes were on J'avet and the *Chimera*.

I quickly tucked the chip into my pocket and knelt beside J'avet.

His hand fell away from the bandage, allowing me to peel it back slightly. I sucked in a wince.

The wound on his head was shallow, but long and ugly. At first glance, it didn't seem to be infected, but it would leave an epic scar.

I replaced the bandage and turned my attention to the rest of him. He looked pretty beaten up. Fading bruises covered his face and what I saw of his neck. A long cut ran from near one eye, all the way down to his chin.

"We need to get him to the infirmary," I said. "I'll give him a full body scan to check for nanobots, then the doctor can treat his injuries."

The head security officer nodded. She waved for the others to bring a gurney which sat off to the side of the docking bay.

They wheeled it over and pressed a button on the side, which lowered the top of the gurney to the ground. From there, they carefully moved J'avet onto it, then brought it back up and walked away in a hurry.

None, I noticed, was a Freytaurian. I hoped their caution was misplaced. If the nanobots could make anyone a host, we'd all be in for a galaxy of trouble.

I placed a hand on the trackpad at the end of the gurney and guided it toward the door.

They say modern technology is supposed to make life easier, but I would have preferred an old-fashioned handle. One I could grip and push the thing around. A slip of a finger on the trackpad and the gurney would move sideways, or run into a wall.

Yep, they still haven't perfected the shopping trolley.

Brinley walked beside me, with half the security officers behind. The other half stayed with *Chimera*.

I presumed they would check her over for— I didn't want to think they might find dead bodies on board. Nope, I was not going to go there unless I was told implicitly they'd found some. Even then, I would have to see for myself.

"What do you think happened?" Brinley asked.

I looked down at J'avet and shook my head. "I don't know,

but it's nothing good. Hopefully he'll be able to give us some answers soon."

It was all I could do not to shake him awake and demand them. I wouldn't give in to emotion. Doing that could kill him. He was an asshole, but I didn't want him to die. Quite the opposite, for some reason.

I needed him to live, and it was more than just wanting answers. He was the last person in the universe I should give two fucks about, but seeing him lying there...

Only the rise and fall of his chest and shallow breathing told me he was alive. If I had it my way, he would stay that way for a long time.

"The others will be fine," Brinley said. "They're probably on a pod, a few hours behind. You know how J'avet is. Maybe he wanted to make a dramatic entrance."

I snorted softly. "If anyone was going to kick everyone off a ship to make himself look good, it would be him." Only...even he wasn't that big a jerk. I knew Brinley was trying to make me feel better, so I did my best to play along. The effort was half-hearted at best.

"Edie..." Brinley said gingerly.

"I'm okay," I said quickly. "We need to concentrate on J'avet right now." By 'we' I meant me. Professionally, my patient deserved all of my attention. Personally—that was something I didn't need to think about right now.

"Of course," she said.

I turned my face to glance at her. "I'm sorry. I know this is as important to you as it is to me. They're your family too."

"The guys are like brothers," she said. "You're like a sister. If you hurt, I hurt. If they're in trouble—"

"You'll come with me to punch some motherfuckers?" I suggested.

She responded with a low laugh. "Yes, exactly. Or blaster them, at least. My right hook leaves something to be desired."

"I'm sure it's awesome," I told her. "But you're right, blasters are easier."

J'avet groaned and shifted.

"Stay still." I wasn't sure if he could hear me, but I got some petty pleasure from bossing him around for a change.

He stopped moving. Although it probably had nothing to do with me, I nodded in satisfaction.

"Good. Keep still." He might have broken bones or internal injuries. To have him die on the way to the infirmary would suck. "We're almost there."

It felt like days, but it was only a handful of minutes before I guided the gurney through the doorway. I didn't even hit it into the wall.

Go me.

While the doctor on duty, a nervous-looking Freytaurian, stood back and watched, I manoeuvred the gurney toward the body scanner. Someone already had the forethought to move the bed which usually lay underneath it. All I had to do was guide the gurney into place and turn the scanner on.

Finger on my lips, I watched as it slowly made its way from his feet, all the way up to his face.

"Several broken ribs. Blaster burns." Those looked painful. He must have changed his shirt at some point, they weren't visible on the one he wore now.

"Severe dehydration, empty stomach. Minor head wound.

No sign of nanobots." I double checked his teeth, but none hid in there.

The entire infirmary let out a collective sigh of relief.

The doctor, a blue skinned man named Barek, stepped forward.

"Bring him over to the examination room. We'll get him on a bed and have a good look over him. We'll start with IV fluids. Nurse, get me a bag."

I nodded and went to do as I was asked, as though a moment ago I wasn't their last line of defence between them and a nanobot invasion.

I grabbed a bag out of the fridge, while the doctor selected the right antibiotics and anti-inflammatories for a Parvoran.

As far as I knew, J'avet could take the same medicines as I could, but I wasn't certain enough to make that call. I mean, if I had to, I would. Okay, I would consult the database, then decide what to give him.

Doubtless, Doctor Barek had done this a hundred times before.

I set up the bag on a pole and hovered nearby while Barek slid a needle into J'avet's arm.

"He should be fine," the doctor said. "Looks like he hasn't had sufficient fluids for at least a week."

I frowned. "*Chimera* should have water—"

"Yes, she should," he agreed.

I heard the inflection in his tone and nodded. Intimate knowledge of the ship's food and water stores weren't within his skill set. Fair enough. They weren't mine either.

"Any idea how long it might be before he wakes?" I asked.

"It depends on the head wound." Barek nodded toward it. "Remove the bandage and wash it."

"Yes, Doctor." I hurried to get a basin of water and some cloth.

"He'll be okay?" Brinley asked. She hovered near the door, looking worried.

"He's got a hard head," I said. "I'm sure he'll be yelling at us all this time tomorrow."

She smiled briefly and stood back against the wall, where she'd be out of anyone's way.

As gently as I could, I peeled back J'avet's bandage. It was covered in dried blood, and didn't smell too clean.

He twitched as I worked the last corner loose.

"Sorry," I said, even if he couldn't hear me.

I threw the bandage in the bin, then washed my hands before I started to wipe away the blood caked around the wound.

"Ouch, that looks painful," I said. It didn't look life-threatening to me, thankfully.

"Indeed." Barek finished with the IV and two different needles, then moved to where he could see better. "We'll glue him back together."

Not actually glue, he secured a tube from a shelf and an applicator and started to apply a clear substance to J'avet's head. It would form a kind of shell that would allow the skin underneath to heal quicker.

The shell would give him an even harder head than usual. At least on that part. His head would match his pubic plate. That idea almost made me laugh and I had to bite it back.

"Get some scissors," the doctor said. "Remove his clothing." He nodded to another nurse to help.

Okay, I won't lie. More than once I imagined taking off J'avet's clothes, but not with scissors. Usually it involved fingers and maybe teeth. What? My imagination is creative, okay?

I started at the hem of his pants, while the other nurse cut into one of his sleeves.

His legs seemed more or less intact, the short red fur lay undamaged but needing a good, long soak in a nice, hot bath.

My knuckle brushed past the front of his thigh and I marvelled at how soft he felt. I could have patted him for ages, except for the whole thing about him loathing my guts. I was big on consent.

I tugged at the fabric and it tore all the way up to his waistband. Everyone should rip fabric once in a while, it's therapeutic.

I cut his waistband and his pants fell away, revealing tight, white underwear. Big surprise, right? I mean, I wasn't expecting *Transformers* or *Spider-man*, or anything like that. A thong, maybe? Naw, he had a stick up his ass, not a piece of fabric.

Recognising this as an entirely inappropriate line of thought towards a patient, I shoved the musings away and went to get a basin of clean water. While he was mostly naked, I would sponge J'avet off. He'd likely prefer to wake up clean. I know I would. Dirty on the inside, clean on the outside. Unless you're talking about covering someone with chocolate. That was a different story.

Yeah, I hadn't gotten laid in a month and it showed. The guys had spoiled me before that, in the best possible way. Now my body ached to be touched, filled, wet.

"Oops." I slopped a little bit too much water on J'avet's leg. I cleaned it up while the doctor glanced at me. He'd finished with the glueing and was now clicking his tongue at the scorch marks on J'avet's chest.

"Singed the hair," Barek said. "And the skin. He was incredibly lucky. He should go and bet on the durva races."

I smiled.

I knew from Slek and Danec that durva birds had big teeth and loved to stop mid-race to bite each other, then bury their way into the ground and disappear. The chances of betting on one who actually finished, much less won, was incredibly difficult. So of course, it was one of the more popular pastimes on Frey-T.

"All in all, he's in reasonable shape, for someone who took a beating," the doctor concluded. "We will need to wait for him to wake up before we can determine if any lasting damage was done to his brain. Someone must be on watch at all times."

I nodded. "I'm not busy. I'll stay with him." It wasn't because I cared about him at all. No way. I just...happened to be unoccupied. Nothing more.

"Good." Barek moved toward a data station and slipped in behind the chair. No doubt to enter J'avet's details into the database.

I cleaned up around J'avet's bed and washed my hands.

Only as I turned off the water, I remembered the chip he handed me before he'd collapsed.

3

I GLANCED over my shoulder before I pulled the chip out of my pocket. I gave it a closer look. To my untrained eye, it looked like nothing special. Slek would probably tell me the specifications down to the last decimal point, but it would be meaningless to me.

I placed the chip under a small scanner. Designed to look more closely at head wounds, broken fingers and antennas, using it hopefully wouldn't draw too much attention.

I peered at the screen and exhaled softly. As far as the scanner could tell, it was bot-free. Hopefully it wasn't infested with something worse.

"I wondered what he slipped you," Brinley said over my shoulder.

I jumped. I hadn't even seen her approach. Lucky I hadn't gone into spying as a profession. I would suck at it.

"Yeah, it's J'avet," I said. "He wouldn't slip me anything good."

She stifled a laugh with her hand. "We should probably take that to the captain."

I ran a hand over my crazy curls. The ones on my head. "I suppose we should. I just..." I glanced back toward J'avet. "He wanted me to have it for a reason. He could have given it to security."

Brinley looked apologetic before she said, "Or you were the closest person."

I lowered my hand to my lap. "That's possible too," I agreed. "I might be reading too much into this. It is J'avet after all. Given a choice, he'd give it to anyone but me." I said the words, but I didn't believe them. He had staggered toward me. He looked at *me*, albeit only a fraction of a glance. I was sure he meant it for me.

"We could put it into a computer and find out," I said. "One not connected to the rest of them."

"Right. It might have a nasty virus J'avet didn't know about." Brinley looked thoughtful. "Just a wild guess there isn't one like that here."

"I wouldn't think so," I agreed. "Slek would know."

"So would the captain," she reminded me.

"When did you become such a goody goody?" I asked teasingly.

She smiled faintly. "Since we all almost died. I'd prefer that not happen again."

The uncertainty in her eyes matched my own. This chip might contain a virus, or the answers as to whether or not the guys were alive.

"I think I can find us a tablet where the chip should fit inside," Brinley said slowly. "I'll get it and bring it back here. I'll try not to be long. Maybe hide that until I get back. If we hand that to the captain, we may never find out what's on it."

I swallowed hard and nodded. "That's true. That would suck." We'd get the whole 'don't worry your pretty little heads about it' spiel and that would be that. We'd be lucky if we ever found out what, if anything, the IF did about what information was on there. That didn't sit right with me at all.

"I need to check on the patients," I said. I pulled the chip out and tucked it back into my pocket. If J'avet would wake, it would save a lot of trouble and speculation, but he was still out.

He looked so peaceful lying there, but part of me wanted to give him a hard poke to wake up.

I resisted the temptation. He needed to rest. Time for answers would come soon. Not soon enough, but soon.

I walked around the infirmary, checking on the handful of patients who were currently resting there. Most had broken bones, or had just given birth. Most inflictions were healed so quickly these days, no one stayed for long.

By the time I'd made a coffee for one patient and changed the sheets for another, Brinley was back, tablet in hand.

We sat down near J'avet and tried to look as though we weren't up to anything suspicious. I was sure we didn't quite pull it off, but no one gave us a glance.

I pulled out the chip and pressed it into the port of the tablet. Brinley turned it on and we waited.

After a moment, the tablet screen showed a file icon for the video.

Brinley and I exchanged glances before she pressed the icon.

My heart jumped when Slek's face came onto the screen.

"If you're watching this—" He ducked out of view. "Fuck,

that was close." The vision shook and something behind him rumbled. "There's a lot of Iri here. Too many to..." The screen crackled and several words were cut off. "Putting coordinates on this chip. Get it to the IF... main headquarters..." He was breaking up badly now.

"Too many to stop at once... Need to get inside. We're gonna try..." The screen crackled again. Slek glanced over his shoulder, then back at the screen and smiled.

"Zarex says hello."

The whole screen seemed to shake, then the video ended.

"Shit," I breathed. "There should be another file on there."

Brinley closed the video and searched through the files for a moment. "There's a small file, but it won't open." She pressed on it a couple of times. "It might be password protected."

I frowned toward J'avet. "He might be the only one who knows it. Unless we can guess."

"I don't think it will be '123456,' or 'sexypants,'" Brinley said.

I barked a short laugh. "Probably not. Knowing him, it's something obscure." I sighed. "Slek would be able to hack it."

"Maybe Slek put the password on there," Brinley suggested. "Something only you would know."

I thought, but drew a blank. I had no idea what he would choose, that I would remember. He had no cutesy nickname for me. I didn't have one for him either. Danec called him Slekie once.

I took the tablet from Brinley and right clicked on the icon. An option to put in a password popped up. I keyed in 'Slekie' and pressed return.

The screen responded with, 'Incorrect password.'

I ran a hand over my hair and tried, 'Danny', Slek's nickname for Danec.

"That's wrong too," I said, frustrated. I tried a few more words, including 'orgasm' and 'sex'. I even tried 'puny,' which I used to tease him and his enormous muscles.

"I'm starting to think I don't know him," I said, frustrated.

"What about where you met?" Brinley suggested.

"On board *Infinity*." I tried that. Still nothing. I keyed in 'Kalvix,' the doctor who he flirted with, but who was later killed, a causality of the conflict between the Freytaurians and the Iritauri.

The file opened.

"Holy shit!" I said, louder than I intended. There on the screen was a series of numbers. "We did it."

"*You* did it," Brinley said. "The question is, what do we do with it?"

I closed the file and handed the tablet back to Brinley. "We go after them," I said firmly. "Slek wanted to let us know where to look." If he and Zarex had gone in themselves, they might be dead now, or worse, hosts.

"If they got the chance," Brinley said. "That video... They might have been taken before they could try anything."

"All the more reason for us to go looking," I said. After a moment, I added, "You don't have to come."

"Can you fly a ship?" she asked.

I hesitated. "I could learn," I said finally.

"You don't have time to learn," she said. "I'm coming. On one condition, and it's not negotiable."

I looked at her sideways. I trusted her implicitly, but I was always doubtful when anyone put conditions on things.

"What is it?" I asked carefully.

"We have to wait for J'avet to wake," she said. "He knows what happened. We need to see what he has to say before we go off half-cocked."

"I always prefer to go off full-cocked," I said absently. "Fine, that's a good idea."

I was also eager to see if he was okay or not. I mean, not *too* eager. It was professional courtesy, that's all. Yep, that was it. I didn't care about him in any other way. Okay, maybe a little. He kept life interesting, even if he was an infuriating motherfucker.

I stood and gave him a once-over. The IV seemed to be doing its job; restoring fluids to his body. His breathing was deeper now, stronger. If he'd arrived a day or two later, it might be a very different story. He'd be dead and the captain would have the chip. The IF might not have the coordinates, but they'd know the mission went badly. They'd probably send in a fleet of ships with lasers and destroy everything in that part of the galaxy. Maybe they should do just that.

A sensible person would go straight to the captain and give him the chip. I could go on to Agus and forget about all of this.

The very idea was absurd. As if I was sensible, or had a selective memory. No, I would wait until J'avet woke up and go from there.

What, I asked myself, *will you do if he wants to take the chip to the captain?*

Myself, I replied, *I have no idea.*

I had to cling to the thought that J'avet wanted me to have the chip so we could act. Because, I reminded myself, he thought of me as a hothead, who couldn't contain her emotions. He said he didn't like that about me. I think maybe he lied. Or now he was trying to monopolise on my rashness. Why though?

Hells, I could speculate all day and never come to a conclusion.

"If he was me, I'd wave coffee under his nose," I said. "Or chocolate. That would wake me up."

Brinley grinned. "Me too. Or a glass of rum."

I grimaced. I was more of a wine girl myself, but each to their own.

"Maybe we should wave some beer under his nose," I said. I had no idea what he drank, or even if he drank, but the smell was pretty strong.

"Or we could wait patiently," Brinley said.

"Bah." I waved dismissively. "If we keep talking, he'll wake and tell us to shut up."

"Now that sounds like him," Brinley agreed. "He isn't much on small talk."

"He really isn't," I agreed. "Or talk of any kind. He prefers to growl and glower." I was babbling on, with one eye on J'avet. With any luck, he would hear and get annoyed.

"Yes, he's good at glowering," Brinley agreed.

"The best. I've never seen a better cranky face than his."

Brinley looked like she was enjoying herself way too much here.

I was too, to tell the truth. It was nice to tell J'avet what I thought about him, without him responding angrily. Unless he could hear, in which case, I was probably in for it any moment now.

I cocked my head at him, but he did no more than a twitch. I couldn't rule out the possibility his head wound was worse than the doctor thought.

J'avet might never regain consciousness. In that case, what would Brinley and I do? Her condition would be out the window. Honestly, as badass as we were, I wasn't sure the two of us were equipped to take on an army of Iri.

I turned to face J'avet. In my sternest voice, I said, "Listen here, you arrogant jerk. We have better things to do than sit by while you sleep. You need to get your shit together and wake the hells up. You didn't limp all the way back here, on a ship, alone, without a perfectly good reason." Gods help me, I needed to know what it was.

I used Slek's favourite words. "Stop being a gwarp and wake up."

J'avet stirred. At first it was just a small, sharp move of his head. Then his eyelids flickered and his mouth drew back.

I stepped closer, until my nose was a handspan or two from his face.

"J'avet?" I said. "Come on, you can do this. We need you to wake up."

His nostrils flared and his eyelids flickered again.

He let out a long, slow, pained breath. Then, without opening his eyes, he said, "Would. You. Shut. Up."

I couldn't help it. I threw myself over his chest and hugged him.

4

"YOU SHOULD BE on Agus by now," J'avet said between spoonfuls of soup. Doctor Barek wouldn't let him eat anything more substantial.

"He hasn't consumed a proper meal in too long. His stomach will reject it," Barek said firmly.

The IV would fill him up as well, so I didn't argue. To my surprise, neither did J'avet. Maybe because it was the doctor's orders and not mine.

"Aren't you lucky I'm not?" I retorted. "You'd have some other nurse bossing you around."

"And you'd be safely away from here," he said evenly.

"You're worried about my safety?" I asked. I fixed him with a level glance. If he had something to say, now was his chance.

He shovelled another couple of spoonfuls into his mouth and shrugged. "I'm concerned for the safety of everyone in the IF," he said finally.

"Right," I said. He was frustrating, but that was nothing new.

"For what it's worth," he added, "I was worried about you. You're good at getting into trouble."

"It's a skill," I said dryly. "I have a few of them."

"I'm sure you do." He actually smiled, albeit faintly.

"How does your head feel?" I asked.

"It doesn't hurt, currently." He looked as though he wanted to ask something, but stopped as another nurse walked past.

When she was gone, I said, "Brinley and I watched the video."

I licked my lips. Here came the bit I didn't want to ask, but I *had* to. I'd held it back for long enough.

"Are the others… Are they alive?"

J'avet exhaled. "I don't know. After Slek made that recording, he hid the chip under the navigation console. The Iri attacked and *Chimera* was boarded. We fought back, but there were too many of them. I was knocked out. When I came to the ship, it was empty."

He closed his eyes and looked pained. "*Chimera* was being towed toward Tarathu. I managed to break the ship free and evade them. I knew I needed to get that chip back to the IF."

My heart ached for what they all went through, and for the expression of despair on J'avet's face.

"I'm sure you would have preferred to stay and blow up every Iri in the area," I said. "But a one guy rescue mission wouldn't have turned out very well."

"No." He averted his face. "Neither will a full on attack by the IF."

I frowned, trying to figure out what he meant. After a moment, it clicked in my brain.

"You think they let you escape, hoping you'd get to IF space and rouse an army?" The Iri did have a way of letting people live, if it served their own purpose.

"All those Freytauri would turn into hosts. All the metal on the ships. They'd be unstoppable."

His words made my blood run cold.

"That's why we can't go back with an armada," J'avet said. "We need stealth."

I blinked. "You just said *we*."

"Did I?" he asked, as if he didn't realise. "You understand the situation. You're human. Brinley too. That makes you immune to nanobots. Nothing we saw suggests they've solved that puzzle yet. Slek managed to access their database for a short time. So far, they can only turn Freytauri into hosts. They…" He hesitated. "They're focusing on turning Agusians. Slek thought they were close."

"Shit," I muttered. If they'd made Slek, Danec and Zarex into mindless hosts, then what would I do?

I knew what I *wouldn't* do. I wouldn't panic. That wouldn't help anyone, especially me. I would be cool and calm. Save my fury for the Iri.

"You're taking this surprisingly well," J'avet remarked.

"Would you prefer I throw myself on the floor and kick and scream?" I asked sweetly.

He smiled again, still just slightly. "No, but it seems more in character for you."

I regarded him for a moment. "If I didn't know better, I might think you're teasing."

His eyebrows twitched. "I don't tease."

"Of course you don't." I didn't believe that. Nothing he said contained malice. "You must have taken quite the hit to the head. You're almost being nice."

"I'll work on that some more," he said.

I took his empty soup bowl and handed him a cup of water with ice floating in it.

He nodded in thanks and sipped slowly.

"So when are we going?" I asked. "You should heal first. Maybe just Brinley and I should—"

He cut me off. "No. I'm not letting the two of you go by yourselves. I shudder to think of the trouble you'd get yourselves into."

"Wow," I said slowly. "It's almost as if you care."

He gave me a 'yeah, right' expression, but his eyes said something more.

Perhaps lust wasn't a one way street. How about that?

"I suppose it would be difficult with two," I said. Not that I was going to let him tell me what to do, but I was a nurse, not a soldier, pilot or a navigator... "*Chimera* is a bit big for us anyway. It would feel too empty."

"We're not taking *Chimera*," J'avet said. "She's too noticeable and too damaged. We'll take one of the pods."

I sat back and stared at him. "You mean one of the pods designed for short trips? Like, a few hundred kilometres and then they run out of fuel? Those pods?"

"We'll take spare fuel," he said evenly. "It will only be three of us."

I shook my head. "Now I *know* you're trying to get me killed."

His smile was wider this time. "Only as much as you seem to be."

I snorted. "I am never trying to get myself killed," I said firmly. "Trouble finds me wherever I go."

"Only since you left Earth," he reminded me.

"That old argument." I waved a hand. "You need to make up your mind. Do you want me to help, or go home?"

"Both," he said. "You'd be safe on Earth, but this mission is vital to the whole IF."

"No pressure then," I said.

"Not at all," he replied with a gusty sigh out his nose. "You don't even have to come. There are other humans…"

"I'm going," I said firmly. "Brinley will too."

I missed Zarex and Slek. Both would have thrown in several innuendos by now. Danec would have his bags neatly packed and ready. Within the hour we'd be out the door, so to speak.

"Was… was there any sign of Danec?" I asked gingerly.

"He wasn't one of the ones who attacked us," J'avet said. "We never saw him. I have no reason to assume he's anything but alive and deep inside the Iri compound on Tarathu."

"That's something, I suppose." I hoped the part of him that was him, was still there. How long did it take before the host gave up fighting and surrendered to a life full of nanobots? Did that ever happen? I didn't know. I couldn't count out the idea he was gone forever, but I wouldn't give up on him until I knew for sure. Who was I kidding? Even then, I still wouldn't give up. He was mine and I was his. I would get him back, whatever it took.

"If Slek is a host, that will be more problematic," J'avet said. "His skills are ones we need. He taught me a lot about the things he did to disable the nanobots, but if they've evolved, then…"

"We'll deal with it," I said firmly. I didn't want to think about

378

Slek as an Iri either. He would hate it even more than Danec. Slek was a free spirit, in every sense of the word. His engineering abilities, in the hands of the Iri, I didn't bear thinking about either. The only reason I did was that, from what I had seen, the nanobots, or whoever programmed them, did the thinking. The hosts were just bodies. In that case, they couldn't make use of Slek's skills, unless the head asshole accessed them.

"Is there anyone else we could trust, who could help?" I asked.

J'avet put a hand to his head, as though to scratch near the wound. His frown when he touched the hardened healing substance almost made me laugh.

He gave me a dry look and lowered his hand. "I'm sure you understand by now I don't trust very many, very often," he said.

"No shit," I replied. "Is that a no?"

"I know a man," he said, as though he hadn't heard my question. "Another Parvoran. You met him on board *Infinity*."

I scrunched up my brow and thought. "The guy who was with you when you told me I was too dumb to play chess?"

"The same." J'avet didn't look even slightly sorry for the things he'd said that day. "E'rel doesn't have the ability or imagination Slek does, but he'll be adequate."

"High praise," I said sarcastically. "What do you say about people you actually like?"

"I tell them they should go somewhere safe," he said.

It took me a moment to grasp his meaning. When I did, I snapped my fingers. "I *knew* you were hot for me. Too hard to admit it, hmmm?" I glanced at his groin to emphasise the double meaning.

"I'm getting tired," J'avet said. "You're exhausting."

Rather than being offended, I smiled. "I've heard that. In the best way possible though."

He smirked. "Keep telling yourself that." The grumpyass was back, but I thought we'd reached a new understanding. One in which we didn't hate each other. I would call that progress.

"Do you want me to talk to E'rel?" I asked. I had seen him around the station. He'd always looked like he was avoiding me, but truthfully I hadn't given it, or him, much thought. Any friend of J'avet's was unlikely to be a friend of mine. Until now.

"No, I will," J'avet said. "He'll have as much patience for you as I do. I don't want him to give an outright no because you irritate him."

"If that's his attitude, this is going to be a long journey," I said with a sigh.

"You can still say no," J'avet said.

"And miss all the fun? Not a chance." I took his cup and placed it on the table beside his bed. "If I can put up with you, then I can put up with two assholes."

There was that faint smile again. "Are all humans so stubborn?" he asked.

"Are all Parvorans?" I asked in response. "Is it true all your women stay home on Parvora while the men go out to space?"

J'avet grimaced. "On Parvora, space travel is considered a lesser activity. Most women wouldn't lower themselves to try it. Some do. Most do not."

I frowned. "So if you go home, you're looked down upon?"

"I would be, but I don't go home," he replied.

My mouth formed an O. He looked so sad I almost wanted to cry for him.

"That explains why you're cranky all the time," I said. "Bitter and twisted from being treated so badly. But then, in turn, you treated me like crap."

"I was just being honest," he said, but I sensed he knew he was running out of wiggle room here.

"Sure." I drew out the word. "You mean you want to keep people at arm's length, so they don't do anything horrible to you. You put up walls as high as the galaxy."

"And you cannot respect my desire to keep people on the other side of that wall," he stated.

"Nope," I replied easily. "No one should be stuck behind a fortress. It's not healthy."

"You're a psychiatrist now?" he asked.

"No, I have common sense." I ignored his snort and added, "Everyone needs to have someone care about them. It would be a lonely life without that."

I knew that all too well. The past month, if it wasn't for Brinley, I would have been lonely as hells.

5

"For the record, you should be resting," I told J'avet. "I'm mentioning it in case later someone thinks you weren't told."

"Noted," J'avet said. "Consider your ass covered."

"Hey," I protested. "I'm not *just* trying to cover my ass." I also knew he wouldn't listen anyway, even if I insisted.

"Did you say it because you care?" He glanced at me over his shoulder.

"Hells no," I said lightly. "You're still an asshole." I placed another can of food into the locker at the side of the pod.

"Glad we cleared that up." He went back to tapping at the pod controls.

I turned back and frowned at the back of his head for a while. The doctor had removed the healing shell that morning, and murmured sounds of approval.

"Come back each day so I can check your progress." Barek gave J'avet a nod and moved away, to see another patient.

Apparently J'avet took that as permission to leave the station after only two days.

"The doctor is going to be pissed," I pointed out. I closed the locker door, leaned against it and crossed my arms.

"You surprise me." J'avet glanced up. "I thought you would be the one pushing to leave."

I shifted from foot to foot. "The sooner we go, the better. But if you drop dead from that head wound, you'll be no use to us, or the others." That included the whole crew of the *Chimera*, not just the guys. A few hundred of various species, although only two apart from Slek were Freytauri.

"Then it's your job to make sure that doesn't happen," he concluded.

"I can check your wound, but you're not going to listen when I tell you to rest." I cocked my head and gave him a challenging look.

He smirked. "Of course not. I haven't listened to you yet. Why would I start now?"

I shook my head. "You're such an ass."

"You're such a pain in my neck," he retorted.

"It's not my fault you can't recognise awesomeness when you see it," I joked.

"Of course I can," he said. He looked so smug I wanted to sock his arm.

"Well then," I said with a sniff. "You could show more appreciation for it."

He shook his head and stood. For a moment I thought he was leaving the pod. Instead, he moved like a flash of lightning.

Before I could take a breath, he had me pressed against the

locker with the full length of his body. His nose was a finger width from mine. His breath brushed my lips.

"Is this what you had in mind?" He curled his fingers in my hair and pressed his mouth hard against mine.

I could only respond with a moan. I had imagined what it would be like to kiss him, but this was more than I could have expected. His lips were firm, demanding, like a lifetime of pent up desire that needed release.

His tongue traced my lips and slipped inside my mouth when I opened for him.

He broke off the kiss, gave me a scorching look and moved back into trail heated kisses down my cheek and neck.

"Edie," he said, his mouth muffled by my skin. "I want you."

"Mmm. I want you too." As frustrating as he was, the attraction was undeniable. The guys had all given me their permission to explore relationships with other guys, including each other and J'avet. Zarex, in particular, encouraged it. He always said he couldn't fulfil all my needs, so I should have more guys in my life to cover every angle, so to speak.

J'avet—well, he gave me a challenge. I never knew what he would do or say next. Someday I might have to choose a guy, but we had to get the others back first.

J'avet slid a hand under my shirt and ran it lightly over the front of my bra. Through the fabric, he pinched my nipple.

I twitched, but made no effort to pull away. The slight sensation of pain drove a knot of arousal right to my core.

His hand was still in my hair while the other started on working down the zipper on the front of my shirt. Lucky I hadn't put on the one with a bajillion buttons on the front this morning.

I slipped out of my shirt and somehow my bra joined it a moment later. Evidently J'avet was better with those than Slek. I hadn't even felt him unhook it.

My pants went next, then my panties, until I was naked and J'avet was still fully dressed.

"Your turn," I said. I helped him with his shirt, then leaned my head back to get a good look. He was as muscular as the other guys. Every bit of him was covered in the same fine fur as his face, but it did nothing to hide the definition of his abs, or his biceps. His stomach was flat and smooth, down to the V of his hips. Those disappeared into his pants until I pushed down the zipper and worked them off.

They were the same type of underpants he'd worn in the infirmary. At least until he tugged them down and out of the way.

I blinked at the expanse of smoothness at his groin. He had a plate of bone, like an eyelid across his pubic area.

"So," I drew the word out, "how does this work?"

He smiled and the plate of bone slid up, retracting into his belly as though it had never been.

Gingerly, I put out a hand, but I could barely feel where it had gone. Only a hint of something hard, as long as my hand, gave any sign of it.

"That's amazing," I marvelled. Also pretty amazing was the erect cock which had hidden under the plate. "How the hells did you fit that under there?"

For the first time since I'd met him, he grinned.

"Just one of those things." He gripped my hair tighter and jerked my head back so he could kiss my neck again.

His other hand, he dipped between my legs. With slow, firm strokes, he rubbed at my clit and entrance with his whole hand.

I moaned and started to buck against his hand.

He pushed one of my legs aside more and pressed his hand inside me. No finger-at-a-time, for him. No, he shoved in every finger and he shoved it hard.

"You're so warm, so wet already," he said, as if he talked about the weather.

"I try," I said breathlessly.

Before I could say another word, he yanked his hand out and turned me away from him. He pushed me forward until my upper body lay over the nearest console. His hand tight in my hair, he guided his cock to my entrance and slammed into me.

I gasped out loud at the sudden, almost violent penetration. He was big too, bigger than Slek. When he pounded harder and harder, I was sure he'd split me in two.

He groaned with the effort and slammed into me deeper, until each thrust filled me with delicious pain.

"J'avet," I said breathlessly. I drew closer and closer to coming, but not over the edge. Whatever he was doing, somehow it wouldn't quite let me orgasm. I was on the brink one moment and back from the brink in another. Then on the brink again.

He grunted and tugged on my hair until I had to throw my head back to keep him from tearing out my curls. He was definitely the one in charge here. Strangely, I didn't mind letting go, letting him do whatever he wanted to my body.

He slowed a little and his spare hand snaked around to pinch my nipple again. He gripped it and twisted so hard I cried out in pain and pleasure.

That drove him harder and faster than ever.

He squeezed my nipple so tight tears sprang to my eyes. That was what it took to drive me all the way over the edge, into the most intense, powerful orgasm I'd ever had. I was lost in a whirlpool of pleasure that sucked me in, held me under and turned me every which way.

A trickle of water made it last even longer. Or maybe I came again. It was so close to the first time, I couldn't tell. It didn't matter.

J'avet moaned and ground into me as he came too. His wet heat flooded my pussy. His moans flooded the rest of me, every nerve in my body tingling with a mixture of my pleasure and his.

Then he sagged against my back and finally let go of my hair.

We panted in unison while we came down from the rush we gave each other. After a hundred lifetimes, he pulled his cock out of me. Although I ached, my pussy immediately missed him.

There will be other times, I told myself.

"We should consider the sleeping arrangements on this journey," J'avet said in my ear. He put his hand lightly around the front of my neck and pulled me off the console.

"Yeah," I said, still trying to catch my breath. "I want to do that again. Unless you snore."

I felt his chest rumble in response.

"You're insufferable," he said, but this time there was a touch of affection in his tone.

"You too," I retorted. "What did I say about resting?"

His chest shook now and I caught the sound of him chuckling softly.

"You said I should rest, then you led me astray. This is definitely your fault."

"Fuck off," I said, before I realised he was teasing. I twisted around until I was face to face with him, my ass hard against the console. "We should get washed up."

He dipped his head to kiss me lightly on the mouth.

"Yes, we should. E'rel and Brinley will be here soon."

My eyes widened. I had totally forgotten about them. They could easily have walked in on us. They still might.

"I call first dibs on checking out the pod's shower." I slid out from between him and the console, and bent to gather up my clothes.

He pinched my ass and made me jump.

"Hey!" I stood up straight just as his pubic plate slid back into place. "Not fair, I can't knee you in the groin now. Not without hurting my kneecap."

He looked unapologetic. "Why do you think I have that?" He nodded downward.

"Dirty cheat," I muttered, but I grinned. "Shame there's only room in the shower for one person at a time." I could barely lift my arms, much less share.

He shrugged and started to pull his clothes on. "Don't use up all the water."

"It gets recycled, smartass," I told him. Unless someone stole the water, as the Iri presumably had with the *Chimera*, then we'd never run out. It might taste a little stale after a while, but it would keep us alive and clean.

He arched an eyebrow at me and turned away. Just like the usual, grumpy old J'avet. Frustrating bastard.

I watched him slip back into the chair behind the console

before I heard a voice outside. I bit back a squeak of alarm and hurried into the tiny bathroom before Brinley or E'rel stepped aboard.

They might wonder at my timing—having a shower in the middle of the day. Let them wonder. They'd figure out what was going on soon enough. I just hoped I could figure it out first. Was this just attraction and lust, or the start of something more? Hells, we had to go into the heart of the enemy, get the others out and escape with our lives, before we could even think about romance.

I dumped my clothes on a small shelf and stepped into water slightly too hot for comfort. I would need every muscle relaxant I could get after that session.

6

I MIGHT AS WELL HAVE PARADED AROUND naked. Brinley took one look at me and grinned.

E'rel barely glanced in my direction before he slid into a seat in the cockpit.

Brinley swung her bag onto a bunk and raised an eyebrow at me.

"What?" I asked. I started to arrange the new box of cans E'rel had brought on board and left near the door.

Acting like an ass wasn't just a Parvoran thing, but they did it so well. They could teach the average politician a trick or two.

"You know what." She picked up her pillow and made a face at how thin it was. "You and J'avet."

I shrugged, although my face suddenly felt warmer. "Just two consenting adults doing what adults do."

She snapped her fingers. "I knew you two didn't hate each other. It was so obvious."

"Apparently to everyone but us," I said. "Who said we don't still hate each other? He's still an ass."

J'avet stepped aboard, bag over one shoulder, yet another box of cans in his arms.

"Don't forget it either," he said dryly. "Don't start thinking I'll be nice."

"I wouldn't dream of it," I told him. "What did you say to Vaw? I don't think it's gone unnoticed that we're stocking this pod."

"Officially, we're meeting up with the *Vulcan*," J'avet said. "That will take us to Agus."

I narrowed my eyes. That sounded so plausible, I wouldn't put it past him to plan just that.

"But we're not, right?" I asked. I expected him to hesitate, to avert his eyes. Instead, he looked straight at me.

"No. We're not. Unless you've changed your mind and still want to—"

"I haven't," I said firmly. Okay, a small part of me would have liked to run away to Agus, but I had a month to do that. Honestly, I never really thought about it as a viable option. For so long, I figured the guys would turn up. Now, they needed me. There was nowhere else in the galaxy I would be but here. Okay, maybe a larger ship, with a metric butt load of experienced, heavily armed soldiers.

J'avet turned to Brinley. "There are other pilots."

"I'm going," she said firmly. "Wherever Edie goes, I go."

"I wouldn't make that a hard and fast rule if I were you," J'avet placed his bag on the bunk above mine. "Edie doesn't always make the best choices."

I sniffed. "Ain't that the truth." I looked at him down my lashes and held back a smile.

"Very much so," he agreed. "We'll be lucky to get out of this alive." He left the box of cans at my feet and went to sit beside E'rel.

"See," I said, "he's still an ass."

"So I see." Brinley looked like she was holding back laughter. She patted me on the shoulder and moved to sit in the pilot's seat to start the preflight check.

Muttering to myself, I went on unpacking cans until the lockers were full and boxes were empty. I carried the empty boxes off the shuttle and put them beside the docking bay door in a neat pile.

Many people left them lying around, but I figured this would make life easier for the station's maintenance people.

Of course it also made me anxious that J'avet would close the pod door and leave without me. To my relief, the door was still open when I got back.

I took a last glance around the pod bay, then stepped up the gangway and into the pod. Who knew if we would ever be back? Even if we survived this crazy mission, we might not come this way again.

Part of me was sad about that. As stations went, this was a nice place to spend a few weeks. The rest of me got stir crazy after the first day, and couldn't wait to leave.

I pressed my hand against the palm pad. When it flashed green, I pressed the button to close the door. I half expected to see a contingent of security officers come running to stop us from essentially stealing a pod.

No one came. I guess J'avet's story and rank was enough to convince them we weren't up to something.

"I'm inputting the coordinates to the rendezvous site," Brinley said over the pod's comm system.

"You're cleared for departure," a voice said in reply. "Safe travels."

"Thank you," Brinley said brightly. She turned off the comms and pressed a few of the buttons in front of her. The pod hummed and lifted up a couple of handspans above the docking bay deck.

"As soon as we're clear, I'll modify the coordinates," she said. "We're going to have to travel a hundred kilometres in the wrong direction first though."

"It can't be helped," J'avet said. "I'd prefer not to waste fuel, but they'll send a ship after us if we head right for Iri space. The pod can't outrun anything except another pod."

"That's a cheery thought." I leaned against the cockpit door and crossed my arms. "If the Iri come after us—"

"I have a plan," J'avet said.

"Care to share?" I asked.

"Perhaps you could allow the pilot to concentrate," E'rel suggested coldly.

I regarded him for a moment, then smiled. "That's Parvoran for 'you like Brinley.' How adorable."

He twisted around to give me a dirty look, but J'avet seemed amused.

"I'm merely suggesting you be quiet," E'rel said before he turned away.

"Sure." I nodded. "I'm happy for you both. You'll be adorable together." They really would.

Brinley looked back at me and gave me a wink. So she felt it too, hmmm?

Wait, why did I suddenly get the feeling this wasn't a new thing? I had been somewhat distracted for the last few weeks. They could have been seeing each other for ages and I hadn't noticed. I made a mental note to ask Brinley for the details later. In the meantime, I felt like a pretty crap friend for not seeing this sooner. Talk about being self absorbed.

I was dragged from my thoughts by the opening of the docking bay doors. We passed through them, into the airlock and out into space.

I don't think I would ever be tired of looking at the open expanse of space spread out in front of us. Stars upon stars twinkled like fairy lights. A small fraction of what I saw out the window was IF space. Beyond that were more unexplored galaxies than a person could count. I knew the IF planned to send their people out there some day, when technology advanced more.

Personally, I had only seen a small portion of the galaxy. When this was over, I wanted to see more. Frey-T, Parvora, not to mention Agus. It felt like years since I left Earth, headed straight for there. 'Straight' turned into a wiggly line, with a few loops thrown in.

I sighed and moved into the main sitting space of the pod. From here, I got a good view of the station disappearing behind us.

"Undapan Station to Commander J'avet." The voice startled me. My heart began to race.

J'avet looked uncertain for a moment, but opened the comms. "Commander J'avet here."

"You are requested to return to the station immediately," the voice said. "Doctor Barek has not cleared you for travel."

J'avet turned his face enough that I saw him grimace. He looked back toward the comm panel. "I feel fine," he said firmly. "I have a nurse with me to see to my needs."

I scowled at the back of his head. His needs? He made me sound like a servant.

"You didn't clear this mission with Doctor Barek?" I asked.

J'avet glanced over his shoulder. "He would have said no."

I shook my head. "You're such a rebel." I was going to be in a world of trouble now, aiding him in his escape from the station.

"We didn't have time to waste." J'avet ran a hand over his head and winced as he touched the wound.

"Commander, you're ordered to return to the station until further notice. Failure to comply may result in disciplinary action."

"When you put it that way," J'avet said. He turned off the comms. "You might as well change those coordinates now. They're going to come after us no matter what we do."

Brinley nodded, keyed in the change and pushed the pod to move faster.

"Commander, we've detected an unauthorised course change." The station couldn't hear us, but we could hear them well enough.

J'avet sighed and turned the comms back on. "Yes, we seem to be experiencing some trouble with navigation. We—"

I stepped forward and held my fingers in front of his face, slightly apart.

J'avet frowned, then nodded. "Undapan Station, I think we have nanobots on board. They're... taking over the pod. We have no control over..." He turned off the comms again and sat back.

"There. That should keep them off our backs for a moment," he said.

"Unless they decide to blow us up." E'rel looked unimpressed.

"Blowing us up won't kill the bots," Brinley said.

"*Chimera* is the only ship currently on the station which is equipped with a laser," J'avet said. "And she's out of commission for a while." He looked smug.

I regarded him for a moment. "J'avet. Did you sabotage the *Chimera?*"

He smirked. "Just enough to give us time to get away."

"You really are a rebel," I said, impressed.

"I also commandeered some devices Slek made that could help us."

I waited for him to elaborate, but he didn't. "I'll go and keep an eye on the station. They might send someone after us anyway."

J'avet nodded. He looked weary. That wasn't surprising. He'd been beaten up, injured and left more or less for dead, with no food or water. If it was me, I would want to rest for a year.

I ran a hand over my hair and wondered if I should insist we turn back. If J'avet died because he was away from a doctor's care for too long... I sucked in a breath and reminded myself that, barring further injury, there wasn't anything a doctor could do that I couldn't do as well.

I plopped into a seat and watched the station out the window. For a while, I actually thought they'd let us go.

Naive, right? I know. This mission was important. If we

succeeded, the whole IF would thank us. After they tossed us in the brig for a few years and threw us out of our jobs.

When they figured out what we'd done, they'd appreciate us, right?

A speck of black appeared in the side of the station. At first I thought I was seeing things. I blinked a few times and focused my eyes. Nope, it was definitely there and getting bigger by the moment.

"The docking bay doors are opening!" I called out. "There's a ship coming through."

E'rel brought up the rear camera and put the vision on a screen at the back of the pod.

"You couldn't do that before?" I muttered. It would have saved my eyes.

He said nothing.

"It's the *Gamma*," Brinley said. "They aren't messing around."

"That sounds bad," I said.

"She's a small vessel, but fast," Brinley said. "Equipped with sonic canons and—" She listed a bunch of features which meant nothing to me, but sounded like a galaxy of pain.

"We can't outrun her," J'avet said.

"Especially if she's come to blow the shit out of us," I said.

"Especially then," he agreed. He rubbed his hand over his forehead.

He looked so defeated, all I could do was watch the screen.

I guess this was the time to kiss my ass goodbye.

Shit. I *really* had not planned to die today.

I pressed my lips together and watched the *Gamma* draw closer.

7

"This might be a good time to let them know we don't have any nanobots on board," Brinley said.

E'rel and J'avet both turned and scowled at me, as though it was my fault for making the suggestion in the first place.

I scowled back. "You didn't have to tell them that. You could have ignored me like you usually do."

The side of J'avet's mouth twitched upward. I couldn't tell if he was apologetic or thinking he should stick to ignoring me.

Either way, he turned away and opened the comms again.

"*Gamma*, this is Commander J'avet. We were mistaken about the presence of nanobots on board. My apologies. Stand down."

He sounded so firm I would have done what he told me to do. Maybe. Depending on what it was.

The *Gamma* took a while to respond. When they did, it was a female voice which spoke.

"Commander J'avet, that is what I would expect the Iritauri to say."

I suppressed a snort, which ended up as a cough. She had us there.

"I'll turn on the vidscreen," J'avet said. "You'll see two humans and two Parvorans." He pressed a button and a light turned on, right in my eyes.

I waved and smiled at the camera. It didn't hurt to look friendly.

"Captain Vaw has ordered your return to the station." The vidscreen went both ways. The woman who spoke was also human, to my surprise, with an insignia which marked her as captain of the *Gamma*.

J'avet nodded curtly. "I'm fine," he said. "We have an important mission to carry out. We can't delay any longer, not even for my health."

I'm pretty sure *Gamma's* captain matched my eyebrow rise at the arrogance in his tone. He was right though. Not even for him could we turn back.

"If you think the whole station doesn't know you're headed back to Iritauri space, then think again," she said dryly. "Your organisation didn't go unnoticed."

J'avet swore under his breath.

I moved to stand behind him. "Why let us go then?" I asked.

"Because we need you to go," she replied. "This way, it doesn't involve Captain Vaw, or anyone else in the IF. We can all turn a blind eye, having made an effort to order you to turn back."

"Should you be telling us this?" I asked.

She smiled. "Probably not, but I'll have this recording deleted when we're finished. Officially, we fired a warning shot, but you evaded us."

"Warning shot?" Brinley asked.

Light flashed from the front of *Gamma* and something blasted over our heads, close enough to rock the whole pod.

The only one standing, I was knocked off my feet and thrown hard into the far wall. Tears of pain sprang to my eyes.

"Edie!" Brinley called out.

I struggled to my feet and rubbed my shoulder where I'd hit. Nothing was broken, but I would have a nasty bruise to show for it.

"I'm okay," I said, glaring at the screen where *Gamma's* captain looked unapologetic.

"Lucky for you, it was only a warning," she said coolly.

I was tempted to tell her to fuck right off, but she might change her mind about letting us go.

J'avet looked furious and his face was redder than ever. That was saying something, since he was red anyway.

I got another surprise when he said, "You could escort us part of the way there."

E'rel scowled at him. I was starting to realise that was his default expression in response to everything. He was even less cheerful than J'avet.

I'd probably be pissed too if my whole planet treated me like I was a lesser being, just because I wanted to go to space.

"It would save fuel if we spent some of the journey in their pod bay," Brinley said.

J'avet gave the smallest of nods. The corners of his eyes crinkled as though he was in pain. When had he taken pain relief last?

I glanced at my watch. Long enough. He was due for more.

"*Gamma* does have an infirmary," I said. "That would satisfy Doctor Barek. We might not even get in too much trouble when we get back." Maybe.

If we get back. There was always a chance we wouldn't. Okay, a *big* chance.

"Thanks for the offer," *Gamma's* captain said, "But I prefer not to be court martialed."

"Scared to take *Gamma* near Iri space?" J'avet asked, his chin raised in challenge.

"That too," she agreed. "Now hurry up and evade me before I change my mind."

"Evading," Brinley confirmed. "Edie, buckle up."

I hurried to do as she said. I'd witnessed enough for her evasive flying to know I might get thrown around again.

Hard pass.

"Good luck," *Gamma's* captain said before the screen went black.

"We'll need it," I muttered.

"Any damage from her warning shot?" J'avet addressed the question to E'rel.

The other Parvoran shook his head. "No. It was calculated to rattle the pod, not do us any harm."

I rubbed my shoulder again. "She did us some harm," I pointed out.

"Any *significant* harm," E'rel said without looking at me.

J'avet glanced back and gave me a questioning look. He actually seemed worried.

Well of course he did, we both knew he cared about me, even if he wouldn't let on too much.

"I'm fine," I said. "Just bruised. Nothing broken."

His mouth turned up at the corners in the tiniest of smiles.

"Good. Stay belted in until we're clear of the station, and *Gamma*." Something in his eyes suggested he'd like to see me restrained for a while longer, and not in a pod harness. Okay, maybe in a pod harness, but not with clothes on.

I smiled knowingly. "I'm not going anywhere," I told him. "Except to get you painkillers when we're clear. And to make you lie down."

"I could use a lie down," he said.

"Alone," I added.

He scowled, but I was used to him by now and just smiled again.

"You can't help anyone if you're dead," I pointed out.

"She's right, you know," Brinley said. "Also, I think the *Gamma* is following us. They've dropped back to make it look like they aren't, but they are."

As long as they didn't fire anymore warning shots, it would be nice to know they lurked back there. We might need them before we got to Iri space, especially if J'avet argued with me about resting. As important as this mission was, I wouldn't hesitate to call them and make him—okay, *try* to make him—go to their infirmary and rest.

"So, Vaw knew about this the entire time," I said conversationally. "That explains a lot. Like, why no one seemed to mind us taking so many cans. And why this seemed so much easier than it should have been."

"And why no one stopped me from taking a drum or two of fuel," Brinley said. "More than we would need to rendezvous with the *Vulcan*."

"We could have avoided a lot of sneaking around," I said with a sigh.

"The sneaking around was kind of fun," Brinley said. She smiled at E'rel before returning her attention to the ship's controls.

E'rel's face turned darker, which I interpreted as a blush.

"Yeah, well no sneaking now," I said. "We'll have to do our best to keep out of each other's way." In a ship smaller than an inner city apartment in most cities on Earth. Yeah, right. We'd be lucky if we didn't throttle each other halfway there.

"Two take the day shift, two take the night," J'avet said simply.

"That works," I said. As long as I wasn't on the same shift as E'rel. One cranky Parvoran was enough. J'avet I could handle, more or less. E'rel, well, I'd leave him to Brinley.

"I should get to work," E'rel said. "These devices that Frey-taurian gave you are crude at best."

"I hope you're not referring to Slek as 'that Freytaurian', are you?" I asked, my hackles immediately up.

E'rel rose, gave me a glance and moved to the back of the pod.

"Well, he's charming," I muttered sarcastically.

"Don't mind him," Brinley said. "He's better with machines than people. It takes him a while to get comfortable with someone."

"Sounds familiar." I looked pointedly at J'avet. "Speaking of you, it's time you rested. And don't even try to argue, or the three of us will drag you onto a bunk and tie you down."

Slek would have asked, "Do you promise?" but J'avet just looked resigned. He touched his head lightly and winced.

"I could use something for this," he admitted. At least he was man enough to know when he'd reached his limit. I wasn't sure the other three did. Not to mention every other guy in the history of guys. Okay, I'm exaggerating, but I'm a nurse. I've seen it over and over again for years. People hate to admit they're hurt, no matter what species they are. The fact J'avet could admit it made me respect him more.

Although, the fact he said anything might also mean he was in a lot more pain than he let on.

"Come on then." I jerked my head toward the bunk room. "I'll tuck you in."

"Is that what they're calling that now?" Brinley asked teasingly.

I stuck my tongue out at her and stepped back to let J'avet out of the cockpit.

"I'm starting to think you should have been lying down since before we left the station." I clicked my tongue at him.

"Someone needed to deal with Captain Marshall," he said.

"Was that her name? Oh, is that Jenny Marshall? I've heard people complaining about her. She takes no shit from anyone."

He gave me a lopsided half smile, half grimace. "Like you."

"Exactly." I followed him into the bunk room and helped him pull his shirt carefully off over his head.

From the look on his face, even that much effort took a lot out of him.

"I really should have left you back at the station." He sat while I got out some pain relief.

"I would have followed you," he growled. "Without me, you would have gotten yourself killed by now."

"I would not," I protested. "Give me some credit. I'd last at least a full day out here." Probably a bit more, but I would humour him if it kept him still while I checked his wound. It was healing nicely, but not as nicely as it would have if he'd rested.

I applied some healing salve and gave him an injection of pain relief which would work better on him than good, old fashioned tablets like humans prefer to pop.

Before we left, I'd scoured the medical database for information on Parvoran physiology. I'd downloaded it to a tablet, then to the ship, but I'd read as much as I was able to. I needed as much knowledge in my brain as I could get. If he started to crash, I wouldn't have time to consult a computer.

"Okay, lie back," I said. I plumped his flat pillow a couple of times before he placed his head on it.

"Hey, that's a first," I said.

He eyed me. "What is?"

"You did what I told you to," I said with a grin.

He snorted. "Don't get used to it. You're still a pain in my ass, like all humans."

I sniffed and pretended to be offended. "I'll have you know, us humans are awesome."

He brushed a soft, lightly furred hand over my cheek. "Yes, you are. You and Brinley, at least. The rest I've met, I could live without."

"You say that, until the *Gamma* saves our asses," I said. "I think you'll be happy to see Captain Marshall then."

"Possibly." He brushed his thumb over my lips.

"You should sleep," I said.

"Only if you lie next to me." He scooted over to the wall.

"There's barely room for two sticks of dried spaghetti," I said. In spite of that, I lay down in the small space left and lay facing him. It was a tight squeeze, but comfortable enough.

He placed a hand on my hip and closed his eyes. For a long time, I watched him sleep, then I drifted off myself.

8

"THAT CAN'T BE GOOD," Brinley said.

"What can't be good?" I asked. That sentence was right up there with 'we need to talk' for sending shivers down my spine.

I know, priorities, right? An awkward conversation is so much worse than an emergency in space.

Brinley scratched the side of her head.

J'avet moved to stand behind me, his hand lightly on my shoulder.

"What is it?" he asked, even though he could read the controls as well as she could.

I glanced back to take in his expression, but he gave nothing away. At least he didn't seem panicked. If anything did that to him, it would probably be too late for us all.

"*Gamma* to rogue pod." Captain Marshall's voice came through the speakers and made me jump. "I presume you've seen the ship approaching on a course to intercept you."

Brinley looked to J'avet questioningly.

He nodded.

She opened a comm channel, without visuals for now.

That was lucky, my hair looked like a bird had tried to make a nest in it, but gave up because it was too messy.

After all these years, they still hadn't developed the technology to permanently tame curly hair. If they put as much effort into that as they did making nanobots, they'd have a solution by now. Never mind the fact the nanobots were created by Freytaurians and none of them had curly hair. Surely someone could have had the foresight...

I gave myself a mental head shake.

Ship?

Shit.

"We saw, Captain," Brinley said. "We can't tell from here if they're IF or Iritauri."

"Have you tried to contact them?" J'avet asked bluntly.

"Not yet," Marshall replied. "Just checking if you wanted to do the honours."

"If it's Iritauri, I would prefer to stay out of their way," J'avet said.

"I thought you might," Marshall replied. "I'll have a little chat with them. *Gamma* out." The comms went silent.

"They aren't going to do what I think they're going to do, are they?" I asked.

"I think that depends on what you think they'll do," Brinley said.

"You know me, I have a wild imagination," I said. *And damn, J'avet is massaging my shoulder.*

"We'll have to wait and see," J'avet said. "Prepare to evade the incoming ship, in case it's necessary."

Brinley nodded. "I've already plotted an alternate course."

That explained why she was tapping buttons the moment she mentioned the ship.

J'avet nodded. "Good." He said nothing else, but I felt his tension in the way he dug his fingers in slightly too hard.

I flinched. "Ouch."

He didn't apologise, but he did lighten up.

The comms buzzed before Marshall spoke again.

"They didn't respond. I made them an offer to leave IF space before I fire on them. You'll note their change of course."

"They're heading toward the *Gamma*," Brinley said.

"Change course," J'avet said. "Take us away from both ships."

"Getting the hells out of here so we don't end up as a ship sandwich," Brinley said with a nod.

"Definitely the worst kind of sandwich," I agreed.

"I don't think a laser sandwich sounds like much fun," Brinley remarked.

I grinned.

"No, but a canon sandwich—"

"I see being annoying is a human thing," J'avet said dryly.

"I don't think so," I replied. "I think it's universal. You're pretty annoying too." I gave him a smile over my shoulder.

The side of his mouth twitched. "I don't think you can make a comparison between us."

"That's true," I replied. "I'm nowhere near as annoying as you."

Brinley stifled a laugh.

"You're all equally irritating," E'rel said. He looked as though he'd just woken up.

"Did we wake you?" Brinley sounded genuinely concerned.

His scowl softened slightly when he looked at her. Yeah, he had it really bad.

"I should have woken an hour ago," he said. His scowl was back in place again.

"You were sleeping so peacefully, I thought I'd let you sleep for a while longer," Brinley said.

I exchanged glances with J'avet. If he also thought they were too cute for words, he gave no indication. His expression gave me no hint as to what he was thinking.

"Next time, don't let me oversleep," E'rel snapped. He turned and stalked back toward his corner to work on various gadgets, or whatever he did back there.

Halfway there, he stopped, and turned his face back to say, "Please."

Brinley nodded, although she looked unimpressed.

If he was interested in her, he was going to have to work harder than that. J'avet, for all his flaws, at least displayed moments of reasonable, compassionate behaviour. He was frustrating and confusing, but I knew there was someone decent in there. More or less. When I didn't want to kick his ass. Which was often, but it went both ways. Sometimes I even deserved it, but not often.

"The unidentified ship is almost in visual range," Brinley said. "I'll turn on the screen when it is." To me, she added, "Having screens running uses more fuel."

"That makes sense," I said. "Don't want to end up with a flat battery."

"Not out here," she agreed. "And not right now. That would be bad."

"There's *Gamma*," J'avet said.

The ship soared past us, at an angle so she wouldn't collide with us on the way past. For a small ship, she was enormous compared to our pod. A cruise ship beside a dinghy. A whale beside a tuna. An elephant beside... Well you get it.

"There it is." Brinley turned on the screen. At the edge was a dot. The dot was moving quickly and getting bigger by the moment. It soon became clear that whoever piloted the ship, she was a lot bigger than *Gamma*.

That made us the dot.

I peered closely at the screen. "Wait, is that..."

"It looks like it," Brinley agreed.

"*Infinity*," J'avet said.

"Wasn't she at Dendra Station, getting repaired?" From what Slek had said, she'd be there for months. I wasn't the best at adding up, but I was almost certain it hadn't been months since we left Dendra.

"She was." J'avet looked troubled. More than I ever saw him before.

That, in turn, made me worried. "Then why—"

"I don't know," he said, cutting me off. "Brinley, can you listen in to any conversations between *Infinity* and *Gamma*?"

"Sure. If they have any. So far, I'm not picking up anything from *Infinity*."

J'avet hesitated, then nodded. He stepped back and asked, "E'rel, have you finished upgrading the Iri scanner?"

I frowned and swivelled around in my chair. Iri scanner? That sounded very much like a Slek thing. My heart ached at the idea of anyone having to work on his creations. He should be here, with his ridiculously big muscles and ready smile. The guy's heart was at least as big as the rest of him. So was his goofy side.

I swallowed down a knot of emotion. I hadn't let myself wallow, because I knew it wouldn't help anyone, but I acutely missed all of the guys right now. How in the worlds would I choose one, when I cared about them all?

I sighed loudly.

"We'll get them back," Brinley said. "Whatever it takes, okay?"

I nodded. "I know, I just wish they were all here. If they were, we'd all be somewhere else." I frowned at my own, slightly confusing logic, but it made some kind of sense.

Brinley smiled. "I know what you mean. We'd all be on Agus by now. I hear they have bathtubs."

Now we both sighed.

"Here." E'rel pushed a long, thin device toward J'avet. "You need not plug it into anything, just aim and press that button. The screen there—" he pointed, "—will show Iri signatures."

"Nice work." J'avet said.

"I merely worked from the plans I was given." E'rel shrugged and moved back to his corner.

J'avet aimed the device toward the *Infinity* and pressed the button as E'rel said.

"One… two hundred life signs," he said, distracted by his attention on the small screen. "All Iritauri."

"Fuck," I muttered.

"Yes indeed," J'avet said. "They might have missed some nanobots when they cleared out the ship."

Or they'd invaded Dendra station, and who knows where else.

He didn't say any of that, but I was sure he was thinking it.

I was.

"Um," Brinley said. "They've launched a pod. It's on a course toward us."

"Increase our speed," J'avet said. "We need to get out of here."

"The pod is equipped with a laser," E'rel said from his corner.

"And using it in sight of *Infinity* will make us a target," J'avet said.

"Putting the pedal to the metal," Brinley said.

J'avet gave her a funny look, but said nothing.

"Would you actually fire on them?" I asked. "Those on board are there against their wills. They're innocent." More or less.

"If it's them or us, I will," J'avet replied. "Until then, let's try to outrun them. There's a comet field not far from our current position."

Brinley groaned. "Comet field? Do you know how hard it is to fly through those?"

"Harder than dying?" J'avet asked dryly.

She snapped her fingers. "Good point. Okay, comet field it is. The other pod is on our tail. If we can evade them for a day or two, they'll run out of fuel. That is, if they don't start firing first."

"They must want the pod in one piece, or they would have done that by now," J'avet said thoughtfully.

"Or they want us alive," I said. "I mean, it is us."

J'avet snorted. "I can't dismiss that possibility."

"*Infinity* is firing on *Gamma*," Brinley said, her voice higher than usual. She brought the visuals up on the screen for us all to watch in silent horror.

Gamma shot back with what looked like a long laser. *Infinity* shook with the impact.

"Laser and sonic canon," Brinley said. "You can't see the cannon until it hits. When it does, it packs a punch." She sounded awed, but a little scared at the same time.

I frowned. "I thought *Gamma* didn't have lasers?" I glanced toward J'avet.

"She didn't. Now she does," he said. Yep, that pretty much summed it up.

Infinity fired back, just a regular old torpedo, but it looked as big as our pod.

Gamma destroyed the torpedo before it even got close and *Infinity* rocked with another blast from the sonic cannon.

"*Gamma's* small, but she takes no shit from anyone," Brinley said.

"Like us," I said with a satisfied smile.

Gamma moved away from *Infinity*, but the bigger ship made no move to follow.

"She's dead in the water," Brinley said. "I would guess she wasn't ready to leave Dendra, but they took her anyway."

"Now we just have to worry about the pod chasing us," I said. I realised without *Infinity*, those on board might become more desperate.

I finished that thought when a loud bang sounded right above my head, and our pod shook. Instinctively, I ducked down, even though the reflex wouldn't save me from anything.

"We're hit," Brinley said.

We began to slow. Where the pod previously vibrated with movement and power, it shuddered and fell still. A moment later, it was filled with smoke.

That didn't seem like a good sign to me.

"They hit a fuel tank," Brinley said. "We can't fly under our own power."

J'avet looked back. "There is a chance the pod may explode. If it does that—"

"We're totally boned," I finished for him. Frankly, I was getting tired of feeling like I should kiss my ass goodbye.

"Yes," he said softly. "We need to get off this pod."

I cocked my head at him. "That much is obvious. The question is how?" Escape pods didn't generally come with lifeboats.

"When the other pod catches up and clamps on, we'll have to let them board," J'avet said. "That's the only chance we have."

"Well shit," I said under my breath. Looks like we skipped plans A and B and went straight to F. F for fucked up.

9

WE DIDN'T HAVE to wait long. Four or five minutes after we came to a stop, the other pod drew up alongside us.

"Oh look, roadside assist is here," I muttered. Yeah, people still drove cars on Earth, but the joke went over J'avet's head.

Brinley looked too anxious to even smile. "I think it's more like carjacking," she said.

"Right." I grimaced. "We packed blasters, didn't we?"

"Yes, but you won't be using one," J'avet said. "You'll shoot off your own foot. Or mine."

"Hey, I've used blasters before, and we're both still intact." I narrowed my eyes at him. "Actually it was *you* who almost shot off *my* foot."

He looked back at me, face entirely expressionless. He didn't even look slightly apologetic.

I guess we *were* fighting for our lives at the time. Better I lose a foot than my life, although neither was ideal.

"You and Brinley will go to the bunk room, out of the way," he said. "E'rel and I will deal with the Iri."

I wanted to protest. I could kick ass too. Had I not proven that several times already?

On the other hand, I knew that look on his face. He wasn't going to give even half a hair's width.

Forget stubborn as a mule. Stubborn as a Parvoran; they're much worse. I had a feeling E'rel was just as bad.

"Fine," I said reluctantly. Only because the metallic clang of clamps attaching one pod to another echoed and sent chills up and down my spine.

The Iri would be through the door in moments.

I followed Brinley into the bunk room, but we left the door open. Honestly, I wasn't sure it would close, unless it had a manual setting somewhere I didn't know about. Now was not the time to go searching.

The pod's lights blinked and the air got heavier.

I was no engineer, but I had a feeling the Iri hit more than the fuel tank.

"I'm starting to think we weren't supposed to reach Agus," I whispered. It felt like a lifetime since I boarded the shuttle on Earth. I was scared then, but the trip should have been simple and straightforward. A hop to Moon Station, a trip on *Infinity* for a couple of weeks, get off at Agus.

No fuss, no muss. Instead, it was nonstop fuss and a lot of muss.

"We'll get there," Brinley assured me. "Although, by the time we do, we might be the ones doing the teaching. We've done quite a bit of on the job training." Her English accent sounded stronger now, with her anxiety.

I gave her a wry smile. "You're not wrong there, mate." I accentuated my Australian accent.

She smiled in return, then we both ducked down and watched as the pod door started to glow.

E'rel grabbed a device from his box of Slek-tech and tossed it to J'avet. He picked up one of his own and a blaster.

With straight backs, both guys faced the door, blaster in one hand, device in the other.

"What is that?" I asked.

"I'm not sure," Brinley replied. "But they're both hot fully armed like that."

I grinned. As it happens, she was right. Maybe now wasn't the time for those kinds of thoughts, but they came in my head, um, *into* my head, anyway.

The door glowed brighter.

I squinted.

"They couldn't try knocking on the door?" I said softly.

"Some people have no manners," Brinley agreed. "What must their parents think?"

"No idea," I replied. "Kids these days." Okay, the whole conversation was silly, but it helped settle my nerves. I suspected it did the same for Brinley. It certainly didn't hurt. There were worse ways to pass what might be our last few minutes.

A hole appeared in the middle of the door. It quickly expanded until it was big enough to allow an adult to step through.

The smoke was heavier now. Some came from where we were struck, and even more came from whatever they used to melt the door.

At first, I couldn't see through the breach.

I put a hand over my mouth to suppress a cough. The air was thick, but didn't feel quite as heavy now. The Iri pod must be sharing oxygen with ours. How kind of them.

"Stand down," a voice said from inside the smoke. "Throw down your weapons." The voice sounded unsure and tentative, but almost certainly female.

If I couldn't see, chances were, they couldn't either. If that was the case, they wouldn't know J'avet and E'rel were armed. It was a reasonable guess, but just that: a guess.

"We have no weapons." J'avet must have made the same assumption. "We're on a peaceful mission to take supplies to... Vargo."

I held my breath.

Did the Iri notice his hesitation? What would she make of it if she did? She might assume someone headed for the nearest planet would know its name.

On the other hand, people forget things all the time. Birthdays, anniversaries, planet names. No big deal.

Right?

"This pod is now ours." Apparently it didn't matter if she noticed or not. The Iri wanted the pod, not a friendly conversation.

"I don't think so." The smoke cleared slightly, enough for me to make out J'avet as he stepped forward. His figure wavered, distorted by the thick air. Even though the Iri scared him as much as they scared me, he sounded completely calm. "Actually, your pod is now ours."

I frowned. How did he figure that?

The Iri stepped through the doorway, a blaster in her hand as well.

A shiver passed through me. J'avet could be such an ass, but I didn't want to lose him too.

Hadn't I lost enough already?

No, I reminded myself. The others weren't lost, just... misplaced for a while. We would get through this and I would find them, and then—

I bit back a sob. Brinley's arm went around me and I leaned against her.

"It'll be okay," she whispered. "We'll get through this."

I nodded. My tongue darted over my lips before I said, "Yeah, I hope so."

She gave me a squeeze.

"There's only one of you," J'avet said. "There's two of us."

Now who can't add up? I thought. Of course, he was trying to avoid drawing attention to Brinley and I. I appreciated that. I didn't want to be noticed too much by someone armed and ready to fire.

The Iri cocked her head. The smoke had almost cleared entirely. The glazed look in her eyes was visible. She was consulting with the nanobot hive mind, or whatever it was.

Finally, she straightened her head. "Our numbers are greater than one. On board the other pod, are others."

J'avet leaned to the side to make a show of looking around her. "I see only you."

"There is only one," E'rel stated. He sounded as robotic as she did. "We should take care of her. We're wasting time." He raised his blaster.

She raised hers just before two more Iri appeared in the doorway.

"Our numbers are more than one," she said again.

"So we see," J'avet said.

"Your numbers are more than two." The Iri turned and aimed her blaster toward the bunk room. She got off a shot that missed my head by a hair. Actually from the smell of singed hair, it didn't miss.

"Fuck." I ducked down further. I almost didn't see J'avet raise the device and point it toward the Iri woman.

She froze.

The Iri behind her took aim at J'avet. Before he fired, E'rel used his device on him. He too froze. J'avet froze the third.

"What the—" Before I finished my question, nanobots started to trickle out of the Iritauri, to lie in a puddle on the pod floor.

I should have known. Part of the box of Slek-tech was a couple of anti-bot devices. He'd managed to switch off the bots on the *Halcyon*, but I hadn't known anyone was working on a personal, handheld version.

Cool.

J'avet exhaled loudly, then moved in a blur to catch the woman before she fell to the floor, face Freytauri blue again. He lowered her down and tried to grab one of the men, but only managed to keep him from falling too hard.

E'rel wasn't close enough to help the last man, who toppled sideways against the door before making a graceful slide to the floor.

None were Danec or Slek, or even Zarex.

"Is that all of them?" I asked as I rose to my feet.

"Stay here." J'avet gestured for E'rel to step through into the other pod with him.

Since he didn't specify where 'here' was, I hurried to crouch beside the former hosts. None seemed to be injured, but they would take time to fully recover from being invaded by nanobots.

I glanced through the doorway. J'avet and E'rel stood beside another Freytauri, also a woman, device still in their hands.

"There's no one else here," J'avet said. "We'll need to move everything from one pod to another."

E'rel sighed as if he'd been asked to walk the length of a marathon.

I mean, sure, it was a hassle, but at least we were alive.

"We have another problem," Brinley said. "We're not stocked with enough supplies or fuel for eight." She'd already made herself comfortable in the pilot's seat of the new pod and checked over the controls. At least, I think that was what she was doing.

"We'll need to take them to the *Gamma*," J'avet said. He looked as impressed as E'rel, but this time with good reason. Taking the former hosts to the ship would take time and delay our mission. Still, it couldn't be helped. *Gamma* was a better place for them than here.

"At least we know those anti-bot things work," I said. Even when he wasn't here, Slek was helping us. "Have we got any more of them?"

E'rel looked at me as if he thought I was the last person on board who should have one.

"Three more," he said finally. "I'm working on a fourth. We need many more."

J'avet nodded. "The sooner you get back to work, the sooner we will have them." To Brinley, he said, "Plot a course to meet up with *Gamma* and let Captain Marshall know we're coming."

Brinley nodded. "Done and done. There's four, no five, IF ships approaching. They seem to be heading toward *Infinity*."

"That will keep them busy." J'avet looked satisfied at that. "I'll send them the specifications for Slek's ship-wide...anti-bot device." He gave me the faintest of smiles to acknowledge his adoption of my term. It was as good a one as any.

I shrugged and turned to help the first Freytauri woman to sit up.

"What happened?" She looked dazed and confused.

I couldn't blame her. We had probably come close to dying only several minutes earlier, and she held the blaster. None of that was her fault, but she might not see it that way. It didn't matter what species someone was, people always seemed ready to blame themselves for all sorts of things.

"Nanobots happened," I said. "You're free of them and their influence." I needed her to know there were no hard feelings for anything the bots made her do. None of it was her.

"They're switched off." For now. "We're headed to another ship. They'll take you to wherever you need to go." I offered her a smile.

She replied with a confused frown. "Um. Okay, I guess." She looked around, obviously with no idea how she got there.

From what I'd seen of Iri nanobot infestation, she would remember everything in time. When she did, she'd need a lot of support to deal with it. I didn't envy her, or any of them.

I patted her shoulder. "Come on, we need to get into the other pod. This one isn't safe."

With my help, she stood and tottered on unsteady legs until she could flop down onto a bunk.

The other three managed by themselves, but the effort to move under their own power was obviously great. The strain on their faces spoke volumes.

I left them there to rest, then helped J'avet carry the food and fuel from one pod to the other. Even E'rel helped, once his corner was all moved over.

The old pod cleared of anything but inactive nanobots, J'avet closed the door.

"Disengage the clamps and move us a safe distance away," he said.

"Declamping and getting clear," Brinley confirmed.

We drew closer to *Gamma*, which was stationary until J'avet opened the comms.

"*Gamma*. Anytime you want to laser that pod, we're clear."

Marshall's voice came back. "Commander, I thought you'd never ask." She sounded as though she couldn't imagine anything more fun.

A weapons port on the side of the ship opened. Something inside it moved, like the muzzle of a canon turning to lock onto a target. A flash of laser shot out, so brilliant it lit up the galaxy. At least, our little bit of it.

I squinted against the glare.

The laser slammed into the pod. For a moment, nothing happened. Then the pod exploded, blowing it and all the nanobots into oblivion.

"You're cleared to dock," Marshall declared, satisfaction in her tone. "All aboard."

10

"Welcome to the *Gamma*." The captain and two security officers greeted J'avet and I as we stepped off the pod.

Brinley and E'rel stayed back to gather E'rel's devices. The Parvoran was adamant they not be left behind for a moment, and J'avet agreed. Honestly, so did I. Trust was a hard commodity to find lately, what with all the nanobots running around the galaxy.

"Thank you, Captain," J'avet said, his tone and expression distracted.

"You're welcome, Commander." Captain Marshall eyed him as though amused by something. She was taller than me, and more slender. The hair at her temples was grey. Lines on her face suggested she smiled a lot.

I suspected she didn't miss anything, ever. I bet nothing happened on her ship that she wasn't aware of. I would bet just about anything she took even less shit than I did. That was saying something.

She reminded me of Doctor Kalvix, who died on *Infinity*. That in turn made me think of how Slek had flirted with the doctor. He would flirt with the captain too, I suspected. Hopefully, I would find that out for sure soon.

It couldn't come soon enough.

"Thank you, Captain," J'avet said again. "We'll be on our way as soon as the Freytauri are transferred to the infirmary."

In spite of his firm tone, Marshall smiled. The kind of smile that said he wouldn't like what she was about to say, but that was too bad. "You'll be here a while longer than that. Admiral's orders."

J'avet scowled. "You said we were to be allowed to go on our way. I appreciate the need for *Gamma* to follow at a discreet distance, but—"

"Things change," Marshall said shortly. "You've proven that one small pod is too vulnerable." Her eyes were like pools of steel, hard and uncompromising.

Still, I had to try. "We dealt with the Iritauri," I pointed out. "We just don't have room for more on the pod. We'd run out of oxygen and fuel before we reached Iritauri space." There was no point in freeing the hosts only to have them suffocate along with us a couple of days later. Besides, I didn't want to share the cans of frankfurts with anyone else.

J'avet gave a sharp nod. "We have a greater chance of success—"

Marshall held up her hands to cut him off. "Argue with the admiral. I'm simply following orders. You will all remain on board *Gamma* until we get closer to Iri space."

"Then what?" I asked. I had the funny feeling they wouldn't

simply let us go again, now we were here. Was there room in the brig for four of us?

"Then we await further orders," Marshall said evenly. She lowered her hands as though the conversation was finished.

Evidently it wasn't as far as J'avet was concerned. "Since when did you follow blindly?" he asked, his voice almost a growl.

The side of her mouth twitched in annoyance. "Since the future of the entire galaxy was at stake," she replied. "I know this is hard to believe, but this is bigger than you, Commander."

I choked back an ironic laugh. I'd lost track of the amount of times I assumed J'avet thought himself more important than whatever went on around him. This time though, I *knew* he knew otherwise. He was doing all of this for the good of everyone.

J'avet gave her a cold stare. "I know that, Captain," he said through gritted teeth. "That's why I don't want this mission fucked up by someone behind a desk."

"He has a good point," I said before Marshall had a chance to respond angrily. "J'avet knows where to go. We need to get in there undetected. Someone who has never even met an Iri, much less dealt with one—"

"Is still in charge," Marshall said firmly.

If I didn't think it would get me into trouble, I might have pointed out how rude it was to interrupt. She'd done it three times since we stepped off the pod.

"We've set aside cabins for you all," Marshall went on as though we hadn't spoken at all. "Take what you need from the pod, you'll be locked out of the pod bay. Just in case."

J'avet's eyes flashed. If he could shoot lasers out of them, I'm sure he would have.

We couldn't even argue this point, really. We *had* tried to steal a pod in the first place. Just because we'd been allowed to didn't mean we were off the hook for that.

"Yes, Captain," he said finally. He'd already grabbed his bag. Apparently that was all he needed because he headed toward the pod bay doors without even a glance back at me.

"He's such a charmer," Marshall said dryly.

"He's okay," I said. "Kind of." He had his moments. If he thought I would trot after him, he would have to think again.

"I'll help the others." I stepped aside to let a couple of security officers and the four Freytauri step off the pod. The former hosts still looked dazed, but judging by the haunted looks in their eyes, their memories were returning. I didn't envy them for a moment. The anguish they would suffer for the next while would be immense. Likely, they would never fully recover.

Before they could take more than a couple of steps away from the pod, I stopped them to ask, "I don't suppose you know a Danec, son of Jaek, or Slek, son of Arron, do you?"

They all gave me the same blank look and faint head shake, before the security officers urged them to trudge on.

"Friends of yours?" Marshall asked. She seemed genuinely interested.

"Yeah," I said, but my guard was up. I decided against telling her more, in case she decided I was too close, emotionally, to handle the mission. Unlike J'avet, I didn't work for GASP, so technically I didn't answer to Marshall.

On the other hand, I was pretty sure if she wanted me out of the way, she would do it, and apologise to the medical arm of the IF later. Or not apologise. I didn't think she'd actually be sorry for anything she did. She didn't get to captain a ship without being confident with her choices.

"Go and help your teammates." She nodded toward the pod. "Then get some rest. You look like you need it. And make sure J'avet sees a doctor, or I will." She turned and walked away.

"I'm not his keeper," I said under my breath and to her back. I headed back into the pod.

"I don't suppose there's any chance of sneaking back off *Gamma?*" I asked.

Brinley glanced up from the bag she was placing tools into. "Probably not, no. Why?"

I told her what Marshall said. By the time I finished, Brinley was frowning. E'rel wore his customary scowl.

"I guess we're safer on here anyway," I said, as if I didn't feel defeated.

"Do you think she'll let us off when we reach Iri space?" Brinley asked. "She might be imagining the glory of defeating those nanobots." She grimaced.

"If we don't proceed with stealth, we will fail," E'rel said bluntly. "Her ego may doom the galaxy."

That would make a great tagline for a book or movie, but in real life it scared the shit out of me.

"We'll have to do whatever we can to make sure that doesn't happen," I said firmly. "This is bigger than her, too."

I turned my face slightly to see a security officer standing near the doorway. No doubt he'd heard everything we said. We'd have to watch ourselves. Although, we hadn't said anything we wouldn't want Marshall to hear.

Yet.

"Here." I reached for one of the bags and swung it over my shoulder along with my own bag. "Lucky we didn't unpack when we left the other pod."

Brinley smiled. "Yeah. We didn't even have time to get comfortable."

"No one could get comfortable on a pod," E'rel grumbled.

"Oh, I don't know," I said lightly. "It's better than a tent. Unless you're being fired on."

"I'd rather be fired on in a pod than in a tent," Brinley said. "The chance of surviving is slightly higher."

"Approximately 52 percent higher," E'rel said. "You cannot flee from a pod which is in space." He frowned as if annoyed at himself for taking part in our silly conversation.

"Good point," I said cheerfully. "At least we can flee from this one." I stepped back out of the pod and flashed the Agusian security officer a warm smile.

He gave me a funny look and his antennas bent to follow me as I moved away. For someone of the same species, he didn't look much like Zarex, but the antenna action made me miss the commander acutely.

I wanted to fast forward to when this was over and we were all safe. If only life worked that way.

We stepped out the pod bay doors, only to be greeted by yet more security officers.

"We'll show you to your cabins," one said.

I had a sense of déjà vu. After the attack on *Infinity*, we were 'guests' on board another ship.

Way too many bad things were becoming a habit lately.

"You could just give us the numbers," I said. "We can find it ourselves."

"Captain's orders. She doesn't want to risk you getting lost."

"This ship isn't big enough to get lost," E'rel said. Clearly he was as tired of their bullshit as I was.

The security officer shrugged. "I'm just following orders. I'm sure you understand."

"We do," Brinley said, her tone nicer than I could have managed. "Lead on, please." She sounded like she was asking to be taken to a nice tea room, one that served scones with whipped cream.

Great, now I was hungry.

The Agusian gestured for us to follow him. A Dendran officer fell in behind us.

"I'm having a flashback to Calig," I remarked."Only these guys don't have bows and arrows."

"And they're not going to kill us, or infest us with nanobots," Brinley said firmly.

"I hope not," I replied. I eyed the Agusian. He didn't seem offended by this line of conversation.

Personally, I would be annoyed if someone compared me to people the nanobots reduced to little more than mindless, murder puppets.

"You're perfectly safe on board *Gamma*," the Dendran assured us.

"Until someone fires on us all," I said.

She hesitated. "Until then, yes. *Gamma* is more than equipped to take care of herself, as you no doubt saw."

I nodded. "I saw." That gave me some comfort. She'd stood up to *Infinity* better than we would have on our own. "They are freeing all those on *Infinity* from the nanobots, aren't they?" I asked.

"I don't have any information on that," she said.

She reminded me of the automated voice I had on an old so-called smart watch. Good for setting timers and doing maths my lazy ass didn't want to bother with, but more often than not, it had no useful answers.

"Right. Well, when you know, can you let us know, please?" I couldn't rule out the possibility the guys were on that ship. I would have liked to board *Infinity* to check, but it was unlikely I'd be allowed to. If I was, I probably wouldn't be allowed back on *Gamma*.

All I could do was hope that if they were on there, they would contact me the first chance they got.

"If I can, I will," she said.

I guessed that was about the best I would get.

The officers led us to the back of the ship and waved toward a set of doors.

"You'll have to share. *Gamma* isn't equipped for guests," the Agusian said.

The doors slid apart without a sound.

J'avet stood with his back to us, looking out to space. He didn't turn until the doors closed behind us and we started to place our bags on the narrow bunks.

"Can you believe this?" I asked.

He grunted.

"Yeah, I agree," I said, as though I understood grunt-ese. "It's a total pain in the ass."

He regarded me through narrowed eyes. "You really never shut up, do you?"

"Nope," I said lightly. "Hey look, a shower. I could use a wash."

"I could use some food," Brinley said. She gripped E'rel's hand and pulled him toward the door. "Come on, let's eat."

He looked pained, but left anyway.

"Do you need to eat?" I asked J'avet.

He shook his head. "No." He looked hungry, but not for food. "Come here."

I looked at him sideways, but stepped forward. The moment I was close enough, he tangled his hand in my hair and pushed me to my knees.

"I know one way to shut you up," he growled. With his spare hand, he undid his pants and pushed down the front. His public plate slid aside to reveal his already erect cock. He dragged me forward until he was able to shove his cock into my mouth.

Yep, he was right. I couldn't talk like this.

I ran the tip of my tongue over his cock and tasted his juices.

He groaned and pushed his cock in deeper.

"Suck," he ordered.

Normally I don't like being ordered around, but since I was already there, I might as well.

I sucked gently, while my hand crept up to search his groin. I wasn't sure what I would find there, but my fingers touched balls that felt like those of any other guy I had been with.

He moaned. "Harder." His hips moved back and forth as he fucked my mouth deeper and deeper.

I sucked harder at the same time as I cupped his balls and toyed with them.

I thought he was about to come when he pulled out of me.

"Shower," he said. Apparently the blood abandoned his brain to the point he could only say one word at a time.

He pulled me to my feet and all but tore my clothes off

433

before we were both immersed in hot water. He pressed me against the wall and hooked one of my legs around his hip.

Without another word, he slid three fingers inside me and started to rub me with firm, hard strokes.

In approximately three point two seconds, I was ready to come. I guess I needed this more than I knew.

I panted out a moan and threw back my head, narrowly missing the wall before I stopped. Knocking myself unconscious would be a really crappy thing to do in the middle of sex.

J'avet stroked me harder still, so hard he grunted with the effort.

My hips bucked frantically several times before I came. A fierce growl of pleasure slipped out from between my lips. If anything squirted from my other lips, it was washed away in the water.

I hadn't even started to come down when he drew his hand out of me, bent me so my face was under the flow of water, and slammed his cock into me from behind.

The water was too hot and the pressure so strong, I had to move my head to the side every so often just to get a breath.

His hand, which had left my hair while we undressed, wound into my curls again.

He held me firm under the water while he pounded again and again with no hint of restraint.

My head felt light. I was forced to pull him, hand and all, to the side so I could breathe.

He didn't go easily. I thought he might tear out a handful of hair. The pain was both terrible and exquisite. If he was anyone else, I might have told him to stop. I knew he would if I asked.

That was exactly why I didn't. I let him dominate me, and

that permission, which I could revoke at any time, gave me the power. I had as much say in all of this as he did. If I didn't want him to hammer my entrance, he wouldn't. If I hadn't wanted a throatful of his cock, I wouldn't have had one. I knew he knew all of this, even though he hadn't hesitated for a moment.

"Fuck…Edie," he ground out.

That was the idea here. I might have laughed, but I'd end up with a mouthful of water. That, I didn't want.

He slammed a few more times, then pulled out of me. He turned me around and put his hands under my arms. With almost no effort, he lifted me until I could wrap my legs around him. He guided his cock back into me and thrust again, more sedately this time.

With one hand, he held me in place, while the other explored my breasts and pinched my nipples.

"You are…" he said slowly, each word an obvious effort, "mine. Even when we get the others back. Choose us all if you have to. I'm not giving you up."

He ground his groin against me and pressed me against the shower wall.

The only response I could manage was, "Okay." That was a bridge we could cross when we reached it, but I couldn't imagine not having them all in my life.

He thrust slower, then faster, but always with as much force as he could put behind it. He wasn't a man who did things by halves. Whatever he did, he shoved every bit of himself into it. I wasn't sure if that meant he enjoyed life, or was trying to throttle the hells out of it.

Either way, he made for a fun fuck.

I closed my eyes and let the sensation of desire grow again.

His cock hit me deep inside, in just the right place. Again and again he hit, as though he could force an orgasm out of me. Maybe he could, because I came again, more intense this time and lasting longer. Unlike the first, this time he milked it for every bit of sensation he could get into me.

Then he came with a guttural grunt that sounded so primal, I wondered if he was a wild animal, at least for a moment.

He ground into me for what felt like a lifetime, then sagged forward, out of breath. He wound his arms around me and drew me to him, holding me in spite of how slippery I must be by now.

His cock worked free as I placed my head on his damp shoulder.

My eyes flickered shut and I rested all of my weight on him.

"There, that shut me up," I whispered.

He snorted near my ear. "For a while. I might have to keep you quiet for longer yet."

"Oh yeah? How will you do that?" I asked.

He nibbled at the side of my neck, grazing his teeth over my skin.

"I'll find a way," he assured me. He lowered me down and grabbed up a bar of soap. "But first, we wash." He turned me around and started to run soap up and down my body.

I sighed and let him work his magic while the hot water soothed my muscles.

11

I WOKE up squashed against the wall, J'avet fast asleep beside me.

I checked my watch. It was almost five am. The whole ship would awaken soon. Part of me wished time would hurry. The other part wished it would stop completely. I wasn't particularly comfortable, but I could sleep for a month. Better yet, sleep surrounded by all the guys.

The bed shifted and I found myself with room to roll over. I couldn't manage to fully open my eyes yet. Like every other ship, I'd worked in the infirmary during our time on board. Like every infirmary, there were never enough hours or staff. Even for a relatively small ship, something always needed to be done. In particular, the former hosts needed a lot of care. I'd spent hours talking to them, letting them share the trauma they'd been through.

At least, what they were ready to deal with.

One of the women, an engineer named Kariz, had worked

on the repairs to *Infinity*. She told me how everything was going well enough, until power shut down, seemingly at random. She hadn't seen the nanobots before they flooded into her system, but she and other now Iri engineers turned the systems back on and took the ship out of dry dock.

The next thing she knew, *Infinity* attacked *Gamma* and the bots in her head made her step onto the pod and attack us.

Then she was back to herself again, and grateful for it.

"I knew what was going on the whole time," she told me. "But I couldn't stop it. I couldn't stop *myself*. I wanted to send out a distress beacon, or destroy *Infinity*, but I couldn't."

She cried on my shoulder while I patted her back and said words I hoped would soothe her. Honestly, I wasn't sure I helped much. Only time and therapy would do that.

How hard would it be for Danec to come back after weeks, months as a host? The thought of him struggling to come to terms with everything threatened to break my heart. He would have all the support he could manage, and then some, but the sooner we got him back, the better.

"Edie. Time to get up." J'avet's voice broke through my sleepy musing.

I groaned and rolled over to face the wall.

"Or I can leave you out of this meeting," he said. "You shouldn't be there anyway."

I sat up so fast I hit my head on the bunk above.

"Ouch." I rubbed my head. "I'm going."

"Then you need to get up," he said again. "We won't wait for you."

I cracked open my eyes. He was already dressed except for a couple of buttons he was doing up now.

Brinley and E'rel were nowhere to be seen.

"They've gone to breakfast," J'avet said.

"Are you reading my mind now?" I pushed off the blanket and stood, aware of J'avet's eyes on my naked body. Once, I would have hidden from anyone's gaze. Now, I felt pretty, knowing he looked admiringly and not in a judgemental way.

"I wouldn't," he replied. "I'm sure it's as messy in there as your hair is."

Okay, he was a bit judgy.

I stuck out my tongue at him and started to put on my clothes. Jeans and a cute blue t-shirt that would have looked better on Brinley than me. Whatever, it was comfortable, and more or less said 'I'm not on nurse duty today.' It wouldn't stop me from working if I was needed, of course, but it felt nice to be casual.

"For your information, my mind is an organised place," I said as I sat on the floor to pull on some socks. "Everything is neatly filed away, like a database." Or like a wiki, where people added and deleted stuff at random, so you never quite knew what was real and what wasn't. I didn't know how half the stuff in my brain got in there.

Also, I had a special file for 'weird alien dicks,' but doesn't every girl? If not, then she should. The ones I'd met were worthy of their own file each.

"Are you nearly ready?" J'avet tossed me my hairbrush while I stood.

I managed to catch it and drag it through my crazy curls. I could use a trim. Sometimes I envied the guys their short, military haircuts. I could do that too, but I doubted I would rock the look. I wasn't sure I rocked this look either, but it was the only look I had.

Half way through brushing, I caught J'avet staring at me, a slight frown on his face.

"What?" I asked. "Do I have cum on my face?"

He looked surprised, then actually smiled. "No. I was thinking how strange it is that humans have so much hair on their heads and so little on their bodies."

Hmmm, what do you know, I wasn't the only one thinking about weird alien attributes.

I shrugged. "And I'm pink." If I was covered in the same light hair he was, I might be brown, like a bear. As cute as that sounded, I think I'll stick to peach-coloured.

"More pink in some places than others," he said, looking toward my breasts.

I blushed then and tried to focus on untangling the last of my curls.

"If I didn't know better," I said, brushing furiously, "I would think you're flirting with me."

"Parvorans don't flirt," he scoffed. "We state what we want to say. Your nipples are pink. And you'll be late if you don't hurry." He turned toward the door.

"Parvorans could use some manners," I said. "The polite thing to do would be to wait a moment until I'm ready."

He turned back, his frown deeper. "What would that achieve? We would both be late."

"Yes, but we'd arrive together," I said.

"I see no benefit in us *both* arriving late." He seemed genuinely confused.

"It's not about us arriving late, it's about you being a

gentleman and waiting." I tossed the brush on the bed and crossed my arms.

"Gentle man," he said slowly. "I can be gentle, but you seemed to like it—"

I shook my head. "That's not—" I exhaled in frustration. "It doesn't matter, I'm ready now anyway. Let's go."

With obvious relief on his face, he opened the door. When they said men and women were from different planets, they hadn't meant it literally, but they might as well have. Since we actually did, it made the differences between us greater and more confusing.

I put it out of my mind and followed him down the corridor to the small meeting room. Brinley and E'rel were already there. The moment I stepped inside, Brinley handed me coffee and a slice of toast.

"You are my hero," I told her.

E'rel and J'avet exchanged glances.

"Humans like it when you bring them food," J'avet explained.

"Ah." E'rel flopped into a chair with no indication he was moved by the valuable piece of information he'd been given. He now had the key to moving past fights with Brinley, but he didn't seem to realise it.

"Especially chocolate," I said around a mouthful of toast. "And coffee or tea."

"Or alcohol," Brinley said.

"Or that," I agreed. "It all helps."

"But not too much food," J'avet said. "Human women are often watching their weight."

"Yes we are, but you never, ever get to comment on it." I

narrowed my eyes at J'avet. He had done that once and was lucky I hadn't grabbed a stick and poked him in the eye for it.

"You humans are strange," E'rel said.

"That we are," Marshall said as she stepped into the room. "But we make up for it by being awesome. Now, we're approaching Iritauri space."

The sudden change in subject almost gave me whiplash. I slipped into a chair and sipped my coffee.

"I've spoken to the admiral about whether or not you'll be allowed to proceed in the pod." Marshall leaned against the doorway and regarded us all in a way that suggested she held all the cards and she knew it.

"What was the admiral's conclusion?" J'avet said, effectively reminding us all that the admiral held the whole pack. Marshall was a subordinate, just like the rest of us.

If the reminder annoyed her, she gave no sign outside the twitch of one side of her mouth.

"In spite of my better judgement, the admiral is letting you go," Marshall said. "However, *Gamma* will remain at a discreet distance behind the pod and engage any enemies. The mission remains the same. Stealth. During your time on board, Engineer E'rel has worked with my team to produce more devices such as the one which freed our four former-host guests. My chief engineer reports that she'd like more time to work on them, but we no longer have the luxury of time. We will move forward with what we have."

She rolled her shoulders for a moment. "Because the time on board *Gamma* has minimised the pod's fuel use, I'm able to assign four security officers to accompany you. They will operate under the orders of Commander J'avet." She eyed him. "Don't get them killed."

J'avet's mouth was set in a line. "My intention is never to get anyone killed."

"Yeah. Shit happens," Marshall said. "With four more trained, armed personnel, maybe we can minimise the shit and get the job done."

She turned her eyes on me and I had the idea she was about to say something I didn't like.

"I don't feel comfortable sending a civilian into what might end up as a conflict situation."

"I'd be lying if I said I felt comfortable going," I said. "But I'm still going. I've dealt with Iri before. And former Iri." I lifted my chin. I would stow away if I had to, but I wasn't being left out. My guys were out there and I wouldn't rest until I got them back.

"That's why the admiral is letting you go," Marshall said. "I suggested you would find a way to get back on board that pod."

"Damn right I would," I said. "When do we leave?"

"Within the hour," Marshall replied. "The engineers are finishing up some modifications to the pod, and making sure it's fully stocked with everything you need. Engineer E'rel, I'm sure you'll want to oversee the work." She jerked her head toward the door.

"Yes, I would." He hurried out without a backward glance.

Maybe Parvorans weren't assholes, they just hadn't learnt any manners. I've never been the kind of girl who tries to change a guy, so I guess I would have to get used to it. Who knows, they might pick up a thing or two in time.

"Pilot Brinley, you'll see the controls are now equipped with a tracker. We want to know the pod's whereabouts at all times." Marshall fixed her gaze on Brinley, who nodded.

"However," Marshall continued, "the tracker goes both ways, and has longer reach than the pod's existing sensors. You'll know the location of *Gamma* at all times, as well as any other ships, IF or otherwise, even at a few hundred kilometres distance. You can also shout for help and be heard sooner."

I sat back in my chair and asked, "If we ask for help, will any ship hear it?"

Marshall looked at me as though I asked a really good question. "Yes," she replied. "If you only want to speak to *Gamma*, you'll need to use the pod's usual comms. If you use the tracker, the Iri will hear it, too. We don't have time to modify it further."

"It will do," J'avet said.

"It will have to." Marshall straightened up. "We've done what we could while you were our visitors, but after this, you're on your own. I wish you luck on this mission. I'm sure you know how important it is."

"The future of the galaxy rests on our success," J'avet said.

No pressure.

My heart raced and my palms sweated like crazy. This was so much more than a rescue mission to save the guys. If we failed, the galaxy might well be fucked. Overrun by nanobots bent on domination.

Yep, we only had one option here, as I saw it. Don't fail. Absolutely no pressure at all, no way.

Shit.

THE SECURITY OFFICERS were waiting when we reached the pod. Three were Agusian and the fourth was a Garvian.

One Agusian, a tall guy who reminded me a lot of Zarex, stepped forward.

"I am Rayax. This is Tarvun and Navor." He gestured toward the other two Agusians. "And Hamit."

The Garvian nodded. The movement made his tentacles flip and flop.

Another time, I might have laughed, but my sense of humour seemed to have taken a hike somewhere. Maybe it was the collection of long faces around me. Everyone looked anxious, but determined.

"Edie, Brinley, J'avet," J'avet said. "E'rel should be inside the pod. We all should."

If Rayax was bothered by J'avet's brusque tone, he didn't show it. He simply saluted and waved for us to precede him inside.

J'avet barely acknowledged him, just walked past and into the pod, followed by Brinley.

I gave Rayax a shrug and he responded with a wink. Yep, he reminded me even more of Zarex. Before I could say a word, he spoke softly, "Zarex is my brother. I managed to work it so I could come too. I want him back as much as anyone."

Once I got past my surprise, I smiled and patted his arm. "We'll find him," I promised. "He's probably given them so much trouble by now, they'll be glad to hand him back to us." Hopefully not so much trouble they killed him. No, I wouldn't think about that. I couldn't. Just the idea hurt my heart too much.

Rayan responded with a wry smile. "That sounds like him." His expression faded into one of concern that mirrored my feelings exactly. Zarex has that effect on people, obviously. He's easy to care about.

Rayax stepped away so I could board.

"He's cute," Brinley said as I swung my bag onto an empty bunk.

"You don't think I have my hands full enough?" I asked.

She smiled. "Knowing you, you'd handle one more. Or several." Other women might be jealous, but she was happy for me.

"Maybe you should continue your own collection," I suggested. "That would keep E'rel on his toes."

She glanced speculatively toward Rayax. "Maybe I will," she said thoughtfully. "In the meantime, I better get this pod underway before the captain changes her mind about letting us go."

"I think at this point, if she does that, J'avet will tell you to fly through the pod bay doors." I knew full well that would only result in the destruction of the pod, but I was done being told we can't do this or that. I just wanted to be on our way.

Brinley smiled and hurried to the cockpit, where J'avet already sat. He seemed to be looking over the controls, possibly trying to locate the tracker.

I leaned down so my mouth was near his ear.

"Are you going to disable it?" I asked.

"Why would I do that?" he asked over his shoulder.

"Because if *Gamma* can track us, who else can?" I asked.

He twisted around and gaped at me. Without responding, he jumped up and stalked toward E'rel. He crouched beside the other Parvoran and they spoke in low, sharp tones. Whatever they were saying, J'avet wasn't happy.

After a minute or two, he rose and stalked back to the cockpit. He slipped back into a seat and sat with a straight back. "E'rel doesn't know, but he said it's possible for the Iri to pick up our signal if they know to look."

"They're Iritauri," I said, "they'll *know* to look."

"Yes," J'avet said simply. "There's nothing we can do right now. Let's get off this ship. Find a seat and get strapped in."

"Right." I moved to the passenger section and sat in the first row. I felt a bit like the goodie-goodie at school, but I was as close to J'avet and Brinley as I could be without sitting on their laps. As tempting as it might be to sit on J'avet's, it wasn't safe. Especially if we actually had to punch our way out the door.

"What makes a human hunt Iri hosts?" Tarvun sat down beside me and clicked his harness into place.

"Same as you, I would think," I said. "The desire to free all those Freytaurians from their evil clutches."

"Do you really think they are evil?" he asked.

I paused. "The hosts themselves?" I asked slowly. "No. Whoever is behind them, yes. I mean, you'd have to be evil to plot galactic domination, wouldn't you?"

"I suppose you would," he agreed. "Unless you thought the galaxy was better off as hosts."

"Do you?" I asked. This was a strange conversation, for sure.

"Certainly not," he replied. "Freedom is something all species should have."

"Tarvun fancies himself as a philosopher." Rayax sat behind Tarvun and gave him a fond smile.

"He thinks too much." Navor took a seat beside Rayax.

"Maybe you don't think enough," Tarvun suggested.

Navor scratched his antenna. "It doesn't pay to think too much," he said. "Thinking is overrated."

"How would you know?" Tarvun asked, clearly teasing.

"I've seen you do it for the last year and it hasn't made you happy yet," Navor said.

"Excuse them." Hamit sat on the other side of me. "They're always like this. Captain Marshall should probably break them up, but she hasn't done it yet. Probably because they would complain and drive her to distraction."

"Navor would complain," Tarvun said. "He would miss me too much."

"Says you," Navor said.

I couldn't help but smile at them, especially the glances between Rayax and Tarvun. They obviously had something going on. I couldn't complain about anyone else mixing business with pleasure. I suspected if Brinley started anything with Rayax, Tarvun would come too, as part of the deal. Who ever said we led simple lives? Our love lives were as messy as my hair, as J'avet would say.

The pod engines thrummed and we lifted off the deck.

"Navor might need to know where the vomit bags are," Tarvun remarked.

When I looked at them in alarm, they all grinned.

"Don't scare the poor girl like that," Hamit scolded. "It was only one time he was sick while on a pod."

"Yes," Navor agreed. "I ate too many of those things you humans love. Tacos?"

"Oh." I smiled. "Yeah, they are addictive, aren't they? I mean, not literally." Although…

"Those and nachos. Humans know how to make food," Navor said appreciatively.

"I'm glad we're able to make some kind of contribution to the galaxy," I said. No, really, I was worried all we'd ever bring to the IF were pink nipples and drinking beer out of a shoe. Both of those are amazing, obviously, but nothing in comparison to space travel and the show *Centauri Shores*. Yeah, TV shows are still trashy, but they all go well with popcorn and a few glasses of alcohol.

"I'm sure humans have done a lot to advance the IF," Rayax said. "Like…"

I waited.

He looked apologetic and shrugged. "Humans are cute?" he finally offered.

"No argument from me," I said. What else could I say? He wasn't wrong there.

I looked toward the cockpit window to see we'd already left

the pod bay and were almost clear of *Gamma*. A few moments later, we slipped smoothly out into space.

"Set the course," J'avet said.

"Setting course out of IF space," Brinley confirmed.

I could tell by the set of their backs, they were both anticipating something more than just leaving *Gamma* behind us. Were they waiting for a chance to disengage the tracker? We might be safer without it, but we'd also be that much more alone out here.

In spite of stealth being the idea, I would have loved to have an army behind me. Or in front of me. Around me would work too; I wasn't fussy. Without some sort of help, we might disappear into the dark, never to be seen again. That would suck.

"So, tell us about these Iri," Rayax said. "From what I gather, they can only assimilate Freytauri. What would they want with my brother?"

His companions obviously knew the details, because none looked surprised.

I told them what I knew, from the first meeting with the Iri on Calig, to the last on *Halcyon*.

"They're trying to alter their programming so they can use all the species as hosts, not just Freytauri," I said finally. "Which is one reason we're trying to deal with them quickly. If we're lucky, we can get to them before they crack the puzzle. If not, we're boned."

Hamit blinked at me a couple of times. "Boned?"

"Yeah. Fucked. Screwed." Danec was right, we did have a lot of words for sex. "In big, big trouble."

"Oh." Hamit got that at last. "How interesting your language is. We would indeed be... boned."

"Let's make sure that doesn't happen," Rayax said firmly.

"Sounds good to me." In the corner of my eye, I watched E'rel move toward the cockpit. I think he believed he was being subtle, but he moved like he had a big sign over his head saying 'I'm up to something.'

Five pairs of eyes followed him. He sat in the seat beside J'avet and pressed a bunch of buttons.

Apparently unable to contain his suspicion, Rayax undid his harness and stood. "I don't think you should touch—"

"Commander J'avet." Marshall's voice came over the comms. "Are you aware the tracker is no longer transmitting?"

"It seems to have failed," J'avet said unapologetically. "I'll have my engineer look into it. I'm sure he'll have it fixed in no time."

E'rel pulled a device off the side of the controls and held it in his palm. "I'll do my best," he said, his expression deadpan.

Brinley's face was pink with the effort not to laugh.

I had no such problem. The tracker might get us killed. That was a good reason to crack open a window and throw it out. Figuratively, of course, because doing that literally would kill us all.

"You said it yourself, we needed more time to get the tracker working correctly," J'avet said. "We'll have to take that time now."

Marshall didn't sound convinced when she replied with, "All right. Keep me informed."

"Yes, Captain." J'avet killed the comms connection. "Toss that thing in a box and leave it there. We have more important things to work on."

E'rel nodded and returned to his corner, muttering something about wastes of good materials, under his breath.

"Care to explain?" Rayax asked J'avet.

"Not really," J'avet replied. "Apart from the tracker being a danger to us. Are you really here to help?"

Rayax bristled. "Zarex is my brother, he—"

J'avet rolled his eyes. "That explains it."

"J'avet and Zarex have a clash of personalities," I explained.

"Zarex can be..." Rayax searched for the words.

"Yes, he can," J'avet said. "If you're here to help us, then can you explain why anyone would install a device on this pod which might lead the Iritauri directly to us?"

Rayax rolled back onto his heels. "I have no idea. Perhaps it was done in error? Or simply wasn't thought through."

"If you're trying to save the galaxy from a grave threat, then you think *everything* through, right to the end," J'avet said coldly. "To. The. End."

Rayax slumped against the wall. "You're right."

"What can you tell us about the engineer on *Gamma?*" I asked. "They didn't have silver skin, did they?"

"No. She's human, like the captain," Rayax said.

"I hate to say this," I said slowly, "but I don't suppose it's possible someone wants everyone to become hosts, knowing humans can't?" It wouldn't be the first time humans tried to take advantage of a situation so they could take over a country, a city, whatever.

"There's no guarantee humans can't," J'avet said. "Whatever is going on, we'll have to watch our backs. Literally and figuratively." J'avet gave us all a look like he couldn't trust any of us.

After the last few days, that stung. I would have told him to fuck off if we were alone.

"In the meantime, E'rel can analyse the tracker and see if it's programmed to send information to anyone in particular." J'avet turned away and I slouched in my seat.

I wanted to trust all of them, but right now I wasn't sure if I could trust myself. That was the worst part of all. I was on a pod full of people I liked, but I never felt so alone.

13

"WE'RE PASSING out of IF space," Brinley declared a day or so after we left *Gamma*. "No sign of Iri ships. Or anyone else in front of us. *Gamma* is still on course behind us."

"This has gone very smoothly so far," Rayax remarked.

"I'm as worried about that as you are," I said. I expected to be attacked hours ago, or at least see signs of Iri activity. Ships, pods, debris, floating clouds of nanobots—something.

"The fact nothing has happened may be an indication of something happening," Hamit said.

When I looked at him questioningly, he explained, "They may be avoiding us. Or letting us go in deeper before they act."

"You think they know we're here?" I asked. That wasn't a cheery thought. Not at all. It made me damp under the armpits.

"Possibly," he replied. "Possibly not. Those are merely two theories ."

"Hamit is the most popular member of the team for a reason," Tarvun said. "He's always so positive."

"I'm being realistic," Hamit retorted. "There's no point in pretending we're on a journey to find a pleasant place to eat our midday meal."

"Right, this is no picnic," I agreed. "For one thing, there are no tacos. Are there tacos on Agus?"

"They were one of the first Earth foods to be imported there, yes," Rayax said. He sounded jovial, but his antennas drooped slightly. The worry in his eyes added to the picture. He looked at me and smiled, his antennas suddenly fully erect, but I already saw past his tough guy facade.

"I'm worried about him too," I said softly.

The side of his mouth twitched. "Zarex can take care of himself."

"We all can," I said. "But that doesn't mean we don't need help from time to time."

Honestly, I was scared that if they couldn't use Zarex as a host, they would kill him. They might already have. I could hardly bear the thought.

"That's true," Rayax admitted. "Even I need help sometimes. That's why these jokers are here." He jerked an antenna toward Tarvun and the others.

"We could always, you know, not help," Tarvun said. He crossed his arms and propped his boots on the chair beside him. "It's pretty comfortable here. I might take a nap. Wake me when this is all over." He closed his eyes and smiled, until Navor poked him hard in the ribs with his finger.

"You're in this with us," Navor said.

Tarvun lowered his arms and opened his eyes. "Fine. You'd all get killed without me anyway."

I could easily imagine Zarex and Slek bantering in the same

way. So much so it made me want to cry. I held it back and slipped out of my seat. I wandered the few steps down to the back of the pod, to E'rel's corner.

"How are things?" I asked, for lack of anything else to say.

He looked up at me and scowled. "Did you need something?"

I opened and closed my mouth a couple of times. "I just want to know whether or not whatever you're working on is going to help us."

For a moment, he looked outraged. Then his expression softened slightly. "Brinley told me humans need assurance. You don't simply believe what you're told."

"That's true," I said. "I'm sure the same can be said for any species. Do Parvorans accept every word anyone says?"

"We accept very few words anyone says," he replied. "We are taught to act, rather than wait to react."

"That sounds about right." I sat beside him and crossed my legs. "Do you need some help?"

Again, he looked outraged, then stepped himself back from it. "You could hold this while I attach that." He handed me a tube.

I held the tube while he screwed a mechanism of some kind to the end of it. He could have done it himself, but only with difficulty. It was a job for three or more hands.

"Thank you." He took back the tube and handed me another one.

"How many of these do you have?" I asked.

"Eight." He started to attach a second mechanism to the tube.

"And how long have you been trying to do this by yourself?" I eyed him over the tube.

"An hour," he said.

"Wow, I thought humans hated to ask for help." I handed him back the tube and reached for another.

"Parvorans are proud people." He sat back and exhaled through his nose.

"I've noticed that," I said without any condemnation. There was nothing wrong with being proud, even if you did waste an hour trying to do a difficult task. "Five to go."

He nodded. "Brinley also said humans often state the obvious."

I grinned. "Did you just tease me?"

"Of course not," he said. "I was just…"

"Stating the obvious?" I suggested. "It's okay to tease a little bit. It means you care." As long it wasn't nasty or intentionally hurtful. It was a fine line between teasing and bullying and some people could never tell the difference.

He looked confused at that, but got to work on the last few devices.

"What are these anyway?" I asked. "More anti-bot devices?"

"In a manner of speaking," he said. "They're to isolate the nanobots from the whole…hive. Technically they aren't a hive, because they're not alive."

I waved a hand. "I understand. It's as good a word as any. What happens then?"

"I don't know. The nanobots might leave the host. They may operate on their own. My goal is to find options, because we may need them." He looked troubled by that.

"Slek would have… would do the same thing," I said. At least, I *thought* he would. He always seemed to have a knack for producing useful devices, or messing with existing ones to make them do cool things.

"Yes." E'rel placed each of the finished mechanisms in a line with a gap between them. In the middle of each, he placed the anti-bot devices J'avet and he used on the last pod. Eight of each. "Two devices per person."

"Do you want me to hand them out?" I asked.

Before he could answer, Brinley said, "We're approaching Tarathu. There are several ships in orbit."

"Yes, do that now." E'rel took two and left me to divide the rest between the members of our team.

More than one looked doubtful that the new device would be helpful, but they added them to their holsters along with their blasters.

I just pushed one into each pocket.

"*Gamma* is increasing speed," Brinley said. "At this rate, she'll overtake us in approximately twenty minutes."

"Let her," J'avet said. "She'll make it easier for us to hide. Set a course for the far side of Tarathu. We are a pod of Iritauri, exactly where we are supposed to be, doing what we were told. The vidscreen was damaged. If they give us orders, we follow them."

"Unless they try to get them directly into our brains," I said.

"That can't be helped. We'll have to pretend." J'avet sat back and tried to look calm, but by now I knew him too well for that. He was as anxious as the rest of us.

"*Gamma* is two minutes out," Brinley said. "One of the Iri ships is moving to intercept."

"Us or *Gamma*?" I asked.

"I'm not sure," Brinley said. "It might be us. One minute until she catches up. Wait, brace yourselves!"

A shaft of light blossomed in the back window of the pod,

heading right for us. Just when I thought it would hit, it shot over the top of us, so close I had to throw my hand over my eyes to keep from being blinded.

The laser passed over us and disappeared.

"Plot a course to evade further shots," J'avet said.

"Okay, but the Iri ship is now headed straight for *Gamma,*" Brinley said. "They must have decided we're friendly, because their enemy tried to hit us."

"Let's take advantage of it. Head for Tarathu. Send a message that we are damaged and need to land immediately." J'avet's mouth was set in a line. *Gamma* gave us an opportunity, but she'd brought herself under fire to do it.

I couldn't look. I didn't want to think about all those people who might die so we could succeed.

"Message sent," Brinley said. "The reply is coordinates."

"Follow them," J'avet said.

"Following," she confirmed.

A flash of light drew my attention to the rear window, followed by debris blasted in every direction.

I couldn't tell if it was *Gamma* or another ship that was completely destroyed.

"Focus," J'avet said.

I wasn't sure if he was talking to me, himself or the others. Maybe all of us.

"Approximate time to landing?"

"Twelve and a half minutes," Brinley said, her voice tight. "Twelve."

We passed through the planet's atmosphere with a shudder.

"*Gamma* singed the top of the pod," Brinley said. "Any closer and passing into the atmosphere would have caused the pod to break up. That would have sucked."

"It's a long way down," I agreed. The planet drew closer. It looked blue and green like Earth or Calig. If you'd told me it was either, I wouldn't argue.

"Just a bit," Brinley agreed.

"Prepare to veer off course for an emergency landing," J'avet said. "Everyone get strapped in and brace yourselves."

"I'm not finding a nice, flat field," Brinley said. "This is going to get bumpy." She pressed a button and an alarm started to sound.

I hurried to sit and whipped my harness into place.

"Impact in five. Four. Three. Two."

We hit the ground so hard I was jolted forward, almost hitting my head on the seat in front. I felt as though my neck would snap, but the harness held the rest of me in place.

Outside the window, the world was a blur of green and brown.

Under the pod, trees groaned and snapped, scraping along the hull like nails.

I gritted my teeth and hung on. I liked a good roller coaster, but not like this. This felt like we'd slam into something solid at any moment and be crushed like an aluminium can.

Finally, we started to slow, before coming to a stop in the middle of a stand of trees.

"Everyone get your belongings and get off the pod." J'avet was already out of his seat, while I was still dazed.

"Edie, move!" he snapped.

I blinked. "Right." I caught his expression as I undid my harness. He still thought I should have stayed back, out of the way, but this time there was something more. Genuine concern for my safety. I wasn't just a pest. I was a pest he cared about. That was a step up.

I think.

I didn't waste time pondering the question, just grabbed my bag and followed the others out into the jungle.

"We're approximately fifty kilometres from the nearest settlement," J'avet said. "We'll need to walk there, as quickly as possible. If they think we're Iri, they may come looking. If they know we aren't, they *will* come looking. We need to be gone from here before they do."

I scanned the skies above the trees but saw nothing yet.

"J'avet, did I see a river before we stopped?" I asked.

He frowned. "I believe so. Why?"

"We could attach the tracker to a log and float it down-stream," I suggested. "If they can detect it, they'll follow that and give us more time."

He grinned. Actually *grinned*. "Rayax, get the tracker from inside the pod. Carry it until we reach the river. We'll send them on a wild boar chase."

Wild boar? I remembered Slek mentioning something about taking Danec to hunt Parvoran boar. My heart skipped to think they might be on the same planet. If they were, I would find them. We had made it this far more or less uninjured, we could make it the rest of the way.

I hefted my bag onto my back and followed J'avet into the forest.

14

—————

I watched with satisfaction as the log disappeared around a bend, the tracker tied to the top with a shoelace. Technically a bootlace, but the result was the same.

I gave it a finger wave. "Bye bye. I hope you draw all the Iri to you."

J'avet watched me, but he seemed amused for once. "It should slow them down," he said. "We still need to hurry."

Without another word, he stepped back into the cover of the trees. We all followed close behind.

As fun as sending out a decoy was, I felt vulnerable out from under the cover of the canopy.

Every so often, we heard the sound of distant engines and stopped cold. If they got any closer, only the trees would hide our location.

"We'll get as close as we can, then rest for a few hours," J'avet said. He looked frustrated. "The forest will slow us down, but it's safer."

"Haven't we done this before?" I asked, trying to keep my tone light. On Calig, we'd had Slek and Danec with us. And Humar, who complained all the way. We also hadn't known what we were up against. If I had, I might have run the other way.

"Let's not make a habit of it," J'avet growled. "All this nature. Give me a ship any day."

I smiled. "Really? I had you pegged as the outdoorsy type." Not.

"I prefer my outdoors on a plate," he replied. "Even then, the synthetic version is better."

I made a gagging sound. "Let me guess, you've never had real cheese?" Synthcheese was barely edible, but better than nothing. Just.

"No, should I?" He looked slightly disgusted at the idea.

"Absolutely. When this is over, I'm finding us some real food. Even if I have to take you all to Earth to get it. And before you say it," I held up a hand, "I'm not staying there."

He stepped over a log and scowled as his boots sank into mud on the other side. "If it's anything like this, I see why you prefer to be on ships."

"I don't prefer ships," I said. "I prefer cities. Cities don't tend to get torpedoed into oblivion."

I looked skyward, remembering the ship that was destroyed as we entered the atmosphere. The blueish expanse couldn't tell me if it was the *Gamma*, or an Iritauri ship which was now space junk. Neither option was a great scenario. The Iri themselves were mostly innocent. Presumably some chose the life of a host, but I suspected those weren't many.

"Cities are less muddy," J'avet agreed. He pulled his boot free and found some solid ground to put it back down.

"Do you hear that?" Brinley asked. She stopped behind us. E'rel and Rayax, who walked on either side of her, froze.

I cocked my head and listened. "Sounds like another engine," I said finally.

"Heading in this direction," Navor said from the back of the pack.

"Everyone down," J'avet ordered.

I ducked to a crouch beside him and pressed myself against the trunk of a tree. Our dark clothing and packs would make us harder to see from above.

At least in theory.

The vessel drew closer. It sounded small, like a pod.

I wondered about those on board. Specifically, were any of my guys on there? It was possible, as far as I knew. They might be up there, looking, searching, ready to kill.

Okay, I could be wrong, but I'm pretty sure they would all be pissed off if they found out later they killed me. And Brinley. And the others. And, well, *anyone*.

I squeezed my eyes shut, as though somehow that would stop the pod from seeing me. To my surprise, I felt a warm hand slip into mine. I opened my eyes to see J'avet's face right in front of me.

Anyone else might have given me reassuring words, but he simply locked his eyes on mine and stayed perfectly still.

I supposed that was his way of offering reassurance. I took what I could get.

The pod almost soared right over our heads, but it stopped short at the river. It turned and moved slowly away, presumably following the course of the river's flow.

A buzz was followed by a loud explosion and what sounded like a gush of water.

"I guess they found the tracker," I whispered.

J'avet responded with a barely perceptible nod. "Yes, I think so." He seemed disappointed. Presumably he'd wanted the Iri distracted for much longer than they were. That would have been good, but it couldn't be helped.

We waited while the pod passed over the trees a few more times, back and forth in a pattern that suggested they were searching for something. Or someone. Okay, us.

Gradually, they moved away, before they set down roughly where our pod crash landed.

"When they don't find bodies, they might come looking," J'avet said. "We need to move." He let go of my hand and led the way further in the forest.

The pace was faster now, but nothing I couldn't keep up with, since the forest itself slowed us down. I would have been happy with that any other time. Today, though, I would rather push myself than get caught out here.

"We're lucky this forest is damp," Rayax remarked.

J'avet cast him a look over his shoulder.

"If it wasn't," Rayax continued, "any explosions might set it on fire."

"That's a good point," Brinley said. "I don't fancy running from a forest fire."

"Me either," I agreed.

"Quiet," J'avet hissed. "We don't know how far their sensors can reach and what sound they might detect."

Anything he might have said was drowned out by the sound of an explosion behind us.

"There goes the pod," Tarvun said.

"It was never going to fly again anyway," Brinley said with a long sigh.

"Do we have an escape plan?" I asked.

"We'll find one, now be quiet," J'avet snapped.

That didn't fill me with much confidence, but I'd have to roll with it, like I had with everything else so far.

"We should split up," Rayax said. "Half of us can lead any Iri in the wrong direction. The others can keep going."

J'avet stopped and nodded. "Rayax, Edie and Tarvun, you're with me. Brinley, you'll need to find us another ship. E'rel, you'll need to make sure it works. Navor and Hamit, keep them safe."

He all but cut off the last word and turned around to continue walking. I barely had time to give Brinley a hug before I hurried after him.

"I'm surprised you didn't send me with them," I said.

"I'm not letting you out of my sight," he said without glancing back. "You'll get yourself killed."

"I think we both know by now that isn't true," I retorted. "For example, I'm still alive." I waited, in case I'd jinxed myself, then nodded. "See?"

"For now," he replied. He stopped mid-step and turned his head slowly to one side, then the other.

I heard it too, a moment later.

A pod headed in our direction. No, I corrected myself, not quite in our direction. Close enough to make the hairs on the back of my neck stand up, but not to suggest they knew where we were, or even that we were on the planet. With any luck, they assumed they killed us when they destroyed the pod, and were heading home for an afternoon snack.

Slowly, the Iri pod circled the area. At one point, it almost passed overhead. We dropped to a crouch and waited for it to move away.

Not going for a snack then.

My heart hammered like crazy. By the time it was out of sight and hearing, I was ready to get up and run the rest of the way. I all but leapt over fallen logs and ducked under branches so fast, J'avet had to put out a hand to stop me.

"Slow down before you get yourself hurt."

"Sorry, I got a surge of adrenaline." I slowed up a bit. "I just want all of this behind us."

"We all do, but we still need to be careful." J'avet gave me that look again. The one that suggested he wasn't sure I should be here at all. Well, it was too late for that.

"The sun is starting to set," Rayax pointed out.

"Right." J'avet consulted his watch. "We're approximately two kilometres to the Iri base. This would be a good time to stop for a few hours. When it's full dark, we'll use our night visors to see our path."

He lowered his bag to the ground.

"Okay. I could use a nap." I lowered my bag beside his and sat on a patch of dry ground. I opened the neck of my bag and pulled out one of the IF's famous protein bars. When I say famous, I really mean infamous. The things tasted as good as they looked, and they looked like a piece of brick. The texture is almost as hard. Apparently they're the healthiest thing anyone in the galaxy can eat. Or almost eat. Personally, I'd kill for a burger about now.

I bit into my bar and chewed while I wondered how Brinley

was doing. I saw no indication from the Iri pod that they spotted them. That didn't mean they were safe though.

"I have a theory," Rayax said. He seemed to be enjoying his protein bar. I knew he must be flawed in some way.

"What's that?" Tarvun asked, when it became evident no one else was going to.

I had a mouthful, so I couldn't.

"I think the IF is heading here for a full blown attack on Tarathu."

I cocked my head at him sharply, but J'avet didn't look surprised.

"They think we'll fail?" I asked. That was...rude.

"I think they're hedging their bets," Rayax said. "If we succeed, they help mop up after us. If we don't, then they destroy everything."

"But the Iritauri are IF citizens when they aren't hosts," I protested.

"The Iri are a threat to the galaxy," J'avet said, his voice low.

I swung my face toward him. "You knew about this?" If he did, I might shove the rest of my protein bar up his—

"No," he said firmly. "But I suspected. The tracker was to help lead them here, but also to lead the Iri to us. If we were destroyed before the IF could rescue us, then it wouldn't be much loss to the IF."

"I resent that," Tarvun said. "I would be a great loss."

"Me too," I agreed. "At least to myself."

J'avet's mouth twitched up slightly on one side. "I didn't say I agree with them. They would get the chance to attack the Iri and say they were provoked. After that, they could justify any attack on this planet."

"They still can, if *Gamma...*" My tongue darted over my lips and I couldn't finish the sentence. I sucked in a breath. "Surely the *Infinity* would be enough of an excuse. And *Halcyon.*"

"The IF is a bureaucracy," Rayax said. "It's anyone's guess why they do what they do. It means we need to work quickly, because they'll fire first and ask questions later."

"For the record, I would really object to becoming collateral damage," I said.

"We'll do all we can to ensure that doesn't happen," J'avet said.

I twisted my mouth sideways. "I suppose turning the tracker back on led the IF right here."

"It's likely, but it was a chance we had to take," J'avet said.

"*Gamma* would have told the IF," Rayax reasoned. "There's probably an armada a day or two away."

"I feel less than valued as a member of the IF," I said. "When this is over, I might have to have some words with the IF government." What sort of fuckers sent their people into what might be a trap, unconcerned about whether or not we live or die?

Oh, who was I kidding? Governments of Earth have done it since forever. The IF was no worse and no better. And, let's be real, they had the whole galaxy to think about. Eight of us were practically nothing, even if we were in my top eleven most amazing people in the galaxy.

"Get some rest," J'avet advised. "It's going to be a long night."

"Promises, promises," I said with a cheeky smile.

He smiled back and I saw in his eyes he'd rather be somewhere alone with me than out here.

Me too, buddy. Me too.

15

I ADJUSTED my visor for the tenth time in about three minutes. It didn't need adjusting, and fixing it made no difference whatsoever. It was just my nerves which made me restless, and my desire to get this over with before we were blasted to smithereens by friendly fire.

"Keep still," J'avet hissed, before he adjusted his visor. He'd done it at least as many times as I had.

I smirked, even though I knew he wouldn't see it. I would razz him about it later.

Now, I peered into the darkness and let the visor lock on the building down the slope from us. After a moment, the structure came into focus, showing me almost as much as I would see in daylight.

The best thing about the Iri was they needed sleep as much as the rest of us. That meant the building was quiet except a handful of guards who walked this way and that.

J'avet gestured to Rayax and Tarvun and waved for them to

head down to the left. He pointed to me and himself and waved to the right. He really *wasn't* going to let me out of his sight. He pulled out his anti-Iri device and nodded for us to do the same.

When he started down the slope at a slow, silent pace, I followed close behind. Not so close I would run into the back of him, but close enough.

He snuck behind a small stand of trees and we again took stock of the path ahead. Two guards stood near the corner of the building. Two stood at the opposite corner. Rayax and Tarvun would have to take care of the latter two. We would focus on the ones in front of us.

J'avet beckoned me forward and moved out again.

Barely a handful of steps from the guards, he started to trot, device in his raised hand. He pointed it right at the guard furthest from him and pressed the button on the side.

I did the same with the closer guard.

Almost in unison, they were struck down, frozen in place. Their nanobots poured out in a flood and lay deactivated at their feet.

We caught both guards and lowered them silently to the ground. I made sure mine was more or less okay, then glanced over to see that Rayax and Tarvun had done the same with theirs.

I let out a long, slow breath. This was far from over, but we'd taken that first step. We got this.

I hoped.

J'avet nodded toward the door which led into the building. At least, I think that's what happened. His visor jerked in that direction.

I fell in behind him and managed to contain a squeal of surprise when Rayax and Tarvun appeared behind me.

Heart in my throat, I followed J'avet toward the door. I was surprised to find it open. Then again, this was a planet of Iri who more or less shared the same mind. They had no reason to keep each other out.

We stepped into an empty room. A door at the back led into another.

"I'm starting to think this building is a decoy," Rayax whispered.

I pressed my lips together. I hoped it wasn't, because it might end up being a trap.

Mice caught in it—us.

"There's something here." J'avet covered the glow of his watch with his hand, then turned it off. "Through there." He pointed his device toward the rear door.

If you get us killed, I thought in his general direction, *I'm going to be pissed.*

We stepped through the doorway, into a room larger than the one we'd left.

J'avet was right, there was something here. Or rather, someone. Several of them. They lay on the same kind of beds the ships all had in their infirmaries.

Human, Centauri, Dendran and Agusian, they were all attached to tubes like an IV, which ended at a needle in their bare arms.

"Just a guess, they're trying to figure out how to make them hosts," Rayax said. He moved between the beds.

I murmured my agreement and did the same. I couldn't hold back a short, low cry at the sight of a familiar face lying on his back, eyes closed.

"Zarex," I breathed. I put a hand to his wrist. His pulse was strong and even.

I shook him gently, mindful that he might be injured.

He didn't stir. The tube must be keeping him unconscious.

I chewed my lips. It was also possible the tube was keeping him alive. If you could call this living.

Without stopping to think further, I slid the needle out of his arm and let it fall. It slapped against the side of the bed, loud against the deafening silence.

"Zarex," I whispered in his ear. "Wake up."

For approximately a century, nothing happened. Then, finally, he stirred.

"Edie?"

I clamped a hand over his mouth to keep him from talking too loud.

"Shhh," I urged. "We need to get you out of here."

He nodded that he understood. I removed my hand.

I hadn't noticed Rayax was beside me until he clasped hands with his brother and helped him to sit.

"It's 'bout time," Zarex said, sounding sleepy.

Rayax snorted. "We need to free the rest of them too."

I nodded and left them to do their male, brotherly reunion bonding thing and started to check everyone out before pulling their needles free as well. I had to take a moment to staunch the blood each time, but there was no point in freeing them only to have them bleed to death.

J'avet and Tarvun followed me around the room, helping to keep everyone quiet as they woke.

A room full of traumatised, possibly screaming, people would draw too much attention to us.

Fortunately, everyone seemed to understand the need for silence. Or they were too scared to make a sound. Honestly, I couldn't think about it too much right then.

I finished with the last needle and helped a Centauri woman to her feet.

"Rayax, you get them out of here and into the forest. The further away they can get, the better."

"I'm staying with you," Zarex whispered.

J'avet hesitated.

I was sure under his visor he was thinking of arguing. Finally he shrugged.

"Suit yourself, but if you're weak and get us killed—"

"I won't." Zarex sounded more alert by the moment. He even managed to smile at me before I gave him a quick hug.

"It's good to see you," I whispered.

"It's good to be seen," he said. "And not be a host."

"Bonus," I agreed. "You'll have to tell me all about it later."

J'avet interrupted our moment. "Did you see enough to know where to find whoever or whatever is behind this?" he asked bluntly.

"I have a vague idea," Zarex said. "There's a bunker underneath this building. I heard them talk about it before they put me under."

"That sounds ominous," I said.

Zarex smiled and bent to kiss my forehead, above my visor. "I'd give you more, but that will have to wait until your face isn't covered."

"I look forward to it," I said.

J'avet cleared his throat. "Worry about that later." He reached into his bag for a spare visor and handed it to Zarex. "We don't have weapons to spare, so you'll have to stay close."

"I can do that." Zarex took my hand and moved so our bodies were touching.

He was incredibly distracting.

I reminded myself to focus.

By now, Rayax herded everyone else out the door. With any luck, they'd make it into the forest without being seen.

"How do we get into this underground bunker?" J'avet asked.

"Back out the door and to the left," Zarex said.

We followed J'avet with Tarvun close on our heels. Sure enough, at the end of the first room in the building was a doorway. It was so far over, our visors hadn't seen it, showing us shadows instead.

Now I *could* see it, it gave me a strange chill. It wasn't just the air, it was the impenetrable darkness beyond the doorway. Even the visors made out only vague shapes.

"Just wondering, are you sure this isn't a trap?" Tarvun asked.

"I'm almost certain it is," J'avet said. "It's also the only way to go, unless you see another?"

"Can't say I have," Tarvun said.

"Right. Be on your guard," J'avet said to us all.

From the moment I laid eyes on Zarex, I wanted to ask him… I could hardly even think about it. I wasn't sure I could handle the answer, but I had to know.

"Have you seen Slek and Danec?" I held my breath.

"Not since I arrived," Zarex said softly. "And only Slek. I haven't seen Danec since we were all on *Halcyon*."

I nodded. I *had* to believe he was alive. Slek too. Until I knew otherwise, I refused to give up hope.

"Quiet," J'avet snapped.

I froze in place.

Someone was coming, but I couldn't tell from which direction.

J'avet waved us back toward the wall, deeper into the shadows.

I gripped my anti-bot device tight in my hand, ready to use it if I needed to. Honestly, it would be all too easy to aim it in no particular direction and fire. It wouldn't do any harm to anyone friendly, and any Iri I hit would be free.

Of course, there was always the possibility I would hit nothing and end up wasting the device's power. That would leave Zarex and I both more or less defenceless, unless you count our razor sharp wits. I suspected that may not help against Iri who wanted to kill us. I would prefer to die laughing than any other way, but not today.

Heavy footsteps drew closer.

My head swam and I realised I'd held my breath for too long. I let it out and drew in another, trying to make no sound while doing it.

Nothing suggested Iri had superhuman hearing, but fear does strange things to a person's logic. Even mine. Okay, especially mine.

A shout sounded from the room we'd rescued Zarex from and a light turned on in there.

"Oops," Zarex whispered in my ear. "I think they know I left."

I smiled. Same old Zarex. It was nice to see his sense of humour was intact.

"I think they want you back," I whispered. That was too damned bad. He was mine and I wasn't going to give him up without a fight.

Zarex squeezed my hand, confirming he was in full agreement. Good. I would hate to waste time arguing over something like that, especially here.

I looked toward J'avet and wished I could see his face. I had no idea what he was thinking. Did I ever? No, but particularly now, with his face covered.

Did we run or stay put? If we ran, which way would we go?

I heard him exhale.

"We'll head underground before they find us here," he said. He sounded so decisive it gave me hope that at least someone here knew what they were doing.

He started back toward the darkened doorway and disappeared from sight.

I gripped Zarex's hand hard and stepped after J'avet. If I was the praying kind, I might ask that we be near our goal. I had about all the excitement I could take for one night. Okay, one lifetime. When this was over, I was going to live the most boring life possible.

Yeah, right, as if the guys would let it be boring. I would settle for safe and calm, with short periods of bungee jumping, or something similar.

Once through the doorway, the visors detected a set of steps. I stopped before I fell down them and into...wherever they led.

The shouts from behind us got louder.

I glanced back. "I think we need to hurry."

"Forward," J'avet said. He took a couple of steps down and I started to follow.

Then the lights came on. They were so bright I cried out before I slammed my eyes shut and tore off my visor.

"Fucking hells," I growled. I forced my eyes back open, whirled around and blinked.

Four Iri stood looking in our direction, eyes glazed, silver skin shining in the light.

My heart leapt.

16

"Danec," I said breathlessly. Thank whatever forces or deities might exist, he was still alive.

I was slightly less delighted about the blaster he held in his hand.

"Walk down the stairs," he ordered.

Nothing in his expression suggested he had any clue who I was, or cared. I was an intruder, along with J'avet, Zarex and Tarvun. We would be dealt with.

"Do as he says," J'avet ordered.

I turned back around. Something in the Parvoran's eyes suggested he had a reason why we shouldn't fight back. I thought of one, off the top of my head. If we deactivated the nanobots from the Iri, four former hosts would fall down the stairs and take us with them.

Hard pass. Or hard fall. Either way, no thanks.

There was something more to it, though. As usual, J'avet gave away nothing more.

Pretending to be sulky, which wasn't difficult under the circumstances, I trudged along behind J'avet.

Every so often I glanced over my shoulder. I needed to reassure myself I wasn't seeing things. Danec was really alive. Not that I doubted it. No way. Okay, a bit. So much time had passed, it felt like another lifetime since I'd seen him last. I hoped with everything I had that he was still in there.

If he wasn't... A tear slid down my cheek, but only one. I didn't have time to break down right now. I would save that fun for later.

We reached the bottom of the stairs and stopped.

"Turn to the right," Danec ordered.

I watched J'avet for a sign we should do something.

His expression remained unchanged, he turned right.

What the fuck? He must have a plan. If he did, I hoped he'd let us in on it soon. I wasn't sure how much longer I could keep from using my anti-bot device on Danec.

We walked down a long corridor lit with a small bulb every few metres. It smelled of moisture and dank. I guess the Iri weren't too fussy about their underground bunkers.

"Well, isn't this fun?" Zarex said conversationally. "It's always nice to be around J'avet. Nothing ever goes wrong."

"It's a non-stop party," I said. I gave Zarex a look. J'avet was doing the best he could. Whatever he had in mind, would surely give us the best chance of getting out of this alive.

Right?

Zarex tilted his antennas at me as if he wasn't surprised I was defending J'avet now. I guess he saw something might happen between us, given half a chance.

"I wouldn't be anywhere else," Zarex said.

"Nor would I," J'avet said.

I frowned at the back of his head. There was a double meaning to his words. It wasn't too hard to figure it out. Let Danec show us the way. The way to where though? Hopefully not to a place they'd lock us in and throw away the key. Or simply kill us outright.

"This is definitely prime real estate," I said ironically. "It's like every baddie's underground bunker."

"How many baddie's bunkers have you been in?" Zarex asked.

"This is the first," I admitted. Hopefully the last. "You know I watch a lot of movies. Danec does too, right Danec?" I glanced back at him, but his eyes were still glazed. He gave no sign of having heard a word.

I was tempted to slap him, to see if he'd react, but I suspected he'd respond by shooting me. If he survived and was de-botted, he would have to live with that. I objected to not being around to help him through it.

"Through that doorway," Danec said. His words were redundant, because there was only one way to go.

Eyes on J'avet, I stepped through.

J'avet stopped.

My heart pounded. I waited for him to turn around and fire, but he didn't. He just... stood.

"J'avet?" I whispered.

I thought I caught the shake of his head, but I could have imagined it because I wanted to see something. *Anything.*

The room we stood in was cold and as dark as the rest. They really didn't do 'hospitable' here. I suppose it's true what they say; it's all about location, location, location.

"It could use a coat of paint and some comfy furniture," I remarked.

Danec was unmoved. At least he wasn't pissed off. Not that I could tell, anyway.

Yet.

"It is a little empty," Zarex agreed.

"Now you mention it, it is," Tarvun agreed. "Are we waiting for something?"

"Or someone?" Zarex added.

J'avet's mouth was set in a line. Was that it? He was waiting to see what might happen?

Honestly, I wasn't a fan of playing the wait and see game, but he was the one in charge. If he knew what he was doing, then I would go along with it. What choice did I have? Okay, a few, but I would still follow his lead for now.

Footsteps approached from the direction we'd come. The sound of booted feet on the stairs, moving closer. They reached the bottom of the stairs and started down the corridor.

My hands sweated. I gave J'avet a scared look, silently begging him to know what he was doing. If he didn't, we were fucked. We'd be dead before the IF attacked the planet. I didn't want to die in a hole in the ground. That would suck.

My heart sank when familiar faces appeared in the doorway and stepped through.

Brinley, E'rel, Hamit and Navor. They all looked tired, but in good spirits.

I frowned. Better spirits than they probably should be, considering they were prisoners of—

I gaped.

"Slek?" I send another thanks to the various deities of the

universe that he too was alive. His skin was silver, but he was alive.

Shit.

I guess it was only a matter of time before the Iri made him one of them. Only—

There was something about him that didn't seem quite the same as the rest of them.

His eyes.

He looked in my direction and I saw recognition in them.

My heart leapt. I almost took a step forward, but J'avet hissed, "Don't move."

I opened my mouth to argue, but the firmness in his eyes made me close it again and stop.

To Brinley, J'avet said, "You were supposed to find a way out of here."

She smiled ruefully. "We tried, but we got a bit sidetracked by this Iri guy. He insisted we come down here." She jerked her head toward Slek.

"Move over with the rest," Danec said.

Brinley looked at him sadly, but moved to do as she was told. She stepped over to stand beside me.

"What's going on?" I said out of the corner of my mouth.

"Same shit, different day," she replied, which told me nothing. "It's good to see you're all okay."

"Yeah, you too." I was getting more and more confused. I noticed Brinley kept her hand at her side, as if she held something in it.

"Yes, we're fine," she said. "I would say I missed you, but it's good to spend some time apart."

I blinked, slightly hurt by her words. Why was she saying this? It made no sense.

"I suppose that's true," I said slowly.

"Yes," she agreed. "Sometimes you just need to *disconnect*." Her eye twitched in the direction of her hand.

It took me a moment to realise what she was trying to say. When I did, my eyes widened.

"Yes," I said slowly. "Disconnecting is good. It's not healthy to be connected all the time."

"Right. Slek found that out too." Brinley nodded toward him.

"How long should we disconnect for?" J'avet asked.

"Hmmm." Brinley looked thoughtful. "I would say about three."

J'avet nodded. "Three it is." He tapped his heel on the ground once.

Twice.

Three times.

We pulled out the devices I had helped E'rel finish and pointed them at the Iri. I aimed mine squarely at Danec and pressed the button on the side.

He jerked.

His eyes closed, then shot open again. He looked bewildered, scared.

"Please lower your blaster," I said. I had no idea how he might respond. I might provoke him into killing me. I might—

He lowered his arm.

I let out a breath through my nose, then swallowed hard and tried to get my head around all of this. "He's still Iri," I said softly.

"Yes, but he's under your control," Brinley said. "He can go anywhere the rest can, but the hive can't tell him what to do."

I held back a sob. "How is this any better?" I asked. I wanted him and Slek to be free of the fucking bots, once and for all. "They still aren't themselves."

"We can think for ourselves," Slek said, his voice still robotic, but the words were his. "It was my idea not to get the bots out yet."

"Yeah." Navor cleared his throat. "I pulled the wrong device and disconnected him rather than de-botting. He suggested we wait."

"Okay." I drew the word out. My head swam with the implications. I stepped toward Danec and put a hand on his. "Danec? Are you in there?"

"I-I am." His stammer was the most Danec thing I ever heard and it made my throat choke up with emotion. "We need to... need to...need to."

"The nanobots make it hard to think," Slek said slowly and deliberately. "It's been longer for him."

That was true.

"Right." I exhaled.

"What do we need to do?" J'avet directed the question to all of the Iri. Or—whatever they were now. "We need to get to whoever or whatever is behind the nanobots."

Whatever? I thought. *Shit, Please don't let there be a giant computer at the centre of all of this.* That might be difficult to destroy.

Maybe it was a crazy person who hid behind a curtain, giving orders, like in *Wizard of Oz.*

"There is a place," Slek said. "Down."

"Deeper underground?" J'avet asked. "Show us."

Slek stood still.

"Show us," Navor said uncomfortably.

Slek turned away, toward the doorway.

"He only follows the orders of the person who used the device on him," Hamit said.

"I don't care," J'avet said. "As long as he leads us there. The rest of you, tell your Iri to follow, blasters in hand. We should look like prisoners."

We quickly did as he said, but I hated turning my back on Danec, even for a moment. I wanted to drink in the sight of him. His hair was longer, and his skin silver, but he was still one of the guys I loved. Slek too, but I could watch his ass as I walked. Dammit, I missed that ass.

"Did you find a way off this rock?" J'avet asked.

"Yes, we did," Brinley replied. "Slek showed us a ship we can take. It seems to be in working order."

Seems to be? Well, she would know. And Slek. I certainly wouldn't.

J'avet ran a hand over his head. I thought he might suggest Brinley and I leave, get to safety. I was ready to argue, but while his lips moved, no words came out. He must be thinking hard.

"These disconnectors can be used more than once," he said. "Navor, you have more than one connected to yours?"

"Yes," Navor replied. "At least, Slek's bots haven't regained control again."

Slek grinned. "Nope. They're pissed off about it too."

"Good," J'avet said, looking satisfied. "We may need to disconnect more."

"A lot more," I said. Wasn't that the point here? Disconnect, then free the hosts.

That reminded me of a conversation I had with Slek some time ago. "Slek, do you like being a host?"

He must have remembered the conversation, because he grimaced. "I consent to them being deactivated when the time comes. They can fuck right off."

I smiled. That was him all right, sass and all. "We'll be happy to oblige." Over my shoulder I said, "Danec, how about you?"

"I-I want them gone." His speech was strained. "When...when."

"When it's time to get rid of them?" I asked.

"Yes, when," he agreed. "We need to...to end them."

"We will," I promised. We would end every nanobot and free all the Freytauri to live their own lives again.

"We need to go that way," Slek said. He headed down the corridor to the left of the stairs, toward another set of stairs. "Time to go down."

I grinned. Same old flirty Slek, bots or no bots.

I took a deep breath and followed him down.

17

I want to say the deeper we went, the more inviting the place became. Maybe some pink paint here, a disco ball there. Heck, some mood music wouldn't have gone astray, either.

Instead, it was more of the same. Dark, dank and increasingly cold.

"It occurred to me," I said, halfway down a third flight of stairs. "An IF attack might not destroy this baddie bunker. We must be pretty far down."

Zarex, who managed to work his way through to walk beside me, said, "I was thinking the same thing. We would survive for a while before we ran out of air if they collapsed the entrance."

"Yeah, no thanks." I wrinkled my nose. "The Iri would die the same way."

"The nanobots might not though." He slipped his hand into mine and drew me closer to him.

"They might lie dormant for a thousand years until some

well meaning Freytauri archaeologist excavates them and it starts all over again." That wasn't a cheery thought. I felt bad for the fictional, far future folk.

"We'll do what we can to make sure that doesn't happen," he assured me. "Whatever we need to do, we'll make sure they're destroyed forever."

"I know," I said. "I just…this place is getting to me, I suppose. It's so miserable here. Give me some sunshine and a nice beach any day. Or a park. Or a view of the stars. I'm not picky."

I wasn't. Weren't dungeons located underground to add to people's despair? Okay, maybe not, they were probably placed there for convenience, but additional misery was likely the result.

"You could go back out." He gave me a quick, sideways glance.

"You're starting to sound like J'avet," I told him.

"My wisdom must be rubbing off," J'avet said from ahead of us. "It's about time."

Zarex chuckled softly. "I wouldn't say that. I just want to keep Edie safe."

J'avet glanced over his shoulder. "Me too," he said softly.

"Same with me," Slek said. He sounded tired. The strain of thinking with a head full of angry bots must be draining.

"M-me t-t-to." Danec's stammer was getting worse.

"Sounds like we're all in agreement," Zarex said.

"I'm still not going back," I said. "Especially not alone."

Slek stopped a few steps from the bottom of the stairs. "The bots are more excited. We're close."

My heart skipped. I admit it, part of me wanted to turn tail and run. Get off this rock and let the IF blast it all the smithereens. What was a smithereen anyway? I would have to look it up later.

We descended more slowly now and in silence. Or as near to silence as that many people could go.

We reached the bottom of the stairs and into a better lit section of the building.

Also a more heavily populated one.

We were immediately passed by a handful of Iri, none of which spared us more than a glance. Those that did kept moving at the sight of the blasters. Clearly they thought their fellow hosts had the situation well in hand.

I would have liked to free them all on the spot, but we couldn't risk doing that here. Not yet anyway.

Regretfully, I followed Slek toward a room so bright I had to half close my eyes to let them adjust.

When they did, I gaped.

At least twenty Iri moved around the room, all with the same robotic expression. Computer banks lined the walls, flashing with lights in every colour I could think of. It was as close to a disco ball as I had seen here. Turn off the overhead lights, crank up some tunes and you had the perfect underground club. Apart from the whole baddie den vibe.

I took all of that in, in a flash. Then I was distracted by the sight of several Freytauri hunched over screens.

Freytauri.

Not Iritauri.

Their skin ranged from Danec's blue to Slek's purple and every shade in between. Truthfully, they all looked paler, like the shades were washed out slightly. Spending too much time underground will do that to a person.

"We bring you prisoners," Slek said in a robotic voice. "They helped the specimens escape from the laboratory."

Beside me, Zarex stiffened.

I guess he objected to being called a specimen. Fair enough, it was a shitty term, for sure. It made those people sound like a piece of plant.

One of the Freytauri, a woman with long, dead straight hair, turned slowly to look at us. Her eyes, cold and dead, seemed to look right through me. I had the feeling she thought more highly of pieces of plant.

"You have done well," she said, her voice so monotone she might have been a nanobot herself. "You serve the Tauri Empire well."

Uh-o, that didn't sound good.

"Tauri Empire?" I asked. I didn't think she would answer. You know, me being lower than a plant and all.

She turned to me and blinked slowly. She had lashes so long I wanted to hate her just for that. Straight hair and perfect lashes, everything I never had. I bet her nails were perfectly manicured too, but my eyes never left her face.

"The Freytauri are weak," she said slowly. That was the first sentence she said which had any inflection at all. "Biological life is weak. Enhancing life with technology makes them strong. The Tauri Empire will show the way."

"So, you're trying to make everyone into cyborgs?" I said.

"All life will be better," she stated.

"That's a matter of opinion," I said under my breath. "Can I have a word with the Emperor? He seems to have the wrong idea." I had a suspicion, which she confirmed a moment later when she drew herself up and glared at me.

"There is no Emperor," she hissed. "I am Empress Yinika."

Whatever or whoever she claimed to be, she seemed unhinged to me.

"You will serve the Empire or you will die." The other Freytauri had turned from their screens and stood beside her now.

"Do they all agree with your vision?" I nodded toward the closest of them.

"If they do not, they will become hosts," Yinika stated.

More than one Freytauri licked their lips or shuffled their feet.

"Surely they want that?" J'avet asked, addressing them. "To be enhanced. To be better."

"They will achieve that," Yinika said.

"When you learn how to control the nanobots without them," J'avet guessed. "Or can control them separately."

"That's not so hard," Slek said with a grin. He stretched his arms out to either side.

Yinika looked at him in shock. Clearly she hadn't expected us to figure out how to separate hosts from the hive.

"How—"

The Freytauri around her looked terrified.

I might have felt sorry for them, but they were in this up to their eyeballs.

Instead, I smiled. "I guess you all get a dose of nanobots. Do you have any to spare?"

"I have a few I don't want," Slek said. He turned and looked right at me.

I took that as a cue. I raised my anti-bot device and hit the button. I expected Slek to freeze, and for the bots to flood out of him.

His eyes widened slightly, but then he grimaced and started to writhe.

"Mother of fuck," he said in clear discomfort. "That tickles."

I bit back a smile. I'd thought he was in pain, or dying, or something equally bad. Tickles sucked, but he could deal.

Yinika looked outraged at the sight of nanobots pouring out of Slek to lie on the ground at his feet.

He stepped back quickly. "There you go, they're all yours."

"Edie…" Danec's voice was a whisper.

I turned my device toward him. When he nodded, I pressed the button to finally free him from the vermin which invaded his body and held him prisoner for too long.

He twitched, but barely moved while his skin turned back to blue. His eyes watered and a couple of tears accompanied the bots on their way out.

Finally free, he sagged before Zarex caught him and helped him to stay on his feet.

"They will be reactivated," Yinika spluttered.

In one moment, Danec was leaning on Zarex. In the next, he'd leapt toward Yinika, blaster in hand, fury flashing in his eyes.

"Danec, no." I grabbed for him, he was too quick for me.

"If you kill her, you'll have to live with that," J'avet told him. "You'll be as bad as she is."

Danec stopped, blaster aimed square at Yinika's terrified face.

"Think carefully," she said coldly, having regained some of her composure. "You were better with those bots inside you. Faster, smarter, part of a hive. As a Freytauri, you were never a part of a community like the Iritauri are. The Empire nurtured you. Cared for you."

"Edie cares for me," Danec said, his voice almost as chilly as hers.

"I care for him too," Slek said. "But I don't boss him around."

"I boss him around, but I care as well," J'avet said.

I snorted a laugh.

"I haven't had much chance to boss him around, but he's a part of my community," Zarex said.

"Mine too," Brinley said. "And E'rel will when he gets to know him. Right E'rel?"

E'rel looked surprised, but he shrugged one shoulder, then nodded. "Yes, of course."

Danec smiled with one side of his mouth. "See, I don't need bots to belong."

I made a mental note to have that printed on a t-shirt, and stepped closer to Danec.

"You see how happy they are without the bots?" I said to Yinika.

"Happiness is irrelevant," she said. "Only productivity and strengthening the Empire matter."

"Said every dictator ever," I replied. "Happiness is *everything*. Without it, there's no point in living." To her co-conspirator Freytauri, I asked, "Do you want to be a mindless drone? Do you honestly think people are better off like that?"

"She … offered us power," a guy with blueish-purple skin replied slowly. "The galaxy at our feet."

"If you follow her, the galaxy is going to be at your door," I said. "Bashing it down to get in and stop you."

"An IF fleet is a couple of days away," J'avet said. "This is your last chance to surrender."

"Never," Yinika hissed. She twisted and lunged for a button on the console behind her. Before she could hit it, a flash from a blaster shot out toward her. It hit her in the centre of her chest. She let out a gurgling cry and sagged onto the console. With her fingertips, she made a last swipe at the button, but slid down the console and onto the floor.

There she lay, surrounded by nanobots.

Danec looked stunned.

For a moment, I thought he shot her. Then I saw a blaster in J'avet's hand and satisfaction on his face.

"Now *you* have to live with it," I said softly.

His brows rose slightly. "Better me than Danec."

I wasn't sure it was that simple, but it was done now.

"I'll accept unconditional surrender from all of you," J'avet said to the remaining baddies.

I couldn't think of them any other way. They were all complicit.

"You have mine," the man said.

"And mine," a weary-looking woman agreed.

"Mine also," said a third.

Before anyone else could speak or move, a ripple passed through Yinika's body. The hole in her chest, where she was hit by the blaster, became wider and wider. A trickle of nanobots drained out of her, onto the floor. The trickle became a flood. They headed for the consoles and started to eat through the metal.

"I think we need to switch these off," I said.

"Now," J'avet said. He swapped his blaster for his anti-bot device and started to fire. "Is there a master switch?"

"Yes," the Freytauri man said. "Over on the—"

"Just use the fucking thing," J'avet snapped.

"Yes, of course." The man stepped carefully around the bots and hurried to the console on the other side of the room.

J'avet and Zarex followed and I was close behind. Danec slid a hand into one of mine and Slek moved in close enough for our arms to touch.

"We have company," Brinley said.

I glanced toward the door. Every Iri in the complex looked to have congregated and were pushing through the door toward us. The ones who had already been in the room formed a half circle around us.

"Quickly," J'avet snapped.

The man nodded. "This will take two to three minutes."

"We might not have that long." J'avet waved Slek and E'rel over. "Help him. The rest of you, use your devices."

I turned so my back was to Slek and fired off a few shots from the anti-bot device. I missed one, but hit three who froze, slowing down the Iri behind them until they fell. The Iri stepped over them, only to be shot as well.

The bunker creaked.

The nanobots ate their way up the console, almost to the ceiling. Their numbers were double, maybe triple by now.

"Faster," J'avet snapped. "They'll bring this place down around us."

"Almost there," Slek said. "It's a complicated algorithm, but I see what he's doing."

"No, not that," E'rel said.

I was curious what he was referring to, but too busy shooting at Iri to stop and look.

"Take that," I said as I got one in the chest. "And that. I wish we had more devices." I aimed at an Iri woman, but my device clicked and nothing happened. "I'm out of juice."

"So am I," Navor said. He switched to his disconnector, so I did the same.

It slowed down the first few Iri, but their numbers seemed to grow, rather than die down. They must be pouring down the stairs. That would have to stop soon, right?

"Are we there yet?" I asked in my best exhausted, fed up voice.

"In five," Slek said.

"Four."

"Three."

"Two."

"One."

I waited.

The Iri kept on coming.

"Slek?"

"Sorry, now it's one," he replied.

A second later, every Iri in the room stopped dead. The nanobots went still.

I held my breath.

Let it out.

An eerie silence fell over the room until it was broken by the groans of Freytauri as the bots fell dead on the floor. Hundreds, thousands.

In moments the floor resembled a shining beach, covered in black sand. It crunched with every step anyone took.

I sagged and lowered my devices.

"As far as I can work out, that will have deactivated every bot in the galaxy," Slek stated.

"Thank you to whoever put in a kill switch," I said. They must have realised the bots might get out of hand. I wasn't sure Yinika realised the extent of the trouble they would cause.

But then again, I wasn't sure she was in control. The bots inside her must have found a way to use her to do their work. She might have been as innocent as the Iri.

It didn't matter now, I supposed, she was as dead as the bots.

"Everyone take a few minutes to rest," J'avet said. "We'll need it to get everyone out of here."

Everyone was also going to need a shit load of therapy after this. Especially Danec, who pulled me into his arms and held me like he had no intention of ever letting go.

I wasn't sure I would let him go either, so I was okay with that.

"Are you all right?" I asked in his ear.

"I am now," he said. "I'm so sorry about…everything. Doctor Mazic…"

"That was the bots, not you," I said firmly. "You wouldn't hurt a fly."

"A what?" he asked.

I snorted. "It doesn't matter. The point is, you wouldn't hurt anyone."

"I would have shot Yinika." He sounded so hurt my heart broke a little.

"I'm not sure she was a person anymore," I said. "She was more bot than anything. I don't think J'avet will feel too bad about it."

"I suppose." He rested his cheek on the side of my head.

"I missed you," I said softly. "Obviously. I did come all the way out here to save your ass." Speaking of that, I cupped his butt and gave it a squeeze.

"Thank you. I'll spend forever showing you how grateful I am for that."

"Me too." Slek wrapped his arms around us both. "I was not host material. I told them that. Do you think they listened?"

"I'm guessing not," I said and gave him a slight smile. "They didn't seem big on independence and consent."

"Yeah, they really weren't," Slek agreed. "Hey, J'avet, can we get out of here now?"

"Do you all need a reminder of how to speak to me with respect?" J'avet rubbed the side of his face. He looked like a guy who had the weight of the galaxy on his shoulders.

I suppose he had.

"Naw," Slek replied. "I never knew, and I'm okay with that."

J'avet grimaced and shook his head.

"I don't think I'm cut out for military life," Danec said. "I may retrain as a librarian, or something less exciting."

"Hey, books are exciting," I protested. And a metric fuckton safer than this.

"They are," Slek agreed. "So, about getting out of here."

J'avet nodded sharply. "Those who can, help those who need it. We'll go slowly if we have to, but everyone leaves here in one shot. No one is coming back down here. Ever."

I let Danec go and reached a hand out to a young Freytauri woman who looked dazed and pale.

"Come on," I said in my best cheery nurse voice. "Let's get you out of here."

She nodded her thanks and let me put an arm around her shoulders.

A mass of slow-moving bodies, we made our way to the stairs as a loud bang rocked the bunker.

The ground began to shake.

"Shit," J'avet muttered. "So much for the IF being two days away."

18

"WAIT, WHAT?" I stared at him for half a second before he waved us to keep going.

"Everyone get out!" he shouted. "As fast as you can. We have no time to waste. But don't stampede!" he added as the mass of Freytauri began to panic and rush at the stairs.

They pushed and shoved and several were almost knocked to the ground.

"Anyone else who shoves, I will use my blaster on you," J'avet growled.

They slowed slightly after that, enough to move up the stairs like a swarm of ants escaping their flooded nest.

Another explosion sounded from above and the whole place shook. Rock, dirt and other debris rained down on us.

"I didn't come this far to get buried alive," I said under my breath. I willed everyone to hurry, but to do it carefully. Since those things didn't go so well together, I hoped we'd make it out in one piece.

We reached the top of the first set of stairs as a third blast shook the bunker. A chunk of rock narrowly missed my head, but struck my shoulder before it bounced into the wall and crashed to the floor.

Tears of pain filled my eyes. I felt warm wetness on my upper arm, but didn't have time right now for a good look. I wasn't injured so badly I needed to stop. That was all that mattered.

"Edie?" I hadn't realised Zarex was right behind me until he spoke.

"I'm fine," I said firmly. To the Freytauri woman I supported with my good arm, I said, "We're almost there." She probably knew the place better than I did, but my words seemed to offer her some reassurance.

We reached the second flight of stairs and started up. Why do baddies need to build underground bunkers? A nice little cottage beside the beach would make a nice lair, surely? Or a chalet beside a lake. If I was a baddie, I would definitely have a chalet. Or a chateau. No underground *anything*.

The lights went out.

"Fuck." I turned on the light on my phone with the end of my nose—a trick that usually didn't work. Go me.

It didn't illuminate much, but as others turned their own watches on, it gave us enough light to stagger up the last flight.

I might have imagined a hint of daylight, but I clung to that with every bit of hope I had left.

My legs burned with the effort of walking up so many steps. I wouldn't need to go to the gym tomorrow anyway. I hadn't had such a good workout since—ever. Honestly, I'd be happy if I never had another one like it.

The press of bodies surged forward and I was almost pushed to my knees. At the last moment, I caught myself and trudged up the last few steps and into the open of the top floor of the building.

"Everyone out," J'avet ordered. He tapped his watch. "IF ships in orbit, this is Commander J'avet. Cease your attack on Tarathu *immediately*."

Okay, I admit it, his bossy tone was kinda hot. Also the fact he was trying to stop us from getting killed.

The sky lit up with another laser, which struck the building with a deafening crack.

"We might be too close to the building for comms to work," Slek said.

"Or they ignored us," Zarex added. He turned on his own watch and repeated the message, but with his own name.

Finally, a voice responded.

"How do we know it's you and not a bot?"

Legit question, I thought. Unfortunately.

"Because it's me!" J'avet all but shouted into his watch.

Another laser shot out of the sky. It hit the building square on. Everything went silent, then the ground started to shake.

The building crumbled. It imploded in on itself and disintegrated into the levels below it. Soon all that remained was a hole in the ground.

"Well fuck, that could have been us," I said.

"We need to get out in the open," J'avet said. "Somewhere they can see us."

"If they bother to look." I hadn't seen Zarex look worried before, but he did now. And scared. Fair enough; I was about ready to pee my pants.

"What about the ship Brinley found?" I asked. "Can we get off here?"

"Not without the IF shooting us down," J'avet said. He didn't look scared, he looked furious. "We need to convince the IF we're us, or they'll keep on shooting."

As if on cue, another laser blasted a small building close by.

"There's a field that way." Slek pointed east. "Away from any ships or buildings. Away from anywhere they might aim, hopefully."

"Lead the way," J'avet said.

Normally Slek would stop for a wisecrack, but not today. Now, he simply led us at a slow jog away from the buildings, toward what looked to be farmland. If it wasn't for lasers from the sky, it would be a nice place to rest for a day or three. Maybe build a cottage. Import some cows and chickens.

Another laser took out another building.

"The nanobots have all been deactivated," J'avet was saying into his watch. "If you look at your scanners, you'll see several hundred Freytauri, a couple of Parvorans, some Agusians, a Garvian or two and some humans. IF citizens, every one of us. No Iritauri."

"Stand by," a voice replied.

"Standing by," J'avet muttered angrily.

We reached the middle of a field of grain and many of us flopped to the ground, too tired to move another step, or even stand. If the IF didn't believe us, we were dead anyway, so we might as well be comfortable.

I leaned again Danec, who looked utterly spent. The Frey-tauri I was helping leaned against me.

We waited.

"Commander J'avet." A new voice came through both his watch and Zarex's.

I jerked upright. "Captain Marshall?" Relief flooded through me. I didn't know how the *Gamma* survived and I didn't care. I was just happy it had.

"This is J'avet," he said simply. "Good to hear a voice we recognise." He didn't add, 'and who recognises me.' The sentiment was obvious.

"Commander Zarex here too, Captain." Zarex sounded cheerful but he, too, looked tired.

I suspected I only knew a fraction of what he'd been through in the last few weeks. Only now, out in the light, I saw bruises which had almost faded on his cheeks and neck. His antennas were intact, but they both drooped slightly as though showing his exhaustion in a way the rest of him couldn't.

"Nice to hear your voice too," Marshall said. "J'avet says you're all bot-free."

Slek leaned over and spoke into Zarex's watch. "Bot-free and feelin' fine."

"Reports are coming in of deactivated nanobots all over the galaxy," Marshall said. "Was that anything to do with you?"

Slek, in true Slek style, pretended she was giving him the chance to claim all the glory. "That was everything to do with me, Captain, but I had a bit of help from my friends."

J'avet rolled his eyes, but almost smiled. "We would appreciate it if you didn't destroy all the ships, so we can get off this planet."

"We thought about that," Marshall said slowly.

My heart sank. Surely the IF wasn't going to leave us out

505

here, alone, with no way off? I mean, I guess we could make a life here, if we had to. I had my guys and Brinley, crops, water...

"We thought we'd bring *Gamma* to you," Marshall finished.

The ship burst through the atmosphere above us and began a slow descent.

"Yeah, that works," I said to myself. "As long as they actually believe it's us." I waved skyward for good measure.

A few others did as well. Since the *Gamma* didn't fire on us, presumably they knew we were friendly. Well, most of us anyway. E'rel had a way to go. He currently sat beside Brinley, close enough to touch.

They talked in low voices I couldn't overhear, but I wasn't trying hard.

I leaned against Danec again and he put an arm around me.

"I thought about you," he said softly. "Every time I was able to think for myself. Sometimes the bots were listening for orders, or waiting. Then, it was like they looked away for a moment. I wanted to run away from them, but I couldn't move unless they wanted me to. I was..." He sniffed.

"I know," I said softly. I didn't really know, but I could imagine how it might feel to be stuck in your own body. It sounded pretty shit, to be honest.

"If there's ever anything I can do to help you," I said. "Anything to get you through the pain."

"Just be here," he said. He leaned in to press a soft kiss against my mouth. "That's all I need."

"I can be here," I said, "as long as it's not *here*. Anywhere but this planet."

He gave a short, bitter laugh. "Yes, anywhere but here would be great."

"Very great," I agreed. I glanced up. "It won't be long now." I wasn't sure I wanted to be on another ship, but if it meant escaping Tarathu, I would take it.

I took a breath and got to my feet. Danec stood beside me, with Slek on the other side. After a moment, J'avet joined us and Zarex a hair behind him.

At that moment, I realised something. It was almost over. Everything we'd gone through since Danec and I met, all the craziness and heartbreak. The separations and worry. I wanted to cry, or get really, really drunk. Maybe both.

We stepped back to give *Gamma* more room, even though she had plenty. She kicked up a bunch of dirt and wind as she lowered her struts and landed in the field. From here, she looked huge.

I suppose she was, compared to me. I didn't mind feeling small, she would have to evacuate a lot of people from the planet. We'd be lying on top of each other, so to speak, but I don't think anyone would mind too much. At least for the first while.

Gamma settled on the ground and a ramp lowered slowly. When it was in place, the door slid aside.

As expected, several security officers stepped out first, blasters in hand. Those were lowered when Tarvun walked forward, followed by Rayax. The 'specimens,' as Yinika had called them, must have seen the ship and hurried out from wherever they'd hidden. The forest nearby, perhaps.

"Come on," J'avet said. Where once he'd have strode on ahead, he now waited for the four of us to move forward with him. Or he wanted us there to hide behind, but I didn't think that was it.

Marshall nodded to us when we drew close enough. "I see you succeeded at your mission," she said.

"Yes, we did," J'avet said. "I see the IF had enough faith in us to hold off on the attack for a while." His expression was as bitter as his tone.

Marshall shrugged. "The order came from above me. I told them to stop when I heard your voice. I wasn't sure they would listen. Lucky for you, they did."

"Lucky for all of us," I said dryly. "The IF would have killed a lot of its own people."

"Yes," Marshall replied. "They gave me an hour to evacuate the planet before they resume firing. They don't want to leave any chance of the nanobots becoming a problem in the future."

I didn't think they would be, but I said nothing. It wasn't like I would be listened to anyway.

The IF would do what the IF did, and I would have to do what I did.

In this case, that was to ask, "Please tell me you have coffee on board."

"Uh, FUCK YEAH." I cradled the mug in my hands and inhaled the smell. Marshall was kind enough to give me a spoonful of coffee from her own stash. Even with synthmilk and whatever passed for sugar out here, it smelled like pure heaven. The fact all my guys were here in one place made this perfect. As perfect as sharing a tiny bunk room with Brinley, E'rel and two former hosts could be.

Slek smiled. "I feel the same way about this." He held up his half eaten sandwich.

Sometimes it's all about the small things.

I closed my eyes and sipped my coffee. It wasn't the best cup I ever had, but it tasted amazing.

Zarex sat against the wall, eyes half closed. "So the IF has ordered Yinika's companions to be locked in the brig until they can be interrogated properly. They've all been talking. A lot. I don't think that will save them from a lifetime in prison."

I couldn't bring myself to feel bad, frankly. They could rot there for all I cared. I only wanted to know one thing.

"What about this Tauri Empire she went on about?" I asked. "Is that a thing?"

"They all agree it was just her dream. Or the nanobots inside her," J'avet said. "They seem to have been some of the original ones who were banned so long ago. Somehow they hijacked her and made her do everything."

"At least she had that as an excuse," I said. "The others didn't. Unless they had bots too?"

"If they did, they deactivated along with the rest, but I think it was all their own actions. The kill switch was something the one who helped us put in. According to him, Yinika didn't know."

I frowned. "Why didn't he use it?"

J'avet scratched behind his ear. "I suspect he was scared it wouldn't work. Or at least, not fast enough that he wasn't killed while he waited."

Zarex made a sound of agreement. "They were all terrified of Yinika. She seemed to know everything that went on."

"Not everything," Slek pointed out.

"Enough of everything," Danec said. "The nanobots were scared of her too. Or, not her…" He looked uncertain.

"The idea of her," Slek said. "What she and her bots represented."

"Yes, that," Danec agreed. He and Slek exchanged a look.

I liked that they got along, but I hated that they had something so horrible in common. At least they had each other for support. They would both need it.

Silence fell for a long moment.

"Are we all going to Agus?" Zarex asked, breaking it.

"I am if you guys are," I said.

"I am," Danec said softly. "I have decided I will retrain. I think I'll go into something easy, like engineering."

"Hey," Slek protested. "Engineering is not easy, I—" He stopped when he realised Danec was teasing. He patted his shoulder. "I can teach you everything I know."

Danec smiled briefly. The first one I'd seen from him since he was freed. "I'd like that."

"I'm going too," Zarex agreed. "I'll be teaching computer stuff."

I grinned. "That's wonderful."

All eyes turned to J'avet. His brows rose. "You would all get into trouble if I wasn't there."

I laughed. "More like we'll follow you into it."

He snorted, but didn't deny it.

"This works out perfectly, because I've decided which of you I want to choose," I said.

Now all eyes were on me.

I let them wait for a while, then cleared my throat.

"I've decided I can't choose between you, so I want to choose you all. If that's okay with you guys?"

I held my breath while they looked at each other.

"Works for me," Slek said finally.

"And me," Danec said.

"You know how I feel," Zarex said. "If they all give you what you need that I can't, then I'm in."

J'avet sighed. "I told you you're mine. I'm not letting you go. Besides, I'm getting used to you all."

"I think that's his way of saying he likes you," I said. "That's great, because I love all of you."

"We love you too," Slek said.

All the other guys nodded and gave me fond smiles.

"How long is this journey?" I asked. "Because it's going to be a long time before I'm alone with any of you."

"We'll find a way," Slek said. "We always do."

"Yeah," I agreed. Whatever we had to endure, we always found a way to get through it. Together, we could survive pretty much anything.

I sipped my coffee and smiled. We could take on the galaxy.

THE END.

~

JUST FOR YOU, I'd like to give you an exclusive, reverse harem novella. Get yours now.

IF YOU LIKED THIS BOOK, leave a review. If you loved this book, and want to read more about Edie and her alien mates, tell your friends. If enough people love it, then the galaxy is the limit.

Thanks for reading!

ABOUT THE AUTHOR

Maggie Alabaster writes reverse harem and, paranormal, sci-fi and fantasy romance.

She lives in NSW, Australia with one spouse, two daughters, one dog, and countless birds.

Sign up for my newsletter! Sign Up!

Join my reader group! Join here!

Follow me on Bookbub! Click here to follow me!

Check out my website- www.maggiealabaster.com

ALSO BY MAGGIE ALABASTER

Dark Masque

Book 1 Bait

Book 2 Prey

Book 3 Trap

Saving Abbie

Book 1 Pitch

Book 2 Pound

Book 3 Session

Book 4 Muse

Book 5 Rhythm

Book 6 Encore

Novella Venomous

Ruthless Claws

Book 1 Ivory

Book 2 Crimson

Book 3 Elodie

Harmony's Magic

Book 1 Summoned by Fire

Book 2 Summoned by Fate

Book 3 Summoned by Desire

Shifter's Vault

Book 1 Discarded

Book 2 Deceived

Book 3 Disgraced

My Alien Mates

Book 1 Star Warriors

Book 2 Star Defenders

Book 3 Star Protectors

Academy of Modern Magic

Book 1 Digital Magic

Book 2 Virtual Magic

Book 3 Logical Magic

Complete Collection

Summer's Harem

Book 1: Shimmer

Book 2: Glimmer

Book 3: Flicker

Complete collection

Short reads

Taken by the Snowmen

Jingle All the Way

www.ingramcontent.com/pod-product-compliance
Lightning Source LLC
Chambersburg PA
CBHW020240120726
47904CB00001B/32